THE DRIFT

During a deadly snowstorm, Hannah awakens to carnage, all mangled metal and shattered glass. Evacuated from a secluded boarding school, her coach careered off the road, trapping her with a handful of survivors.

Meg awakens to a gentle rocking. She's in a cable car stranded high above snowy mountains, with five strangers and no memory of how they got on board.

Carter is gazing out of the window of an isolated ski chalet that he and his companions call home. As their generator begins to waver in the storm, the threat of something lurking in the chalet's depths looms larger.

Outside, the storm rages. Inside one group, a killer lurks.

But which one?

And who will make it out alive?

C.J. TUDOR

THE DRIFT

Complete and Unabridged

CHARNWOOD
Leicester

First published in Great Britain in 2023 by
Michael Joseph
an imprint of Penguin Random House
London

First Charnwood Edition
published 2023
by arrangement with
Penguin Random House
London

A catalogue record for this book is available
from the British Library.

ISBN 978–1–4448–4996–7

Published by
Ulverscroft Limited
Anstey, Leicestershire

Printed and bound in Great Britain by
TJ Books Ltd., Padstow, Cornwall

This book is printed on acid-free paper

SPECIAL MESSAGE TO READERS

THE ULVERSCROFT FOUNDATION
(registered UK charity number 264873)
was established in 1972 to provide funds for
research, diagnosis and treatment of eye diseases.

E

- The
  Ho:
- The
  Orr
- Fur   nt
  at t   ty
  of I
- The   te
  of C
- Twi   lmic
  Ho:
- The
  Aus

You
by r
contri   ke
to he   er

T

Leicester LE7 7FU, England
Tel: (0116) 236 4325

website: www.ulverscroft-foundation.org.uk

For my family

They circled the body in the snow. Scavengers. Looking for anything they might strip from the corpse.

It was half buried, frozen in the drift. Legs and arms splayed. A perfect snow angel. Bright blue eyes surrounded by frosty lashes stared up at an equally bright blue sky. The storm had passed.

Eventually, one of the group grew braver. It landed on the chest of the dead human and poked tentatively at its face, pecking at the lips and nose. Then it stuck its beak into one of the blue eyes. It tugged and tugged, and finally pulled the eye free with a small pop.

Satisfied with its prize, it hopped away and flapped off into a nearby pine tree.

The rest of the crows, emboldened, descended upon the corpse in a bluster of black wings.

Within minutes, the body was completely faceless, unrecognizable.

Later that night bigger predators would come. By morning, there would be nothing left but a ragged carcass.

A week later, a hunter would shoot a wolf. A sickly-looking thing, but wolf meat was as good as any to feed his family.

Soon afterwards, the hunter would fall ill and die. Then his family. Then his family's friends.

And the crows would fall from the sky.

The Earth is Full of
Dead Good Guys

Hannah

A watch alarm was beeping. Someone was being sick. Loudly, close by. Several people were sprawled at odd, impossible angles over the uprooted coach seats. Blood pooled in eyes and dripped from gaping mouths.

Hannah noted this dispassionately, clinically. Her father's nature kicking in, her mother would have said. Always able to detach. Sometimes, this lack of emotional empathy made life difficult. Other times, like now, that side was useful.

She unclipped her seatbelt and eased herself out of her seat. Wearing the belt had probably saved her life when the coach tipped over. It had rolled twice down a steep slope, causing most of the carnage, and then come to rest softly, propped half on its side, embedded in a snowdrift.

She hurt. Bruises, scrapes, but nothing seemed to be broken. No massive bleeding. Of course, she could have internal injuries. Impossible to know for sure. But for now, in this immediate moment, she was okay. Or as okay as she could be.

Others were moving. Hannah could hear groans, crying. The hurler had stopped, for now. She looked around the coach, assessing. There were a dozen students on board. They hadn't really needed such a big coach, but it was what the Academy had provided. Of the students, she'd say almost half were dead (mostly those who hadn't bothered with their seatbelts).

There was something else, Hannah thought, as she

took in the scene. A problem she hadn't fully compre-
hended yet. Snowstorm outside, coach tipped over
and half buried in a drift. What was it? Her thoughts
were interrupted by a voice shouting:

'Hey. HEY! Can someone help over here? My sister, she's trapped.'

Hannah turned. At the back of the coach an overweight young man with a mass of dark curls was
crouched over an injured girl, cradling her head on
his lap.

Hannah hesitated. She told herself she was just
gathering her wits, preparing. Not that she was hoping someone else would move forward, step up, so
she didn't have to. She didn't like close physical or
emotional contact. But no one else was in any fit state
to help, and as she had medical knowledge, it was her
duty. She started to move forward, awkwardly, stumbling her way along the lopsided gangway, stepping
over bodies.

She reached the man and his sister. Straight away,
she could tell, as they said in the movies, that the
girl wasn't going to make it. This had nothing to do
with the stuff Hannah had learned in the classroom
during her medical training. That was just a plain,
honest gut reaction. Hannah was pretty sure the girl's
brother knew it too, but he was clinging to hope, as
people do in these situations, because it was all they
had.

The girl was pretty, with pale skin and thick, wavy,
dark hair. The sort of hair Hannah had always wished
she'd been blessed with, instead of the fine, mousy
strands that she could never do anything with and
always ended up yanking back into an untidy ponytail. Hannah realized it was probably odd to feel

6

envy when the girl was dying, but human nature was unpredictable.

The girl's eyes were glazed, her breath short and wheezy. Hannah could see that her left leg was trapped beneath two coach seats that had been forced together in the crash. A mess of mangled metal and crushed bone; she probably had multiple fractures. But the blood loss was the real problem, and that was before you got to the wheezy hitch of the girl's breathing, which made Hannah think she could have other, less visible, injuries. Those were the ones that would get you. The British princess — Diana — had died from a small tear in the vein of her lung that no one knew was slowly, fatally, bleeding out.

'We need to get her leg free,' the man was saying. 'Can you help me move this seat?'

Hannah looked at the seat. She could tell him that it wouldn't make any difference. She could tell him that the best he could do would be to stay here with his sister for however long she had left. But she remembered her father telling her: '*In extreme situations, feeling like you are doing something makes a difference psychologically, even if it has no effect on the outcome.*'

She shook her head. 'We can't move the seat yet.'

'Why?'

'It may be the only thing stopping that leg from bleeding out more than it is.'

'Then what?'

'Are you wearing a belt?'

'Err, yeah.'

'I need you to take it off and make a tourniquet here, above the knee. Then we can try to move the seat, right?'

'Okay.' He looked dazed, but nonetheless fumbled

7

beneath his coat to take off his belt. His stomach spilt over his jeans. His sister stared up, lips moving but unable to force words out. Every effort concentrated on fighting the pain, sucking in those vital gasps of oxygen.

'You look a little young for a doctor,' the man said, handing her the belt.

'Medical student.'

'Ah, right.' He nodded. 'One of Grant's.'

The Academy did not specialize in medicine. Generally, it specialized in parents rich enough to buy their offspring an obscenely expensive college education. But a few years ago it had been chosen by the Department as the location for a new medical research centre. An extra wing had been built and Professor Grant, one of the world's leading virologists, installed to oversee the development. Now, brilliant young students from around the world were selected to study at the isolated mountaintop campus.

'Wrap the belt around here,' Hannah instructed. 'Pull really, really tight. Okay. Good.'

The girl groaned a little, but that was a good sign. If she was still conscious enough to feel discomfort, her brain hadn't started shutting down yet.

'It's okay,' the man whispered into the girl's hair, tucking some of his own dark mane behind his ear. 'S'okay.'

'Right,' Hannah said. 'Let's try and lift this.'

The man laid his sister's head gently down and joined Hannah in trying to heave up the coach seat. It was no good. It creaked and gave a little, but not enough. They needed another person. Two to lift. One to pull the girl's leg out from underneath the twisted metal.

8

Hannah could hear more voices, movement around the coach, people coming to, ascertaining whether their companions were still alive, or not.

She turned and yelled: 'Hey, we need a hand here! Can someone help?'

'Kind of busy over here,' one smart Alec from further up the coach replied.

But then a tall, slim figure stood and made his way towards them. Pale, short blond hair, matted on one side with blood. It looked bad, but Hannah knew that even small headwounds bled like bastards.

'You called?' His voice was cultured, with a slight German accent.

'We need some help lifting this chair so we can free her leg,' Hannah said.

The blond man looked at the girl, then back at Hannah, and she saw the cool appraisal in his eyes. She shook her head slightly and he nodded, understanding.

'Right then. Heft-ho!'

Hannah allowed the two men to do the lifting while she eased the girl's leg out from underneath the seats. It took a couple of attempts, but finally, the leg was free.

The girl's brother moved his sister to a slightly more comfortable position, whipped off his jacket and placed it underneath her head. Beneath his coat, he was wearing a baggy sweatshirt that read: *Excuse me for a moment while I overthink this*. Weird, Hannah thought, the small stuff you noticed.

She felt a hand touch her arm and turned back to the blond-haired man. Aryan, Hannah thought. He'd look at home in lederhosen and a hat with a feather in it.

9

'How many do you think are dead?' he asked.

'Four or five — others may be injured.'

He glanced at the girl and nodded. 'D'you remember what happened?'

Hannah tried to think. She had been sitting on the coach, dozing. It was snowing heavily outside. A horn blare. A squeal of brakes and suddenly they were swerving off the road, rolling and rolling, and then blackness. Crazy that they had even tried to make the journey in this storm, but the Academy had been eager to get the students out to the Retreat. To safety.

'Not much,' she admitted.

She looked around the coach again. Her eyes skirted over the bodies, the people sitting around, moaning, crying. She was trying to recall what she had missed before.

The coach had landed, tilted on its right-hand side. From where Hannah stood, looking up the coach towards the driver's cab, the windows on her left were intact, facing up towards the darkening sky. Snow whisked around in lacy sheets, large flakes already beginning to settle. The worst of the damage was on the right: crushed metal, smashed glass. That entire side of the coach was buried in a thick drift, meaning . . .

The door, she thought. *The door is buried. We can't get out.*

'We're trapped,' she said.

The blond man nodded, as if pleased she had reached the same conclusion. 'Although, even if we could get out, we wouldn't last for long in these conditions.'

'What about the emergency exit?' Hannah asked.

'I have already tried that . . . it appears to be jammed.'

'What?'

The man took her elbow and guided her a little way along the coach. On their left, three steps led to the toilet and another door. A sign above it read: IN EMERGENCY PULL RED HANDLE. PUSH DOOR TO EXIT. The blond man pulled at the handle and pushed at the door. It didn't give.

He stepped aside and gestured for Hannah to attempt it. She did. Several times, in increasing frustration. The door was stuck firm.

'Shit,' she cursed. 'How?'

'Who knows? Perhaps it was damaged in the crash?'

'Wait —' Hannah remembered something. 'Shouldn't there be a hammer on board, to break the windows?'

'Correct. That is the other conundrum.'

Hannah frowned. 'What d'you mean?'

The man stepped back and pointed towards a case mounted just above the windows on their left. Where the hammer should be there was an empty space.

'There should be another up here, for the skylights.' He gestured towards the roof. 'That has also been removed.'

Hannah's head spun. 'But why?'

The blond man smiled without humour. 'Who knows? Maybe some *Arschgeige* stole them for a prank. Maybe no one checked this coach before it left —' He let the sentence hang.

'We need to call for help,' Hannah said, trying to batten down the panic.

Which was when the other realization hit.

'Our phones.'

All phones had been confiscated when the students boarded and stowed away with the luggage. No communication en route.

11

No one must know where they were going.

Hannah stared at the blond man. No way to call for help. No way of knowing how long it might take for rescue to come. How long until they were missed? And even then, who would come to their aid in this storm?

She glanced back out of the windows, looking towards the sky. Already snow was piling up, cutting out the faint grey light.

They were trapped. With the dead. And if rescue didn't come soon, they would be buried with them.

Meg

Rocking. Gentle at first. A lullaby. *Rock-a-bye baby.* Then harder. Rougher. Her head banged against glass. Her body rolled back the other way and she was falling. On to the floor. Hard.

'Ow. Shit.'

Her heart spiked and her eyes shot open.

'What the fuck?'

She rubbed at her throbbing elbow and stared around. Her eyes felt like someone had rubbed grit into them. Her brain felt like wet sludge.

You've fallen out of bed. But where?

She sat up. Not a bed. A wooden bench. Running around the side of an oval-shaped room. A room that was moving from side to side. Outside, grey sky, swirling flakes of snow. Glass all around. Nausea swept over her. She fought it down.

There were more people in here, sprawled on the wooden benches. Five of them. Bundled up in identical blue snowsuits. Like her, Meg realized. All of them here in this small, swaying room. Buffeted by the wind, snow caking the glass.

This isn't a room. Rooms don't move, stupid.

She pushed herself to her feet. Her legs felt shaky. Nausea bubbled again. *Got to get a handle on that*, she thought. There was nowhere to be sick. She walked unsteadily to one side of the room-that-was-not-a-room. She stared out of the glass, pressing her hands and nose against it like a child staring out at the first snow of Christmas.

Below — *way below* — the snow-tipped forest. Above, a frenzy of flakes in a vast grey sky.

'Fuck.'

More rocking. The roar of the wind, muted by the thick glass all around, like a hungry animal contained behind bars. Fresh white splatters hit the glass, distorting her vision. But Meg had seen enough.

A groan from behind her. Another of the blue-clad bodies was waking up, unfurling like an ungainly caterpillar. He or she — it was hard to tell with the hood on — sat up. The others were stirring now too. For one moment, Meg had an insane notion that when they turned their faces towards her they would be decomposed, living dead.

The man — mid-thirties, heavy beard — stared at her blearily. He pushed back his hood and rubbed at his head, which was shorn to dark stubble.

'What the fuck?' He looked around. 'Where am I?'

'You're on a cable car.'

'A *what*?'

'Cable car. You know, a car that hangs on cables —'

He stared at her aggressively. 'I know what a cable car is. I want to know what the hell I'm doing on one.'

Meg stared calmly back. 'I don't know. D'you remember getting here?'

'No. You?'

'No.'

'The last thing I remember is . . .' His eyes widened. 'Are you . . . are you going to the Retreat?'

The Retreat. The deliberately ambiguous name made it sound like a health spa. But it didn't imbue Meg with any feelings of wellbeing. On the contrary, it sent schisms of ice jittering down her spine. *The Retreat*.

14

She didn't reply. She looked back outside.

'Right now, we're not going anywhere.'

They both stared into the grey void, more patches of snow obscuring the glass. A snowstorm. A bad one.

'We're stuck.'

'*Stuck?* Did you say we're stuck?'

Meg turned. A woman stood behind her, around her own age. Red hair. Pinched features. Panic in her voice. Possibly a problem.

Meg didn't answer right away. She regarded the other people in the car. One was still curled up asleep, hood over his face. Some people could sleep through anything. The other two — a short, stout man with a mop of dark curls and an older, silver-haired man with glasses — were sitting up, stretching and looking around. They seemed dazed but calm. Good.

'It looks that way,' she said to the woman. 'Probably just a power outage.'

'Power outage. Oh, great. Bloody marvellous.'

'I'm sure the car will be moving again soon.' This from the bearded man. His previous aggression had dissipated. He offered the woman a small smile. 'We'll be fine.'

A lie. Even if the car started moving, even if they reached their destination, they were not going to be fine. But lies were the grease that oiled daily life. The woman smiled back at the man. Comforted. Job done.

'Did you say we're on a cable car?' the older man asked. 'I don't remember anyone mentioning getting on a cable car.'

'Does anyone remember anything?' Meg asked, looking around.

They glanced at each other.

'We were in our rooms.'

'They brought some breakfast.'

'Tasted like crap.'

'Then . . . I must have fallen asleep again —'

More confused looks.

'No one remembers a thing after that?' Meg said. 'Not till they woke up here?'

They shook their heads.

The bearded man exhaled slowly. 'They drugged us.'

'Don't be ridiculous,' the red-haired woman said. 'Why would they do that?'

'Well, obviously so we wouldn't know where we're going, or how we got here,' the short man said.

'I just . . . I can't believe they would do that.'

Funny, Meg thought. Even now, after everything that had happened, people struggled to believe the things that 'they' would do. But then, you can't see the eye of the storm when you're inside it.

'Okay,' the bearded man said. 'Seeing as we're literally stuck here with time to kill, why don't we introduce ourselves? I'm Sean.'

'Meg,' said Meg.

'Sarah,' the red-haired woman offered.

'Karl.' The short man gave a small wave.

'Max.' The older man smiled. 'Good to meet you all.'

'I guess we're all here for the same reason then?' Sean said.

'We're not supposed to talk about it,' Sarah said.

'Well, I think it's pretty safe to assume —'

'To assume makes an 'ass' out of 'you' and 'me'.'

Meg stared at Sarah. 'My boss used to say that.'

'Really?'

'Yeah. Used to annoy the fuck out of me.'

16

Sarah's lips pursed. Max broke in. 'So, what do you . . . I mean, what did you all do, before?'

'I taught,' Sarah said.

Quelle surprise, Meg thought.

'I used to be a lawyer,' Max said. He held his hands up. 'I know — sue me.'

'I worked in bouncy castles,' Karl said.

They looked at him. And burst into laughter. A sudden, nervous release.

'Hey!' Karl looked affronted, but only mildly. 'There's good money in bouncy castles. At least, there used to be.'

'What about you?' Meg asked Sean.

'Me? Oh, this and that. I've had a few jobs.'

A gust of wind caused the cable car to sway harder.

'Oh God.' Sarah clutched at her neck. She wore a small silver crucifix. Meg wondered how many more reasons she could find to dislike the woman.

'So we're an eclectic bunch,' Max said.

'And 'ass' or not, I *assume* we're all heading to the Retreat?' Karl said, raising his bushy eyebrows.

Slowly, one by one, they all nodded.

'Volunteers?'

More nods. Only two types of people went to places like the Retreat. Volunteers and those who had no choice.

'So, is now the time to discuss our reasons?' Max said. 'Or shall we save that for when we get there?'

'*If* we get there,' Sarah said, looking at the steel cables above them nervously.

Sean was eyeing the sleeping figure in the corner. 'Do you think we should wake up Sleeping Beauty?'

Meg frowned. Then she stood and walked over to the prone figure. She shook his shoulder gently. He rolled off the bench and hit the floor with a thud.

Behind her, Sarah screamed.

Meg suddenly realized two things.

She knew this man.

And he wasn't asleep. He was dead.

Carter

'There's a storm coming in.'

Carter groaned and rolled over on the sofa. He knew that voice. Caren. *With a C.* As she had told him at their first introduction. Like it made a difference. Like he was going to send her a frigging Christmas card.

'You know, Carter, a hangover isn't going to get you out of the grocery run.'

Caren sounded perky. She always sounded perky. Carter wedged one eye open and stared at her. Yep. Running tights, vest, hair pulled back into a bouncy ponytail. She was probably on her way to the gym. Carter closed his eyes and buried his face in a stale-smelling cushion.

Caren continued her aural assault. 'We need to be stocked up, in case the storm cuts us off again.'

The sound of the fridge opening and closing, chopping and the whirr of the food processor. Then a clunk as Caren plonked a glass down on the coffee table next to him.

'Drink. It'll help.'

Carter peered out from behind the cushion. A glass of reddish liquid sat on the table.

'Bloody Mary?'

Caren raised an eyebrow and stalked off. Carter pushed himself into a sitting position, reached for the drink and took a swig.

'*Jesus!!*'

Fire in his mouth. Burning. Christ, the burning!

19

He sprang to his feet and ran for the sink. He spat out the fiery liquid, turned on the cold tap and wedged his mouth underneath, gulping at the ice-cold water. Finally, he splashed his eyes and face and stood, dripping, over the floor.

He turned. Caren was watching from the doorway, arms folded, smirking.

'You said it would help.'

She shrugged. 'You're up, aren't you?'

* * *

After a shower and a shave, he felt almost human. The mirror told a different story.

People here had got used to Carter's appearance. They no longer shrank in horror at his approach. It was easy to forget what he really looked like.

Frostbite had decimated the right-hand side of his face. His cheek, much of his forehead and chin were blackened and dead. The centre of his face was a gaping cavity and his lips dragged to one side where the muscle had been destroyed. When he ate or drank, he often dribbled. Only his eyes remained. Blue, sharp. A reminder of the person he had once been.

Carter tried hard not to mourn him. He had never been handsome. Overweight in his youth and later, his features had always been a little raw. But sometimes, he woke from dreams where his face was whole again, and the realization of reality left his pillow damp with tears. He was not a crying man. Nor a vain man. But it's the little things that get to you. Like having a nose.

He slouched back downstairs to find Nate, Miles and Julia lounging around in the large living area, drinking coffee. A Monopoly board had been spread out on the coffee table (Miles was no doubt winning, again) and Julia was rolling a joint — which would piss Caren off when she returned from her workout.

Jackson and Welland, the final members of the group, were nowhere to be seen. Jackson was probably meditating or doing yoga. Welland was probably buried in a snowdrift. With any luck.

They were an eclectic bunch here at the Retreat, thrown together by circumstance and necessity, but they managed to work and live together without killing each other. For the most part.

Fortunately, the Retreat was large. And luxurious. The living area was all polished wooden floors, thick, shaggy rugs and worn leather sofas. There was a massive flatscreen TV and DVD player, games consoles and a stereo. A wooden sideboard housed stacks of CDs, dog-eared novels and a collection of board games. The kitchen was modern and sleek with a huge American fridge freezer and a polished granite island.

Residents at the Retreat were well looked after.

For the most part.

Nate glanced up as Carter walked in. 'Man, you look like shit.'

'I know my usual good looks threaten you.'

Nate blew him a kiss. 'I love you for your tight ass, dude.'

'Don't. You're making me blush.'

Nate grinned. Even with a hangover, he was all stoned-surfer good looks — shiny muscles, sun-bleached hair wrapped in a bandana. By rights, Carter should hate him, but somehow, over the last three years, they had become friends.

'What time did you guys make it to bed?' Julia asked, pushing a dark dreadlock behind her ear and popping a filter in her joint.

A skinny, tattooed Californian, Julia had grown up in a commune and still looked like she would be most at home in a yurt or behind a placard, protesting something.

Carter frowned. It hurt. 'Maybe a couple of hours after you went up.'

Miles arched an eyebrow. He didn't seem the least bit hungover. He looked as dapper as ever, in a polo shirt and chinos, like he was about to punt a boat along the Thames.

'It was a little later than that,' he said in his cultured English accent. 'But I think you might have passed out by that point, Carter.'

'It's my party piece.'

'Passing out?' Miles queried.

'Some people smoke cigars out of their backsides. I pass out.'

'They really do that?' Julia asked.

'With my own eyes.'

Nate chuckled. 'Man, why do we do it to ourselves?'

'Because there's nothing much else to do?' Julia said.

They all smiled and nodded, even though the truth of that statement cut deep.

Of course, there was *stuff* to do at the Retreat. Day-to-day tasks to keep the place running. Maintaining the various areas, inside and out. Cooking, cleaning, looking after the supplies. They all had their assigned roles — Miles made sure of that. There were leisure facilities: the gym, the pool, the slopes. Oh, and there was the grocery run.

Carter walked over to the rota pinned on a large cork-board in the kitchen. Sure enough, it was his name there. Again. Time in this place. It seemed to move differently.

He hated doing the grocery run. Not least because it wasn't exactly a quick scoot to the corner shop. It involved skiing down treacherous slopes all the way to the village, then a hard, uphill trek dragging the sack of groceries, tethered to the skis.

Carter was easily the worst skier in the group. Unlike the others, he had never gone on winter holidays 'to the mountains' when he was a kid. Winter sports to him meant careering down an icy quarry slope on an old car bonnet with his sister.

It took him the longest to get down to the village, not to mention the slow climb back. And that was before you figured in the wildlife in the woods.

He could feel his headache edging in again.

'Does it have to be today? I mean, we've plenty of —'

'No way.' Julia shook her head. 'You know the rules.'

The rules. Yeah, he knew them.

'Julia's right,' Miles said in an irritatingly reasonable tone. 'Besides, there's a storm coming in, fast.'

Carter stared out of the huge plate-glass window that took up almost an entire wall of the Retreat. It was an awesome view, out over the slopes, the vast pine forests, all the way to the spiky ridge of the rocky mountain range.

After a while, it became like wallpaper. You barely even saw it.

And Miles was right. Snow was already gusting down, and an ominous cloud loomed in the distance. A sign that a bad storm was rolling in. Depending on severity, that might mean they couldn't get out again for days, even weeks.

'Got to be today, man,' Nate said. 'Gonna get Biblical.'

Right on cue, the door to the downstairs entrance hall thudded open, sending an icy blast of wind and snow up the spiral stairs into the living area. Footsteps thudded up the staircase.

'*Man*, it's really shitty out there.'

Welland. Overweight, acne-spattered Welland. At twenty-five, he was the youngest of their group, but he was also the one who knew the most about running the Retreat. So, despite the fact he was a miserable, whiny sack of shit with a sly underbelly and a fondness for stirring, they were forced to tolerate him.

Still, along with Welland came a more welcome arrival: Dexter, who bounded into the room and launched himself into Carter's arms, covering his face and hands with his wet, smelly tongue.

'Hey boy. You been out for a walk?' Carter lowered his face into the terrier's cold, wiry fur and whispered, 'Did you piss on Welland's leg? Yeah? Good boy.'

'How is the generator looking?' Miles asked.

Welland shook out his matted dark curls and stamped his feet. 'Okay, but I'm bummed about that lag. Those outages are getting more frequent.'

His positivity was another of his fine attributes.

'Okay, well, no need to fret. I'll check —'

'I'm not *fretting*, man. I'm just *sayin'*. Six seconds is too fricking long. You know what happens if the power goes off —'

'I *know*,' Miles said in a tone that stilled the room.

Welland reddened and bent to pull his boots off. 'Think I've got fucking frostbite,' he mumbled. 'All I need is my toes going all black and falling off —'

24

He glanced up, eyes falling on Carter. 'Oh. Shit. Sorry, man.'

He wasn't sorry.

Carter smiled and put Dexter down. 'S'okay.'

It wasn't okay.

But he didn't have time to dwell on it because suddenly — like Welland was some hairy soothsayer of doom — the power died with a low whine and the alarm went off.

'Shit!' Welland cried. 'I told you.'

Miles raised a hand. He stared at the watch on his other wrist. Counting. One, two, three, four, five . . .

A beep as the generator kicked in and the power came back on. The alarm cut off mid-wail.

Nate let out a whistle. 'That felt long.'

'Six point two six seconds,' Miles said, and lowered his wrist. 'A minor concern.'

'How minor?' Carter asked.

Miles considered. 'The outage would have to last for at least eight seconds for it to be a problem.'

'Why eight?' Nate asked.

'In the event of a power cut, the automatic locks release. But it isn't instantaneous. Residual power means a delay of eight seconds,' Miles said. 'During an unexpected outage, the generator *should* start within four to five seconds, so the locks remain secure.'

But it felt narrow, Carter thought. Too narrow.

'I should have a look at the locks in the basement,' Welland said. 'Think about re-setting the controls down there. If the lag is getting longer —'

'I *said*, we'll monitor the situation.' Miles looked around at them. 'Are we clear on that?'

This time, even Welland got the message. 'Clear,' he mumbled.

Everyone else nodded.

'Good.'

'Right then,' Nate said, standing. 'I'm gonna hit the gym, sweat out last night's beer. Anyone else?'

'I could do with half an hour in the sauna.' Julia drew on her spliff then ground the joint out in an ashtray. The pair of them wandered out of the room towards the elevator.

Welland was still hovering, pulling off his snowsuit. 'See you're down for the grocery run, Carter. That's gotta suck.'

'Yeah, well, everyone has to do it.' Carter clicked his fingers. 'Oh wait. Except you. You've never done it.'

'I can't ski.'

'Join the club.'

'I have asthma.'

'Funny. I wouldn't have thought that someone with your condition would have passed the vetting process to work here.'

'Yeah, well, at least I didn't just turn up out of the blue, like —'

'Can you two quit the lovers' tiff?' Miles snapped. 'And Carter — I need to talk to you before you leave.'

'Why?'

Miles glanced at Welland, who had finished shedding his outer layers, leaving them lying in a wet pile on the floor, and was now investigating the kitchen cupboards for food.

Miles stood and walked towards the elevator. 'Come with me.'

Carter sighed. 'Okay.'

On his way, he brushed past Welland, close enough to whisper: 'I know you don't have fucking asthma.'

The elevator doors slid open and they stepped inside. Miles pressed his pass against B on the control panel. The elevator moved silently downwards.

The Retreat was built over four levels and set into the mountainside. The living area, kitchen and gym were on the first floor. On the second floor: sleeping quarters — two large dorms and twelve single rooms for the staff. On the ground floor there was a huge hallway, a swimming pool and steam rooms. Plus, the utility and storage areas.

The basement was off limits to everyone except Miles (and whoever he deemed trustworthy enough to take down there with him).

The doors opened and they stepped out into a bright, white corridor. It was always cool down in the basement, but that wasn't why the hairs on Carter's arms shivered. The lighting was motion sensitive, snapping on as they advanced along the corridor, revealing a line of doors to their left. Two were offices, now empty. Miles stopped at the third, pressed his pass against another entry pad, and they stepped inside.

Shiny stainless-steel workstations ran along one wall. A large refrigeration unit and metal storage cabinets stood against the other.

'So, what's up?' Carter asked, as casually as he could.

Miles regarded him coolly. Carter had seen corpses with a warmer gaze than Miles.

'Someone has been stealing stock.'

'What?'

Miles opened a drawer in one of the cabinets.

Inside, row upon row of packets — antibiotics and painkillers.

'Looks pretty well stocked to me.'

Miles delved beneath the top row of packets and selected one from the bottom. He opened it. And held it upside down. Empty.

'I'd say about half of the packets have been tampered with.'

'What about —' Carter nodded at the refrigeration unit.

'I couldn't see anything missing so I decided to randomly test some of the vials.'

'And?'

'Several contain a placebo.'

'Like, not real plasma?'

'Water.'

Carter felt his tension notch up. The next question was obvious.

'How? I mean, you've got the only pass.'

'That we know of.'

True.

'Which brings me to our other problem,' Miles continued.

'There's another problem?'

'Jackson is missing.'

Carter stared at him. '*What?* Are you sure?'

'He didn't sleep in his room last night. I can't find him anywhere.'

Carter considered. Jackson was probably the person he knew least well here. A quiet, self-contained man in his late thirties. Teetotal, vegan. Fond of yoga and meditation. Despite that, Carter had never had a problem with him. But then, there wasn't enough there to have a problem with. The man was a ghost.

'You think he's the thief — and he's cut and run?'

'Maybe. But to where?'

Miles had a point. There was only the village. The airfield was an hour away and just one narrow, twisting road ran in and out. And where would Jackson get a vehicle? That left the cable-car station. But that wasn't really an option.

'Maybe it's not what it looks like,' Carter asked. 'Maybe he's just . . . taking a hike?'

Miles gave Carter a look. 'Without his snowsuit?'

Another good point.

'We keep this between us for now,' Miles said. 'If something has happened to Jackson, it's bad for morale, especially after the unfortunate incident with Anya.'

Unfortunate. Right. Carter swallowed. 'And if we find him?'

Miles's lips curved. Carter's balls crept up into his throat.

'Then he's a dead man.'

Hannah

The survivors gathered at the back of the coach.

The dead were mostly at the front.

Hannah had checked on them all herself. Five young men and women who would not see their next birthdays. Death had been sudden, and violent. That was often its nature. There were no beautiful corpses here. There seldom were.

It was fortunate, in some respects, that most of the students on the coach were strangers or casual acquaintances. Apart from the man and his sister, who were still huddled together on the floor at the back, no one was crying for a partner or best friend. On the other hand, none of them had any reason to look out for each other. Every man or woman for themselves. That could be a problem. Of course, right now, there was a far bigger one. But Hannah wasn't prepared to broach it with anyone. Not yet.

In addition to her Aryan helper, the dying girl and her brother there were three other survivors: an athletic-looking young man with dark hair and a blandly handsome face, a slender girl with short, brown hair and glasses and a lanky youth with a ponytail and facial piercings, the puker. They talked among themselves.

'How are we getting out of here?'

'Have you seen the storm? We'll freeze to death out there.'

'We might die in here.'

'So, what are we supposed to do?'

'I can't believe they took our phones.'

'I can't believe no one smuggled one on board.'

'How long will it take them to find us?'

'Oh God. We can't be stuck here all night. Not with dead people.'

Hannah could have told them that the dead were the least of their worries. The more immediate concern was going to be the drop in temperature. It was already getting cold in the coach. They all had thick jackets and jeans on, but not thermal snowsuits, and if they were stranded here overnight, hypothermia could set in rapidly.

Other concerns — food. They had snack packs prepared by the Academy, and water. But those supplies were only supposed to be for lunch. They might need to make them last much longer. There was a toilet and, despite its awkward, lopsided position, it should be usable, so those needs would be taken care of. For now.

Outside, the snow was still piling up on the coach, the glass. How long before it buried the vehicle from view? The storm might cease before then, giving them more options. Or equally, it might not.

'Okay. Everyone — quiet down!'

The tall blond man stood and stared around at the students. Despite them all being a similar age — Academy students ranged from eighteen to twenty-three — he had a commanding presence and the group slowly hushed.

'Firstly,' he said, 'to make communication easier, I suggest we introduce ourselves. I am Lucas.'

'Josh,' the athletic young man said.

'Ben,' the pierced youth followed.

'Cassie,' said the slender girl.

31

'I'm Hannah,' Hannah said.

She glanced behind at the young man tending to his sister. He looked up.

'Daniel — and Peggy.'

'Very good.' Lucas nodded. 'Okay. The situation is this: we can't call for help. We can't get out.'

'Great pep talk, man,' Ben muttered.

'What about the emergency exit?' Josh asked.

'It's stuck,' Hannah said.

'Are you sure?'

'Try for yourself.'

Josh rose and disappeared up the coach. Within a few seconds he was back.

'Yeah. It's busted.'

'Fuck,' Ben cursed.

'And it appears that we are not equipped with the necessary tools to break the windows,' Lucas continued.

'Say what?' Josh queried.

'The emergency hammers are missing,' Hannah said.

'Christ!' Ben rolled his eyes. 'I can't believe they put us on this heap of shit.'

A valid observation, Hannah thought. The coach was old. The Academy hadn't replaced its transport in some time. Perhaps it hadn't been deemed a priority. Most students arrived by limo or helicopter.

'It's a moot point,' Lucas stressed. 'None of us would survive for long out there in this storm.'

'So, what do you suggest?' Josh asked.

'Sit tight and wait for rescue to come.'

'And if it doesn't?'

'We reassess. We *may* be able to find a way out. In which case, we nominate the two most capable people to try and get help. But there's no point send-ing anyone out there if they're not going to survive.'

'He's right,' Hannah said. 'We're better off waiting.'

'And why should we listen to you?' Cassie demanded, eyeing her coolly.

Hannah noted that the girl hadn't questioned Lucas's authority. She kept her voice pleasant and reassuring: 'I've done some training in crisis manage-ment.'

She hadn't exactly, but her father had.

'In a situation like this,' Hannah continued, 'our best bet is to stay where we are, at least until the storm has passed. We have food, we have shelter, and most importantly we have each other.'

'You want us all to hug?' Cassie asked sarcastically.

'Yes,' Hannah replied. 'Because our greatest chal-lenge if we are stuck here tonight is going to be the cold. We need to keep together to maximize body warmth.'

'You think we'll be stuck here that long?' Ben asked, looking worried.

'Maybe. It might not be possible to send rescue until the storm has eased.'

'They will *send* rescue, won't they?' Cassie asked, directing her question at Lucas.

'Yes,' Lucas said, so emphatically that even Han-nah almost believed him. 'Why go to all this trouble to get us out, to safety, just to abandon us now?'

It made sense, but Hannah knew that part of the reason the Academy was so keen to get the students out was so it had no liability for any more deaths.

Ben raised a hand, and this pleased Hannah because it meant that the group were accepting her and Lucas as leaders of a sort, and that would make things easier.

'Yes?' she said.

'Should we, like, check if any of the others have phones, just in case?'

'By the others, you mean the dead?' Hannah said.

He looked awkward. 'Well, yeah. And, I mean, they don't need their jackets or their food, do they?'

Hannah glanced at Lucas. It was a good suggestion.

'We *should* make use of all available resources,' he said.

'So, who's going to, you know . . .' Josh said.

'I will,' Hannah said.

'I'll come with you,' Lucas offered.

She nodded. They walked up the coach.

'Actually, I wanted to talk to you,' Lucas said in a low voice.

'And I wanted to talk to you.'

'Okay.'

'You go first,' Hannah said.

'Did you notice anything about the dead?' Lucas asked.

'How do you mean?'

'They're all students, yes?'

'Well, yes.'

'And all the survivors are students —'

'Your point?'

'Where's the driver?'

She stared at him. Of course. She should have noticed. Where was the driver? *Careless, Hannah.* She looked around, as if he might suddenly pop up from behind a seat. Surprise!

'That's impossible,' she said.

'Do you remember what he looked like?' Lucas asked.

Hannah frowned. She had seen the driver outside the coach, smoking, as she boarded, but she hadn't taken much notice. He had been short, she thought. And slim. That was about it.

'Not really.'

'But you don't see him here?'

She looked around again. 'No.'

'Then there are only two solutions. There is a way out —'

'Or?'

'He escaped out of the emergency exit and disabled it afterwards.'

'But why?'

'Why indeed?' Lucas smiled. 'Now, what was it you wanted to tell me?'

Hannah swallowed, a little thrown by the sudden change of subject. 'We have five dead students.'

'Yes?'

'Four, as you would expect — trauma from the crash.'

'What about the fifth?'

Hannah led him forward. In one seat, a frizzy-haired youth was sprawled, a sizeable bloody dent in his head.

'He probably died from blunt force trauma to the head,' she said.

Lucas looked at her quizzically. 'So, he also died in the crash.'

'Yes, but . . . he was already a dead man walking. Look at his eyes.'

Lucas bent forward. She heard his sharp intake of breath. The student's corneas were a distinct pinky-red. *Redeye*.

Lucas paled. 'But we were all tested?'

The tests were supposed to be foolproof.

'Something must have gone wrong,' she said.

'*Verdammt*. Do you think —'

'No way of knowing until someone else displays symptoms.'

'You just told them all to hug.'

'Or we might die of hypothermia.'

'But we could infect each other.'

'It's too late to worry about that. We've been breathing the same air, touching the same things for hours now. Either we're lucky . . . or we're not.'

She let this realization settle.

'So, even if rescue comes,' Lucas said slowly. 'Some of us will die.'

He was smart, but he still didn't get it.

Hannah shook her head. 'If rescue comes, and the Department realizes there's an infection on board . . . none of us will make it to the Retreat.'

Meg

The dead man's name was Sergeant Paul Parker and she had worked alongside him in Homicide. Later, they were both transferred to Infection Control and Public Unrest. Or as everyone in the division called it: 'Shoot and Burn'.

'You've got to remember, Hill, they're not like us. We're doing them a mercy.'

A mercy. Yeah. Meg remembered. Sometimes she wished she could burn those memories. Scoop them out like a lobotomy. Forgetting could be a mercy too.

Of course, all of that was incidental now because the name on the lanyard tucked beneath the man's snowsuit read: *Mark Wilson — Security.*

'Who is he?' asked Sarah. 'Is he okay?'

'His name is Mark Wilson.' Meg repeated the lie. 'And he's dead.'

Sarah clapped a hand over her mouth. 'Oh my God.'

'How?' asked Sean.

Good question. She touched his neck. Not for a pulse. Meg knew when dead was dead. More to get an idea of his body temperature. Cool, but not yet cold and waxy. She reached for his arm and lifted it. Still loose and flexible. So rigor mortis hadn't set in which meant he had died recently, probably within the last couple of hours.

'Could it be a reaction to the drugs we were given?' Max asked.

It was a good suggestion. Reasonable even. Meg knelt beside the body. Just a body now. Not Paul or

37

Mark or whatever he had been calling himself. She examined his face, his mouth. A mouth she had kissed. Out of lust, loneliness, convenience, desperation. Never love. Not even at the start. Relationships have been built on less. But they needed more to survive.

Now she parted his lips and peered inside, looking for traces of vomit, an indication of overdose. No vomit, but she could see blood around his teeth. She could smell it too. She frowned. Then she reached for his snowsuit and unzipped it. Underneath he wore a white thermal T-shirt. Or what used to be a white T-shirt. Now, the front was stained maroon.

'Holy shit!' exclaimed Karl. 'Is that blood?'

'Yeah.'

Meg gritted her teeth and edged up the T-shirt, grimacing slightly at the stiffness of the blood-caked fabric and the feel of it pulling away from flesh. The wound was just below the breastbone. Between the second and third ribs. A strike to his liver, she thought. Precise, fatal.

'He's been stabbed,' she said flatly, and turned back to the group.

They stood around her, looking frightened and confused. Their predicament, the sway of the stranded cable car, momentarily forgotten in the face of the dead man. Meg wondered if any of them had seen a dead body up close before.

Even with everything that had happened over the last ten years, some people were removed from the true horror. They saw bodies on the television, of course. Or at least they saw what the media wanted them to see. But many rural areas had been spared the worst of the outbreak. As had those rich enough

38

to live within one of the private gated communities that had sprung up outside the major conurbations. If you didn't live in the cities, you might never have encountered the carnage up close.

'Why would someone do that?' Sarah asked in a wavering voice, clutching at her crucifix.

Meg shrugged. The woman's constant near-hysteria made her want to be brutal with her. 'Who knows? But they knew the best place to stab him to make the wound fatal — unless they just got lucky.'

'You seem to know a lot about knife wounds,' Sean said.

'I used to be a police officer,' she admitted.

'Used to be?' Karl asked.

'Yeah.'

She stared around at them, challenging them to ask her more. No one did. Everyone had a past these days. And no one wanted to discuss it.

'Can you tell how long he's been dead?' asked Max. 'I presume he must have been stabbed before we boarded.'

'And they just put a dead body on here?' Karl said.

'Maybe no one realized,' Sean said. 'We all thought he was asleep, right?'

Meg looked back at the body. It was possible no one had noticed, but it seemed unlikely. Perhaps they just didn't care.

'Possibly,' she said. 'He hasn't been dead long. No more than a couple of hours, I'd say.'

'What other alternative is there?' asked Sarah.

'One of us stabbed him,' Karl said, looking at Meg. 'That's what you're thinking, isn't it?'

'But we were all unconscious,' Sarah said.

'Supposedly,' Max said.

Sarah threw up her hands. 'This is ridiculous. No one stabbed him. None of us even knows him.'

Meg remained silent. Sarah folded her arms as if to say, '*There you go then.*'

Max scratched his chin. 'Of course, the assumption that he was killed before boarding does not preclude the possibility that one of us is responsible.'

Sarah stared at him. 'What?'

'He means,' Sean said, 'just because one of us didn't stab him on board doesn't mean we didn't kill him before we got on.'

'Oh, for goodness' sake!'

Max looked at Meg. 'Bearing in mind, one way or another, we are going to be stuck with each other for some time, I'd like to be sure no one here is carrying a weapon.'

'We all had our belongings confiscated,' Sean said. 'I mean' — he looked down at his snowsuit and boots — 'these aren't even my clothes.'

Meg considered. Then she started to unzip her snowsuit. Underneath she was wearing a white thermal T-shirt and shorts. Just like Paul. Not hers. She had been re-dressed while unconscious. She pulled her boots off then stepped out of the snowsuit, immediately shivering.

'What are you doing?' Sean asked.

'Proving I have nothing to hide.'

She threw the suit at Sarah. 'Check the pockets.'

Sarah looked about to argue then shut her mouth again. She patted the snowsuit down. 'Empty.'

'Great.'

She passed the suit back to Meg, who stepped into it gratefully.

'Okay. Who's next?' Meg asked.

Max was already undoing his suit. Sean followed. Sarah rolled her eyes but reached for her zip. They exchanged snowsuits, patting the pockets and shaking them out.

Karl was the last. He looked around as if someone might give him a last-minute reprieve. Then he shook his head and reached reluctantly for his zip. As he eased his snowsuit off, Sarah let out an audible gasp.

Karl's arms and legs were covered in ugly black tattoos. From the crudeness of the inkwork, Meg would guess they were done in prison: swastikas, skulls, the number 1 4 8 8, the Aryan circle and fist, the words 'Blood and Honur'. Not an inch of unblemished skin remained below his neck. They all knew what those tattoos meant. Hate-filled symbols of white supremacy.

Karl met Meg's gaze defiantly, but Meg could see the shame in his eyes. She felt the others looking at her. Of course. She was a black woman. The tattoos should upset her more. Her burden, not theirs.

She smiled thinly at Karl. 'You know they spelt 'honour' wrong.'

He bowed his head. 'Yeah, I know.'

She nodded. 'Give me your suit.'

Karl stepped out of his suit and held it out. Meg reached for it.

Something hit the floor of the cable car with a clunk.

A small, bloodstained knife.

Carter

He stood at the top of the run, just outside the boundary to the Retreat. The old sign — the one no one used any more — clanked and swung on its hook.

Carter checked again that he had everything, and steeled himself. It took about twenty minutes to make it down to the village on a good day, if you were a good skier. He was not a good skier and today — judging from the gathering clouds, the wind and the snow swirling about his goggles — was not a good day.

And then there were the woods. There was no avoiding them. About halfway down, row upon row of tall pines closed in on either side. Dense, sinister. Full of things that watched and whispered . . . and whistled.

Carter hated woods and forests. Always had. He blamed his dad. When Carter was a kid, his dad had told him this story about some kids he once knew who had found the body of a girl in the woods. She had been dismembered. Limbs hidden under piles of leaves. They caught the dude who killed her, but never found her head.

Carter wasn't sure if it was true or not. His dad had talked a lot of shit, especially when he was drunk. But that story had stuck. Carter would wake from nightmares about the dead girl, her missing head crawling towards him like some kind of mutant human spider. Dr Moreau's worst nightmare. Nothing good ever happened in dark, dark woods. He should know.

Carter adjusted his ski goggles and took a deep

breath. Fuck it. He pushed off with his poles. Not elegantly, not fast. Like a kid on the learner slopes. He hated that feeling of losing control, of being taken by gravity and the slippery, crystallized ice. Give him a car or even a bike. Anything but two slabs of wood and some fucking sticks.

He imagined Caren watching from the huge plate-glass window, smirking at his shaky, unsure progress. He caught Caren watching him a lot. He didn't harbour any crazy idea that this was because she had some secret crush on him. Not unless she had a thing for the grotesque. It was more like she could see through him. Like he was as naked to her as the emperor in his shiny new clothes.

Carter tried to shove thoughts of Caren with a C from his mind and concentrate on not breaking his neck. Sweat broke out and cooled on his back. The wind whipped snow into his face and he had to keep risking his balance to raise an arm and wipe his goggles clear again. The weight of the black sky bore down on him. He needed to be quick today. He couldn't risk getting caught in the storm.

He reached a plateau in the slope and managed to swerve to a halt. Below, the run narrowed, the tall pines leaning in closer. He tried to quell his unease, then pushed off again as fast as he dared, keeping his eyes trained straight ahead, away from the woods' shadowy folds. It was still early but the storm was already ushering in a premature twilight. The trek back up would be the dangerous part.

Ahead, he could see the slope widening, flattening, and his breath started to come a little easier. To his right, the rusted remains of an old ski lift drew into view. Once, it had ferried people to the top of the slopes. Now, half of it had collapsed, chairs buried in the snow, like some great beast slayed and brought to earth.

Carter coasted past the wreckage, down into the village. Not a big village, but in its hey-day it must have been bustling. Allegedly, there used to be a chic boutique hotel, a couple of smart bars and restaurants, a chemist's and one small supermarket — Quinn's Convenience Store. Just enough to serve the skiers who holidayed here.

But no one had taken holidays for a long time. The boutique hotel was now a boarded-up, graffitied shack. The restaurants and bars were similarly derelict. The chemist's had struggled on for a while, but eventually it couldn't get the drugs, and then it was looted, so that went too. Which just left Quinn's.

Carter suspected that, in the event of a nuclear apocalypse, the only things left would be cockroaches and Jimmy Quinn.

He took off his skis and walked along the main road, catching a flash of brown out of the corner of his eye: a fleeing deer. He tensed in case any predators followed — cougar or wild dogs. But the high street remained empty. Carter relaxed, a little.

Quinn's was halfway along. The storefront was dirty, the windows were barred; barbed wire decorated the roof. Multiple security cameras swivelled in Carter's direction as he approached. However, when he pushed open the door, it still jangled with an old-fashioned bell.

Inside, the store was dimly lit and dusty and always smelt of fish and something sour. The shelves were stocked high with tinned goods from various continents, and two massive refrigerators housed hunks of

44

meat of dubious origin. Carter had never summoned up the courage to ask what they were, lest he find himself joining them.

The rest of the shop was given over to a bizarre and eclectic selection of items which never seemed to change. Carter walked past a display of Easter eggs, women's twenty-denier tights, inflatable pool floats, cocktail shakers and packs of video cassettes. Not even DVDs — video cassettes. And Betamax at that. Carter wondered if, back in the day, the store had been smarter, stocked with fine wines and fresh delicacies. Or maybe not.

Quinn had stock flown in once a month via the small airfield an hour's drive out of the village. He also had two of his four sons stationed there, so nothing came in or went out of the village without Jimmy Quinn's approval. Including people. The Retreat and Quinn had formed an uneasy alliance. Carter doubted it was possible to have any other sort of alliance with Jimmy Quinn.

Miles had once told Carter that Quinn's family used to run a large crime syndicate in the UK and Quinn still had connections with organized crime. Carter was willing to believe it. Although how Quinn had ended up here, thousands of miles away, running a convenience store in the mountains, was anyone's guess. Carter had a feeling it was probably better not to know.

As Carter reached the front counter, Jimmy Quinn sprang from the back room.

'Hey, Carter. How you doing, man? Long time no see. Thought you might be dead.'

If Jimmy Quinn was five foot four, that was being generous. He was a tiny, tightly coiled man with a head of Brillo-like black hair and a wide smile that didn't quite align with his hard, grey eyes. If his face said 'Welcome,' his eyes said 'but watch your back.'

Carter smiled. 'Hey, Mr Quinn.' Always Mr Quinn. Never Jimmy. 'Not dead yet.'

'Good. That's good, right? Best we can hope for, yeah?'

Jimmy Quinn talked at a rapid-fire pace, like Yoda on speed. If Yoda spoke with an almost impenetrable Liverpudlian accent.

'You got everything on our list?' Carter asked.

Miles phoned their list through to Jimmy every fortnight.

'Yeah, yeah, most.' Jimmy nodded. 'I made a couple of substitutions. You know.'

Carter did. Jimmy Quinn once substituted tins of beans for wood sealant and flour for a fake pot plant. It was pointless asking what the substitutions were so Carter just nodded.

'No problem. Miles agreed payment, yes?'

'Yeah. Miles is sound. Not like some. Some customers I have to send my sons to see, you know?'

Carter had never seen another living customer in Quinn's shop. But he had once seen the remains of one being dragged out by one of Quinn's two burly minders.

He fished a parcel out of his pocket. 'Miles added a few extras, for your good service.'

Jimmy Quinn eyed the parcel greedily, grabbed it and shoved it beneath the till. 'Nice work. Miles is a good bloke, right?'

Wrong, Carter thought. But it was all relative.

He waited as Jimmy disappeared out back and returned with his sons. Carter had never been formally introduced, but he was pretty sure the threatening-looking dude with black tattoos creeping out of the collar of his shirt was called Sam and the scary-looking dude with slicked-back hair and a Bond villain scar running from eye to chin was called Kai. But he could be wrong. He always thought of them fondly as Thing 1 and Thing 2.

'Here go you, lad.' Jimmy winked.

Carter cleared his throat. 'Erm, could I use the toilet?'

Jimmy Quinn stared at him.

'It's a long way back up the mountain,' Carter added.

Jimmy chortled. ' 'Course. You don't want to shit your pants, right?' He nodded to Thing 2 on his left. 'Let him use the crapper.'

Thing 2 accompanied Carter to the toilet located just to the left of the counter. He took out a key from a chain around his neck and opened it. The smell of sewage assaulted Carter's nostrils. Thing 2 smiled as he blanched.

'Enjoy.'

Carter stepped inside and shut the door behind him. Then he reached into his snowsuit, delved into his underwear and pulled out two clingfilm-wrapped parcels he had tucked inside. He lifted the cistern lid and dropped the parcels in. Then he flushed the toilet. A signal to Thing 2 that he was done. When he exited, Thing 2 would slip inside and retrieve them. By tomorrow, one of the parcels would be on its way to a small suburban town many miles away. The other, Thing 2 would keep.

Even in families like the Quinns' there was no such thing as absolute loyalty. Thing 2 and Carter had come to an arrangement. Carter needed to send the parcels without Jimmy (ergo without Miles) knowing. Thing 2 was happy to siphon off a little extra to sell for himself.

Carter stepped out of the toilet. Thing 2 didn't even look at him. Carter walked over to the groceries, which Jimmy Quinn and Thing 1 had already strapped to the skis outside.

'Goodbye, Mr Quinn.'

Jimmy grinned. 'Till next time, if you're not dead.'

Carter laughed and waved, even as he thought that Jimmy wasn't so far from the truth.

Sending the parcels was a big risk. But it was one he'd been willing to take. For her. Now the stakes had risen. Miles knew about the missing stock.

The question was — how long before he worked out Carter was the one stealing it?

★ ★ ★

Carter had hoped to get back to the Retreat before dark. But the encroaching storm had other ideas. It was barely mid-afternoon, he was only halfway up the slope, and already the light was failing, miserably. Skulking away to its room like a sulky teenager.

The wind buffeted his body, trying to shove him down the slope. Snow whipped and frenzied in the air. Not pleasant. Not one fucking bit. Carter grunted and dug his poles harder into the snow, heaving the groceries strapped on to the skis behind him.

It would be easier to trek closer to the woods. The snow wouldn't be as deep, and he'd be shielded from the wind. But the woods were full of wildlife, grown emboldened in recent years. Fewer humans and less

48

civilization had put them back on a more even footing. Humans were no longer the lords of all they surveyed.

And then there were the Whistlers.

Carter found himself casting glances towards the woods. Here the trees were still fairly sparse. Further up the slope they grew denser, creeping in on either side, dragging shadows like tattered shrouds.

He swallowed. Tried to force himself to focus on the task at hand. There was still a little light left in the day, despite the burgeoning black clouds. The Whistlers preferred full night. Pitch black. The sun was bad for their fragile skin. Whistlers were preternaturally pale, almost translucent. Like ghosts. Except, unlike ghosts, they didn't drift around silently. Their arrival was preceded by the awful wet, whistling noise they made as they tried to drag in oxygen through their pitted and scarred lungs.

Stop it, Carter.

He stuck one boot in front of the other, stabbing the snow with his poles to drag himself up the slope. The clouds puffed out their chests and glowered darkly above him. Snow plastered itself against his goggles. Carter gritted his teeth. Wiped his goggles again. And then something caught his eye.

Movement up ahead. A blob of black amidst the whiteout. He blinked. A crow? Too big. An animal? Too tall. A figure, he realized. Stooped, staggering, falling on to the snow then righting itself again. Carter was still too far away to tell whether the figure was male or female. Or Whistler.

He paused. The figure was blocking his way back to the Retreat. He unhooked the straps around his waist that tethered him to the makeshift sled behind him. Then he dug his poles into the snow and anchored the skis to them. The snow was deep. They should hold for a while. He didn't want to have to chase the damn groceries all the way back down the slope to the village.

Released from his load, Carter advanced towards the figure. If it had seen him, it didn't show any signs of it. It seemed confused, circling raggedly in the snow. Lost? Injured? As Carter drew closer, he could see it was male. Shaven head. Dark clothes. No snow-suit. Carter's unease increased. There were ruby-red splodges around the man, staining the snow. One arm was missing, torn from its socket, leaving a gaping, raw stump. An animal had been at him. Or maybe he'd been attacked by Whistlers.

Then the man turned, and Carter understood why he had been staggering around so blindly. He was blind. One eyeball had spilled from its socket and was stuck, frozen, to his cheek. The other was gone completely, along with half of his face. Eaten away, leaving nothing but gristle and bone.

Despite the mutilation, Carter still recognized him. Jackson.

What the hell had he been doing out here? How had he got this far without dying from either blood loss or hypothermia? In addition to the other injuries, frostbite had already begun to eat its way into Jackson's flesh. It was a miracle he was still alive. Without medical attention, that situation wouldn't last much longer.

Carter glanced back towards the makeshift sled. Even if he'd wanted to, he couldn't drag the groceries and Jackson back to the Retreat. If he returned without the groceries, his conversation with Miles would be short, and unpleasant. But he couldn't leave

Jackson to die out here. Not like this.

'Fuck,' he cursed. Then, shouting into the void: 'FUCK!'

You're either a good guy or you're a survivor, someone had once told him. *The earth is full of dead good guys.*

It was a salient piece of advice. Of course, the person who had imparted it was dead.

Carter had shot them.

Jackson fell forward, more blood seeping from his body and reddening the snow around him. He tried to claw his way towards Carter. From its new and unflattering position on his cheek, his remaining eye seemed to stare up accusingly.

Carter reached into his pocket and pulled out a gun.

Jackson's mouth opened in a silent plea.

You're either a good guy or you're a survivor.

There were times, Carter thought, when being a survivor really sucked.

'I'm sorry, man,' he whispered.

And then he raised the gun and shot Jackson in the head.

Hannah

'We can't tell the others,' she said firmly.

Lucas raised his eyebrows. 'Why?'

'Because they might panic. Right now, we need to keep everyone calm.'

'So what do you suggest?'

'We take the clothes and supplies as planned. Then we move the dead to the front of the coach, lay them across the seats, hide the infected body underneath, hope that no one checks.'

'And hope that no one else shows symptoms?'

Hannah bit the inside of her lip but nodded.

'I concur,' Lucas said.

They stripped the bodies. The first couple they did somewhat gingerly, feeling the intrusion, the indignity. Several times, Hannah had to stop herself from apologizing to the dead person she was manhandling.

By the third, they worked quickly and less carefully, dragging off the clothes, checking pockets for anything useful, tipping snacks and water into a carrier bag they had found on one of the girls. Perhaps she used to get travel sick, Hannah thought, and felt a momentary twinge of empathy. No more travel for that girl. Never again.

She swallowed it down and carried on. Depending on sizes, they could double insulate with the extra outerwear. They now had more water, protein bars and fruit. It wasn't much, but it would keep them going. Until rescue came. *If* rescue came. And then what? What about the infected student?

If you don't inform the Department, Hannah, you are complicit in spreading the virus and endangering others.

She tried to shut out her father's voice. But it lingered. Hannah knew the policy set out by the Department. As one of the world's leading virologists, her father had helped to write it. Contain the infection at all costs. Shut it down. People presumed that meant isolation, quarantine. But this was a virus like no other. Spreading like no other. The only sure-fire way to shut it down was to shut down the carriers. Permanently.

If they wanted to get through this, they couldn't let anyone know about the infected body.

Hannah sighed and looked at the young man she had just relieved of his trousers. Apart from the unnatural angle of his neck, he was remarkably unscathed. Dressed now in just a T-shirt and a pair of long johns, he could be sprawled out, chilling. She frowned. Something caught her attention. An unnatural bulge in the crotch area of the long johns. She bent over and stretched out a hand.

'What are you doing?'

She jumped and turned. Lucas. He was holding a bundle of clothes and staring at her curiously.

She flushed. 'This student. He has something . . . in his pants.'

One eyebrow raised. 'I see.'

She felt annoyance rise. 'Look.'

He followed her gaze. 'Oh. I do see.'

She leaned forward and touched the rectangular bulge. Hard, metallic. She glanced back at Lucas and then slipped her hand inside the long johns, trying to ignore the bristly feel of pubic hair. *Cold* pubic hair. She fought down a shudder of distaste. Her fingers

53

closed over the object, and she drew it out.

A mobile phone.

Lucas smiled. 'I think, as you say in England — bingo.'

'Maybe.' Hannah looked at the phone. She pressed the home button. It sprang into life. The screensaver was a picture of a different young man: tousled blond hair, shaved down one side, piercings all the way along one ear, and in his nose and lip. He grinned and made a peace sign at the camera. A boyfriend, perhaps? Again, Hannah felt that twinge of sorrow. This boy had had a partner who loved him, who was perhaps, even now, waiting for a message or call, and here she was stealing from his dead body.

You'll never make it as a doctor if you let emotions intrude.

Her father again.

Empathy is a distraction. They are patients, not people. You will discover there is a world of difference.

Okay. Fair point. Right now, she needed to be clear-headed.

'Is there any signal?' Lucas nodded at the mobile.

Hannah held it up. Zero bars. Of course. 'That might change if the storm clears,' she said. 'But it's a moot point — it's locked.'

Lucas tutted. 'It will need a password. *Scheisse.*'

Hannah glanced back at the dead student. His face was unblemished, eyes open, not yet clouded with death.

Patients, not people.

'There is another option.'

'What?'

'Face recognition.'

Lucas frowned. 'Will it work? I mean, has the

54

software some way of detecting whether, you know —'

'— we're dead or alive?' Hannah shrugged. 'Only one way to find out.'

'HEY!'

They both jumped at the shout from the back of the coach.

'My sister could do with some water down here?' Daniel.

'I'll go,' Lucas said. 'You see if you can unlock the phone.'

She nodded. Lucas headed back down the coach with the bundle of clothes and the bag of snacks and water. Hannah turned back to the body.

'Okay.'

She leaned over and held the phone up in front of the student's face. The first attempt failed. Damn. She reached behind his head to prop it up. It moved on his neck with a sickening ease. She positioned the phone more directly in his line of vision. Success. The small padlock at the top of the screen unlocked. So much for cybersecurity. She quickly swiped up to access the phone and made her way back to the others. The group were sorting through the clothing and supplies. They looked up at her approach.

'We're dividing up the food and water equally,' Lucas said.

'The clothing we're splitting according to size,' Josh added.

'Then we thought we might do a fashion show,' Cassie drawled.

Hannah wondered again what the girl's problem was. Perhaps she wanted to be in charge. Or perhaps it was just authority — *any* authority — she didn't like. But Hannah didn't have time for petty power games.

55

'We found this on one of the students,' she said briskly, holding up the phone.

'Man, I told you someone would sneak one on board,' Ben said, grinning.

'I've unlocked it, but there's no signal.'

Hannah saw the hope rise and fall on their faces.

'It's possible we may get a signal when the storm has eased,' she added.

'What about a text?' This from Daniel. He sat a little apart from the others, holding his sister's hand while he dribbled water into her mouth. She was still holding on, Hannah thought, but barely. And what would that mean for Daniel when she died?

'If there's no signal —' she started to say.

He interrupted: 'Sometimes signal quality isn't good enough to allocate the necessary bandwidth for a voice call, but you can still send and receive texts because the bandwidth you need for that is really narrow.'

Hannah stared at him. He gave a small shrug. 'I worked at a phone shop for a while.'

'It seems worth a try,' Lucas said.

'But who should we text?' Ben asked.

They looked around at each other. It was a good point.

'We need to contact someone involved with the evacuation,' Lucas said. 'Someone in charge.'

'You mean Professor Grant?' Ben said. 'He's the main man, right?'

'Right.' Cassie snorted. 'Anyone just happen to have the Prof's number on them?'

Hannah hesitated. They didn't know. She had never told anyone at the Academy. Nor had he. That was how they both preferred it. But now?

56

'I do,' she said. 'Professor Grant is my father.'

They all stared at her.

'Man, *there's* a third-act reveal,' Ben said. 'Your dad is the head of the Department?'

'You never mentioned it.' Cassie stared at her suspiciously.

'I never thought it needed saying,' Hannah replied. 'No one at the Academy knew. I used my mother's surname — Weston.'

They all remained silent for a moment.

'So, if the Prof is your father, why didn't he take you with him on his helicopter when he evacuated at the start?' Josh asked.

Hannah felt a flush creep into her cheeks. 'I didn't want to go,' she said, which was true. 'I still had work I needed to finish.' A lie.

'You refused a chance to hightail it out because of *work*?' Ben said.

No. Because her father had never asked her to go.

'Yes.' Hannah nodded.

'I don't believe you,' Cassie said.

'Why would I make it up?'

'To make yourself look important.'

Hannah sighed. 'I'm only telling you now because I have to. Because it might help.'

'Fine.' Cassie nodded at the phone. 'Text Daddy then.'

Her father was the obvious person to contact, but something in her still resisted. *Shutdown. Contain the virus at all costs.* But what choice did she have? She looked down at the screen and realised that a text conversation was still open.

The last messages the dead student had received. He must have been replying when they crashed.

57

Is Mr Jet on board?

In the luggage hold.

You know what to do?

Arrive, confirm and put Mr Jet to bed.

A thumbs-up emoji — **Feeling fine?**

Feeling fine. Followed by three emojis — a party popper, a bottle of champagne and fire.

She frowned. *Mr Jet.* Who or what was Mr Jet? And what about the emojis?

'Forgotten his number?' Cassie asked.

Hannah looked up. 'No. It's just . . . these texts. They're a little odd.'

She saw Cassie and Josh exchange glances.

'Look.' She handed the phone to Lucas.

He read them and gave a small shrug. 'Students, you know, maybe some sort of joke?'

'Can we see?' Josh asked.

Lucas handed him the phone. Cassie and Ben crowded in to look at it.

'Could be a drugs deal,' Ben said.

'Maybe Mr Jet is . . .' Josh mimed sniffing up a line of coke.

'Did you say *Mr Jet*?' Daniel asked from the back.

The group turned. *Reluctantly*, Hannah thought. Like they were trying to forget he was there, sitting with his dying sister. A little too much reality.

'Yes. Why?' Josh asked.

'Can I see?'

Ben passed the phone over. Daniel read the message. Hannah watched as his face fell.

'What is it?' she asked.

'Well, I might be wrong . . . it might mean something else entirely, but —'

'What?'

He looked up at her. His eyes were very blue, she thought. Startling.

'I used to work in a theatre,' he said. 'Selling refreshments.'

'I thought you worked in a phone shop?' Lucas queried.

'I've had a few jobs.'

'Go on,' Hannah said.

'In most public buildings, you have codes, for when you need to evacuate people without causing a panic. For example, if there's a fire, the code for that is Mr Sands. Mr Sands is in the building.'

They all nodded. Hannah felt something unpleasant twist in her gut.

'So, what's Mr Jet code for?'

Daniel cleared his throat and looked around. 'A bomb.'

Meg

They stared at the knife.

'It's not mine. I've never seen it before!' Karl looked around the group with wild eyes. 'You have to believe me.'

'We don't have to believe anything *you* say,' Sarah snapped. 'It fell out of your pocket.'

'Someone must have planted it there.'

Sarah snorted. 'Right. Like they planted those Nazi tattoos on you.'

'It is a possibility,' Max said evenly. 'The knife, I mean. Why would Karl agree to be searched if he knew the knife was there?'

'He was last. He didn't want to take his clothes off,' Sarah said.

'Because of these. Okay?' Karl held out his arms, face flushed and angry. 'I didn't want you to see them.'

'Really? You didn't want us to know that we're sharing our space with a racist white supremacist?'

'I'm not sure there's any other type of white supremacist,' Meg said evenly.

Sarah stared at her. 'It doesn't bother you?'

Before Meg could open her mouth to tell her that of course it did but it should bother *all* of them, Karl broke in:

'I'm not a racist or a white supremacist. *I had to*. I was in prison, okay? It was the only way to stay safe.' He looked around at them all pleadingly. 'I had to,' he finished weakly.

'What were you in for?' Meg asked.

A hesitation. He didn't meet her eyes. 'Fraud.'

'Right.' Meg nodded slowly. Then she held out Karl's clothes. 'Get dressed.'

'*No.*' Sarah snatched the clothes away. 'He doesn't get these back until he confesses or explains.'

Meg stared at her. 'That's not how we do things.'

'We? Who the hell is we? The police? In case you hadn't noticed, you're not police any more. It's just us in here.'

'So what? We abandon all decency?'

'He could be a killer.'

'Innocent until proven guilty.'

'Meg's right,' Sean said. 'Give the man his clothes back.'

Sarah stared at them all then chucked the clothes on to the floor and stalked to the furthest corner of the car. Which wasn't very far. That was the problem with throwing a wobbly on a cable car, Meg thought. Nowhere to run.

Karl retrieved his clothes gingerly and stepped into them, almost tripping in his haste to get dressed. Meg felt some pity for the man. He had been humiliated and scared. And she knew what it was like for people like Karl in prison. Weak and new to the system. They were targeted, violated, living in constant fear for their lives. The only way to survive was to affiliate with a gang, for protection. Sometimes, we all had to do what was necessary to survive, however unpleasant it might be.

The knife was damning, yes. But her gut was telling her that Karl wasn't a killer. His shock at seeing the weapon had seemed genuine. Which meant that the knife had most likely been planted on him either before — or after — they got on the car. If it was after, then someone in here wasn't drugged. Someone was lying.

'I didn't do it,' Karl mumbled again. 'I don't even know the guy.'

Meg could have told him that plenty of people killed strangers. In most cases, killing a stranger was easier. But there was usually a motive of some kind: anger, alcohol, cash, sex. Right now, she couldn't see why a former bouncy-castle salesman would want to stab a former police officer. Unless . . .

'Are you sure you don't know him?' she asked Karl.

'What? Yes. I'd never seen the guy until, well, just now.'

'His lanyard says he's security,' she continued. 'A lot of security are ex-police. You never had a run-in? Saw a chance at revenge?'

He stared at her with hurt eyes. 'I thought you were on my side.'

'I'm not on anyone's side, Karl. I'm just trying to get to the truth.'

'And who put you in charge?' Sarah suddenly said.

Meg smiled coolly. 'We're just having a conversation, Sarah.'

Before Sarah could muster a reply, Meg turned back to Karl. 'Well?'

'No. I didn't know him — and even if I did, why the hell would I kill him on here? I mean, we're about to be stuck with each other for months. Plenty of time to exact' — he made quote marks in the air — ' ''revenge'.'

He had a point.

Max was looking thoughtful. 'Doesn't the fact that the weapon was concealed on one of us make it more likely that *someone* on this cable car killed Mr Wilson?'

'How do you figure that?' Sean asked.

'Well, if the perpetrator had struck at the holding facility, he or she would have had more places to dispose of the knife.'

'Maybe,' Meg said. 'Maybe not. Perhaps the intention all along was to frame one of us.'

'Okay.' Sean sighed. 'The way I see it, it doesn't really matter who killed him —'

'It matters to *me*,' Sarah said. 'I don't want to be shut up with some psychopath who's going to stab me in my sleep.'

'Okay,' Sean said. 'But what do you think will happen to us if we rock up at the Retreat with a dead guy and a bloody knife? We'll all be arrested, locked up, or worse.'

'We should let the relevant authorities deal with it,' Sarah said primly, and folded her arms.

Sean caught Meg's eye. Max looked down at his feet.

'I don't know about the rest of you,' Sean said, 'but I'm not the biggest fan of the relevant authorities.'

'I would have to second that,' Max said.

'I can't go back to prison,' Karl muttered.

Sarah pinned her gaze on Meg. 'You used to be a police officer. Tell them.'

So, suddenly, it mattered that Meg used to be police. She looked back at Paul/Mark's body. Why was he here under an assumed name? Why was he here, in these remote mountains, at all? Meg hadn't seen him for years. He could have moved departments, countries. Perhaps he was here on some kind of undercover assignment. But if so, that meant they were all suspects in the murder of a police officer.

She looked back at the bloody blade on the floor.

'We need to get rid of the knife,' she said.

'*What?*' Sarah stared at her incredulously. 'Cover up a crime?'

'No,' Meg said smoothly. 'But without the knife, they can't pin this on one of us.'

'But we know one of us did it. *Him.*' She pointed at Karl.

'I didn't kill him,' Karl said again, starting to sound angry. He glared at Sarah. 'How do we know you didn't do it? You were sleeping near us. You could have stabbed him and hidden the knife on me.'

'Don't be ridiculous,' Sarah snapped.

'Okay.' Meg held her hands up. 'We don't know anything. And right now, the best way to cover our backs is to get rid of the murder weapon.'

'And how do you suggest we magic it away?' Sarah said. 'We're in a cable car suspended a thousand feet in the air.'

'There's a hatch,' Sean said.

Meg looked at him. 'What?'

'In the floor. For emergencies. Like' — he raised an eyebrow — 'getting stuck.'

'Oh, the irony,' Meg said.

'Yeah.'

And now they could see it. A small square set in the metal.

'How do we open it?' Max asked.

Sean frowned. 'I guess we need some kind of tool to release it. But' — his eyes fell on the knife — 'I could probably do it with that?'

'Okay,' Meg said.

'And if I could make one other suggestion?' Sean added.

'Go ahead.'

'We dispose of both the knife and our late companion.'

'Oh, great,' Sarah said. 'This just gets better and better.'

Meg looked at Sean. 'We never said anything about dumping the body.'

'Hear me out. No one will ever find it in the snow. It'll get eaten by predators. We could say that he freaked out, panic attack, opened the hatch, there was a gust of wind and he fell out. If we all stick to the same story, no one can prove otherwise.'

Meg stared at him coolly. 'I see you've thought this through.'

He shrugged. 'Just trying to see a way out of this for all of us.'

'We should vote.' Meg looked around. 'All those in favour of dumping the body, hold up your hand.'

Sean stuck his up. Followed by Karl.

Max frowned. 'I don't know. It seems like an admission of guilt. I abstain.'

Typical lawyer.

'And I vote against,' Sarah said. 'It's criminal. He should have a proper burial.' She shot Karl another evil look. 'It's obvious who the killer is. He was in prison. And those tattoos — they tell you exactly what sort of man he is. I don't know why we're even debating. We get to the Retreat, hand him over.'

'Looks like you have the deciding vote,' Sean said, looking at Meg.

She considered. It had been six years since she and Paul had split up, five since she had last seen him. It had been an acrimonious split. Any past feelings she had were just that — in the past. And ultimately, whatever she might or might not have felt for Paul, he was dead now. Worse, he was a problem. One they could do without. One *she* could do without. If anyone discovered their connection, she would be the prime suspect. Sean was right. They couldn't arrive at the Retreat with a dead body on board.

'Okay.' She nodded at Sean. 'Let's dump the dead weight.'

Sarah threw up her hands. 'I want no part in this.'

'No one says anything about it,' Meg said. 'That's the deal.'

Sean worked the hatch open quickly, finding the lock and releasing it with a click. Meg got the impression he was no stranger to breaking into things. Karl and Max carried the body over and laid it next to the hatch. Meg tried not to look at Paul's face.

'Everyone step back,' Sean said. 'It's going to be windy and cold, and you don't want to fall through.'

The rest of the group moved away.

'On three,' Sean said to Meg. 'One, two, three —'

Together, they lifted the metal trapdoor. It fell back with a clang. Immediately, a gust of freezing air and snow blizzarded into the car. The roar of the wind was deafening. It had felt cool before. Any remaining warmth was now evaporating.

'We need to do this quickly!' Meg shouted to Sean over the wind.

He nodded and dropped the knife out of the hatch. It disappeared in an instant.

He turned to the body. 'Ready?'

It was on the tip of Meg's tongue to say yes when, suddenly, she thought of something. She grabbed Sean's arm.

'Wait!'

'What?'

'We haven't searched him.'

'For what?'

'I don't know.'

He gave her a look of exasperation but nodded.

'Make it quick. We're losing heat fast.'

She leaned over the body, patting it down, stuffing her hands in pockets. She didn't know what she was searching for. In fact, she thought she was going to come up short when her fingers closed over a small piece of card.

She pulled it out. An old photo.

'Can that wait?' Sean yelled.

'Yeah, sure.'

She stuffed the photo in her pocket. They rolled the body to the edge of the hatch. Their eyes met. Meg nodded. They shoved the body overboard and watched as it was swallowed by the hungry storm, within seconds just a black speck against the white.

Meg stared after it, the wind making her eyes tear. And then a sudden gust of wind rocked the cable car. She fell backwards. Another gust rocked it back the other way. She felt herself slide towards the hatch, feet kicking into open air. Sean caught her arm, hauling her back. Behind them, someone screamed. And then, it all happened quickly. As the cable car swayed, Max grabbed a handrail, but Karl staggered forward, off balance. Sarah moved towards him; arms outstretched. Her fingertips touched his back . . . and with one shove, she sent him toppling head first out of the open hatch.

Carter

You weren't supposed to leave the bodies. It was one of the rules. The risk, however small, of a sixth-degree infection.

The virus was primarily airborne. The problem was that there were many variants. Blood, faeces, bodily fluids, tissue, bone marrow. All channels for infection. Even cooked meat had been proven to harbour traces of the particularly unpleasant Choler variant.

Carter stared at Jackson's body. He hadn't been prepared to drag a live Jackson back to the Retreat so he sure as hell wasn't going to drag a dead one. Not with the dusk dropping faster than a teenage boy's pants at third base and the snow falling harder every second. And not with the howl of the wind disguising any other sounds.

Of course, the storm would help. Jackson would be buried within minutes. No one would know, and by the time his body was found — *if* it was found — it would be so decomposed there'd be no way of telling how he'd died.

Carter would have permitted himself a small smile if his face hadn't already been frozen into a rictus grin. He put his head down and pushed on up the slope.

★ ★ ★

The first sign that something was not good, not yet *bad* — that would come — but definitely *not good*

68

was when Carter finally reached the top of the ski run. Ahead of him, he could see the electric security fence that bordered the Retreat. Outside, to his right, sheltered among the pine trees, was the incinerator. Hidden from view, for obvious reasons.

But it was the Retreat that had caught his attention and caused the breath to snag in his throat. The large picture window was dark. Carter frowned. He could see other lights on, dotted around the building. But no lights in the main living area.

That was odd. Mostly, the lights were left on all the time. Unlike most urban conurbations, they didn't need to be too careful with their power. Their electricity was supplied by a combination of two massive wind turbines further up the mountain and solar panels. A battery stored the energy and supplied the Retreat at a constant rate when required.

At least, it was supposed to.

Over the last few weeks, Welland had noticed a problem. The battery was leaking energy. This meant that its supply was inconsistent, causing power spikes and outages. The back-up generator could compensate, but they only had a limited supply of propane . . . plus, there was that lag between the power cutting and the generator kicking in.

Welland had seemed at a loss as to how to fix the problem. Generators and heating were not Miles's speciality. Science and medicine were. As Welland was fond of saying, 'Doctors can perform brain surgery, but they still need someone to keep the lights on while they do it.' Carter had to give him that one.

He advanced slowly towards the Retreat. That dark expanse of glass gave him a bad feeling. Fortunately, as he neared the gate, he could still hear the low hum of the electric fence. He fumbled off one glove to punch in his code, pulling it hastily back on as his fingers tingled with cold. The gate buzzed and he pushed it open, dragging the groceries behind him. The hairs on the back of his neck prickled, as they always did. Crossing the boundary, from danger to safety. Lowering your defences. A final moment of vulnerability before the gate clicked back shut and he was secure.

Of course, the fences and gate were only an illusion. In reality, Carter knew he was in as much danger inside as out there. Just different enemies. While he remained useful to Miles, he was safe. But Welland would love an excuse to throw him under a bus (or off the nearest mountaintop). The feeling was mutual. Caren tolerated him, and while Carter liked Julia and regarded Nate as a friend, the fact was they were all survivors here. And survival was a solitary business.

Carter approached the front door, tapped in a second code and let himself in, dragging the groceries into the huge entrance hallway. The door swung shut heavily behind him. He pulled off his gloves and looked around, listening.

Everything sounded quiet. Too quiet? The alarm wasn't sounding, which was good, he guessed. He glanced towards the darkened spiral stairway which led to the main living area. If no one was up there, he wouldn't expect to hear any noise. But still, that silence.

And what about Dexter?

While not the world's most alert guard dog — he had been known to sleep through the alarms — he usually noted Carter's absence and came bounding down to greet him on his return.

Instead, silence.

Carter lugged the supplies over to the storeroom, unhitched the bag from the skis and shoved it inside. He'd unpack it later. Then he propped the skis in the rack, pulled off his gloves and boots and peeled off his snowsuit. Beneath, he wore a sweatshirt, jeans and thick socks. He could feel the warmth from the underfloor heating immediately start to permeate up through his feet.

The door to the pool and spa was ahead of him. To his right, the storeroom and utility room, which housed the fuse boxes and system controls for the Retreat. The elevators and stairs were on his left. Carter walked towards them and then paused. No one was going to be sitting around in a dark living room. He turned back and walked over to the door which led to the spa and pool. He pushed it open. It was heavy and soundproofed, like all the doors in the Retreat.

He walked into the open-plan changing area. Benches lined one side and lockers the other. There was a small dressing area in the centre with mirrors and hairdryers. To his left, a frosted-glass door led to the showers and toilets. To his right, a small corridor led to the pool.

The changing area was empty. Carter pulled out his gun and tentatively checked the showers and toilets, pushing open the cubicle doors one by one with his foot. No one home, not even a floater.

He crept back into the changing rooms. He could hear the faint sound of water lapping from the pool. He walked down the short corridor. At the end, small sprays shot water into a shower tray. Carter peeled off his socks and stuffed them in his pocket, then splashed through and out into the pool area.

The humid air shrink-wrapped itself to his skin.

71

The smell of chlorine made his eyes sting. The lighting here was dim. Uplighters were arranged around the stone walls. Loungers lined the sides. At the far end, another picture window mirrored the views of the living area upstairs. The pool itself was half Olympic length, but narrower. Underwater lighting lent it a beautiful azure tone.

A body lay at the bottom.

Long dreadlocks floated up like seaweed. Drifting in a cloud of red.

'Fuck.'

Carter moved forward, needing to be sure, even though there was really only one person it could be. No mistaking that hair.

Julia.

Cool, hipster Julia. They hadn't been close, but he'd liked her. Found her company easy. And now she was dead.

He swallowed, trying to keep calm. How? Why?

Fuck. He needed to find Miles. He turned and headed back through the changing rooms, pushing open the door into the hallway. The door to the utility room opened.

Carter spun around, gun raised, finger tensed on the trigger.

Welland wobbled out, nodding away to whatever was playing on the headphones clamped over his ears. He looked up and spotted Carter.

'SHIT!' His eyes widened. 'Why the fuck are you pointing a gun at me?'

'What were you doing in there?'

'Trying to sort out the power.'

Carter stared at him. Hair yanked back in a ponytail, sweat patches under the arms of his T-shirt, belly only just contained by the stained fabric. But no bloodstains.

He lowered the gun. 'What the hell's going on?'

'You tell me. The power went out again. When it came back on, only half the systems were running. Miles sent me down here to see if I could fix it.'

Which he obviously hadn't.

'How long have you been in there?'

'About an hour. I think the lights to Main 1 might have fused, but fuck knows where the spare fuses are. I'm gonna have to try and re-route some of the power —'

'Julia is dead.'

'*What?*'

'Julia is dead. In the swimming pool.'

Welland continued to stare at him, mouth hanging open like someone had unhinged his jaw.

'I don't — *Julia?*'

Carter nodded.

'Drowned?'

Carter thought about that cloud of red.

'I don't think so.'

'Fuck.'

'Where was everyone when you came down here to look at the power?'

'Er . . . Nate was making something to eat. Julia was watching TV. I don't know where Caren was . . . or Jackson.'

'Jackson is gone.'

'Gone?'

'He left.'

'When? Where did he go?'

'Who knows? He's probably already wolf meat.'

Welland blinked at him. Like someone had put him

on power-saving mode.

'Where's Miles?' Carter asked more urgently. Now was not the time to discuss Jackson. Not yet, anyway.

'He went down to the basement, to check everything was secure.'

Carter felt his throat constrict. 'How long was the lag this time, Welland?'

Welland blinked again. Then his large face crumpled. 'I *told* him. I told him it was getting worse, man.'

'How long?'

'Eight seconds.'

Eight seconds and the automatic locks in the basement released.

'Jesus Christ.' Carter ran a hand through his hair. 'And did you see Miles come back from the basement?'

'No, man. He told me to get down here right away and try to fix the problem.'

Oh, they needed to fix the problem. Question was — just how big of a problem did they have?

'We need to find the others,' Carter said.

Welland nodded, lip and chins wobbling.

'Have you seen Dexter?'

Welland shook his head.

Carter glared at him. 'And take those fucking headphones off.'

★   ★   ★

They walked across the hallway. Welland headed for the elevators. Carter caught his arm. 'We take the stairs.'

'Why?'

'Because we don't want to announce our arrival.'

74

Although, Carter thought as they started to climb the spiral, open-plan stairway, if anyone was up there, they had undoubtedly already heard them by now. He stared up. Darkness enveloped the top. He pulled out his torch.

'You got a torch?' he whispered over his shoulder to Welland.

'Yeah.' Rustling, grunting and a sudden blinding beam of light that illuminated the whole stairway.

'For fuck's sake,' Carter hissed. 'Keep the beam low.'

'Oh. Okay.'

The light dimmed. Carter sighed. They might as well have congoed to the top and set off some fireworks.

They finally reached the living area. Outside, the storm howled and raged, audible even through the triple glazing. Huge wads of snow clung to the glass, almost obliterating the outside world, cocooning them inside a tomb of white.

The rest of the room was eerily quiet. Carter shone his torch around.

'Man, I don't like this,' Welland murmured.

'Really?' Carter replied. 'I'm having a fucking ball.'

The torch illuminated small patches of the room, made unfamiliar by the darkness. But Carter could see that the seating area looked as if it had been hastily vacated. Mugs of coffee sat on the table, half finished. An ashtray contained a partially smoked joint.

'There's no one here,' Welland whined. 'Can we just —'

A moan. From their left. The kitchen. Carter flicked his torch over. The worktops were a mess. Spilled food, vegetable cuttings everywhere. Which, to be fair, was usually how Nate prepared food.

Carter walked quickly over, Welland a panting, sweating shadow behind him. As they rounded the large island, Carter pointed his torch down. Nate lay on the floor, half curled on his side. His white T-shirt was stained maroon with blood.

Carter crouched down. 'Nate?'

Another groan, but one eye flickered open. Thank fuck.

'Hey, man. It's Carter.'

'Cuh-ter?' Nate mumbled. It looked like a tooth had gone.

'What happened?'

Nate struggled to sit up, wincing in pain. There was more blood on the floor beneath him. Carter put a hand around his friend's shoulders.

'Welland,' he instructed. 'Get him some water.'

Welland hustled to the sink and clattered about clumsily, coming back with a glass of water, which he slopped everywhere. He handed it to Carter, who placed it to Nate's lips. Nate half drank and half dribbled water down his top. Carter gently took the glass back off him.

'Can you remember what happened?' he asked.

Nate frowned. 'I was making some food . . . and —'

'The power went out,' Welland interrupted. 'That's when Miles sent me down to the utility room to check what was going on.'

'Thanks, I got that,' Carter snapped. He focussed his attention on Nate. 'What happened to you?'

Nate blinked slowly. Carter didn't like it. He glanced back at the bloody T-shirt.

'I'm just going to lift your top, okay?'

Nate continued to stare at him blankly. Carter

pulled up the damp cotton. Nate's torso looked unblemished. No visible wounds. Maybe the blood was from the missing tooth. But that was a lot of blood on the floor.

'I was making some food —' Nate slurred.

'And Julia?' Carter prompted.

'Julia . . .' Nate squinted, like it hurt to force the words out.

C'mon, man, Carter thought.

'Candles,' Nate said triumphantly, like he'd just solved the meaning of the universe. 'She went . . . for candles.'

Candles. Right. So that explained why Julia had gone downstairs, but not how she had ended up dead in the pool.

'Did you see her?' Carter asked Welland.

Welland shook his head. 'No. You're not gonna pin this on me.'

'Julia —' Nate said again.

'Julia's dead,' Carter said, seeing no point in sugar-coating it. 'I found her in the pool. Looked like she'd been stabbed.'

Nate rubbed at his eyes. 'Julia.'

'I'm sorry.' Carter sighed.

He knew that Nate and Julia had been friendly. Maybe more than friendly on occasion.

'Nate,' he said. 'We need to find who did this. Did you see who attacked you?'

'I was —' Nate paused. Then he leaned forward and threw up, coffee and bile splattering the floor.

Carter jumped up, dodging the spray.

'Christ, man!' Welland cried. 'What the fuck is wrong with him?'

Nate remained, half bent over, drool hanging

from his lips.

'I don't know. Maybe he has concussion,' Carter said as the bitter smell of sick rose into his nostrils. 'We need to get him somewhere safe, then find out what the hell is going on.' He bent and helped Nate to his feet. 'And we need some fucking light,' he added to Welland.

'I was *trying*, man.'

'Well, try harder. Let's get Nate downstairs. You take him to the utility room. Lock yourselves in.'

'What are you going to do?'

'Try and find Miles.'

'What about Caren?'

'She can look after herself.'

'So can Miles.'

'Yeah, but we *need* Miles.'

Carter hooked Nate's arm over his shoulder and they staggered back down the stairs and into the light of the hallway. Carter felt himself breathe a little more easily. Crazy, the security light gives us. Like we still believe it will make all the monsters turn to dust.

Of course, now they *were* back in the light, Carter could see Nate properly. He looked bad. Really bad. And that was coming from a man who was no oil painting himself. *Hang in there*, Carter thought. *I don't want to lose you, man. I've lost enough.*

'I was just making some food,' Nate slurred.

'Yeah, you said.'

Nate's eyes were unfocussed, and the bandana was starting to worry Carter. Maybe there was a bad head wound beneath it. Nate swayed. Carter caught him.

'I was just making some food.'

'Why does he keep *saying* that?' Welland wailed.

Carter didn't know. But he did know that Nate had

been wearing a grey bandana this morning.

This one was dark red.

'Nate, I think we should just take a look at your head, okay?' he said.

Nate gaped at him. Carter unknotted the bandana and gently peeled it off.

The top of Nate's head slid off and hit the floor with a wet slap.

'*Jesus fucking Christ!*' Welland turned and retched.

Carter stared at Nate's gently pulsating brain. Grey and crinkled like a shrunken sponge. The tip had been skimmed off, along with his skull. Then he'd been wrapped back up again, like a zombie parcel.

Who the hell would . . .

'Carter,' Welland croaked.

And that was when he heard it. Of course.

Whistling.

They both slowly turned.

An emaciated figure in a bloodstained blue jump-suit stood behind them. His skin was pale, almost translucent. Cracked lips stretched over yellow teeth and his eyes were dark crimson. In one hand, he held a cleaver, still crusted with Nate's blood.

And *there* was the 'minor' problem.

Eight seconds and the automatic locks released.

And medicines weren't the only thing locked up in the basement.

The Whistler wheezed as he stared at them, red eyes gleaming with hatred.

Carter's finger tensed on the trigger. But he didn't shoot. Not because of any empathy or sympathy. But because they couldn't afford to waste him.

'I don't want to kill you.'

The Whistler grinned, showing black gums. He

took a step forward.

'It doesn't have to be like this,' Carter said.

The Whistler charged. Carter aimed at his leg. A shot rang out. The Whistler's head exploded. He staggered a few steps, cleaver still raised. A second shot and bright red blood bloomed in the centre of his jumpsuit. The cleaver fell with an echoing clang, and he crumpled to the floor. The whistling slowed and stopped.

Carter turned. Caren stood halfway up the stairs, gun clasped in both hands, still pointed at the body on the floor.

'What the fuck did you do that for?' Carter yelled.

She lowered the gun and glared at him. 'Save your ass? Oh, you're welcome.'

'You know the deal. No kills unless absolutely necessary.'

'True. Saving your life isn't *absolutely* necessary. But I've got mine to think of.'

Caren trotted down the stairs and walked over to the body. She pushed at it with her foot.

'Supply 01,' she muttered. 'I should have guessed.' She turned away. Her eyes alighted on Nate. 'Jesus.'

Nate stood swaying, drool hanging from his mouth. There was the sound of water trickling. A large dark patch spread out over the crotch of Nate's joggers and a small puddle formed on the floor.

'He's pissed himself!' Welland cried.

'Where the fuck is his head?' Caren asked.

Nate stared at them plaintively. 'I was just making some food.'

Carter felt his heart give. 'I know you were, man. I know you were.'

He raised his gun. But there was enough self-preservation left in what remained of Nate's brain for his eyes to widen. He turned and half stumbled, half ran towards the door to the pool. Carter fired off a shot, but he was wide, hitting the wood as Nate disappeared through.

'Shit,' he cursed.

'Great. Wound your prey,' Caren muttered.

He glared at her. 'He's not fucking prey. He's my friend.'

They ran after Nate, through the changing rooms and out into the pool area. Julia still lay at the bottom of the pool.

'*Shit!*' Caren cried. 'There's a body in the water.'

'I know,' Carter said. 'It's Julia.'

Nate lurched along the side. Then, he stopped. He stared at the pool. 'Julia.'

Carter didn't know whether Nate's depth perception had gone, or he'd simply forgotten that he couldn't walk on water, but he stepped straight out into the deep end. He hit the water like a rock. Old Nate could swim like an Olympic champion. But that part of him was lost. He surfaced, eyes wide, mouth working into words he couldn't find, slapping at the water with his hands like he was trying to grab it to stay afloat.

'I was just making some food,' he spat. 'Food.'

Carter lowered his gun.

Nate sank beneath the water once more.

Caren shook her head. 'He's done.'

Man, she was a cold bitch.

Carter waited. This time Nate didn't surface. Something briefly squeezed at Carter's heart and then, like Nate, it was gone.

He turned to Caren. 'We need to get down to the basement and check the isolation chambers.'

'Are you sure that's a good idea?'

'No.' He paused. 'But we need to see what else got loose.'

Hannah

'Did he say a bomb?'

Everyone talked at once. Voices clamouring over each other to be heard. Not panicking was obviously no longer an option.

'We have to get out of here.'

'We could be blown up any second.'

'He could be wrong.'

'Why would someone bring a bomb on board?'

'Okay! Okay!' Lucas attempted to shout over them. But this time, even his authoritative tone wasn't cutting it.

An ear-splitting, high-pitched wail reverberated around the coach. They covered their ears.

'Jesus!' Hannah cried.

Just as suddenly, it stopped. Daniel stood at the back, holding up the phone. He waggled it. 'Panic button,' he said. 'If you don't want me to press it again, shut the fuck up.'

'Hey, man,' Ben said. 'You're the one who told us there's a fucking bomb on board.' He coughed and reached shakily for a bottle of water. He looked pale. Hannah stored that thought.

'No,' Daniel said patiently. 'I said that Mr Jet is *sometimes* code for a bomb. We don't know for sure that's what the texts mean.'

'He's right,' Josh said, sounding as if he was trying to convince himself as much as anyone else. 'It could just be a coincidence.'

'But what if it isn't?' Ben asked.

Voices started to rise again.

'One at a time,' Hannah said. 'I know we're all scared, but we need to stay calm.'

'Okay,' Cassie said. 'So, let's look on the bleak side. If there *is* a bomb on board, what do we do . . . apart from die horribly, in pieces?'

'Why blow up a bus full of students?' Josh asked.

'Maybe the bus isn't the target,' Lucas said thoughtfully. 'The text says *Arrive*. It's more likely that the target is our destination — the Retreat.' He glanced at Hannah. 'And, possibly, your father.'

Hannah considered. Anti-science terrorism was growing, particularly among the young. They'd seen attacks in the capital, and in other countries. Activists had started to form organized groups and give themselves names like Stormers and, more recently, Rems (after the band who wrote: 'It's the End of the World as We Know It'). A centre like the Retreat, where new, experimental drugs were trialled, would be high on any group's list. As would her father.

She nodded. 'You could be right.'

'O–kay,' Josh said. 'So, if the target is the Retreat . . . then the dead guy will have been planning to set off the bomb when he got there, which he can't do now because, you know, he's dead.'

'Unless the bomb is on a timer,' Daniel said.

'Great,' Ben muttered.

'How likely is that?' Hannah asked.

Daniel pushed his dark hair behind his ears. 'Well, most improvised bombs are detonated either by a timer or manually, by a phone signal. We know mobile reception is bad here. If these guys are at all organized, they wouldn't risk not being able to detonate the bomb because of a poor signal.'

Hannah stared at him. She had to admit that she had misjudged Daniel. Because of his weight, his dishevelled appearance. She had marked him down as slow, lazy, stupid. It was her prejudice, one that had been drummed into her by her mother from an early age. *Fatties*, as her mother had disdainfully called them, were greedy, lazy creatures. Sitting around all day stuffing their faces. They had no self-respect. No self-control. No discipline. Her mother had been very proud of her own discipline, rigidly maintaining her size-six figure through a combination of diet, exercise and slimming tablets. An elegant mess of bones.

She had expected the same discipline from Hannah. She had weighed her only daughter constantly, restricted her food and made her skip on a rope until she collapsed in exhaustion. Aged ten, Hannah had still been wearing the clothes of a six-year-old.

After her mother died, Hannah had sat on the kitchen floor and eaten her way through the contents of the fridge: almost an entire cold chicken, half a trifle, a block of cheese, a hock of ham, olives, left-over pizza, fizzy, full-fat Coke. Indulgent food that her mother would buy for her father but never touch herself. Hannah ate until her belly was so distended she looked pregnant and could barely move for the shooting stomach pains. Somehow, she had made it to the bathroom and vomited up her pain and grief for most of the night. When her father returned from work, he had found her lying, passed out, in a small puddle of her own sick.

He had left her there.

'So, how much time do we have?' Josh asked.

Lucas checked his watch, a chunky and expensive-looking Rotary. 'It's 3.45 p.m. now. We left the

Academy at midday. We must have been travelling for about an hour and a half when the coach crashed —'

'But we don't know how far we have to go, how far away the Retreat is,' Cassie pointed out.

'I do,' Hannah said. 'I went there once with my father. I'd say it's probably a good five-hour drive from the Academy in good conditions, so maybe six or seven hours today.'

'That means we have an approximate ETA of 7 p.m.,' Lucas said. 'I would imagine our bomber wouldn't risk setting the timer before 8 p.m., so that gives us at least four hours.'

It wasn't much, and it was still a guess.

'We have to find the bomb and get rid of it,' Josh said.

'Yeah. Let's do that,' Cassie drawled. 'Oops. Small problem, dude. We're trapped in here, and it's minus ten out there.'

As she spoke, Hannah noticed her breath puff out in a small cloud of white. It was getting colder in the coach too.

'So, what do *you* suggest we do?' Josh asked, sounding irritated.

Cassie nodded at Hannah. 'The Prof's daughter could alert Daddy, for a start. Then, I guess we look for something we could use to break a window, so someone can get out and try to reach the luggage hold . . . if they don't freeze to death first, of course.'

Decent suggestions, Hannah had to admit. Although breaking a window would also increase the chances of them freezing to death in *here*. But that was a risk they would have to take.

Daniel was tapping at the phone.

'What are you doing?' Hannah asked.

'Changing the auto-lock to 'never'.' He handed the phone back to her. 'So you don't have to face ID a corpse each time you want to unlock it now.'

'Thanks,' she said. But right away Hannah noticed another problem. The battery was already on half power. It certainly wouldn't last the night. She opened a new text. Her father might not reply to an unfamiliar number. He might think it was a prank, but she had to try. She started to type:

Dad, it's Hannah. This phone is borrowed. The coach has crashed. Seven survivors. IED in luggage — possible detonation time of 8pm. Please send help ASAP. Hannah.

She pressed send and watched the blue bar creep up. Closer and closer to completion. And then it stalled. Fuck. An exclamation mark inside a red circle popped up. *Message send failure.*

'It didn't go,' she said dully.

'Shit, man.' Ben dragged his fingers through his scraggy hair, pulling it loose from the ponytail. 'We're toast.' He coughed again and shivered.

Hannah looked up. 'I can keep trying, but the battery is already on half charge. It might be better to conserve power and try again if I can get more signal?'

She took their lack of argument as acquiescence.

'Okay.' Lucas clapped his hands together. 'Plan B. We try to break a window to reach the luggage hold. *Los!* Let's go.'

They moved up the coach, some more willingly than others. Lucas and Josh led the way, Hannah followed, then Cassie. Ben slouched behind them, and Daniel brought up the rear, obviously reluctant to leave his sister.

Hannah couldn't help thinking that this was probably a pointless task. The glass was toughened, so they needed something heavy to stand a chance of breaking it. Plenty of the coach seats were half uprooted from the floor, but not enough that they could be pulled free.

'Hey, over here!'

Josh and Lucas crouched down between two seats on the right-hand side of the coach: the side half buried in the drift.

'This window is already broken,' Lucas said as Hannah and the others joined them.

Hannah looked at the glass, splintered into a crazy mosaic of shards. It might be possible to kick the glass out. But there was still a problem.

'It's buried in the snow,' she said. 'How d'you plan on getting out?'

Josh looked around. 'Did any of you do survival training?'

Cassie raised an eyebrow. 'Too busy drinking and taking drugs.'

Josh ignored her. 'One of the things we learned was how to make a snow tunnel, to shelter in extreme conditions. If the coach is resting on a big enough drift, there might be enough loose snow beneath to tunnel out?'

Hannah considered. 'But won't the snow be too compacted by the weight of the coach?'

'Not necessarily — and only one way to find out.'

Lucas frowned. 'It is a brave idea, my friend, but first we have to clear enough glass to make a hole big and safe enough to crawl through. Then there is the risk of the snow collapsing and burying you.'

'I'll take the risk,' Josh said. 'I've made snow

tunnels before.'

'It's dangerous,' Lucas said, voice tightening. 'With only a small chance of success.'

'But a small chance is better than no chance,' Daniel said. 'If we can find that bomb, we get to live tonight. But there's other stuff we could use in the luggage hold, to help us survive until rescue comes. Phones, food, more clothes. I left painkillers in my bag. Strong ones. Peggy needs them.'

He was right. This wasn't just about survival tonight. It was about survival period.

They looked at each other.

'Let him do it,' Cassie said. 'I mean, no one has any better ideas, do they?'

'We should let Josh decide,' Hannah said.

Everyone nodded, although Lucas still looked a little put out. Hannah got the impression he was comfortable in charge, less so when his authority was questioned.

'I want to try,' Josh said firmly.

'Very well.' Lucas sighed. 'Then we will help.'

Josh nodded. 'We'll need gloves or something to cover our hands with to remove the glass — and to dig.'

'We found some gloves on the other students,' Lucas said. He turned to Ben, who was slumped against a seat.

'Ben,' Lucas said. 'Can you go and fetch the gloves from the clothing we procured?'

Ben offered him a slightly dazed look. 'Gloves?'

'Yes. It's important. We need your help.'

'Right.' Ben slowly stirred back into life. 'Okay. Sure.'

He stumbled back down the coach, coughing

again. Hannah tried to contain her concern. She turned back to Josh.

'How long d'you think the tunnel will take?' she asked.

Josh considered. 'Hard to say. It really depends on the consistency of the snow and just how deep the drift is. An hour. Maybe two.'

Hannah glanced back out of the other windows. She could just see grey sky. But it was darkening. 'We probably only have an hour or so of light left.' She slipped the phone out of her pocket. 'You should take this. You can use it as a torch.'

'But then you don't have any way of contacting anyone for help.'

'If this goes wrong, we're all dead anyway,' Lucas reminded him. 'The phone will be more use for you. Once you open the hold —' He suddenly paused. '*Verdammt!*'

'What?' Josh said.

'The luggage hold . . . it will be locked.'

'*Shit,*' Hannah hissed. Why hadn't she thought of that before?

'The driver must have had a key,' Cassie said.

Hannah and Lucas glanced at each other.

'Hannah,' Lucas said steadily, 'why don't you see if you can find the driver's keys?'

She nodded. 'Okay.' She started to turn.

'I'll come with you,' Cassie said.

Hannah wanted to say no. But that would just look suspicious.

'Fine.' She forced a degree of pleasantry into her voice.

'Fine.' Cassie offered an insincere smile.

They climbed over the crumpled seats to the front

of the coach. It was probably Hannah's imagination — it wasn't long enough or warm enough for decomposition to have started — but it seemed as though there was already a slightly unpleasant smell coming from the dead bodies. She saw Cassie staring at them.

'I'm sorry if you knew any of them,' she said.

'I didn't. I didn't have any friends at the Academy.'

'Oh.' Hannah stared at her.

Cassie met her gaze. 'What? Did you think I was Miss Popular?'

Hannah shrugged. 'It makes no difference to me.'

They had reached the driver's cab. The disappearing driver, Hannah thought. Everyone else probably presumed he was dead. Only she and Lucas knew the truth. *Where was he? Had he managed to escape? Had the exit door only jammed afterwards?*

'You know — you really do take after your dad,' Cassie said.

Hannah turned sharply. 'I'm sorry?'

'Didn't I mention? I took your dad's class. Virology. Helped out in the lab sometimes too. He's a brilliant man. But very . . . what's the word? Clinical.'

'He's a scientist,' Hannah said tightly.

'Guess that must have been difficult.'

'I don't know what you mean.'

'I just got the impression . . . he's a hard act to live up to. Guess that's why you took general medicine, not research.'

Hannah fought down the bristling anger. 'You may have been one of my father's students, but that doesn't give you any insight into him or me.'

She slid into the driver's seat, indicating the conversation was over. The driver's jacket was still slung over the back. Standard green, the logo of the school

91

on it. Size S. Hannah tried to breathe out the anger. *Don't let emotion intrude. Don't be like your mother.*

She looked at the dashboard. The steering wheel was a good arm stretch away. She could barely reach the pedals, and she wasn't especially short. Something scratched for attention in her brain.

'Is there a key?' Cassie asked, interrupting her thoughts.

Hannah peered beneath the steering wheel. 'It's a push-button start.'

But you still needed the key fob to be nearby for that to work. Hannah picked up the jacket. *Small.* That scratching again. She shoved her hands in the pockets. Something bulky had been stuffed into one of them: a baseball cap with the Academy logo on. She frowned and then rummaged in the other pocket. *Yes.* Her fingers closed around a key fob with a smaller key attached. She pulled it out triumphantly.

Even Cassie managed a small smile. 'You know,' she said, 'the power to the engine probably cut in the crash. But if the battery isn't too badly damaged, there might be some residual power — for lights and maybe heat.'

When she wasn't drowning in a pool of her own sarcasm, Cassie could actually be helpful, Hannah thought. It was going to get dark soon, and colder. If they could eke out a few hours' light and heat, it would help.

She pressed the ignition. The engine made a spluttering sound and immediately died, but the dash and lights flickered on, and Hannah smelt the faint burning smell of the heating kicking in. It probably wouldn't last for long, but it was something.

'You have power?' A voice shouted. Lucas.

'Yes!' Hannah shouted back. 'And a key.'

'Excellent.'

But no driver, she thought, and the scratching scratched again. Small jacket. But she couldn't reach the floor pedals and the steering wheel was a stretch, indicating the driver was tall, with long arms and legs.

'What is it?' Cassie asked.

'D'you remember what the driver looked like?'

Cassie scrunched up her face. 'Big guy. Dark hair. Hat. Only saw him from the back.'

Hannah stared at her. 'Big guy?'

'Yeah. I mean, I didn't pay much attention, but I got that impression. Why?'

Hannah thought back to the figure she had seen standing outside the coach, smoking. Slight, short, wearing the official Academy cap. Probably the right size for the jacket over the seat.

'The jacket here is a size small,' she said to Cassie. 'But the seat position indicates a much bigger individual.'

'So, maybe the jacket belongs to a different driver?'

Hannah stared at her. *Of course*. A different driver.

'It wasn't the same driver,' she muttered. 'Someone took his place.'

'So?' Cassie said. 'Why does it matter?'

Hannah debated with herself. Could she trust Cassie?

'Okay,' she said. 'You mustn't tell anyone, but the driver has disappeared.'

'*What?*'

'He's not among the dead.'

Hannah watched as Cassie processed this.

'You think he got off the coach somehow?' she asked.

'Yes. But the question is how, and why?'

'Maybe he was the bomber's accomplice.'

'Maybe.'

'You don't sound convinced.'

'I don't know,' Hannah admitted. 'I feel like there's something else.'

Cassie looked thoughtful. Then she glanced quickly down the coach to check no one was in earshot and lowered her voice: 'Okay. There's something I need to tell you. Earlier, I said that I worked in your dad's lab.'

'Yes?'

'I helped with some of the testing for the evacuation.'

Hannah stared at her. 'And?'

'Obviously, pupils with negative tests were to be evacuated to the Retreat, to quarantine. Anyone with symptoms or a positive test was to remain at the Academy.'

'Yes. Of course.'

'Yeah. That's not what went down.'

'*What?*'

'I know at least two students on this coach tested positive.'

Hannah stared at her. 'Are you sure? Maybe you got them confused.'

Cassie smiled sourly. 'The thing about being the unpopular girl nobody notices is — you notice a lot. I know exactly which of the students I tested came up positive, and two of them boarded this coach.'

Hannah considered. 'Was one a skinny kid with frizzy hair?'

'Yeah. Jared. How do you know?'

'When I was stripping the dead, I thought that he

94

showed signs of infection.'

'But you didn't say anything.'

'Neither did you.'

'Touché.'

Hannah's mind ticked over. 'It doesn't make sense. My father would *never* let infected students leave the Academy . . .' She faltered.

Her *father* would never let infected students leave the Academy. But it wasn't just down to him. There were governors, investors and students with rich, powerful parents.

Hannah had noticed that most of those left at the Academy seemed to be staff and scholarship students. She had dismissed it as a coincidence. But what if it wasn't? What if some of the infected students had been allowed to leave, to appease their parents? What if her father had found out? She could imagine his reaction. *Never let the virus travel. Contain the infection at all costs.*

But would he really go so far as to engineer a coach crash and make it look like an accident? Would he let his own daughter die?

Yes, she thought. He would. *Shutdown.*

That was why the emergency exit had been tampered with, why the hammers had been removed.

'I think the driver crashed the coach on purpose,' she said to Cassie. 'None of us was supposed to reach the Retreat.'

'Are you serious?'

Hannah nodded. 'I know my father.'

'He'd let you die?'

'Without losing a wink of sleep.'

Cassie shook her head. 'Clinical, right?'

'Right.'

They both fell silent as they let this sink in.

Hannah realized there was another question she needed to ask.

'You said you knew that two of the students who boarded had tested positive. One is dead. Who's the other one?'

A long pause. Then Cassie said: 'You.'

Meg

'You killed him.'

Sarah stared at Meg with wild eyes. 'I was trying to save him.'

'You're a liar. You just murdered an innocent man.'

'Hardly innocent.'

Meg strode forward, fist clenched. Sean grabbed her arm. 'No. That's enough.'

She yanked her arm out of his grip. 'Is it? Before, we just suspected we had a killer on board. Now we *know* we have one.'

Max put an arm around Sarah as she cowered away. 'You're crazy,' she mumbled.

'Meg,' Sean said in a low voice. 'You were prepared to give Karl the benefit of the doubt. Don't you think Sarah deserves the same?'

'I *saw* her push him. Didn't any of you see it?'

'I couldn't be sure,' Max said. 'It all happened so fast.'

Sean sighed. 'I don't know. It could just have been an accident.'

Meg shook her head. 'Fine. Believe what you want. I *know* what I saw.'

They stood and glared at each other. A stand-off. The hatch had been shut. Both Karl and Paul were now frozen corpses in the snow. Except Karl had been alive on the way down. He had experienced the rush of freezing air, the terror of the fall, the knowledge that his life was about to end. Only seconds. But the seconds before death could feel like an eternity. She

97

should know.

'Look,' Sean said. 'I don't know if this makes any difference, but Karl's story, about being in prison —'

'What about it?' Max asked.

'I think he was lying.'

'I told you,' Sarah snuffled.

'I'm not saying he killed the security guy. But those tattoos. You don't pledge yourself to a gang for protection and get tattoos like that if you're just some no mark in jail for fraud.'

'What are you saying?' Max asked.

Meg knew. She just hadn't wanted to commit herself to that line of thought.

'I'm saying,' Sean continued, 'only one type of prisoner becomes a lackey for the gangs to avoid being killed.'

'Sex offenders,' Meg said with a sigh.

Sean nodded.

'I knew,' Sarah said. 'See. I knew there was something wrong with him.'

' 'Course you did,' Meg muttered.

'You sound like you're familiar with the prison system,' Max said to Sean.

Sean hesitated and then said: 'I was in prison for almost ten years.'

Now they all stared at Sean.

'What for?' Max asked.

'Theft.'

'Ten years seems a bit harsh,' Meg said.

'I stole a vehicle. There was an accident. People died. It was my fault.' He swallowed, looking uncomfortable.

'I was in prison too,' Max said.

'I thought you were a lawyer?'

'I was. I accepted some money from the wrong people.'

'So,' Sean looked around at the others. 'Are any of us here volunteers or are we all recruits?'

'I volunteered for the Retreat,' Sarah said. 'I saw it as my Christian duty.'

Of course you fucking did, thought Meg.

'And what are the Bible's thoughts on pushing people to their death?' she asked sweetly.

Sarah shot her a poisonous look. 'And why are you here?'

Good question.

Once upon a time a young woman had a daughter and she loved her very, very much. She would have given her life for that little girl. But she couldn't. Her little girl had died and there was nothing she could do. No way to heal the huge open wound in her heart. She had tried. Alcohol, drugs, sex. Nothing worked. The woman had realized that life had lost all meaning without her daughter. Just an endless treadmill of hurt. Every day was a fresh reawakening of pain. Ripping the raw wound open again and again. She was too weak. She couldn't take it.

She decided she would join her daughter. She tried to hang herself, but a friend found her. She didn't die. But she did end up in a psychiatric unit. The next time, she tried pills. She ended up back in the unit again. She tried to ingest bleach that a cleaner had carelessly left in the bathroom and, once they had pumped her stomach, they put her in a straitjacket and a padded room. Over the next few years, she spent more time in the padded room than out. She attacked the staff because they were keeping her from her little girl. Because they wouldn't just let her die.

99

And then she was offered a chance. She had been slumped in the dayroom, dosed up with pills, along with the rest of the slack-jawed and glassy-eyed residents of the unit, when the men in suits came. Grey men with weary faces and well-worn shoes.

They asked her questions. She ignored them. Then one of them mentioned 'the trials'. *The trials*. She had heard about them. Most people had. In whispers. On pirate media channels. Through the usual conspiracy theorists. Secret laboratories in remote places where the Department carried out trials on live 'recruits'. To try and find a way to beat the virus.

'We know you had a daughter who died,' one of the grey men said. 'By helping us you could stop other children dying.'

'Maybe I don't want to,' she had slurred. 'Maybe I want their mothers to feel the pain that I'm feeling.'

The grey man had shaken his head and stood, retreating to another table. The second grey man remained, staring at her curiously.

'I don't think you mean that,' he said.

'What the fuck do you know?'

'I know you want to die. And they won't let you.' He straightened the papers on the table in front of him. 'I think we could help each other out.'

She eyed him suspiciously. 'How?'

'The trials are high risk. Most recruits won't survive.' He shrugged. 'But at least their deaths mean something. For the good of humanity, right?

'Fuck humanity.'

'Suit yourself.' He started to stand.

'Wait?' She looked up at him. Her brain felt fogged and she couldn't disguise the desperation in her voice. She tried her hardest to form her words:

'*Most* don't survive?'

He leaned down and winked. 'I've yet to meet one.' He pushed a sheet of paper over the table to her and held up a pen. After a moment's hesitation, she took it.

He smiled. 'Sign here . . . and here.'

That had been over six months ago. They had got Meg off the drugs. Cleaned her up. Declared her an ideal subject. And now here she was, stuck on a broken-down cable car, fuck knows where, with a possible psycho killer. *For the good of humanity*. Right.

She looked around at the expectant eyes. 'Does it matter why we're here? If we don't want to go to jail, we need to get our stories straight. We've got *two* missing bodies to explain now.'

★　★　★

Karl had freaked out, tried to open the hatch. Mark, the security guy, had tried to stop him. They had both fallen out in the struggle. That was the story, and they all needed to stick to it like glue.

Meg sat down in the corner of the cable car furthest away from Sarah. The car rocked again. Her stomach lurched. At least a little murder and the disposal of a dead body had distracted her from her motion sickness. *When* were they going to get the damn power back on? Surely someone at some point would get the car moving?

She went to look at her watch then realized she wasn't wearing one. It had been taken, along with the rest of her belongings. No watch. No phone. No way of telling the time. How long had they been hanging here? Two hours? Three hours? More?

At the opposite end of the car, Max and Sarah sat together talking in low voices. Meg couldn't hear what they were saying over the roar of the wind outside, but their faces looked serious. Sean stood in the middle of the car for a while, staring out at the haze of white, and then he came and sat down beside Meg. Lines had been drawn, she thought.

'Hey,' he said.

'Hey.'

'You okay?'

'Not really.'

'Yeah.'

The cable car shuddered again. Meg's stomach rolled. And then she shivered. It was definitely getting colder in here. She could feel a faint heat coming from the air vents under the seats. There was lighting around the roof of the car. Powered separately by some kind of battery, she presumed. But how long would that last? Come night, temperatures would really drop. If they lost that scant bit of power, they would be hanging here in minus temperatures in the pitch black. It wasn't an inviting prospect.

Sean leaned in closer. Meg resisted the urge to move away. It wasn't that she found him a threat. And he certainly wasn't ugly or repulsive. He had a pleasant face with vivid blue eyes. He obviously worked out a lot. She could tell from the definition of his muscles when he had taken his snowsuit off. But she still didn't know him. And Meg didn't really like anyone edging into her personal space. The last people who had been up close and personal with her had been restraining her while they pumped her full of drugs.

'When you searched the security guy, you found something?' Sean whispered.

102

Of course. The photograph. She glanced across the car. Sarah and Max were still talking. If she couldn't make out what they were saying, she guessed they couldn't overhear her and Sean either.

'Yeah. Almost forgot.' She reached into her pocket and took the photograph out.

They bent over and stared at it. The picture was a selfie, taken against a snowy backdrop. A large building — church, university? — could just be seen in the background. A young man stood with his arm around a girl. The young man was swarthy, with a wide, chubby face and a mop of long, curly hair. The girl was stunningly pretty. Brunette waves, a pixie face with large blue eyes. Meg frowned. She didn't know either of these people. She glanced at Sean, who was also staring at the photo intently.

'Any ideas?' she asked.

He shook his head. 'Maybe they were relatives of his — kids.'

Meg looked back at the picture. She was pretty sure that neither of these people was related to Paul, and she knew he didn't have children.

'I don't know,' she said. 'He didn't look old enough to have kids this age. They look like they're in their late teens or early twenties.'

'Siblings then?'

'Maybe.' She turned the photo over. Written on the back were two names.

Daniel and Peggy. Invicta Academy.

'Mean anything to you?' she asked Sean.

'Nope. You?'

Invicta Academy. It rang a bell. A very distant bell, but Meg was sure she had heard the name before, somewhere. She stared back at the photo. Why had

Paul had this on him? Who were these people? If not friends or family, could they be suspects, victims? Or was she presuming too much? She hadn't seen Paul for years. He had a new life. Perhaps he had new friends, or stepchildren. And yet gut instinct told her that wasn't it. Something about the picture was off. *Invicta Academy*. What was it?

The car juddered again, creaking loudly from above. Sarah yelped. Meg raised her eyes to the roof. The whole cabin was coated in snow, more and more landing, settling. Overnight, it would freeze. And then, more would fall.

'What is it?' Sean asked.

'Just wondering how much weight these cabins are designed to carry.'

'At least twenty people, I'd say. Why?'

'Thinking about all that snow.'

He glanced up. 'I'm sure it's designed to cope with snow.' He paused. 'But then, normally, the snow would be cleared off at the terminus. The car wouldn't be stationary long enough for it to accumulate.'

'The cables will stand it though, right?'

'I don't know.'

Another alarming creak. At the other end of the cabin, Max stood up and walked, unsteadily, over.

He smiled awkwardly. 'We have a bit of an issue.'

'What?' Sean asked.

'Well, it's a little sensitive.'

Meg raised an eyebrow. 'More sensitive than pushing a man overboard?'

'Look, I don't condone . . .'

'Just spit it out,' Sean said.

'It's Sarah.'

Meg glanced over his shoulder to where Sarah sat,

bent over, arms wrapped around her stomach.

'What about her?' she asked without sympathy. 'She's ill? Dying? Having a crisis of conscience?'

Max sighed. 'She needs a shit.'

Carter

They stood in the hallway and stared at the elevator.

There were no stairs to the basement. No emergency exits. The sole access was via the elevator, with the security pass that only Miles possessed.

As far as anyone knew.

Which left Carter in something of a predicament.

'How are we supposed to get down there if Miles has the only pass?' Welland asked.

'Good question.' Carter looked at Welland. 'Is there any way you can bypass the security controls?'

'I don't think so.'

'Could you try?'

Welland considered. Carter could practically hear the cogs turning and see steam coming out of his ears.

Welland shook his head. 'No, there's no way.'

Welland really was a 'can't do' kind of guy.

'So?' Caren said.

Carter debated with himself. They had no idea what they would find down there. Miles might already be dead. In which case, at least he wouldn't be able to kill Carter for lying to him.

'Okay.' Carter started to reach into the hidden pocket in his jeans where he kept his stolen pass. Lifted off the body of a girl he once knew.

Before he could retrieve it Caren had stuck a hand down the neck of her T-shirt and pulled out . . .

Carter stared at her. 'Is that —'

She held up the basement pass up between her

fingers. 'Not that I don't trust Miles, but —' She shrugged.

'Where the hell did you get that?' Welland asked.

Caren smiled perkily. 'Ask me no questions, I'll tell you no lies. Now — are we doing this?'

Carter nodded. 'I guess so.'

He hit the call button.

'Do we all have to go?' Welland asked, twisting his T-shirt between his hands and treating them all to a glimpse of his pale, furry belly. 'I mean, shouldn't someone stay up here and be, like, a lookout?'

'Good idea,' Carter said. 'Split up. Always works well in horror movies.'

'And you most definitely do not look like the guy most likely to be killed before the opening credits,' Caren added, displaying a sense of humour unseen in the three years Carter had tried to avoid her. Perhaps all it took was a little horrific slaughter to bring out the best in some people.

Welland let out a deep sigh. 'This sucks, man.'

The elevator pinged. Caren and Carter raised their guns. The doors opened.

Something small, brown and white and furry leapt out, barking excitedly.

'Dexter!' Carter exclaimed.

Caren lowered her gun and wrinkled her nose. 'He stinks.'

Carter scooped the little dog up into his arms. 'Hey, fella. Did you get stuck in the elevator?'

'Well, he hardly called it himself,' Caren added, sticking a foot in to stop the door closing. 'Looks like he's left us a little present too.'

Carter ruffled the dog's ears. 'Aw, did you do a little shit? Did you?'

Caren rolled her eyes. 'Okay, the animal love is great. Can we get on now?'

Carter put Dexter down. 'Okay. Stay up here, buddy.'

They stepped in, trying to avoid standing near the deposit in the corner. But Dexter wasn't about to relinquish his new-found company. He bounded in after them.

Carter looked at Caren and shrugged. 'Looks like he's coming with us.'

She pressed her pass to the controls and hit 'B'.

'Great. When we all end up dead, he can feast on our corpses.'

* * *

The elevator slid silently down. Carter and Caren drew their guns as the doors opened.

The corridor was empty and lit by the emergency lighting, green strips along either side. Helpfully, it cast a ghoulish glow to proceedings.

'Man, it's like fucking Halloween down here,' Welland moaned.

For once, he wasn't wrong, Carter thought.

They stepped out. Carter led, Caren behind him and Welland trailing at the rear like a sulky child. Dexter scampered around their legs. The doors on their left were open, which was wrong. Normally, when the power was working, they were closed. The systems really had gone haywire. He glanced at Caren.

'You ever actually use that pass to come down here?'

'Once or twice,' she said. 'Just to check.'

'On what?'

'What do you think?'

108

Guns still drawn, they walked towards the first open door and peered inside. This had been the junior doctors' office. Three desks, ancient laptops gathering dust on top. People weren't so devoted to their computers or devices now. What was the point? The internet and phone networks were patchy, the news was all propaganda, TV was the same regurgitated shows and social media wasn't remotely social.

On the other wall, a large cork pinboard hung, peppered with curling pieces of paper. Jokes, cartoons, 'funny' workplace mantras. A take-out menu from the restaurant in the village. And a page from a newspaper:

INVICTA ACADEMY.
New research wing opened by Professor Grant.
Carter stared at it for a moment then turned.
'Let's check the next one.'

They withdrew and entered the second office. *His* office, Carter thought. The Professor. There was just one large mahogany desk in here, with an expensive-looking leather chair behind it. A heavy sideboard stood against one wall. Once upon a time, it had contained cut-crystal glasses and bottles of fine wine and whiskey. Those had long since been drunk. Straight out of the bottles.

The desk was bare except for a glass paperweight and a picture in a wooden frame. A girl, with fine mousy hair and cool grey eyes. Not quite beautiful. Her nose was too long and her face a little thin. But striking. Determined.

'Carter?'
'Yeah?' He turned.
Caren was frowning at him. 'There's nothing here. C'mon.'

109

He picked up the picture and laid it face down. 'Coming.'

They exited the office and checked out the labs. All empty. The only sounds were their own footsteps and the hum of the refrigeration unit.

'No one home,' Caren said.

'So, shall we go back up?' Welland asked, hopefully.

Carter gave him a look. 'Sure. *After* we check the chambers.'

* * *

There were a dozen isolation chambers in the basement. Officially. Unofficially, it was a baker's dozen. There was a thirteenth chamber, remarkably secure, and remarkably well hidden. *Officially*, of course, none of the chambers existed. Their true purpose was known only to a few important people. And the survivors.

Carter could smell the iron tang of blood before they even turned the corner. Dexter bounded ahead. When he reached the door to the isolation chambers he stopped and whined.

Know the feeling, buddy, Carter thought.

The door to the chambers, normally sealed, was half open. They stared at it.

'So, are we all ready?' Caren asked, as if they were about to begin a high-impact aerobics class rather than enter the seventh circle of hell.

No, Carter thought, but he nodded tersely and stepped inside. Caren followed. Welland whimpered, 'Oh man,' and trudged behind them.

Carter had been right. Dark red blood. All over

the floor and up the walls. Smeared across the glass screens of Chambers 1 and 2. The source lay about halfway down, between Chambers 3 and 4.

'Jesus fuck,' Welland moaned from behind him.

Caren just let out a low whistle between her teeth. Dexter sat down and started to lick his balls.

Carter moved forward. Tentatively, trying to make sure he didn't touch any of the blood. They were all vaxxed, but that wasn't a hundred per cent foolproof. As had been proven in the past.

He reached the body. Not Miles. Another Whistler. Blue jumpsuit, long grey hair. Face caved in — a catastrophe of smashed bones and blood. What was her name? Carter couldn't remember. She had been one of the nurses, Miles had told him. Carter had only ever known her as Supply 02.

He stood and looked back at the others. 'Dead.'

'Two down,' Caren said.

He nodded. *Where the fuck was Miles?*

They stepped over the body. In Chamber 3, a wasted figure crouched in the corner, face hidden by long, matted hair. This one didn't have much left in him. All but drained. A skeleton sheathed in skin.

'He was a doctor, before he became infected,' Miles had told Carter. 'He would bring female recruits down here sometimes, sedate them and, well, you can surmise the rest.'

Carter turned away. Dexter had finished his male grooming and trotted ahead of them. He stopped outside Chamber 4 and sat, panting happily. Caren and Carter exchanged glances. Three Whistlers had been contained down here. Three lots of supplies. Two were dead. One wasn't going anywhere.

Which left . . .

They walked up to the reinforced glass. Each chamber contained a bed, a chair, a wall-mounted TV, a small bookcase and a sectioned-off washing and toilet area. A small red light on the door indicated that the chamber was locked.

Miles was sitting inside, flicking through an old paperback and looking bored. He glanced up at their approach.

'Finally.' He shut the book and chucked it on to the bed. 'I wondered how long it would take you to find me and let me out.'

Hannah

She was ten when her mother killed herself.

Her father always said it was a cry for help. The sleeping pills and alcohol were just too much for her mother's frail body. But Hannah knew that her mother never did anything unintentionally. If the overdose was a cry for attention, it was intended to be her final one. She controlled her death as rigidly as she had controlled her life.

Aside from Hannah, control was all her mother had. Hannah's father had been a distant figure in both their lives for as long as Hannah could remember. A fleeting shadow in the corner of her eye. A transient ghost who walked in and out of rooms but never settled. Hannah had known bad smells that lingered longer.

'It's your fault my mother died!' she had yelled at him once, in a rare display of teenage angst. 'You didn't love her enough.'

Her father had fixed her with his chill gaze and said, 'Love cannot save people, Hannah. Only science can save people. One day you will understand that.'

Hannah did. She understood that her mother didn't want to be saved if she wasn't loved. She understood that science saved the many, not the few. And right now, if she wanted to survive, she would have to save herself.

Statistically, if Hannah was infected, she had a 98 per cent chance of showing symptoms. If she did show symptoms, she had a 75 per cent chance of dying. If she survived, well, that was the other percentage she didn't want to think about. Of course, they had about a 99.999 per cent chance of being blown to smithereens in the next two hours so maybe it didn't really matter.

'We keep this between us,' she said to Cassie. 'At the moment, our priority is the bomb.'

'Sure thing.' Cassie nodded. 'Way I see it, we're not getting out of this alive anyway. The only question is whether we get out in one piece.'

Hannah stared at her. 'And I thought *I* was a pessimist.'

'I prefer to think of it as being a realist. The fact is, if just one of us is infected, we probably all are —'

'That doesn't mean we'll all die,' Hannah said.

'No. But if the alternative is to end up a fucking Whistler —'

'Don't call them that,' Hannah snapped.

'Why?'

'It dehumanizes people.'

Cassie raised an eyebrow. 'I thought we were already dehumanizing them by putting them in the Farms —' She broke off and covered her mouth. 'Oops — probably not supposed to call them *that* either. What's the official term — Seclusion Centres?'

Hannah felt her jaw tense. 'What would you have the Department do? Those people may have survived, but they're still infected. They won't recover. Some are dangerous with the Choler variant. The Seclusion Centres are a humane solution.'

'Locking them away. *Using* them against their will.'

'That's not true.'

'Y'know,' Cassie mused, 'I seem to recall another

114

time in history when people were rounded up and put in places like that. What did they call them, back then? Oh yeah, concentration camps.'

'It isn't remotely the same,' Hannah said tightly.

Cassie smiled. 'I guess I should have had you down as a denier, bearing in mind who your dad is.'

'I am not like my father. And you shouldn't believe wild conspiracy theories on social media.'

'*Still* defending him when he's willing to let you die. That's devotion.'

Before Hannah could retort there was a shout from behind them.

'HEY!' Lucas's voice. 'Could you save the gossip for later? We need the keys.'

Hannah pushed past Cassie. 'Not a word,' she hissed.

She clambered back down the coach and handed Lucas the keys. 'Here you go.'

Josh and Lucas had cleared the glass and Josh had already made a decent-sized tunnel in the snow. Lucas had scooped the excess into a large pile that was melting nearby. Hannah was surprised. This might just work.

'Impressive.'

'Yeah,' Josh panted, wriggling his way back out. 'The snow isn't too compacted. It looks like I can get enough depth and then start to tunnel back up.'

'Do you need some help?'

He shook his head. 'Thanks, but this is kind of a one-man job. Plus, no offence, but I don't want anyone else screwing it up.'

'Fair enough.'

He shuffled himself back into the tunnel, only his feet now poking out. Hannah sat back and folded her arms. The faint heat from the air vents was already dissipating. Without the engine running it was simply residual. Soon, it would start blowing cold. They would be lucky to get another half an hour's worth of power from the battery. She rubbed at her arms. If they didn't get blown up first, there was the distinct possibility they might go to sleep tonight, fall into the arms of hypothermia and never wake up.

Cassie had sat down nearby, pointedly ignoring her. Daniel was at the back of the bus again, tending to his sister. An uncharitable part of Hannah (her father's part) wished the girl would just hurry up and die. At some point, she would become a liability. A drain on their resources. Already Daniel's time could have been better spent helping Lucas and Josh. He was a big guy. Another pair of hands would have given Lucas a break. She frowned. Talking of another pair of hands — there was someone missing.

'Where's Ben?' she asked Lucas.

'Oh, he, err, had to use the lavatory.'

Great. That should add to the already slightly ripe aroma inside the coach.

The toilet flushed and Ben stumbled out, wiping at his mouth. His lank hair was plastered to his scalp and dark circles bloomed beneath his eyes. He looked like he had been relieving himself at both ends.

'You okay?' Hannah asked.

He nodded, then coughed. 'Man, I wish I'd taken that Pedialyte out of my bag. You err, might not want to go in there for a —'

A thud shook the roof of the coach. They all jumped.

'Shit!' Ben cowered. 'What the hell was that?'

'Avalanche?' Cassie suggested. 'Meteor strike?'

Another thud. They raised their eyes to the roof.

116

The thud was followed by scuffling sounds. And then a grey silhouette slunk past the snow-caked windows.

Lucas clicked his tongue against his teeth. 'I think we have visitors.'

'Wolves,' Hannah said, her heart sinking.

Josh eased himself back out of the snow tunnel. 'Did you say wolves?'

More thuds, and the scrape of claws, this time from further down the coach. Everyone's eyes tracked the windows.

'I thought wolves were scared of people,' Ben said.

'Usually,' Hannah said. 'But they don't know we're people. Right now, all they smell is prey.'

And animals that were desperate and hungry grew bolder and more aggressive. Infected animals even more so. But no point mentioning that just yet.

More scuffling on the roof. They were scenting, Hannah thought. Searching for a prey they could smell but couldn't reach. And then a howl. First singular then joined by four or five more. For the first time, Hannah understood the meaning of blood-curdling.

A large figure stumbled down the coach. Daniel.

'Do you know there are wolves out there?'

'You catch on fast,' Cassie muttered.

'We know,' Lucas said coldly.

'What do we do?'

Lucas sighed. 'We wait. When they realize they cannot reach us, they will look for easier prey elsewhere.'

'But how long will that take?'

Lucas gave a small shrug. 'Hard to say.'

'What's the time?' Josh asked.

Lucas checked his watch. 'Five fifty-seven p.m.'

Around two hours left, if their calculations were

117

correct. Maybe longer. Maybe less.

Josh shook his head. 'I'm going to keep tunnelling. We can't waste the time.' He crawled back into the snow.

The rest of them stood, ears straining, eyes trained on the roof of the coach. Aside from Josh scraping in the snow tunnel, it had gone quiet.

'I can't hear them any more,' Ben murmured.

No, Hannah thought. And for some reason, that made her more nervous.

'Maybe they've gone,' Cassie said.

A faint scrabbling sound, this time to their right.

'Or maybe not,' she added.

The soft scrabbling continued.

'They can't reach us though?' Ben said nervously. 'I mean, there's no way in.'

But there was, Hannah suddenly realized. The tunnel. Shit.

'They can dig,' she said, looking around.

'What?' Cassie asked.

'Wolves. They can dig. They dig out prey.'

'Are you sure?'

'Yes. I saw it on a documentary.'

'*Scheisse*,' Lucas hissed.

Hannah bent down. 'Josh, get out of the tunnel!'

'What?'

'Get out. Now!'

Lucas grabbed Josh's ankles and hauled him back into the coach.

'What the hell —'

The tunnel collapsed in a small avalanche of snow. Cassie shrieked as a pair of snarling jaws burst through the white, smearing it with pink saliva.

'Fuck!' Josh yelled, scrabbling away.

Lucas kicked out at the wolf with his feet. Josh joined him, pushing back at the snow with his heels to block the probing snout.

'Kill it, man!' Ben screamed.

'What the fuck with?' Josh shouted back.

'It's just hungry and desperate. We need to scare it off,' Hannah cried.

'The phone. The alarm!!' Daniel yelled.

'Where is it?'

Josh reached into his pockets. 'I must have dropped it,' he said. 'In the tunnel.'

'Wait,' Lucas said. 'I see it.'

So could Hannah. Near Josh's feet, half buried in the snow.

She dived forward. The wolf's snout burst through the snow by her ear. Hannah felt its hot breath, saw the flash of yellowing teeth.

She raised the phone and pressed the alarm. The ear-splitting siren pulsed out. The wolf howled, but this time in fear, not fury. The snout and scrabbling claws retreated. Hannah kept her thumb pressed on the alarm. Eyes squeezed shut, heart pounding. She couldn't stop, couldn't move. Someone grabbed her. She turned and almost punched them. Daniel caught her arm.

'Enough. It's enough. It's gone.'

Hannah released her thumb. His voice sounded oddly distant. Her ears were ringing. She sat back, breathing hard.

Everyone fell into a stunned silence. The wolves had gone. But so had the tunnel Josh had created. Snow had caved in on the broken window again.

'Guess the tunnel is fucked,' Cassie observed.

'What do we do now?' Ben moaned.

'We dig it out again,' Lucas said briskly, looking at Josh.

Josh nodded wearily. 'This time I might need some help.'

'You shall have it.'

'What if the wolves come back?' Daniel asked.

Lucas's lips thinned. 'We work fast.' He nodded at Hannah. 'And we still have the alarm.'

But for how long, Hannah thought, glancing at the phone. The battery was down to a quarter.

And then she realized something else. There was a new message. The phone must have briefly found some signal. She looked up. The others were preoccupied with the snow tunnel.

She clicked the message open.

When the storm eases, we will find you. Soon. P.G.

P.G. He could never bring himself to sign *Dad*, or even *Father*.

But he had received Hannah's text. He knew they were alive.

We will find you. Soon.

Hannah debated with herself.

And then she quickly deleted the message.

They were running out of time, in more ways than one.

Meg

It was never like this in the movies. When disaster struck — a plane hijacking, terrorists taking over a skyscraper, the zombie apocalypse — no one ever stopped to say, 'I really need a shit.'

Logistics were discussed. It was eventually decided that Sarah would 'go' in one corner, collect the deposit with one of her socks and dump it back out of the hatch. The rest of them stood in the opposite corner, facing out through the glass, staring at the rapidly darkening sky, trying to pretend they couldn't hear any noises or smell the rank aroma.

A small part of Meg shared the other woman's shame. Being forced to crap in the corner of a cable car marooned a thousand feet up in the sky was not on anyone's bucket list. On the other hand, karma.

Finally, Sarah walked over, looking embarrassed. Sean pulled open the hatch and she dropped the soiled sock and its contents out of the car. The smell, and a faint smear of brown on the floor, remained.

'Thank you,' she mumbled to Sean.

'Hey, we all have to do it.'

'Yeah.' She gave him a grateful look.

'Y'know, perhaps we should consider this situation,' Max said.

'I'd really rather we just forgot about it,' Sarah said.

Difficult, Meg thought, when the whole cabin smelled of shit.

'What I mean is,' Max continued, 'if we're going to be stuck here for a while, we may all need to relieve ourselves one way or another.'

'Well, Max and I can just pee out of the hatch,' Sean said.

'Bully for you,' said Meg. She looked around. They didn't have any containers, no empty bottles. No food or water, she thought, which could soon be another problem.

'Our boots,' she said suddenly.

'What?'

'If we need to pee, we can pee in a boot, then empty it out of the hatch.'

'Oh, dear God,' Sarah muttered.

'Well, if you have a better idea?' She stared at Sarah.

Sarah dropped her eyes and shook her head. 'I suppose not.'

'Hopefully it won't come to that,' Max said in a reassuring tone. 'I mean, I'm sure people are trying to fix the power right now.'

Sean and Meg exchanged looks. She knew what he was thinking. 'People' weren't as reliable as they had once been. Even those who worked for the Department. Everything was fractured now. Society, order, infrastructure. Add to that the fact that 'the trials' were secretive projects run by a select few. Officially, they were gradually being phased out. If anything happened, there were far fewer 'people' to put it right.

'It's probably best to be prepared for every eventuality,' Sean said.

'Fine.' Sarah fingered her cross. 'But I've said a prayer and I'm sure we'll have power again soon.'

It was on the tip of Meg's tongue to ask her if she had squeezed in the chat to God while she squeezed out her shit, but before she could speak there was a lurch . . . and the cable car began to move.

Sarah gave Meg a triumphant look. 'See.'

The car crawled slowly upwards. Meg pressed her face to the glass. Ahead, she could see the tip of the mountain and a grey sphere jutting out that must be the upper terminal. Her heart began to lift. It could only be another few hundred feet. Closer and closer.

There was another lurch, a hideous screech of metal. Meg turned. The cabin swung wildly forwards then they were hurtling backwards, down the cables. The reverse velocity was so fast and unexpected Meg found herself lifted off her feet and flung against the opposite wall. Dazed, she scrambled for something to hang on to, fingers grabbing a pole. Max hit the floor hard, his head smashing into the side of a bench. Sarah hung on to another pole and Sean fell against Meg. There was a second jolt, throwing them all back the other way, and then the car ground to a halt, rocking gently. They remained clinging on to whatever they could, breathing hard.

For a moment, no one spoke. Sarah was crying.

'Jesus,' Sean breathed. 'Everyone okay?'

Meg nodded. Sarah whimpered. Max groaned from the floor.

'What happened?' Meg asked.

'I think there was a surge of power . . . and then the haulage cable snapped,' Sean said.

'Oh God. We're all going to die,' Sarah cried.

'No,' Sean said. 'There's a support cable. That jolt was the emergency brake kicking in.'

'You seem to know a lot about cable cars,' Meg said.

He shrugged. 'Just basics.'

Max was attempting to sit up. Meg moved across the car to help him. His glasses were cracked, and he

123

had a nasty gash on his forehead where it had struck one of the benches. Blood trickled down his face. Meg looked around for something to wipe it with and settled on the sleeve of her snowsuit. Fortunately, the wound looked shallow, and a bump was forming, which she vaguely remembered was a good thing with head injuries.

'You've got a fair crack on your head there,' she said. 'You don't feel sick, do you? You didn't lose consciousness?'

'No. Argh.' He groaned again. 'My wrist. That's what really hurts.'

Meg gently took the man's arm. She studied his wrist. It was bruised and bent at a slightly unnatural angle.

'Can you move it?'

Max frowned then shook his head. 'No.'

'I think it might be broken.' She looked around hopelessly. 'We haven't even got a first-aid kit.'

Sean started to unzip his snowsuit. Meg stared at him.

'What are you doing?' she asked.

'First-aid.'

He pulled off his T-shirt. Meg noticed a tattoo on his chest. A girl's face. Surrounded by wavy dark hair. Familiar somehow. She frowned. And then it was gone again as he zipped the suit back up.

He ripped the T-shirt down the seam, splitting it into two pieces of fabric, then crouched next to Max. 'This might hurt a bit,' he said.

He took the man's arm and wrapped one part of the fabric around his wrist to keep it stable. The other half he fashioned into a makeshift sling, looping it around Max's neck. He gently eased the man's wrist into it.

Max winced but nodded. 'Thanks.'

Meg eyed Sean curiously. 'You're a man of many talents.'

'Not really.' He offered a small smile. 'I just know a little about a lot of stuff.'

The car rocked again, harder. Above them the cable creaked. They all raised their eyes to the roof.

'You said there was a support cable,' Max said. 'If the power comes back on, will the car move, or do we have to wait for rescue?'

'That I don't know,' Sean admitted.

Another gust of wind. The movement felt rougher. Only one cable now. All of their lives hanging, quite literally, by one giant steel thread. And then there was the thing that everyone was trying hard not to be the first to say.

It was Max who made it real: 'What if rescue doesn't come?'

They all looked at each other, but no one had an answer.

Which, of course, was when the lights flickered and the power in the car went out.

Carter

The takeover had happened before Carter arrived at the Retreat.

There had been an outbreak amongst the medical staff. A bad one — Choler variant. Within forty-eight hours most of the staff were dead. A few escaped. Some were contained in the chambers. To prevent the spread. And for other reasons.

Miles and the other survivors found themselves the Retreat's sole caretakers.

And they wanted to keep it that way.

As far as the Department was concerned, the Retreat was a dead zone. The trials had been winding down for a while. There was talk that they might be abandoned altogether. To all intents and purposes, the Retreat had never existed in the first place. It was easier for everyone if it never existed again. *Shutdown.*

That was three years ago. So far, the Department had shown no signs of wanting to reactivate the Retreat. Perhaps they really had forgotten about it.

But that could always change.

Sleeping beasts could be awakened.

The Department might decide to send people in again.

Especially if they ever found out about Isolation Chamber 13.

★ ★ ★

The four of them gathered in the living area, settling on the sofas. Dexter perched on Carter's lap. Caren had fetched candles from the storeroom and now she lit them while Miles recounted what had happened.

'When the power cut, I headed straight down to the basement to check the security of the isolation chambers. When I got there, 02 was already outside her cell and 01 was on the floor. We know 02 has long exhibited advanced symptoms of Choler variant. I thought she had attacked him. Stupid of me to fall for such an obvious ploy, but it happened so fast. I trained my gun on her but then 01 was up. He knocked me over and bolted for the elevator. I got off some shots, but she charged me, and while I fought her off he made his escape.'

Because you only needed a pass to get down to the basement, not up from it.

'How the hell did you end up inside a chamber?'

'Under the circumstances, with an insane inmate trying to throttle me, it seemed the safest place. The doors lock automatically once they're closed.'

'You locked *yourself* in there?' Caren said.

'Of course. I presumed you'd find me eventually, if any of you were still alive.' He eyed her shrewdly. 'After all, I'm not the only one with a pass to the basement, am I?'

Caren met his gaze. 'It's just for back-up.'

'Someone has to gatekeep the gatekeeper, right?'

'Right.'

Miles nodded, then said in a harder voice. 'I'll need that pass, Caren.'

She hesitated. But not even perky Caren with a C argued with Miles. Reluctantly, she pulled the pass out and handed it over.

'Thank you.' Miles slipped it into his pocket.

'What if we hadn't found you?' Carter asked, keen to change the subject.

'I had my gun. A bullet would have sufficed.'

'So you didn't kill 02?'

'No. In fact, I watched as she smashed her own brains out against the glass.'

'She did that to *herself*?' Welland exclaimed.

Miles shrugged. 'We know what Choler does to the infected. She wanted to die. She was the sacrifice so that 01 could escape.'

'He wanted to die too,' Carter said. 'But he wanted to take us with him.'

Miles nodded. 'Understandable. If I was being kept down there, I'd probably want to do the same.'

They considered this. Mostly, Carter thought, they tried *not* to consider the occupants of the isolation chambers and what they were used for. Necessity might be the mother of invention, but it was also the father of fuck you.

Miles was the only one who went down there regularly, to extract blood plasma for the vaccines. Taken from living survivors of infection, it was the only way to provide reliable immunity. Traditional vaccine methods didn't work. The Department's scientists had tried and tried. The greatest minds. Billions of dollars. Secretive 'trial' centres such as the Retreat. But the virus always evaded them. Only plasma from the source could provide protection. And regular boosters were needed.

Hence the Farms. Huge detention centres outside the cities where the living infected were contained (for their own good) and 'milked' for plasma. For the greater good.

128

Funny, how many terrible things were done for the 'greater good'. Carter sometimes wondered at what point the balance tipped. When did the greater good become the fortunate few — and screw everyone else?

But then, Carter wasn't in any position to moralize. The Whistlers had been kept here for the exact same reason. Regular boosters. *Supplies.*

The blood groups had to match, of course, but they had been lucky. 01 was O+, 02 was AB+ and 03 was O− (the universal donor). Good donor bloods. But now they were down to one, weakened supply.

'So, what do we do?' Caren asked. 'We only have 03 left. He's almost done. That's not enough.'

'But there are only four of us left now,' Welland said.

'Yeah, let's look on the bright side,' Carter intoned drily, stroking Dexter.

Caren frowned. 'What about Jackson?' She looked between them. 'Has anyone *seen* Jackson?'

Carter and Miles exchanged glances.

'Jackson has left the building,' Miles said.

'*What?* How?'

Miles sighed. 'It is likely that he was stealing plasma. He ran. He's probably dead.'

'*Jackson?*' Caren said in the same disbelieving tone. 'But he wouldn't. He —'

'He what?' Miles pounced on the hesitation.

Caren shook her head. 'Nothing. I just find it hard to believe. I mean, he's not like Anya —'

Carter tensed at the sound of her name. No one talked about Anya.

'Unfortunately, your belief makes little difference to our situation,' Miles snapped, and Carter could tell it had rattled him too. 'The point is,' he continued, 'even though there are now only four of us, we require boosters every four to six weeks. Our current stock will run out rapidly. We could stretch to eight, maybe even twelve at a real push. Worst-case scenario — we could go without. We're safe and isolated here. *But*, in case any of you are forgetting, we still need to supply Jimmy Quinn. If we don't —' He looked around and let the implication hang. Long enough for them to imagine what might shiver and squirm on the end of it.

Up until now, the deal Miles had struck with Jimmy Quinn had suited them all. Even with the Farms, demand for blood plasma outstripped supply. Hence there was a big black market for it — for all medicines, in fact — and Quinn had associates who would pay handsomely. In return for regular supplies, Quinn and his burly sons had left the inhabitants of the Retreat well alone. But it was a deal with the devil. If their supply faltered, their days in the snow were numbered.

'We need fresh supplies,' Miles finished.

Carter shook his head. 'No.'

'We don't have any choice.'

'There's always a choice.'

'The plasma needs to be extracted from living survivors. If you have a better suggestion, I am all ears.'

Carter stared at him, opened his mouth and then shut it so hard he felt his teeth crunch.

'How do we even . . .' Welland stuttered, twisting his T-shirt again. 'I mean . . . do you mean —'

'He means Whistlers,' Carter snapped. 'Okay? He means trapping fucking Whistlers — out there.'

Caren's face paled. Welland looked like he'd just dumped in his pants.

'But how?' Caren asked.

'We have the tranquillizer gun,' Miles said. 'We get in fast, take down the weakest, drive the others away. Then drag the bodies back to the Retreat.'

'You make it sound simple,' Caren said. 'We all know they're not so easy to drive off. Most have Choler. They're dangerous.'

Miles sighed and looked around at them. 'Which is why we shouldn't leave the decision too late. It might take several attempts to get what we need.'

Carter shook his head. 'Fuck.'

'In the meantime,' Miles continued, 'we have more immediate concerns — we need to dispose of the redundant supplies and the other bodies. We can't have corpses hanging around, especially if our immunity is going to be compromised.'

They all nodded. Survivors, even dead ones, could still infect — through shedding and blood.

'We need to clean up and get them into the incinerator asap. I am tasking you with that, Welland.'

'Oh, man,' Welland whined. 'I mean, that's, like, four trips.'

'Indeed,' Miles replied without sympathy. 'Which brings me to my next point. The power situation.'

'More like the lack of power situation,' Caren muttered.

'Indeed,' Miles said again.

Carter could tell he was getting annoyed. Miles's annoyance tended to work in direct correlation to how much he sounded like someone had stuffed a bunch of plums up his backside.

'The automatic locks in the chambers are functioning again. For now. But the system is still compromised. The battery and generator are both failing. Welland does not seem to be able to provide

131

us with an easy fix.'

'I've tried, man,' Welland moaned. 'It's not my fault. They're both fucking junk.'

'Precisely.'

'What?'

'We need to replace them.'

'I don't have a generator up my fucking ass,' Welland grumbled.

'That could be arranged,' Carter said.

Miles's lip twitched. 'I am aware of this, Welland. However, the cable-car station has its own battery and generator, does it not?'

'Well, yeah,' Welland said slowly, like a goat being led into a bait trap.

'So, if we fetch them and bring them here, then we might have a solution to our problem.'

Welland's face crumpled. 'But the cable-car station is, like, a three-mile hike. And it's high, man. With my asthma —'

Carter snorted.

Miles smiled thinly. 'Indeed.'

Uh-oh. Third one. Not good.

'I'm not suggesting you come, Welland. It would be a shame to gain a battery and generator and lose you upon the way. You will provide instructions for their removal. Carter and I will retrieve them.'

Carter felt his world shift a little and imagined his face might look just as pale as Welland's right now.

'We will?'

'Yes.'

'Not to put a dampener on our little hiking trip — but have you seen outside?' Carter nodded towards the picture window, now almost entirely sheeted in white.

'The worst of the storm should pass tonight,' Miles said. 'We'll set off first thing.'

'If we can dig ourselves out.'

'If that's what it takes.' Miles eyes were glacial. Carter knew there was no arguing with that tone.

'What about me?' Caren asked. 'Am I supposed to stay here and bake cookies?'

'Someone needs to hold the fort,' Miles said. 'And keep an eye on Supply 03.'

She sighed. 'Fine.'

Miles looked at Carter. 'Okay?'

No, Carter thought. Very much not okay. But he couldn't explain why, not in front of the others, and Miles knew it.

'Fucking dandy,' he said.

He shifted Dexter from his lap to the sofa, got up and walked towards the stairs.

'Where are you going?' Caren asked.

'To fish my dead best friend out of the fucking pool.'

★ ★ ★

The pool net wasn't big enough. It was designed for fishing out sunglasses and shit, not dead bodies.

The best Carter could manage was to shovel both Julia and Nate along the bottom into the shallow end. It was hard work. Dead bodies always weighed more. And dead bodies in sodden clothes weighed more still.

Carter had already shed his top and was coated in sweat by the time he dropped his pants and waded into the shallows to haul them both over to the side of the pool. He propped the bodies against the steps. Then he climbed out and pulled them on to the poolside.

133

Their skin was white —Whistler white — and crinkly, shrunken. Touching it made him want to retch. When did that happen? he wondered. When did we stop being people that others wanted to touch and hug and become these revolting husks? Or was that what we always were? Lumps of meat given life by a flick of the sorcerer's wand. Perhaps death didn't take anything away. Perhaps it merely restored us to our natural state.

He stared down at them. Something else was wrong. Not just their deadness. Not just the fact that Nate was missing the top of his head. It was Julia.

Carter crouched down and lifted her T-shirt. The water had washed away the blood and he could make out three separate stab wounds. Deep. Jagged. Made with a large blade. A bread or steak knife, at a guess.

But 01 hadn't had a knife.

Carter supposed he could have dropped it somewhere. They could have missed it. But it wasn't in the pool. It wasn't in Julia.

He frowned, trying to imagine the sequence of events: 01 escapes the labs, comes up in the elevator. Does he encounter Julia then, as she's coming out of the storeroom, before going upstairs to the living area? If so, how did Julia end up in the pool and why wasn't there any blood in the hall? And if 01 had killed Julia before killing Nate, where did he get the knife from?

Or did he go straight up to the living area, attack Nate, steal a knife and come back downstairs to stab Julia? No, Carter thought. Not enough time. Julia had only left to fetch candles. She would have gone back upstairs and discovered 01. Besides, why steal a knife and stab Julia if he already had the cleaver? It didn't make sense.

Unless 01 hadn't killed Julia.

'Carter?'

He jumped and stood up.

Miles stood at the entrance to the pool. He glanced at the bodies.

'Is everything okay?'

'Besides the obvious?'

'Yes.'

Carter hesitated. *The knife. Julia.* Then he shook his head. 'It just sucks. All of this shit. It fucking sucks.'

Miles nodded. 'But we always knew it might come to this.'

'Did we?'

'That's why we had a contingency plan — to acquire fresh supplies.'

Carter glared at him. 'Could you stop calling them that?'

'How would you rather I refer to them? Whistlers? The infected? None of that is important. What they *are*. What they *were*. All that matters is what they can provide. You never had a problem with it before.'

'That was different.'

Miles smiled thinly. 'No. It wasn't. Morally, ethically, it was just the same. The only difference now is your personal feelings.'

He was right.

'I saw her,' Carter said. 'In the woods.'

Miles shook his head. '*No.* You saw a ghost . . . someone or something that looked a little like her.'

'What if you're wrong? What if she survived and she's out there?'

Miles tutted. 'And what if she is? You know what she'll have become. Your concern is touching, but it changes nothing.'

135

Carter stared at him, wondering — not for the first time — if he had the guts to kill Miles. To hold his smug, blond head under the water while he thrashed and kicked until the last gasp of air had bubbled out of him.

Carter didn't. The man had saved his life. He owed him. And without Miles, none of them would have survived this long.

'Carter,' Miles said evenly. 'Anya is dead.'

Carter stared at him. 'I hope so,' he said. 'I really fucking hope so.'

Hannah

They took it in turns to tunnel, working to Josh's instructions. He was too tired to do it all on his own. They needed to work quickly, not meticulously. Darkness was falling fast outside, and time hung heavily over them. Less than two hours. Those not tunnelling shifted snow back into the coach, where it melted on the floor.

Tunnelling was the better job, Hannah thought. At least it kept you warm. The heating had died. The lighting had dimmed to a feeble flicker. If they managed to find and dispose of the bomb, night would bring the next real test. Without light or heat they were vulnerable. Cold could be a stealthy killer.

She found herself glancing around at the rest of the group, assessing them. Josh was back in the tunnel, digging. He was physically strong and level-headed. Hannah wasn't worried about him. Nor Lucas, with his steely pragmatism. Cassie might be spiky, but she was tough. Daniel, she couldn't get a handle on. He had retreated to the back again to tend to his sister. When Peggy died — because she would, one way or another — how would he cope?

Right now, Ben was the one who worried her. He had struggled with his tunnelling stint and was curled up on a seat a little way back. His breathing was harsh, his eyes half closed. Exhaustion? Hypothermia? Or infection?

Hannah dumped a pile of snow on the floor. Even with gloves on, the cold was eating into her bones.

She lowered her voice so only Cassie could hear her: 'I'm worried about Ben.'

Cassie glanced up. 'Yeah, he doesn't look so good.'

Their eyes met. The unspoken suspicion passed between them.

'I'm going to get us some more clothes from the back,' Hannah said. 'It could be the cold. None of us should let our body temperature drop too much.'

Cassie nodded. 'While you're there, you might want to tell Daniel he's up to tunnel next, dying sister or no dying sister.'

Hannah climbed over the twisted seats to the rear. Daniel was crouched next to Peggy, administering water to her dry lips. A waste, Hannah couldn't help thinking. Giving her water would do nothing. It just meant less for the living. In a way, trying to sustain her was a cruelty; maybe better to let her go than prolong the inevitable.

But then, Peggy wasn't *her* sister. When you loved someone, you tried to hold on to them because letting go meant admitting you would never hold them again. Few of us were prepared for that. So, we clung on, even when Death's bony grasp would have been kinder.

Daniel looked around as Hannah approached. 'My turn, right?'

'Yeah.'

'Can you watch Peggy?'

'Of course.' And then, because she felt she had to, Hannah asked: 'How is she?'

Daniel regarded her with his sharp blue eyes. Not slow, or stupid, she reminded herself.

'Why don't you tell me?' he said.

Despite herself, Hannah crouched down next to the

girl. Her skin was clammy, her breathing rough. The leg was still a mess. Hannah could smell death upon her. Not a metaphor nor an exaggeration. You really could smell when someone was dying. As the body failed it gave off a distinct acetone odour. Changes in the metabolism affected the scent emanating from the breath, skin and bodily fluids. Part of the deteriorating body's chemical breakdown.

It was a miracle the girl hadn't yet died from blood loss. Although that was probably why her consciousness was intermittent. When oxygen is depleted, the body concentrates on diverting it to the most vital places to keep us alive. Consciousness isn't necessary for survival.

Hannah sighed. 'Not good.'

'She's going to die, isn't she?'

'I think that is the most likely outcome.'

Daniel swallowed back tears. 'Well, thanks for not sugarcoating it.' He looked back at his sister. 'Our parents died young. I always swore I'd look after Peggy. Big brother, you know.'

Hannah didn't, but she nodded anyway. 'I'm sorry.'

'D'you have any brothers or sisters?'

'No, I'm an only child.'

'Right. Well, I guess your parents doted on you.'

'Not really. My mother killed herself when I was ten and my father was always busy with work. I went to boarding school and then came here to the Academy.'

'Right. That sounds . . . cold.'

'I never really thought about it.'

But she had, of course. She had wondered why her father didn't come to take her home for the holidays like other children's parents did. She had wished she

had a mother who could send her lovely parcels decorated with ribbons and notes with hearts on (not
that her mother would have ever done that when she
was alive). The parcels her father sent were dull and
practical. Always signed *P.G.* rather than *Love, Dad.*
For all his brilliance in medicine and science, her
father had never managed to grasp the concept of
love. Unable to comprehend something he couldn't
put under a microscope or dissect.

Daniel was still staring at her. The intensity of his
blue eyes made Hannah uncomfortable.

She smiled tightly. 'Anyway, my father ensured I
had the best education.'

'Well,' he said. 'That's what's important, of course.'

Before she could decide if he was mocking her, he
turned and kissed his sister's forehead. 'I'll be back
soon, Peg.'

She found herself squirming at the gesture. Her
father's daughter. Uneasy around affection. Incapa-
ble of love.

''Scuse me.' Daniel stood, eased his bulk around
her and started to clamber heavily up the coach.

Hannah sat and stared at the girl. She wished she
hadn't agreed to stay with her now. *Why won't you die?*
It would be kinder, she thought. Kinder for all of them.
Peggy's presence at the back of the bus was a distraction.
Bad for morale. In a hospital a nurse would probably
already have upped her morphine, just enough to ease
her away. But they didn't have any drugs here, not even
paracetamol. Hannah looked around. Her eyes fell on
the bundle of clothes. *All it would take would be a coat,
placed over her mouth and nose.*

Her father talking again. But maybe this time he
was right.

She's going to die anyway. And who would know?

Hannah stretched out a hand and picked up a heavy padded parka. She glanced down the coach. Daniel had reached the others. No one was looking her way. It would take seconds. She raised the coat over the girl's face.

'I'm sorry,' she lied.

Peggy opened her eyes. Hannah jumped.

The girl's hand grasped her wrist. She opened her mouth. 'Save her!'

Hannah winced at the smell of decay on her breath. 'Save who?'

Peggy's eyes found hers. The same startling blue as her brother's. 'Please. Save her.'

Just as suddenly, the girl's hand dropped. Her eyes fluttered closed. Hannah sat back, heart thumping.

Save her.

A shout from up the coach.

'He's there!'

She turned. Daniel was staring back at her. Had he seen? Had he guessed her intention? Hannah hugged the coat to her chest, then grabbed a handful of other clothes, as though that was what she had been doing all long. Without looking at him, she hurried back to join the others.

'Did you say Josh had made it?' she asked.

'Yes,' Lucas replied. 'He is just opening up the exit to make it large enough to climb out without collapse.'

Hannah peered into the tunnel. She could just see Josh's feet and the faint light of the phone which — message deleted — she had given back to him. Of course, getting out was one thing. Then Josh had to open the luggage hold, find the bag containing the bomb, get it away from the coach and crawl back inside without the tunnel collapsing and suffocating him.

Still, their chances of survival had edged up. Just a little.

'Why don't we all crawl out?'

The question came from Ben, who had uncurled from his seat and stood, arms wrapped around himself, staring at them through puffy eyes. He coughed. 'I mean, why are we standing around in here, waiting to get blown to smithereens?

It was an obvious question. And one Hannah was surprised no one had asked before. Perhaps because they hadn't really believed that Josh would succeed.

Lucas eyed Ben carefully. 'You don't look so good, my friend. Are you feeling all right?'

'I'm fine, and you haven't answered my question.'

Ben didn't look or sound fine. He was pale, shaking, and the nervous aggression was another worrying sign. Or *symptom*.

'Firstly, my friend,' Lucas smiled, 'the more of us who try to get out of the tunnel, the more chance it collapses and buries us.'

Ben shuffled from foot to foot. 'I'm skinnier than Josh. I could do it.'

'Secondly,' Lucas continued in the same dangerously placid tone, 'the temperature outside is dropping rapidly. It is dark. Wolves and other wild animals will be out hunting. Josh is taking a risk for us. We are safer waiting in here.'

'Not if the whole coach blows.'

'Give Josh a chance to find the bomb,' Hannah said steadily. 'We have an emergency exit if we need it. Lucas is right. We won't last long out there.'

'No.' Ben shook his head. 'I can help Josh.'

142

'Listen, dude,' Cassie said. 'I'm definitely with the not-getting-blown-up stuff. But I'm also keen on not being eaten by wolves or suffocating in freezing snow. So why not just calm down and wait?'

'Fuck you!' Ben snarled. 'I'm not staying here, waiting to die. You guys can wait for your funeral. Not me.'

'Ben,' Lucas said. 'Please do not do this.'

'Who's going to stop me?'

Lucas sighed. Then he punched Ben in the face.

No change of expression, barely an intake of breath. Like a lizard flicking out its tongue to snatch a fly. Hannah might have missed it if she'd blinked.

Ben staggered and dropped like a stone.

'Jesus!' Hannah stared at Lucas, then crouched beside Ben. He was out cold. 'You knocked him unconscious.'

'That was the intention. He was becoming irrational and a danger to himself and us.'

'Not to mention a major pain in the ass,' Cassie added.

Hannah stood. 'So, violence is the answer?'

Lucas stared at her coldly. 'Sometimes, it is the only answer.'

'Guys.' Josh's voice echoed back from the tunnel. 'I'm going to climb out. I'll signal you through the windscreen when I've found the device.'

Lucas bent down. 'Good man.' He looked back at the others. 'I suggest we convene at the front of the coach and wait.'

Hannah scowled at him. 'I'm going to move Ben on to some seats first.'

'As you wish.' Lucas turned and walked towards the front of the coach.

'I'm with Rocky,' Cassie said, following him.

Hannah bent and grabbed Ben under the arms. He was heavier than he looked. Dead weight.

'Here. Let me help,' Daniel said.

Together they grabbed Ben and lifted him on to a coach seat. Hannah checked his pulse (erratic) and pulled back his eyelids. His corneas already had a pinkish hue. If Hannah had been in any doubt before, that confirmed it. Ben was infected, and symptomatic. *Damn.*

'What is it?' Daniel asked.

'Nothing,' she said quickly.

'Are you sure?' He nodded at Ben. 'Because it seems to me that Ben here is showing typical markers of infection — temperature, cough, erratic behaviour?'

She sighed. 'Possibly.'

He nodded. 'You already knew, didn't you?'

No point denying it now. 'We think some of the students on the coach may have been infected when they boarded.'

His eyebrows shot up. 'Fuck,' Then he looked at her more closely. '*We?*'

'Lucas and Cassie know.'

'I see. And when were you going to share that with the rest of us?'

'When it was necessary.'

'Necessary?' He snorted out a brutal laugh. 'Before or after we were all dead?'

'I didn't want to cause panic, to make things worse.'

He stared at her. 'So, chances are we're all infected by now?'

'Possibly.'

He smiled thinly. 'So maybe getting blown to pieces would be the better option after all.'

'We could be fortunate. Some people are more

144

resistant to infection than others.'

'I thought just 2 per cent of people were that lucky.'

'Maybe it's our lucky day.'

Daniel raised his eyebrows. 'You think?'

They looked at each other. Then they started to smile. The sheer crazy horror of the situation forcing it out.

'Couldn't get much worse, right?' Hannah said.

'Sometimes life gives us lemons. Sometimes diarrhoea.'

'I'll remember that one.'

'Something Peg used to say —' He broke off. For the first time, he had talked about her in the past tense.

Their smiles subsided.

'I'm sorry about your sister,' Hannah said. 'If there was anything I could do —'

'I know. You can't save everyone, right.' There was a pause, and then he said: 'If you could, but it meant someone else would die, would you?'

'Well, I'd hope that situation never arose.'

'But if it did?'

She thought. There had been stories of hospitals becoming overrun with the infected. Doctors having to make such decisions.

'My father said it's important not to think of it as a value choice. You're not saying one life has more value. It's about determining who has the best chance of survival long term.'

'So, young before old.'

'Sometimes. Not necessarily.' She frowned. 'Why are you asking?'

Daniel hesitated before replying. 'Guess I have death on my mind.' He straightened. 'Right. I'm going to go and sit with Peggy. I want to be there when . . . well, you know.'

She did. But their conversation had left Hannah feeling unsettled. *Save her.* She was missing something. Again. She shook her head. Then she turned and made her way to the front of the coach.

Lucas sat in the driver's seat. Cassie stood beside him. Most of the left-hand-side windows were now completely covered by snow. Occasionally, the coach creaked with the wind, but otherwise it felt dead with silence. Like they were already slowly suffocating. The front windscreen offered some visibility. Although, mostly all they could see was more snow and the dark edge of the woods. The sky had shaded to charcoal. The sun had sunk deep beneath the horizon. The moon cast a wistful silvery light.

'So, now, we wait,' Lucas said with a small smile.

Hannah flicked him another glance. Maybe she was mistaken, but she thought she had detected a note of satisfaction in his voice. As though a part of him was enjoying the danger of their situation. She thought again about that single sharp punch. Judged perfectly to render Ben unconscious. What was Lucas studying here? What was his background?

There was a clunk and thud from their left.

'The luggage hold,' Lucas said. 'It sounds like he has opened it.'

Hannah found herself holding her breath. How long would it take Josh? Twelve students on board. One large rucksack each. First, he had to find the right rucksack. Then, if he found the device, he had to get it far away from the coach.

'What's the time?' she asked Lucas.

He glanced at his watch. 'Seven forty-nine.'

She felt the tension gnawing at her bones, along

with the cold. What if he couldn't find it? What if their timings were way out? Any second could be their last.

Stop it, Hannah. You are allowing yourself to panic. Focus on what is at hand. Not hypotheticals.

More thumps and clunks from the underside of the coach. She wanted to ask Lucas again what the time was. But she knew it was pointless. Time became sadistic in situations like these. Dragging its feet, stretching out the seconds and minutes just to torture them.

'Perhaps we should play I-spy,' Cassie said. 'I spy something beginning with 's'.'

'Snow,' Hannah said automatically.

'Too easy, right?'

'Look!' Lucas pointed out of the window.

A figure drew into view. Josh. He held something up in his hand. A small rectangular device. The IED.

'He did it!' Cassie cried. 'Fuck me!'

Now he just had to dispose of it, Hannah thought.

'Be careful, my friend,' Lucas whispered.

Josh gestured towards the woods.

'Ditch it, man,' Cassie muttered. 'Get rid of it.'

Josh pulled his arm back and lobbed the IED like a rugby ball. The device flew from his arm and into the woods.

They waited.

Cassie raised an eyebrow. 'Well, that was an anti-clima —'

The *BOOM* shook them off their feet. Orange lit up the sky, momentarily setting it ablaze. The coach rocked with the aftershock, creaking and tipping, settling further on its side. Hannah staggered and grabbed at the seats to stop herself falling. Cassie stumbled backwards, almost landing on the pile of dead bodies.

'Fuck, man.'

Lucas gripped the steering wheel. From the back, Hannah heard Daniel cry out and curse. Whether the impact had set the bomb off or the timer, one thing was certain. It was no hoax.

'Is everyone okay?' Hannah asked.

'Dandy,' Cassie mumbled.

Lucas nodded. 'We are lucky. That was, as you say, just in the nick of time.'

'What about Josh?' Hannah asked.

They peered out of the window. They could just make out Josh's figure, lying in the snow. Alive? Dead? Then the figure moved, and shakily stood. *Thank God.*

Josh dusted snow off himself and waved at them, momentarily silhouetted in orange as flames ate up the woods. Hannah felt a pang. There were animals in the woods. She hoped the snow would dampen the fire, so it didn't spread.

Josh pointed, indicating he was going to walk around the coach. It occurred to Hannah that the coach had shifted; the tunnel might have collapsed. Josh would have to dig his way back in. But almost immediately this concern was overtaken by another, bigger problem.

A bellowing roar echoed from the woods. Agonized, brutal. Something moved at the corner of her vision and then emerged from the shadows of the smoking trees; something huge and black and orange.

There were animals in the woods.

A bear — a grizzly from the shape and size — staggered across the snow. Its fur was singed and blackened, one leg on fire. The beast swung its head

148

from side to side. Its cries reverberated through the coach. Agony, fear, fury. A dangerous combination.

Josh stared at it. No sudden movements, Hannah thought. Stay calm. Move slowly away. But as the bear limped towards him Josh shoved a hand in his pocket. The phone, Hannah realized. The alarm. *No. Not for the bear. It's injured, unpredictable. Don't antagonize it.*

'*Nein,*' Lucas whispered, echoing her thoughts.

Too late. The pulsing siren rang out. The bear shook its head more wildly, roared again and then reared up on its hind legs.

'That's not good,' Cassie muttered.

Almost as suddenly, the alarm cut out. The battery must have died. The bear dropped to all fours. Josh still had a chance. *Don't run*, Hannah silently implored. The worst thing to do is to run. Bears are fast. You can't outpace them. Josh had angered the grizzly, but he could still avoid attack. *Lie down in the snow*, she intoned in her head. *You've done survival training. Lie the fuck down.*

Josh turned and ran.

Fuck.

The bear charged. Even with an injured leg, it made up the ground between itself and Josh in seconds. A swipe of its huge paw took him down to his knees. Josh tried to crawl away. Another paw swipe almost took the back of his head off. Blood spurted. Josh fell forward into the snow.

'Jesus!' Cassie gagged.

The bear fell on Josh, clawing and tearing. The encroaching darkness offered some mercy, shielding them from the worst. But they could still hear the cries. Screams of agony and howls of fury. As the bear yanked its head back Hannah saw slick tubes of red and grey intestines between its teeth. In the fading glow from the fire, the bloody snow looked black.

Hannah turned away . . .

'You should have let me go with him.'

. . . and almost screamed. A thin, pale figure loomed behind her. In the dim light, his skin was translucent, eyes a ghastly red, one swollen half-closed from Lucas's fist.

'B–ben,' Hannah stuttered.

He stared past her then coughed. 'Should have let me go with him.'

Lucas swivelled around. 'Then you would also be dead, my friend.'

Ben's lips drew back from his teeth in a snarl. 'I'm not your fucking friend, and I'm a dead man already. Look at me.' He swayed, catching a seat to steady himself. 'I'm infected.'

'Yes.'

'You knew.'

'We suspected there was an infection on board,' Lucas replied.

Ben started to laugh, a raw, hacking thing. As he breathed in, his breath whistled horribly. Momentarily, Hannah wished he *had* gone with Josh. Better they were both dead out there than this, in here.

'Well, now you're *all* fucking walking dead,' Ben spat. 'How d'you like that, you Nazi shit?' He grinned, then sank to the floor.

Instinctively, Hannah moved to help him.

Lucas caught her arm. 'Do not expose yourself further. Leave him.'

'On the floor?'

'You can do nothing for him.'

'I could get him a coat, and water.'

150

'Why? He will be dead soon — the infection is moving fast. You are wasting resources.'

Hannah shook her head. But then, hadn't she thought the same about Peggy?

'You sound like my father,' she said.

'*Danke.*'

'It wasn't meant as a compliment.'

'I know.' Lucas glanced down at Ben's slumped body, then stepped over it. 'We should get some rest. It's almost dark. We need to conserve energy.'

'You expect us to sleep?' Cassie asked incredulously. 'Ben's dying, and we just watched Josh get his intestines ripped out by a fucking bear!'

Lucas sighed. 'Josh's death is regrettable. But he served his purpose. He disposed of the bomb. The important thing is that *we* are alive.' He smiled. '*Zur Zeit.*' And then he turned and walked back down the coach.

Hannah stared after him. Her German was rudimentary, but she understood enough.

Zur Zeit.

For now.

Meg

'Push me higher, Mummy. Higher.'

The sun was warm on her back. *Should have put some more sunscreen on*, she thought.

Lily wore a sunhat and a pretty yellow sundress with her new pink sandals. Her curly hair was pinned into two pigtails.

'Higher, Mummy.'

'I can't push you any higher. You'll fall.'

'Higher.'

She was a daredevil, Meg's daughter. Six years old and fearless, because fear was learned, inherited. Lily would swing herself across the monkey bars, climb up the slide, jump off the top of the climbing frame. *Higher, higher.* Afterwards, Meg would wonder if Lily had always been trying to reach for the heavens, even while she was alive.

It was a perfect summer's day — or was it? Did it happen? Had there been a perfect summer day while Lily was alive? Sometimes, it was hard to remember. Things had already begun to turn. To change. New rules. A new way of living. But she supposed they had all still believed that they would return to normal again. Or a new normal, at least. This was just a blip. A pothole in the road. Science would save them. Of course. And they had all clung to that notion, faith as blind as that of the religious zealots. There would be a cure, or a vaccine, and humanity could get back to the normal business of consumption, war and destruction, carelessly fucking up the planet for future generations, while the rich took off to space on day trips and the poor begged for food. Normal.

Meg reached for the swing. But it was empty. She frowned. 'Lily?'

She couldn't see her daughter.

'Lily?'

She ran out of the gate. A sign on it read CLOSED DUE TO GOVERNMENT RESTRICTIONS. Meg looked back. The playground was now derelict, the swings knotted around the top of the bars, the slide stained brown with rust, the old roundabout splintered and rotten. The sun had gone in. Storm clouds gathered overhead.

She shivered and called Lily's name again, even though, in the pit of her stomach, she knew that Lily was gone. She had been gone for years. This was just another mirage, Meg's mind playing tricks, conjuring up memories that weren't real. A manufactured, blissful past when, in reality, things had already been fraying at the seams.

They had told them that children were safe, even as the virus spread. Even as it mutated. Even as it became apparent that traditional vaccines weren't working. But they had lied. They had lied about everything. And then Lily got sick, and she was taken to hospital. And she should have survived. She *would* have survived, if the hospital had had enough beds or nurses or equipment. But they didn't, and although Meg would happily have ripped an oxygen mask off an octogenarian if it would have saved her daughter, she couldn't because all the other sick were young people too. Young people who weren't supposed to die. Lies. So many fucking lies.

Meg pushed open the gate, walked back into the

derelict playground and sat down on the rotting bench. Except it wasn't the playground any more, it was the Garden of Remembrance at the crematorium where they had buried Lily's ashes. A small white headstone marked the spot where all Meg's hopes and dreams lay. *Beloved daughter. Forever in our hearts and memories. You lit up our lives and your light will never dim.*

The funeral director had chosen the words, because Meg couldn't find the right ones. There were no right words. Nothing was enough and everything was too much. Trying to sum up her love and loss in a few neat phrases was impossible. The only thing she remembered growling was: *'Don't fucking mention God. If there is a God, then he's a cunt.'*

There had been three of them at the funeral. Only family and partners were permitted, and Meg didn't have any family. She'd lost her mum when she was seventeen, and Lily's real father was dead, which just left Paul (already in the throes of becoming her ex) and her gran, who had advanced dementia and spent most of the funeral asking where Lily was and who was looking after her while they cremated Grandpa.

Meg stared at the headstone. The dates were wrong, she thought. It couldn't have been seven years since Lily died. How was that possible? Lily couldn't have been dead for longer than she had been alive. Just six years. Six precious, short years. A blink. A cipher. A prologue. The rest of her story forever unwritten. How could time be so fucking relentless? *Can't stop. Must hurry on. Much to trample, crush and destroy.* Leaving Meg behind with nothing but memories. And even those were flawed and false.

When the world started to end, not with a whimper

154

or a bang but with a slow, whistling sigh, Meg didn't care. She had watched the news from a numb cocoon of grief and medication. As the infections spread and society crumbled, at first slowly and then like a cliff edge giving way and falling to the sea, she had barely raised an eyebrow. Her world had already been destroyed. Everyone else was just catching up.

She felt tired, so she lay down on the bench. She often used to sleep in the Garden of Remembrance, breaking in by climbing over the fence and drinking vodka until she passed out. She would close her eyes and imagine she could feel her daughter's warm body next to hers. She held it tight and promised that this time she would never let her go . . .

The bench tipped. A lurch. Meg rolled. Her eyes shot open.

Where was she?

Somewhere cold. Dark. Cramped.

And then she remembered. They were lying on the floor of the cable car, trying to sleep. Huddled up together to share body warmth. She had curled herself into Sarah's back. Another body, who she thought was Max, lay the other side, snoring gently.

It probably wasn't that late. They had no watches and no real concept of time. But darkness had fallen and, like animals, they found themselves yawning as the daylight ebbed away, exhaustion felling them. Perhaps that wasn't all. They probably had traces of sedative in their systems still, and there was another possibility. Oxygen deprivation. The cable car wasn't completely hermetically sealed, and they could open the hatch, obviously. But it was still a small space and the air at this height was thinner anyway. It was something to bear in mind.

Now Meg was awake, she could feel the cold creeping in again, could see her breath in the air. Without heating, the temperature had fallen rapidly. It was almost pitch black too, just a faint glimmer of moonlight between the clouds revealing vague shapes. That was when she realized something. Sean wasn't curled up asleep with them. She turned.

He sat on the bench in the far corner of the car, staring out of the snow-caked window. As Meg moved to stand, he glanced over.

'Hi,' he said in a half-whisper.

'Hi.'

She walked over and sat down next to him, wrapping her arms around herself.

'Couldn't sleep?' he asked.

'Not the best of circumstances.'

'No.'

He studied her more intently. 'You're crying.'

'Oh.' She rubbed at her watery eyes and sniffed. 'Just a crappy dream.'

'What about?'

She hesitated and then said, 'My daughter, Lily.'

'You have a daughter? How old?'

'She was six when she died.'

'Oh, I'm sorry.'

'Thanks.'

'Virus?'

'Partly. Partly lack of care, facilities, staff. She should have survived.'

He nodded. 'The masses suffer and die while the elite pay for private care and survive.'

'Same as it's ever been,' she said bitterly. 'They say you can't put a price on life, but they do, all the time. I used to beat myself up, thinking if only Lily had been born to someone wealthy, she would still be here.'

'Yeah.' He paused. 'I know how you feel.'

'You lost someone?'

'Not a child but . . . someone I cared about. A lot.'

'I'm sorry.'

'I always swore I would protect her, but I couldn't. She was all I had.'

Meg nodded. 'Lily was my only child.'

'No dad on the scene?'

'He died in a motorbike accident.'

'Right.'

'There was someone else, for a while — but it didn't work out. My daughter always came first. She was my world.' She swallowed. 'And then my world ended.'

'I guess the apocalypse doesn't mean so much to you.'

'Not really.'

'I can't imagine losing a child. You must be strong to keep going.'

Meg smiled bitterly 'No. I'm selfish.'

'Selfish?'

'Why should I keep living while Lily is dead? Why should I wake up to see the sun shining when she can't? And she's alone. I always swore that I would never leave her —' She paused, a lump rising in her throat. 'That's why I tried to kill myself. More than once.'

'I don't blame you.'

She barked out a short laugh. 'Thanks. Normally people tell me there's so much to live for.'

'Really?'

'I know. Have they looked outside?'

They both smiled. He understood, Meg thought. The deeper the wounds, the darker the humour.

'I thought about killing myself,' Sean said. 'But I couldn't go through with it.'

'Why?'

'Without me, there's no one to remember how special she was. Or to get justice for her.'

'Justice?' She glanced at him in surprise. 'Did someone kill her?'

'Yeah.' He nodded. 'And when I find them, I'm going to make them pay.'

Even in the darkness, Meg thought she could see a shadow cross his face.

'And will that make you feel better?' she asked.

He smiled thinly. 'I'll let you know when the time comes.'

They fell into silence for a moment, staring out at the patches of starry sky through the snow.

'The storm looks like it's easing,' Meg said.

'Yeah.'

'Do you think we'll get out of here?'

'We have to,' he replied, voice suddenly tight. 'I haven't come this far to die up here.'

'Maybe it's what we deserve,' Meg said. 'Like it or not, we covered up one murder and aided and abetted a second. The fact that neither of those things seems to be bothering anyone probably says something about all of us.'

'They were strangers,' Sean replied. 'We've all got so used to death it's hard to find the energy to care about people we don't know any more.'

Except she *had* known Paul. Once. In all senses of the word. So what did that say about her?

'Do you think Karl killed the security guy?' she asked him.

'I don't know. Maybe.'

158

'I saw Sarah push him.'

'Maybe you did. But she'll never admit it, not even to herself.'

He was right, Meg thought. The biggest lies are the ones we tell ourselves.

'I don't like her,' she confessed.

'No kidding. But I agree — she is an odd one.'

'She's a teacher.'

'Well, that's her story.'

'You don't believe her?'

'I believe her as much as I believe any of you.'

'Great. Thanks.'

'I mean, we're all hiding stuff. That's okay. It's what people do. But Sarah —' He shook his head. 'There's something more. The twitchiness, the mood swings. You notice the cross?'

'Hard not to. She's always fucking playing with it.'

'Not a fan of religion.'

'God let my daughter die. He can get fucked.'

'Fair point. Maybe Sarah *is* just religious. But I know a lot of people find God when they lose the bottle.'

'AA?'

'Yeah.' He paused. 'But a lot of people relapse and have to climb back on the wagon.'

He was right. And that might explain a lot. Christ. Was the damn woman in some kind of withdrawal?

'We should keep an eye on her,' she said.

'Agreed.'

Meg considered. 'And what does your Spidey sense tell you about Max?'

'I think he's a lawyer. I think he's been in prison. Probably more than he says. You don't tend to get jail time for a first offence any more — and not a soft one at that. I wouldn't trust him to represent me. But I think he's mostly been honest with us.'

'And me?'

'You? Well, you're a tough nut. You've had to be, and I see why. You're definitely ex-police . . .' He regarded her intently. 'But I think you're one of the good guys.'

'Thanks.' She regarded him more closely. 'And what about you? Are you one of the good guys?'

'I used to think so.' He shrugged. 'But people change.'

A pause.

'I think the killer is still on board,' Meg said, surprising herself by voicing the thought out loud.

Sean nodded. 'I think you're right.'

They looked at each other.

'What are we going to do about that?' he asked.

She turned away. 'I'll let you know when the time comes.'

Carter

He has saved her a hundred times.

And lost her a hundred more.

The end result is always the same.

He wakes crying.

And then he hears the baby.

The corridor is dark. He stumbles along it, slipping and sliding. The floor is covered in ice. Snow blows in from windows somewhere high above him. A storm howls outside.

The newborn wails inside.

He moves towards the sound, trying to hurry, but his feet keep sliding out from under him. He can't seem to get any closer, no matter how hard he tries.

Deep down, he realizes this is a dream. The baby is safe. She is no longer a baby. She is grown. A teenager. And she is the reason he has been stealing the plasma and medicines and sending them to an address in a small suburban town, where he pictures her catching a yellow bus to school and swinging on a tyre in the backyard of her white picket-fence house.

He's never seen her house. He doesn't even know if his parcels are reaching her. But still, he tries. Because he can't lose her. Not her as well.

His feet finally find a grip. He is moving along the corridor and emerging into a room.

It's small and it feels like it's moving, swaying from side to side.

At the end is a crib. It's rocking with the room.

Rock-a-bye baby.

And then it tips. The baby spills out, face first on to the floor. The wailing grows louder. He tries to run forward, but the motion of the room throws him off balance and he staggers.

As he does, he realizes the cries have changed. No longer the full-throated cry of a baby. A different sound. Gasping, wheezing . . . The baby is crawling towards him. And she is pale, so pale. And every time she breathes, she makes a sound. Whistling.

Instead of running towards her, he starts to back away. But the door has gone. He's trapped, backed up against a glass wall as the storm lashes its fury outside.

The baby looks up.

He screams . . . the glass breaks and he's falling into blackness.

★   ★   ★

Fuck. The same. Every time.

Carter sat up. For a moment, disorientated.

He was in his room, in bed. Lying on top of the covers. It wasn't fully dark outside but, after the events of the day, he had needed some rest.

His room was at the far end of the Retreat. Rather than panoramic views out over the slopes, it faced back towards the sheer face of the mountain behind them. Whiteout. Carter was good with that. He didn't need a view. He didn't need a reminder that the rest of the world was out there. On life support. But still breathing.

They had stored the dead bodies in the basement. It was coolest down there. And although no one was saying it: out of sight, out of mind. In the morning, Welland would take them, one by one, to the

162

incinerator. No ceremony. No prayers. No final goodbyes.

None of them was religious, but sometimes Carter *felt* the stripping away of those things; those small acts of ceremony that we clung to, to kid ourselves that we were more than overgrown apes who had learned to tie shoelaces. These days death had been laid bare for what it really was. An ending. Often brutal, seldom fair, rarely kind.

Carter and his sister had lost their parents young. Although, to be honest, their dad wasn't really a loss. He was a charmless drunk who floated in and out of their lives until one day he floated away for good, in a river after an altercation outside a bar. Their mother struggled to cope with his death and a year later hanged herself in their bedroom. Carter found her body. He was nine.

After that, Carter and his sister went to live with their grandparents. They were poor, hard-working and unsentimental. They hadn't expected to be looking after children at their age and made it clear that they were doing it out of duty rather than love. They expected the siblings to help in the shop they ran, complete weekly chores, stay out of the way when their friends came around to play poker, and generally not be a burden.

While Carter soon rebelled, his sister sought to appease. If she could just work harder, smile more brightly, be kinder and more helpful, then she would earn the love she was certain that their grandparents had somewhere deep inside them.

She was wrong. But that was his sister. She wanted to see the best in people. She thought love could change them. While he braced for thunderclouds, she waited for the rainbow.

And now she was dead too. Brutally, unfairly, unkindly.

Carter swung his legs out of bed and sat, taking in his surroundings. It didn't take long. Even these rooms, the former staff rooms, were small and impersonal. Shades of grey and white. Really, there wasn't so much difference between the living quarters and the isolation chambers. They were all prisoners here in a way.

The only difference in his room/cell was the small dog bed tucked in one corner. Dexter eyed him from it sleepily. His stubby tail wagged a couple of times as Carter stood and stretched, then he yawned a wide, doggy yawn, closed his eyes and rolled over. Dexter had belonged to one of the staff. Carter didn't know who. Now, the dog regarded Carter as his owner. Dogs are nowhere near as loyal as we pretend. Really, humans are all just furless blobs to them.

Carter walked up and down, working off some of the cramp that had settled into his muscles after the trek back up the mountain. That seemed like days ago, rather than hours. Despite the lack of light in the living area, things were at least stable again. The generator was working. For now. But if they didn't get a fix on the power outages, then that situation wouldn't last. Welland reckoned they had fuel for about a month, 'give or take'. Give or take what? was the question.

In the meantime, Carter had other things on his mind. Things he didn't want on his mind. Things he wished would get the fuck off his mind. Julia, for a start. And the knife, or lack of one. It still bothered him. It wasn't in the pool. Or the Retreat. Or on 01. So, if it wasn't him, who had stabbed her? And more

164

to the point, why hadn't Carter mentioned it to Miles?

Miles was the one in charge. Their self-appointed leader. But Miles was a man with secrets of his own. Carter knew him better than the others, but that still didn't amount to much. Things he did know: Miles had a medical/scientific background. He was capable of extreme violence without remorse. And he liked to be in control. In his previous life, he could have been anything from a serial killer to a world leader.

Carter didn't really think Miles had killed Julia. Too sloppy for him. On the other hand, he couldn't think of anyone *else* who could have killed her. So, confessing his suspicions about her death to Miles seemed like a bad move.

And then there was Jackson.

Carter had barely given the guy any thought in the three years he had been living here. But suddenly, Jackson was squatting in his head.

Carter knew he hadn't been the one stealing the plasma.

So why the hell had he left the Retreat? Why was he running?

There had to be another reason.

Normally, Carter resided in the murky area between caring very little about anyone else and not giving a shit about anyone else.

But that was when things didn't affect his own status quo. Miles discovering the theft and Jackson's death gave him a problem. A big one. *Not* stealing the plasma was not an option. But nor was being discovered.

Miles's insistence on a trek out to the cable-car station — just the two of them — was only exacerbating Carter's growing unease. And that was before you got to Miles's plan to acquire fresh supplies. Suddenly, in less than twenty-four hours, everything was spiralling out of control. What Carter wouldn't give to be as bored as fuck right now.

He walked into the small bathroom, used the toilet and splashed his face with water. Then he turned and walked through his room, out into the corridor. He heard the tip-tap of tiny claws behind him. Dexter stood at his heels, looking expectant. Carter paused. He could go downstairs, get some food, start on the beer. Or . . . he turned and looked down the corridor towards the other bedrooms. Jackson's was No 6.

He debated with himself. People always think they want to know stuff. Secrets. Answers. Actually, there was plenty of stuff we were better off not knowing. If humans weren't so intent on a quest for knowledge, they probably wouldn't be in such a fucked-up position right now. Not all knowledge was good. And even the stuff that was good didn't always fall into the right hands. Give the wrong idiot a shitload of knowledge and that was when the world imploded.

Nevertheless, proving again how adept he was at not following his own reasoning, he walked down the corridor towards Jackson's room. Dexter followed. At the door, Carter turned. 'Stay, Dexter.'

Normally, Dexter had an impressive ability to ignore most known commands. Carter used to wonder if he had been trained in another language but then decided that he was just a stubborn little fuck. Either way, for once Dexter sat and waited, looking at Carter curiously.

'I know,' Carter said. 'It's probably a bad idea, right?'

Dexter cocked his head to one side, then turned and started to lick his balls. Carter shook his head.

'And if I could do that, I wouldn't be here right now, buddy.'

He pushed the door open. It wasn't locked. As Carter stepped inside it occurred to him that Miles had probably already searched the room. In which case, he was very unlikely to spot anything Miles had missed. But still, the itch to try was there.

Jackson's room looked just like his. But it didn't smell like his room. This room smelt fresh, clean. The bed was neatly made. A digital clock and Fitbit rested tidily on the bedside table. Jackson had always struck Carter, from the scant thought he had given him, as a disciplined individual. Controlled, measured, calm. Not someone prone to irrational or impulsive acts. So what had he been up to? Why had he fled the Retreat? Where the hell did he think he was going?

Carter moved around the room, searching in obvious places even though a) they were obvious and b) he had no idea what he was searching for. He rifled through the clothes in the wardrobe. This didn't take long. The recruits were provided with a few items of basic clothing, as well as toiletries and other essentials. Due to the nature of his own arrival, Carter's clothes had been borrowed from the closets of the dead.

Jackson's wardrobe consisted of the usual mix of leisure and gym wear. Plus, a pair of flip-flops, and trainers. Not much to search, but Carter checked the pockets and tipped up the trainers anyway. *Nada*. He walked into the small white bathroom.

Not many hiding places in here either. But, obviously, the first thing Carter did was lift the top off the toilet cistern and peer inside. Nothing but water. He opened the mirrored cabinet above the sink. Vitamins, shaving apparatus, deodorant, toothpaste. Carter shut it again and stood, turning in a circle. He stared at the shower.

Where would *he* hide something? He stepped into the cubicle, reached up and unscrewed the shower head. He took it off and squinted inside. Empty. He looked down, between his feet to the shower drain. Okay. He squatted and lifted off the circular chrome cover.

Bingo. The plastic shower trap had been removed and a plastic bag containing a mobile phone had been taped to the inside of the pipe.

No one at the Retreat had a phone. They had all been confiscated before arrival. The staff had been permitted to send emails, but communication was strictly monitored. There were no landlines. Only the Professor had his own phone. After the takeover, some of the group had used it to try to call people. Friends, family. No one had replied. They had left messages on voicemails, perhaps hoping that they might be returned. That day never came. After a while, they had stopped trying. Miles kept it charged. For calling Quinn, and emergencies.

Carter stared at the phone in the shower pipe. It was very small. An ancient Nokia. Almost an antique.

If Jackson had run, why had he left his phone here, hidden?

Carter reached in and carefully extricated the bag from the tape sticking it to the pipe. He slipped the phone out of the plastic.

He pressed a random button. The phone lit up. It was charged. And unlocked.

He stared at the green screen.

There was something else.

Jackson had messages.

Now, We are All
Sons of Bitches

Hannah

Sleep seemed a ridiculous notion. Wedged uncomfortably between the twisted seats at the rear of the coach. Trying to ignore the biting cold, permeating even through several layers of clothes, and the smell from the chemical toilet, which had come loose from its fittings and was leaking across the floor now the coach had tilted almost completely on its side.

But fear and trauma had drained them. Despite the cold and the discomfort, the sounds of slow, measured breathing gradually filled the coach, broken only by Peggy's groans and Ben's hacking cough, reminders of death in their midst.

Hannah closed her eyes, but she didn't sleep. Not properly. Even in the best of conditions, she had never been a good sleeper. Since she was a child, she had hated that feeling of slipping into oblivion. A fear that she wouldn't wake up. It had worsened after her mother's suicide. Every time she felt herself falling, she wondered if this was what it was like — death — and she jolted awake. Her father didn't help. Never in bed till past midnight, and up with the dawn, he viewed sleep as an impediment. Something for the lazy and weak-minded.

No human needs more than four hours of sleep. We have become complacent. Wasting time in our beds when we could be working. Our ancestors knew that the darkness hours were the danger hours. Soon, there will be a time when we need to be awake — properly awake — and prepared.

171

Instead of sleep, Hannah had become used to lying in a semiconscious state, letting her brain meander. Unknotting problems that had been bothering her in the day, finishing essays, resolving equations. Sometimes, wandering off on tangents.

She found herself thinking about Indiana Jones. A hero from an old film their au pair had let her watch. She had loved that film and handsome Indiana, until some smart Alec had pointed out that, despite all his heroics, Indiana's role in the whole thing was pointless. The outcome would have been the same had he never been involved.

She felt the same about their situation now. They were still trapped. Despite Josh's sacrifice, their situation had not improved. True, they were not dead, but if what Hannah feared was correct, that was only a matter of semantics. They would be soon. Not only was rescue unlikely, anyone who *did* come looking for them wouldn't be here to help. They would be here to shut them down.

That was why she had deleted her father's message without telling the others. If she had told them about the message, it would mean telling them about the infections, and her suspicion that the crash was deliberate. It seemed cruel to admit that their situation was even more hopeless.

Ironically, right now the storm was their best ally. While it raged, no one could reach them. When it eased, a decision would need to be made. Stay here and hope the Department would be merciful. Unlikely. Or attempt to escape.

They could no longer dig themselves out. The new angle of the coach made that impossible. Even if they *could* get out, they would have to survive freezing

172

temperatures, evade predators, find food and shelter. And that was if none of them showed symptoms or fell ill. All the while, the Department would be looking for them.

You're thinking too far ahead, Hannah. Break the problem down.

Okay. Things she had learned from her father — trying to tackle the whole problem was like smashing your head into a brick wall. Instead, you had to slowly dismantle the wall, brick by brick. Smaller pieces.

Their immediate problem was containment. They could try the emergency exit again. But she was pretty sure that had been sabotaged. Which left? Trying to break a window on the other side of the coach. But they still lacked the means to do that. Perhaps they should check whether any of the seats had loosened more when the coach tipped again.

Her mind paused. Rewind. She was missing something. Something about the coach tipping. The emergency exit? No. Near it. The toilet. Something about the toilet.

How did coach toilets work? They drained into a tank, which had to be emptied. So, there would be a waste pipe running out of the toilet into the tank. Running out. Only a small gap. But if they could lift the toilet out and somehow remove the tank, maybe there would be a big enough gap to squeeze through. Hannah seemed to vaguely recall a mythical aircraft escape in an old movie using such a trope. But was it just a trope? Could it work? And even if it didn't, could they use the toilet itself to break a window? Options, she thought. They just needed . . .

Her train of thought stalled. Her eyes sprang open. Noises. From above her. Faint thuds, making the

173

glass of the window vibrate. Something was climbing over the coach again. She raised her eyes. Could the wolves have returned, attracted by Josh's blood? Or maybe it was new predators: lynx or wild dogs.

Hannah pushed herself up, her muscles protesting, eyes adjusting to the dark. The coach wasn't quite pitch black. That made her think it must be early morning. Maybe two or three o'clock? And perhaps the moon and stars were no longer camouflaged by storm clouds?

She looked around, neck creaking. Cassie was curled into a tight ball in the seat in front of her. Lucas slept almost upright on another seat. Daniel lay lumpily next to his sister.

Hannah found herself wondering about him again. He wasn't a typical Academy student. Academy students tended to fall into two camps, the rich, spoilt offspring of rich, privileged parents — and the scholarship students. The brightest and best in their fields, whether that be science, medicine, literature or art. The Academy could afford to employ the best tutors to teach tiny classes. Like her father.

Daniel didn't really seem to fit into either category. And she didn't remember seeing him around the campus. Of course, it was a large school. Different groups didn't necessarily mix. She didn't remember seeing Peggy, Cassie or Lucas either. Maybe she was just being judgemental again.

More scuffling sounds from above. Hannah didn't like it and she wouldn't get to sleep while they continued. She pushed herself to her feet and started to clamber up the coach. The gangway was almost vertical, so this meant balancing on the twisted seats, trying not to slip. Harder than ever in the dark.

Above her head, the furtive shuffling followed her. *Furtive*. Yes, she thought. That was the word. A different sound to the wolves. More deliberate. Like whatever was making it was aware of the coach and its inhabitants and wary of disturbing them.

She reached the front of the coach. Despite the cold, there was a discernible whiff of staleness emanating from the dead bodies. Gas, Hannah thought. Although it had been less than twenty-four hours, organs started to decompose first. Visible signs wouldn't show for another few days but, inside, the bodies were already breaking down.

Another thump overhead. Hannah jumped. She turned away and climbed into the driver's cab to peer out of the windscreen. The snow had cleared a little, but it was fogged by condensation. She raised an arm to wipe it away.

A face stared back at her.

She scrabbled backwards, fear and shock seizing her voice.

The face was pale, teeth yellowed, corneas red-rimmed. For a second, their eyes met. Then the figure slid from the windscreen and ran back into the dark folds of the woods. Hannah stared after it, heart thudding.

Someone grabbed her shoulder. She screamed and swivelled, fists raised.

'Whoah! *Halt!* It's me.'

Lucas. He stared at her in concern. 'What is it?'

Hannah glanced back through the windscreen, almost doubting her own eyes, her own sanity. No sign of the figure. Just the dark woods, still smoking slightly, and a bloody mass lying in the snow. Josh's remains.

She swallowed. 'I saw someone. Outside the coach.'
'What?' Lucas's face creased in disbelief. 'Rescue?'
Hannah shook her head. 'I don't think so.'
'Then who else would be out there in this storm? A villager?'
But there were no villages nearby. They both knew that. Just the snow, the mountains and the wilderness of the woods. A place where wild animals lived. And other creatures.
She turned, the word slipping out before she could help herself: 'A Whistler.'

★ ★ ★

So called because of the way the virus ravaged the lungs. Making each breath a hideous, wet whistle. No one knew who had come up with the name. But, like many things, it had quickly become absorbed into the language.

There weren't many options for the Whistlers. Those left almost living. Survivors but still contagious. Especially those infected with Choler, a dangerous and dominant variant that affected the brain. That was why her father had created the Seclusion Centres. Secure places where they could be looked after, and help the scientists to battle the virus.

Public opinion was divided on the centres. Some thought they were necessary. Others — like Cassie — claimed the centres were no better than prisons or concentration camps. Critics had coined the name 'The Farms', which had stuck.

Once, when Hannah had dared to ask her father, he had said:

In any war, Hannah, there are casualties. We are

fighting a war against an enemy who is ever changing. In order to protect the world, there must be sacrifices. For the greater good.'

But not everyone wanted to sacrifice themselves. Many of the infected ran, hid, formed their own communities. In isolated places, away from the general population. When they were found, they were rounded up. But a lot of people had sympathy for the Whistlers. They were still people. Still someone's mother, brother or child.

A few years ago, there had been an outbreak at a tiny village not far from the Academy. One of the villagers had sourced some infected meat. The infection had spread rapidly. Her father and his team were called in. The village was quarantined. But the rumour was that some of the infected escaped into the woods. Where they still lived today.

★ ★ ★

'You think they're dangerous?' Cassie asked.

They had re-grouped at the back of the coach. Hannah's scream had woken the others and she didn't see any point in lying about the situation.

'I don't know.'

'Shit,' Daniel muttered. 'This just gets better and better.'

'We've no reason to think they pose a threat,' Lucas said. 'At least, not while we remain inside the coach and they remain outside.'

'But how long are we supposed to sit tight for?' Daniel asked.

'The authorities must have missed us by now. The storm looks to be easing. Maybe they are already

177

putting together a search party,' Lucas said.

Cassie glanced at Hannah. 'D'you want to tell them?'

No, Hannah thought. But it was probably time.

'We may have another problem,' she said.

Lucas glanced at her sharply. 'Which is?'

'The coach crash might not have been an accident.'

'What?'

'Cassie was involved in testing. Two students on board had positive tests.'

'So how did they get on board?' Lucas demanded.

'I don't know. But the point is my father would never have let infected students leave the Academy —' Hannah looked around at them. 'And if he found out, there is no way he would have let them reach the Retreat.'

'But causing the coach to crash . . . that is surely a stretch,' Lucas said.

Hannah shook her head. 'Not if you know my father.'

'So the driver crashed on purpose and killed himself?' Daniel asked.

Hannah saw Lucas's face shift.

'The driver isn't among the dead,' Hannah said.

Daniel stared at them. 'So do you know where he is?'

'Best guess — he got out and sabotaged the exit, leaving us trapped.'

But as soon as she said it, Hannah realized what had been been troubling her about this scenario. The driver had left without his jacket or cap. No outerwear at all. How would he survive out there?

'Of course, there is another possibility' — Cassie smiled thinly — 'He didn't escape.'

'You just said he's not amongst the dead,' Daniel said.

'Exactly. Maybe he's still here and one of us is an interloper.'

'You're joking?' Daniel looked around at them nervously. 'I mean, I can't even drive.'

'Okay.' Lucas held a hand up. 'This is ridiculous. No one is an interloper.'

'What about you?' Cassie asked.

'Me?'

'Yes. You don't seem much like a student. I don't remember seeing you when we got on. Is it you?'

'Can we drop this?' Hannah said steadily.

Cassie shot her a look. 'Let him answer.'

Lucas sighed. 'No, it is not me. But you are right — I am older than most students here. I was forced to take a break in my education after an accident . . . and I only returned two years ago.'

'What accident?'

Lucas bent and rolled up his right trouser leg.

Cassie gasped.

'Fuck, man,' Daniel hissed.

Even Hannah felt a small jolt of surprise.

Below Lucas's knee was a prosthetic leg.

'I lost it in an automobile crash,' he said. 'I almost lost my life. I was lucky to survive, but recovery and rehabilitation meant I was out of schooling for a while.'

He looked around at them meaningfully. 'It also means I am unable to drive a manual vehicle without modifications, so there is no way I could drive this coach.'

Hannah couldn't help noticing he said this with some satisfaction. Cassie had the decency to look a little shamefaced.

179

'I'm sorry,' she said.

Lucas gave a small nod. 'Accepted.'

'Yeah,' Daniel said. 'I think we're all getting a bit stressed out.'

'Hardly surprising,' Lucas said. 'We have just seen an acquaintance killed. We are trapped with a pile of dead bodies, some of which are infected. Not quite the trip we were expecting.'

A long pause.

'Do you really believe your father would leave you to die?' Daniel asked Hannah.

'No, he wouldn't *leave* me to die. He wouldn't leave any of you to die. He would make sure of it.' She let this sink in. 'When the storm eases, his people will come. But not to rescue us. To kill us.'

'Okay,' Lucas said. 'We need to review our options.'

'What options?' Cassie asked. 'We're trapped. Again.'

'We need to find another way out.'

And then Hannah remembered her night-time musings. 'There might be a way. The toilet.'

Cassie raised an eyebrow. 'What? We're going to flush ourselves out like in a cartoon?'

'No. I think it might be possible to remove the toilet. Underneath, there's a tank. If we could dislodge that, the gap might be big enough to crawl out of.'

'*Might* and *possible* working hard there,' Cassie said.

Hannah folded her arms. 'I'm open to any other ideas.'

'It seems worth a try,' Lucas said.

'But what then?' asked Cassie. 'I mean, how are we going to survive out there? Freezing cold, wild animals, Whistlers. And where the hell do we go?'

'If we get out, we can get to the luggage in the hold,'

Hannah said. 'More supplies, food, clothes — and phones. The more people we can make aware of our situation, the less likely it is that the Department will get away with shutting us down.'

Although perhaps the Department *should* shut them down, a small part of her thought. If they were infected, they could spread the virus. Survival was selfish. But then, survival often was.

'What about Peggy?' Daniel asked. 'And Ben. They won't survive out there.'

Hannah stared at him. His devotion was admirable but also deluded.

'Daniel —' she started to say.

Lucas interrupted. 'We must be realistic. They won't survive anyway.'

'So we just abandon them, to die alone?' Daniel turned to Hannah. 'Is that what you think too?'

Yes, Hannah thought. Because there was no other option. And ultimately, we all die alone. No one is coming on that journey with us.

'We may not have a choice —'

Daniel shook his head. 'Forget it.' He rose and climbed over the seats, away from them.

'Where are you going?' Lucas asked.

'To the toilet — or do I need your permission for that too, seeing as you seem to be playing God now?'

'Harsh,' Cassie muttered.

Hannah sighed. 'Lucas is right. Peggy and Ben will die regardless. We can't waste energy or resources on trying to get them out of the coach. The best we can do is make sure they're comfortable for as long . . . as it takes.'

'That may not be too long.' Lucas said. 'Do you hear something?'

'No?'

'Exactly. Ben is no longer coughing.'

He was right. Hannah should have noticed. She glanced up the coach. Ben wasn't lying where they had left him. In fact, she couldn't remember seeing him when she clambered down the coach earlier. Perhaps he had hauled himself on to a seat. She hadn't checked, she thought with a stab of guilt. None of them had. They had already written him off.

'I should go and see —' she started to say.

And then they heard a crash and a shout:

'*Jesus Christ!*'

Daniel stumbled backwards out of the toilet, almost slipping on the leaking waste and disinfectant. He grabbed at a seat to steady himself and Hannah realized that his hands were covered with blood.

Instinctively, she rose. 'What is it?'

He stared at her, face slack with shock. 'I don't think Ben is going to be a problem any more.'

And then he threw up.

Meg

Thirst. Cold. Hunger. All would kill you. Right now, Meg felt like they were waiting to see which would win out first.

Cold they could manage by keeping moving. Despite the fact it made the car rock precariously, walking up and down at least generated some warmth in their muscles. In between, despite their lack of affection for each other, they huddled in one corner together, sharing meagre body heat.

Worryingly, in the morning light, Meg could see that ice had formed in the corners of the car's glass walls. The temperature inside was continuing to drop. The cable car was not well insulated. It didn't need to be. It was only supposed to operate for short trips of fifteen minutes. Without light or heat, it would get even colder, especially if they were stuck here for another night.

Hunger was causing pangs, but they could survive without food for some time. The body didn't need food physically as much as it craved it mentally. It might be painful, but a week or more without food wouldn't kill them.

Thirst was another matter. Their throats were dry and their lips had started to crack. Fortunately, the cold meant they weren't losing much in the way of sweat, but they were all feeling that sandpaper soreness in their mouths. Although, on the other hand, not being able to eat or drink had at least temporarily solved their toileting problems. Every cloud.

'We're going to die in here,' Sarah muttered as she took her turn walking up and down the cable car, clapping her hands together. 'It's just a matter of time.'

'We mustn't think like that,' Sean said.

'He's right,' Max said. 'Rescue could still come.'

'After all this time? They've forgotten us. Or maybe they don't want to rescue us. Maybe the plan was always to let us die in here, like guinea pigs in a plastic ball.'

'Hamsters,' Meg said.

'What?'

'You don't put guinea pigs in a plastic ball. It's hamsters.'

'Or gerbils,' Sean interjected.

'Who cares?' Sarah screamed. 'Guinea pigs, hamsters, gerbils. We're going to die.' And then she burst into tears, sat down in the corner and began to mumble a prayer.

Meg didn't have the will — or sympathy — to comfort her. Even Max seemed unable to summon up the energy to be gentlemanly. He shifted slightly in his seat and winced. He didn't look so good, Meg thought. His face was pale, and his breathing seemed a little laboured. The broken wrist was obviously causing him pain, unsurprisingly, and they didn't have any painkillers.

Meg wasn't sure about Max's age. He obviously kept himself in decent shape, but he must be in his late sixties, maybe older. The shock and pain of his injury plus the lack of food and water and the *fucking cold* must be taking their toll. But then, they were taking their toll on all of them. She worried about the night. Drowsiness was a symptom of hypothermia. What if they went to sleep and didn't wake up? The cable car creaked again.

The wind had died down, the rocking had abated, but every movement still felt precarious. How many more hours, and what if rescue didn't come?

As Sarah sat down, Max stood up. Or at least he tried. He staggered and fell back. Sean went to help him, but Max shook his head.

'I'm fine,' he snapped, pride making his tone sharp.

He pushed himself up again with his good arm and started to walk carefully across the car. His steps were slow and tentative. Meg was reminded that, for every step they took to keep warm, they were also using energy that they couldn't really afford to waste.

Halfway down the cabin on his second stint, Max suddenly paused, his legs buckled, and he crumpled to the floor. Meg and Sean leapt up.

'Max, are you okay?' Meg asked, crouching down next to him.

'Yes. Just a bit unsteady, that's all.'

But he didn't look okay. He looked dazed, and as Meg and Sean eased him up Meg noticed his skin felt clammy and hot. Something was wrong. She caught Sean's eye and could tell he was thinking the same. Shit.

'Let's sit you down,' Sean said. 'And maybe we should check your arm. Make sure you didn't hurt it when you fell.'

'No, no, it's fine. I just felt a bit dizzy.'

They eased him back on to the bench.

'Well, what d'you expect?' Sarah muttered. 'We've had nothing to eat. No water. We're all weak. It's probably stupid even moving around.'

'Thanks for that constructive insight,' Meg said.

'I think we should look at your arm,' Sean said to Max again.

185

'Really, it's okay. I told you —'

'Max,' Sean said. 'I really don't want to have to break your other arm, so *please* let me look.'

The older man sighed. 'Fine.'

Sean eased his arm out of the sling and gently unwrapped the makeshift bandage. Meg's heart fell. The wrist was swollen, which was to be expected, but the skin looked tight, mottled red. Meg could tell, even from looking at it, that it would feel hot. It only took a tiny break of the skin for infection to set in. *Shit.*

'O–kay,' Sean said. 'That's not great.'

Max sighed. 'It's infected, isn't it?'

Sean nodded. 'I think so. Cellulitis?'

He looked at Meg, and she nodded. Double shit.

Max rested his head back against the glass wall. 'I'm sorry. I didn't want to be a burden or a liability.'

'You're not,' Meg said firmly. 'So far, the cellulitis looks limited to the wrist. It hasn't spread and the skin isn't cracked.'

'It hurts.'

'That's probably a good thing.'

'Good?' Sarah barked from the corner. 'The poor man is probably going to lose his arm.' And then she started crying again.

Meg's head snapped around. 'If you can't say anything helpful, could you kindly just shut the fuck up.'

Sarah glared at her, then clutched at her cross. 'Do not repay evil with evil or insult with insult. On the contrary, repay evil with blessing, because to this you were called so that you may inherit a blessing.'

Meg rolled her eyes. 'For fuck's sake.' She turned back to Max. 'When we get to the Retreat, I'm sure they'll have plenty of antibiotics.'

He raised an eyebrow. '*If* we get there.'

'How do you feel, in yourself?' Sean asked, deliberately changing the subject. 'Lucid? Any tremors or shakes?'

'I'm a little shivery,' Max admitted. 'But I'm not sure how much of that is the wrist or the cold and lack of sustenance.'

It was a good point. It would be harder to fight the infection if he was already weak. Sean wrapped up Max's wrist again. Meg's mind ticked over. Food, they couldn't do anything about. But if they could just source some water. *Water, water, all around and not a drop to drink*. Except here, they had snow all around. Fluttering down from the sky and settling on the roof. There must be a fair amount up there by now. If they could only get to it, they could drink it.

Meg looked around the cabin. Glass walls, benches, metal floor with a hatch. She frowned. The floor hatch was all very well if there was an experienced guide on board and equipment to abseil out of the car. But what if there wasn't? She was sure she had seen news stories where people had to be rescued from stranded cable cars by helicopter, which would surely mean . . .

She stared at the ceiling. Sure enough, in the far-right corner there was what looked like another small square. Another hatch?

'I might have an idea,' she said.

'All ears,' Sean replied.

'If we could get to the snow on the roof, we could drink that.'

'Good idea. But how do we get to the snow on the roof?'

'I think there's another exit hatch in the ceiling.'

They all looked up.

'*Of course*. In case of helicopter rescue,' Sean said.

Great minds, Meg thought. She walked over and reached up. She could just touch the hatch with her fingertips, but she couldn't get any traction.

'Let me,' Sean said.

Normally, Meg wouldn't step aside for a man, but here, Sean did have the height advantage. He moved over next to her and reached up. He felt around the edge of the square with his fingers. Then he shoved hard. The square didn't budge. Of course, they were presuming it opened at all. It might not even lead to the roof. It might just be a hatch for electrics.

'Could be the weight of the snow holding it down,' Sean said. 'Or maybe it's frozen shut . . . or it only opens from the top.'

Meg felt her heart fall. 'Fuck,' she cursed.

Sean studied the hatch.

'See here, this is a hinge, which makes me think that it *does* open.'

'Okay.'

'But here —' He pointed to a small hexagonal hole the other side.

'What's that?'

'I think it's a lock.'

'So, we *could* open it from the inside.'

'If we could push it up and if we had the key or some other kind of tool.'

'Like a knife?'

He raised his eyebrows.

'Fuck,' she cursed again.

Behind her, she could hear Sarah mumbling her bloody prayers.

'While you're at it, could you ask God if he could drop us down a screwdriver? We could use some divine intervention right now.'

It was spiteful, Meg knew. Sarah ignored her. Probably for the best.

'Perhaps,' Max said, 'the key is in the cabin somewhere, hidden so no one opens the hatch for fun.'

'I don't know,' Sean said. 'There's not many places to hide something in here.'

'Worth a look though,' Meg said.

And it was more use than praying. She dropped to her knees and started to crawl around the floor, looking underneath the benches. It was about the only place she could think where something could be hidden. Sean hesitated and then did the same on the other side of the car.

The cabin had obviously been thoroughly cleaned. Meg hadn't even found a piece of dried-on chewing gum. She was about to give up when she saw something. Not a key. But something out of place, nonetheless. In the furthest corner, beneath one of the benches, was something black. She reached out to touch it. Tape. A corner of black electrical tape, the edges ragged, like the rest had been ripped off. Meg frowned. Maybe the cleaners had missed it. Or maybe it had been stuck on afterwards. Or used to stick something under here?

'Meg!'

She jumped, banging her head. 'Ouch.' She crawled back out from under the bench.

'I've found it!' Sean said.

'You've got the key?'

'Yes.'

She stared at him as he held up a small silver key, like the ones you used to open a gas meter.

'It was on the floor under the bench here.'

'Right.'

Meg couldn't believe she had missed it, but still. She stood and walked over to Sean. He reached up and inserted it into the lock. He turned it one way and then back again. Meg wasn't sure which way locked or unlocked it. Sean pushed at the hatch. There was a squealing sound and it lifted, just a little.

He looked at her and grinned. 'Okay. I think we're in business.'

Meg joined him, standing on tiptoes, pushing at the hatch as hard as she could. She felt it lift a little more. But the ice and snow — precious, wet, watery snow — were holding it down. Oh, the fucking irony. She looked across at Sarah, who still sat, eyes down, hands clasped.

'D'you think you could take a rain check with God and come and actually help us here?'

Sarah shot them a black look but stood and walked over. With three of them pushing the hatch gave some more. Meg could see a good inch or two of white and feel the chill of the wind.

'Just one more push.' Sean said.

'Allow me.'

They turned. Max stood beside them, looking wobbly but resolute. He reached up with his good arm. As one, they all shoved at the hatch. It creaked and then gave, flipping open with a dull clunk.

Immediately, a small avalanche of snow fell from the roof over their heads and faces. It was freezing, like the coldest ice shower. But they all started shovelling it greedily into their mouths.

'Turn one of your gloves inside out and fill it with snow to save and drink,' Meg said. 'You can stick your hand into your pocket or sleeve to keep it warm.'

They all did as she instructed, scooping the snow into their inside-out gloves. Meg licked at the snow on her hands and face, savouring the icy water, breathing in the freezing air from the hatch. And then she stuck her tongue out. Flakes of snow landed on it.

A sudden, vivid memory struck her. Lily, aged about four, standing in their back garden one March morning. It had been unseasonably cold and had suddenly started to snow. Meg had dressed her up warmly in her Peppa Pig coat and woolly hat and Lily had twirled around and around in circles, tongue stuck out, arms outstretched, catching snow on her tongue.

Meg swallowed, blinking back the tears.

'You okay?' Sean asked.

'Fine.' She nodded, turning away.

She looked around. They all stood, licking at the snow in their gloves like guests at the world's worst cocktail party. It was kind of ridiculous, and hilarious.

'What is it?' Max asked.

'Just look at us,' Meg said.

Sean started to chuckle, then Max. Even Sarah managed a smile. They were probably still going to die, but not right now. Right now, they had water and a tiny bit of hope.

'Okay,' Sean said. 'If everyone's got some snow, we should probably close this hatch before it gets even colder in here.'

He stretched back up to grab the hatch, but now there was a problem. With the hatch flipped open on to the roof he couldn't grab it.

'Crap.'

'Can't you reach?' Max asked.

'I need to climb up,' Sean said. He stepped up on

191

to the edge of the bench and reached as far as he could out of the open hatch.

'Got it,' he said. Then cursed. 'Shit. The snow . . . it's making it slippery. I can't get a grip.'

Meg put down her glove full of snow. 'Climb down and hitch me up on your shoulders. I might be able to stretch further out.'

'No. I can —' His foot slipped and he crashed to the floor. The whole cable car swayed. Max sat down abruptly. Meg and Sarah grabbed for the poles.

'Shit,' Sean cursed from the floor.

'Are you all right?' Meg asked.

'Yeah.' He stood, pulling a slight face as he put weight on his left ankle.

'You sure?'

'Just twisted it a bit. I'll be fine.'

'Can you still lift me up?'

He nodded. 'Let's do it.'

He bent down. Meg climbed on the bench and then on to his shoulders. He clutched her legs and straightened, propelling her up through the open hatch.

She gasped. The wind scraped at her face like sandpaper. The freezing air in her lungs felt like caustic bleach. She blinked back ice from her eyes. Ahead of her, the long line of the support cable stretched all the way up to the grey shell of the cable-car station. It looked bigger up here. *Damn*, she thought. It wasn't that far. Maybe 250 yards. But it might as well be 250 miles.

She reached for the hatch. Her hand knocked something else, half buried in the snow. She frowned and brushed the snow away. An object had been secured to the cable-car roof with black tape. She stared at it.

192

'Meg?' Sean shouted from below. 'Not to be impolite, but you aren't getting any lighter.'

'Okay. Wait.'

She scrabbled at the tape with her gloves, ripping one corner free and tugging the object out.

'Oh, yeah,' she heard Sean groan. 'There goes the hernia.'

She stuffed it down her snowsuit and felt around for the hatch with both hands. Her fingers closed over it. She adjusted her grip.

'Okay. Lower me down.'

Sean crouched and she pulled the hatch shut back over her head. It closed with a metal clang. Something about that clang rang with a gloomy finality. Like a tomb being sealed.

Back in the car, Meg slipped from Sean's back feeling breathless and a little sick. The extreme cold and height had given her momentary vertigo. She bent over, trying to breathe and control the nausea. Eventually, she straightened.

'All right?' Sean asked.

She debated with herself. *Should she tell them?* But what good were more secrets?

'I found something on the roof of the car,' she said.

'Is a parachute or abseiling equipment too much to ask for?' Sean quipped.

Meg pulled out the object she had stuffed inside her snowsuit.

'Oh dear Lord.' Sarah quickly crossed herself.

'Is that —' Max started to say, then trailed off.

It was perfectly obvious what it was.

A gun.

193

Carter

No one ever thinks they're the bad guy.

We all kid ourselves that we're the hero of the story.

And we're usually wrong.

In movies, the good and the bad are clear cut. Black and white. The light side and the dark side. The freedom fighters and the evil empire. In life, it's not like that. The lines are blurred. People are not black and white, and we all see situations in different ways. One person's freedom fighter is another's terrorist. One's crazy genius is another's dangerous psychopath. One person's leader is another's oppressor. That's how society rumbled or crumbled.

An apocalypse doesn't happen because of evil men, zombies or even a virus. It happens because of ordinary people. Because somewhere along the way we lost society, lost cohesion. We forgot to try to see the other side. Instead, we all bunkered down harder in our trenches, refusing to be moved, lobbing missiles at those who dared to challenge our myopic view. No good guys or bad guys. Just a bunch of scared motherfuckers trying to find their way home.

And talking of motherfuckers.

'*Man*, I can't go out to the incinerator in *this*.' Welland stared at Miles plaintively. 'It's still a fucking shitstorm out there.'

For once, he was right. Morning had dawned, not with clearer skies but with more heavy swathes of snow. Not as heavy as the previous night. The wind had died down from a banshee howl to breathless gasps. But the drifts were piled high and visibility was poor. You'd be mad to go anywhere in this weather.

Of course, now Welland had voiced this, Carter was fucked if he was going to agree with him.

'We could always swap,' he said, pulling on his snowsuit. 'Nice trek up to the cable-car station. Fresh air. Be good for you.'

Welland glared at him. 'You know I can't hike with my asthma.'

'Oh yeah, your asthma.' Carter fought the urge to make quote marks with his fingers around the word 'asthma', not least because people who did that were dicks.

Miles gazed at Welland evenly, like a predator eyeing a meal. 'The storm will start to abate in a few hours. Fetch the bodies from the basement and load them on to the sled in the meantime. You are the only one who can work the incinerator, Welland. We are depending on you.' He held up the pass to the basement.

Carter could see Welland was torn between puffing up his chest like Mr Toad and protesting about having to go outside again. In the end, pride won out. He took the pass, snorted and headed across the hall towards the elevator. 'Yeah. Everyone relies on Welland.'

Carter bit his tongue so hard he was sure he could taste blood.

Miles turned to him and raised his eyebrows. 'So, ready?'

No, Carter thought. But he shrugged. 'Guess so.' He paused. 'You think Caren will be okay here on her own?'

'She has Welland.'

'Exactly.'

'Caren can look after herself.'

Carter had no doubt about that. Right now, she was upstairs, lifting weights in the gym. But could she be trusted to look after the Retreat in their absence? As far as Carter was aware, Miles had always been on site to look after things. And by things, he didn't just mean the supplies. He meant Isolation Chamber 13.

Which brought him to another matter.

'You sure about this?'

'No.' Miles stepped into his boots. 'But I don't see that we have much choice. We need a new generator. We need a battery. The cable-car station is our only option.'

Carter would have liked to disagree, but he knew Miles was right. He had given it a lot of thought, trying to come up with ways around a trek to the station, but he'd got nowhere. However, he also knew something Miles didn't, and that might just possibly affect his plans.

'Miles, there's something you should know —'

'What?'

'I was thinking about Jackson yesterday, and what Caren said — about not believing he would steal the plasma?'

Miles continued to stare at him. Carter knew this trick. Let someone keep talking. Give them enough rope to hang themselves.

'So,' he continued, 'I decided to take a look around his room, and —' Carter pulled out the Nokia. 'I found this.'

A small twitch. A tensing of the jaw. 'Where?' Miles asked.

'Hidden in the shower pipe.'

Miles nodded. 'How . . . resourceful. And how clever of you to think of looking there.'

Carter gave a small shrug. 'Just a lucky guess.'

Miles held out his hand. Carter placed the Nokia in it.

'There are messages. Text conversations,' he said.

'With whom?'

Carter paused, priming his grenade. 'Hard to say. The contact is simply Lloyd.'

'A friend, family?'

'I don't think so —'

While some older messages were brief and banal — How are you? What's happening? — the most recent were more specific: questions about the layout of the Retreat, the routines, the basement and 'the plan'.

'I'd say it's some kind of Rem group,' Carter said.

The Rems (also known as X-Men, Stormers and Anons) were a loose affiliation of Doomsday cultists, anti-vaxxers, science sceptics and far-right religious fuckwits who sprang up around the time the virus really started to bite. Some wanted all life to end, some wanted governments toppled, some wanted the status quo reset, some wanted God to come down in his flaming chariot and smite the unbelievers. The usual crap.

What these apocalypse agitators couldn't seem to grasp was that the planet was managing to self-destruct very nicely on its own, thank you. So, all their attacks, protests and assassinations were the equivalent of giving a wedgie to someone who was lying on the floor, bleeding out from every orifice, and expecting them to care.

Carter wouldn't have had Jackson down as one of

them. Despite his new age yoga and meditation crap, he seemed to lack that frothing-at-the-mouth fundamentalism. But maybe he was just a good actor. We all wore different faces for different people, some more palatable than others.

Miles was still scrolling through the messages. 'Why here? What do they want?'

Carter waited. And then Miles paused, thumb hovering over the phone, eyes widening. *There it was.* He looked up at Carter.

'They know about Isolation Chamber 13. They know *he's* here.'

Carter nodded. 'Yeah.'

Miles frowned, considering. 'The last message is three weeks ago: **I'll txt when more news.** Nothing since.'

'Actually' — Carter reached over and tapped the phone — 'there was one outgoing call, not a text, just a couple of days ago.'

'Just before Jackson disappeared.'

Carter had been thinking about this. 'We don't know exactly *when* Jackson disappeared.'

Days could pass and none of them would see Jackson. He rarely joined them for meals, never socialized in the evenings. He used the gym early in the morning, undertook his allotted tasks and shut himself in his room for the rest of the time. Shadows were more obtrusive.

'Well, who else could have made the call?' Miles tapped the phone against his chin. 'But if Jackson was Rem, why run? Why steal the plasma?'

'I don't know.'

'A change of heart? Perhaps Jackson decided to bail?'

Carter had considered that too. 'So what do we do?'

Miles slipped the phone in his pocket. 'For now, we stick with the plan. While the power supply is compromised, we are vulnerable. That remains the priority. I'll give this some thought and then we'll decide what to do.'

'And the others?'

'We keep this between us for now.'

Carter opened his mouth, but before he could say anything there was the sound of barking, closely followed by feet thudding down the stairs. They both turned. Dexter shot down the staircase, yapping frantically. Caren followed. She still wore her gym gear and looked sweaty and worried.

'What?' Miles asked.

'We've got company.'

And now Carter could hear something else. The low whine of snowmobiles. He glanced at Miles. They both drew their guns and headed for the door. Miles shoved it open. Carter stopped to grab Dexter and shoved him into Caren's arms: 'Don't fucking let him out. Got it?'

She grimaced as Dexter panted in her face. 'Are you sure? His breath could deter Godzilla.'

Carter ruffled Dexter's head and followed Miles outside. Three battered blue-and-red snowmobiles pulled up by the fence in a blur of white. Emblazoned down the side of each, worn but still legible: *Bob's Snow-Mo Adventures*. The snowmobiles didn't belong to Bob any more. Bob's adventures had come to an abrupt end some time ago. Like most things in the resort, the snowmobiles now belonged to the Quinns.

As Miles and Carter watched, guns poised, two burly figures in black climbed off, machine guns

199

slung over their backs. Quinn's sons. They swung their guns around and glared at Miles and Carter. This was bad. Jimmy and his sons had never, as far as Carter knew, made the trek up to the Retreat for any reason. And — label him observant — it didn't look like this was a social call.

The third figure dismounted. Small, wrapped up in a white snowsuit with a thick, furry hood, and huge orange goggles.

Jimmy Quinn walked up to the gate. He pushed the goggles up.

'Miles! Carter! Nice place you got here.'

'Thank you,' Miles said evenly. 'I'd invite you in for tea, but we were just heading out.'

The smile sliced off like it had been decapitated. 'You're going nowhere. We need to talk.'

Hannah

The body was lodged between the wall and the toilet. His head had slumped to one side, revealing a gaping red gash across his throat. More ugly slashes ran vertically up his arms. A large piece of bloody, jagged glass lay on the floor nearby.

'Suicide,' Lucas said flatly, peering over Hannah's shoulder.

She didn't reply. She crouched awkwardly in the small space, examining Ben's body. The cuts on the arms were standard for suicide. At least, for a suicide where a person knew what they were doing. A vertical cut spoke of meaning. Not a cry for help. Slicing up the arm meant you would bleed out far more quickly.

The slash across the neck was less typical. Not many suicide victims chose to cut their own throats. It made death far more unpleasant, for a start. Suffocating, choking on your own blood. It took real dedication to press the knife, or piece of glass, hard enough against your own flesh to make the cut. The tendons there were tougher than people realized.

And there was something else. Hannah frowned.

'What is it?' Lucas asked.

She hesitated. What *was* it? At first glance, she would say, yes, even with the neck wound, this was suicide. It made sense. Ben knew he was infected, dying. He had taken some glass from the broken window and ended things sooner, on his own terms. But glass wasn't as sharp as a blade. He would have had to really saw at that artery.

201

On the other hand, Ben was infected. The virus could affect the brain. Hence the rage and aggression. There had been cases of the infected doing violent harm to themselves and others. It was possible that Ben could have slashed his own neck in a fit of viral rage. Choler.

What was the alternative? One of *them* had killed Ben. Who would be capable of that? And then Hannah remembered how she had considered putting a coat over Peggy's face.

Lucas was still staring at her intently.

Hannah sighed. 'Some of the wounds are atypical of suicide, but taking into account that Ben could have been suffering from viral rage, I agree — the most likely conclusion is that he killed himself.'

Lucas nodded as if she had given the correct answer, and she felt that flicker of doubt again. *Who would be capable?*

'Well, that is one problem solved, I guess.'

Hannah wasn't sure if he meant the suicide or Ben himself.

She straightened. 'We need to move him,' she said. 'And clean up in here.'

Lucas looked around at the blood-smeared toilet and grimaced. Hannah knew what he was thinking.

The virus spread in numerous ways. It was the most virulent and adaptive the scientists had ever seen. Water droplets, breath, fluids, contaminated meat and blood. Out of all of them, saliva and blood were the ones most likely to infect. If they hadn't been compromised before, wading around in Ben's blood was a sure-fire way to ensure they were infected.

But then, one of them already was.

Hannah stood. 'I suggest we use some of the spare

clothes to make a stretcher and put Ben with the other bodies. Then we clean up as best we can. We still have water at the moment. Plus, we can use some of the snow from the broken window.'

Lucas nodded again. 'Agreed. Okay. Let's inform the others.'

He turned. Hannah pulled her sleeve down over her hand and gingerly picked up the piece of broken glass. It was thick. Reinforced. She placed it against the wound on Ben's throat. Too thick. As she thought. The cut had been made by something smaller, thinner. Uneasily, she put the glass down again.

★ ★ ★

There's always a moment, in a crisis, where a divide happens. Any group of people, however small, will begin to form alliances, and to display enmity. Discord will grow. Minor to start with, but there will come a crux point.

At the start, there is simply relief at being alive. Worry about the situation follows. Still, at that point, most people are united in a common goal. Survival. But the longer the crisis, the more survival turns inwards. 'We' becomes 'I'. As that happens, resentment and arguments occur.

They dragged Ben's body out of the toilet by his ankles. Death held no dignity, Hannah thought. Ultimately, once those rapidly firing neurons that imbued us with our perceived sense of self had flickered out, we were just lumps of meat, no different to the carcasses slung on a butcher's hook.

Using snow and some torn-up T-shirts, they scooped up the sick and scrubbed and mopped up

203

the blood. Daniel washed his hands and changed into a clean sweatshirt. It was too tight for him, his belly straining against the fabric. He tugged it down self-consciously. Momentarily, something brushed past Hannah's mind like a moth in the dark, and then disappeared again. Probably not important.

Finally, they wrapped Ben's body in two jumpers, knotted at the arms, and used them to carry him up the coach, where they laid him on top of the other dead.

There was a definite smell coming from the pile of bodies now. No denying the process of decay, even in these cool conditions. Add to that the aroma of blood, urine and faeces from the toilet, and each breath inside the coach was starting to feel like something of a test of endurance. Hannah felt her stomach turn. Unusual for her.

They needed to get out of here. Not just for survival but for their own sanity. The human mind was an incredible thing, able to adapt and bend to many different situations. But there came a point where it started to fray, to overload. Right now, they were all on the edge.

'Should we, like, say something?' Cassie said, staring at the bodies.

'What is there to say?' Lucas replied. 'Ben is dead. It is better this way.'

'For whom exactly?' Daniel asked.

'For all of us.'

Daniel glared at Lucas. 'You're a cold bastard, you know that?'

'I try not to let emotion control me.'

'Well, maybe you should.' Daniel gestured at the pile of bodies. 'Look at this. Look at *us*. We've just dumped them here like old coats. These were people with hopes and dreams and families that loved them.'

He stared around at them. Hannah understood. He was looking at the dead students and seeing his sister there. Dumped in a pile with the rest of them.

'We did not kill these people,' Lucas said. 'Ben chose his own exit.'

'Did he?'

Lucas turned to Daniel. 'What are you saying?'

'I've never heard of someone slitting their own throat before.'

'You're accusing someone of *killing* Ben?' Cassie asked.

'Not someone.' Daniel fixed his eyes on Lucas. Tension crackled in the air.

Lucas laughed without humour. 'I see. And why would I kill Ben?'

Daniel shrugged. 'He was a liability, wasn't he? Easier for everyone now he's dead. You said it yourself. Just like it would be easier if Peggy died, right?'

Lucas gazed at him appraisingly. 'I think it would be easier for *you*, my friend.'

Daniel's face darkened. 'You fucker.'

He lumbered forward, arm raised. Lucas was faster. He jabbed his fist into Daniel's belly. The bigger man 'oomphed' and doubled over. Lucas followed with a knee to Daniel's head, knocking him down. He raised his foot. Hannah caught his arm. 'Enough.'

She felt Lucas tense and then relax. She turned to Daniel.

'Are you all right?'

Daniel knelt on the floor, groaning. 'Fine,' he gasped. He looked up at Lucas and scowled. 'Showing your true colours now, bud.'

Then he staggered to his feet and stumbled back down the coach.

Cassie shook her head at Lucas. 'Wrong call — you don't kick someone when they're down.' And then she walked after Daniel.

Hannah remained.

'He tried to hit me first,' Lucas said.

'That was still excessive.'

He sighed. 'You are right. I should apologize.'

'No. Leave it for a while. Let him calm down.'

Lucas nodded. 'We are all feeling the strain. Not cabin but coach fever, yes?'

'Yeah.'

Hannah turned and walked to the windscreen. The morning was lightening. The snow had stopped falling. The trees sparkled. Except for the mess of blood and remnants of flesh that used to be Josh, it looked almost magical, and Hannah was suddenly overcome with a yearning to breathe fresh air again, however fucking much the cold burnt her lungs.

'We need to get out of here,' she said.

Lucas joined her. 'I agree. You really think we could escape through the toilet?'

'I think it's worth a try.'

A couple of birds took wing into the sky, dark silhouettes flapping away. Beyond them, a larger shape drew into view. Hannah frowned.

'Do you see that?'

Lucas was peering at his watch. Now he glanced up. 'What?'

'Over there.'

The object was too big for a bird. Too slow. And now Hannah could hear something. The distant whirring of blades.

206

A helicopter. Circling. Searching. *The Department.*
'Shit.'

They watched as the helicopter hovered, dropped then started to rise again before turning and shrinking into the distance. *They were looking in the wrong place*, Hannah thought. But they were still looking. And they'd be back.

'Do you really think the Department wants to kill us?' Lucas asked. 'You could be wrong. We could be rescued. Get out of this mess.'

'You don't know my father,' she said.

'I know he is a brilliant scientist.'

Hannah barked out a bleak laugh. 'That old trope. Brilliant. Inspiring. Brave.'

Lucas frowned. 'That is funny?'

She looked at him: 'Let me tell you about my father. When I was eleven, not long after my mother committed suicide, my father brought home four beagle puppies. He told me that three of them had to go to the labs, for experiments. But I could keep one. I had to choose.' She paused. 'I picked the smallest, obviously. The one I thought wouldn't survive being injected with poison or having bits cut off and put under a microscope. I called him Buddy, and I loved that little pup for the whole four weeks I had him.'

'What happened?'

'One day, I came home from school to find that Buddy had gone. One of the other beagles had died and the lab needed a replacement, quickly. So, my father took Buddy. I never saw him again.'

Lucas drew in a breath. '*Scheisse.*'

'My father offered to get me another dog, but I had learned my lesson. I asked for a goldfish.' Hannah smiled. 'It's hard to be broken-hearted over a goldfish.'

'That is terrible.'

'Yes.' She turned away. '*That's* my father.'

★ ★ ★

They encountered a problem with Hannah's escape plan right away. The toilet seat was set into a moulded plastic unit. Although the seat was loose, they would need to remove the whole unit to get to the space beneath. The unit was fixed down by six screws. Two had already fallen out. Four remained.

'Don't suppose you happen to have a screwdriver on you?' Hannah asked Lucas.

He shook his head. 'Something I forgot to pack.'

She eased herself out of the cramped, stinking space, not really big enough for the two of them. She felt hot and sweaty. A wave of dizziness suddenly swamped her. She clutched at a seat, taking a deep breath, willing it to pass. Her breath caught in her throat. She coughed.

'Bit of a cough there?'

She looked up. Cassie was curled in a lopsided seat halfway along the coach. She was reading a paperback procured from one of the dead students. *Catch-22*. Appropriate.

'I'm fine,' Hannah said. 'Just dust.'

'Right.'

Hannah didn't like Cassie's tone. She was fine. She had to be.

'Not sitting with Daniel?' she asked the other girl, unable to disguise the antagonism in her own voice.

Cassie yawned. 'No offence, but the dying-sister vibe isn't especially cheery. I wish she'd hurry it up.'

Hannah stared at her. 'And you accused Lucas of

being cold.'

'Nope, that was Daniel. *I* said Lucas kicked some-one when they were down. Which he did.'

She turned a page in the book. Hannah shook her head. Every time she thought she was getting a handle on Cassie, she surprised her again. And not in a good way.

'Do you have anything we could use to undo some screws?' she asked wearily.

'Sure.' Cassie said. 'Let me just get my toolbox.'

Hannah gritted her teeth. She didn't have time for this. 'Well, thanks for your help.'

Cassie raised an eyebrow. 'What d'you want? There's only room for two of you in there. There's nothing I can do for Daniel or his sister. Better to conserve energy. Especially seeing as our food and water are pretty limited.'

She was right, Hannah hated to admit. Her eyes roamed around the coach, hoping she might see something they could use.

'A coin might work,' Cassie added.

'Do you have any coins on you?'

'Nope.'

'Great.'

Cassie gave her a salute and buried her nose back in the book. Hannah sighed and looked down the coach. She didn't want to, but she needed to talk to Daniel.

He was seated next to his sister again. Peggy was still — just — alive. Her breathing was shallow and ragged and her skin pale and clammy. She must surely only have a short time left. But it was hard to tell. Initially, Hannah had thought she would die within the hour. But here she was. Death was a process. It took as long as it took. And it was never like it was in the movies. People always presumed it was either sudden or prolonged, with plenty of time to prepare. But the idea of 'preparing' for death was a fantasy.

Similarly, the most catastrophic injuries could take time to finally kill you. First, the organs would begin to fail. Slowly, one by one. Feeling in the limbs would fade. The brain would shut down higher functions, consciousness would become dulled and intermittent. The need for food or water would fade and many of the dying would lose the ability to swallow. Breathing would falter and, finally, without enough oxygen and with failing electrical impulses from the brain, the heart would stop beating. Depending on the injury, this could take minutes, hours or days. Death came when Death was ready. And no one, in Hannah's experience, was ever prepared. She shivered and swallowed down another cough.

'You don't need to say it,' Daniel said as she approached.

'Say what?'

'Lucas was right. It would be for the best. Peggy is going to die, and this is worse.'

Hannah sat down beside him. 'Lucas isn't right. Death is never for the best. But there comes a time when it's the least painful option.'

Daniel nodded. 'I was hoping that somehow we might get out of this, in time.'

Hannah frowned. In time for what? For Peggy to survive? That had always been unlikely.

'I'm sorry,' she said. A futile platitude.

Daniel raised his eyes to hers. Such striking eyes, Hannah thought again.

'I thought I heard a helicopter,' he said.

'I think the Department is looking for us.'

'And you really think they'll kill us if they find us?'
Shutdown.

'Yes,' she said. 'That's why we have to get out of here. We need to unscrew the toilet base. Do you have anything we could use to loosen the screws? A coin, perhaps?'

Daniel hesitated then fumbled in his pocket and pulled out a tarnished old penny. Hannah hadn't seen one for years.

'Lucky coin,' he said. 'My gran gave it to me. It's not done much good so far.' He held it out. 'You might as well have it.

Hannah took the coin. 'Thank you.'

'You really think this will work?' Daniel asked.

'I don't know. But we have to try. In here, we're sitting ducks.'

'And if we get out? What then?'

A good question. 'We take everything useful from the luggage in the hold. Head into the woods and find shelter for tonight. By daylight we try to find our way to a village or town. Once people know about us, it becomes harder to get rid of us.'

Daniel nodded thoughtfully. 'And how far to the nearest village or town?'

'I don't know,' Hannah admitted. 'Maybe fifty miles, maybe five hundred.'

'And do you really think we'll survive long enough to walk five hundred miles?'

'I'd rather die trying than sit in here waiting for death.'

Daniel smiled. 'You remind me of Peggy some-times.'

'I do?'

'Yeah. She was tougher than she looked —' He

211

caught himself. That pesky past tense.

'Daniel,' Hannah said. 'If we get out, you have to come with us.'

'I can't leave Peggy here.'

'You can't do anything else for her.'

'It's . . . it's not just about Peggy.'

'Then what?'

He didn't reply.

'Look,' Hannah said. 'I know it's hard, but there will come a point when you have to make a choice.'

Daniel looked back at his sister and tenderly brushed a stray hair from her forehead. 'I know.' He turned back to Hannah. 'Will you be here? When the time comes?'

'If you want me to.'

'Promise.'

She sighed. 'I promise.'

'Thank you.'

She stared at him. Was there something he wasn't telling her?'

Save her.

Before she could ask, Lucas's voice called from the toilet. 'Have you found anything to undo these screws?'

She called back: 'Yes. Just coming.'

Daniel stared up the coach at Lucas, his face hard. 'I don't trust him,' he said.

'You can't really think he killed Ben?'

He looked at her. 'Someone got up in the night. I saw them move.'

Hannah frowned. Could she have missed that? She supposed she may have dozed a little.

'Lucas?' she asked.

'Too dark to tell.'

'Are you sure?'

Daniel gave a rueful smile. 'I'm not sure about anything any more. Just . . . be careful.'

★ ★ ★

Undoing the screws was a slow, laborious process, made more unpleasant by the disinfectant and effluence seeping out of the upturned toilet. They lifted the seat out first and then took it in turns with the old penny. By the time the last screw popped free, their fingers were ragged and sore, and Hannah's sweatshirt was soaked with sweat. Despite his torn fingers, Lucas looked cool and calm. He tugged at the plastic unit and ripped it out. Then, awkwardly, he manoeuvred it out of the narrow door.

Moment of truth, Hannah thought.

She crouched down. Beneath the unit was an area of grey plastic flooring and a small outlet hole for the toilet. Hannah pushed at the plastic with her hand. Then she stood and kicked at it with her heel. It felt flimsy, but she still wasn't sure she could break it. Not without cutting her leg to shreds.

Lucas squeezed back in. 'Well?'

'Just this plastic flooring. I think the compartment for the holding tank will be on the other side. If we can get through this, theoretically, there should be an access space.'

'Theoretically?'

'It's all I have.' She looked back at the flooring. 'I just don't think I can break it.'

Lucas raised his leg and kicked hard at the plastic. It cracked a little. He kicked it again. This time his foot burst through up to the ankle. He staggered. Hannah winced. Then she realized it was Lucas's false leg. He tugged it back out, the sharp metal plastic raking against the metal prosthetic.

He smiled at her. 'It has its uses.'

They bent and pulled at the plastic, snapping pieces off, revealing a rectangular space underneath. Hannah peered into it. She could see the holding tank and, above that, a small hatch which must open at the side of the bus, to allow the tank to be removed when necessary. *Yes.* And for once, God or fate or just plain luck was on their side. There was space to get around the tank, and she could see a wedge of light where the hatch door had come open in the crash. Another hefty kick should see it give.

They had an exit. Tight. Awkward. But a way out.

Hannah felt light-headed with relief. She wiped at her forehead.

'We're going to make —'

A coughing fit overcame her. She covered her mouth with her arm. She couldn't catch her breath. Lucas was looking at her. She read the question in his eyes. But before he could say anything there was a yell from the back of the coach.

'HANNAH!'

She backed out of the toilet. Daniel was making his way towards her. He looked dishevelled and distraught.

'It's Peggy,' he said.

She nodded. 'Okay.'

Daniel turned and staggered back down the coach. Hannah followed. Before she even reached the back she could hear the moans of pain. She rounded the twisted seats and her eyes widened. Peggy lay against the window, body convulsing, legs splayed. The crotch

214

of her bleached jeans was soaked in blood.

'What the hell?'

She glanced at Daniel in confusion then dropped to her knees beside the girl. Where had all that blood come from? She placed a hand on Peggy's stomach. Something moved beneath her fingers. No. Hannah gently pulled back the baggy sweatshirt. The girl's belly was taut and distended, pulsing with contractions.

Jesus Christ.

Peggy was dying.

She was also pregnant . . . and in labour.

Hannah turned to Daniel angrily. 'Why didn't you tell me she was —'

The words withered on her lips.

Daniel stood behind her. In one hand, he held a small, sharp flick knife.

'You promised,' he said. 'Save her.'

Meg

'Why would someone hide a gun on the roof of the cable car?' Max asked.

'It must have been Karl,' Sarah said. 'He must have had two weapons.'

Meg considered this. 'But if he had a gun, why bring a knife to the party?'

'Maybe he thought a gunshot would wake us up.'

'We were out for the count.' Meg looked at the gun. 'Plus, we were stripped and searched. All our personal possessions taken off us before we were put on board. So how did he get a knife *and* a gun on to the cable car?'

'Well, obviously, he can't have been drugged,' Sarah said. 'He must have been faking.'

'He would still have gone through the same procedures . . .' Meg trailed off.

They were missing something. *She* was missing something. She thought about the scrap of masking tape beneath the seat. The masking tape sticking the gun to the roof. There was a connection, but she just wasn't seeing it.

Sean looked thoughtful. 'If the dead guy was security, maybe the gun was his.'

'So how did it end up stuck on the roof?'

He shrugged. 'Maybe he wanted to hide it for some reason?'

Or, Meg thought, maybe the killer found it and hid it up there? She considered the scenario: the killer stabs Paul, discovers the gun and panics. What to do?

216

He could ditch the gun, but it could be useful. There's nowhere to hide it inside the cable car, so he secures it to the roof. Crazy, but also kind of ingenious. But then, why didn't he put the knife up there, or ditch the knife? And where did the tape come from?

'Is it loaded?'

Sarah's voice interrupted Meg's train of thought just as she was getting somewhere.

'I asked if it's loaded,' Sarah repeated. 'I don't know about anyone else, but I'm not really very comfortable with you standing there holding a loaded gun.'

'You think I might shoot you all?' Meg said.

Sarah folded her arms. 'I'd rather not find out.'

Meg shook her head. 'Fine.' She clicked open the chamber. Six bullets inside. The gun was fully loaded, but it hadn't been used.

She emptied the bullets into her hand and held them out. 'Who wants them? A gun is no good without bullets.'

Sean stepped forward. 'I'll take them.'

She handed them over. He dropped the bullets into his pocket.

'Everyone happy with that?' Meg asked.

'Why do you get to keep the gun?' Sarah said.

Meg rolled her eyes. 'You want it? Here?' She proffered the gun, holding it by the barrel. Sarah looked at it and then shook her head.

'Actually, no. You keep it.'

'You sure?'

'Yes.'

Meg started to slip the gun into her pocket.

'Actually —' This from Max. He had sat down again, and his voice was a little croaky. 'Why does anyone need to keep it? Why don't we just get rid of

217

it, like we did with the knife?'

It was a fair point. If they made it to the Retreat with a gun, questions would be asked.

'I think we should keep the gun,' Sean said. 'Just in case.'

'Just in case?' Sarah looked at him. 'In case of what?'

But Meg knew. If they remained stuck here, faced with the options of starving or freezing to death, a bullet might not seem such a bad option.

'In case of *what*?' Sarah said again, voice growing shrill.

'In case rescue doesn't come,' Meg said flatly.

'I don't . . .' Sarah's eyes widened. 'You mean, shoot ourselves?'

'Or each other.'

Sarah stared at her in horror. 'No.'

'It's something we might have to consider,' Meg said. 'If our only options are dying slowly of hypothermia or starvation, we might want to take a quicker route. I know which I'd rather choose.'

'Only God decides who lives and dies,' Sarah muttered.

Meg barked out a short laugh. 'Right. So, when you pushed Karl out of the car, that was the hand of God, was it?'

'I *didn't* push him.'

'Can we not do this again?' Sean said. 'I say we keep the gun.'

In the corner, Max started coughing. Meg glanced over. Despite the water, his skin looked ashen and his eyes bloodshot. His hair was matted around the temples. Meg was willing to bet he was running a temperature. They needed to get him help.

'There is another option,' she said.

Sean raised an eyebrow. 'Jumping out of the hatch?'

'No. Climbing out.'

'What?'

'We can see the cable-car station from here. It's not that far.'

'It might as well be a million miles,' Sean said.

'I think it might be possible to climb along the support cable,' Meg said.

They all continued to stare at her. Then Sean burst out laughing. 'Seriously?'

Meg glared at him. After their conversation last night, she had thought they had made some sort of connection, but right now, he was acting like a dick.

'It's possible,' she reiterated. 'It's barely two hundred and fifty yards.'

'And that's not far if you're strolling down a sun-lit boulevard, maybe,' Sean said. 'But you're talking about clinging on with your hands and ankles to a steel cable one thousand feet up in the air in a snowstorm.'

Meg glared at him. '*I* can do it.'

'Can you? Really?'

'I held the police academy record for the assault course.'

'And I won the sack race in primary school,' Sean retorted. 'It's about as meaningful.'

'You should let her try.' This from Sarah, shivering in the corner.

Max regarded Meg through bloodshot eyes. 'Do you really think it's possible?'

'Yes,' she said, although she was in no way certain. 'It's dangerous. But it might be our only chance. If I can get to the station, I can raise the alarm, get help.'

'Look,' Sean said in a patient tone that made her

want to punch him. 'I know you're strong and fearless and all of that shit. *But* you'll never even make it halfway.'

'You have a better idea?' she asked. 'Aside from us all blowing our brains out?'

She saw something cross his face, a strange expression she couldn't read.

'Yes,' he said. 'I'll do it.'

'No,' Meg said.

'I'm stronger than you.'

'You're also heavier. I'm lighter and more agile.'

'I have more stamina.'

Meg glared at him. 'I appreciate the offer, but no.'

He smiled thinly. 'You don't trust me.'

'I didn't say that.'

'Didn't have to.' He shook his head. 'What? You think I'll get to the other side and do a runner, leave you all here to die? Maybe I killed the cop. Is that what you think?'

'No,' Meg said. 'And stop putting words into my mouth.'

They glared at each other.

'All right,' Max said weakly. 'Logically, there are only two reasons why we're still stuck here: one, it's a technical fault. In which case, there could be people working to get us moving right now. It's just taking some time.'

'Or?' Meg asked.

'A catastrophic event. Something has happened to the operators. There's no one to fix the problem. Perhaps no one even knows we're stranded.'

The thought was sobering.

'Either way —' he continued.

'We're fucked,' Sean finished for him.

Max smiled ruefully. 'I was going to say, the longer we're here, the greater the likelihood that it's the second.'

'So we're fucked?' Sean said.

'Basically.'

They all stared through the glass. Snow floated gently down like scraps of lace. In the distance, the sky undulated like a silver ribbon above the grey shell of the cable-car station. They watched, impotent, from inside their glass and metal tomb.

'That only leaves one question,' Meg said. 'How much longer do we wait?'

Carter

No one spoke. No one moved. Even time seemed to have decided to take a rain check.

Pinned by Jimmy Quinn's reptilian gaze, the yawning barrels of the submachine guns pointed at them, the moment seemed to last an eternity. Carter swallowed, feeling sure that the sound could probably be heard by distant deer in the forest.

Miles was first to break the silence. 'I talk better when people aren't pointing guns at my head.'

Jimmy Quinn smiled. 'They're not pointing at your head, Miles. They'll take out your knackers first.' But then he raised his hand and Things 1 and 2 lowered their weapons.

Miles inclined his head in a gesture of thanks and lowered his own gun.

After a moment, Carter did the same.

'So, what's the problem?' Miles asked.

Quinn nodded to Thing 1, who promptly stomped over to his snowmobile and took a package from the rear. As he walked back round, Carter recognized it as one of the parcels he had dropped off with Quinn yesterday morning.

Thing 1 dropped the parcel by the gate.

'Your plasma,' Quinn said.

'Yes,' Miles replied. 'The amount you requested. I don't —'

Thing 1 raised his gun and fired at the parcel, which exploded in a burst of brown paper and shards of glass.

Carter and Miles covered their heads and ducked.

'Shit!' Carter glanced at Miles and then back at Quinn. 'What the fuck?'

Quinn walked over to the obliterated box. He kicked the remains with his foot.

'You think I'm stupid, Miles? You try to sell me shit?'

Carter began to sweat. He had always been careful to rearrange the plasma so that Quinn never got any placebos, but had he made a mistake? Had Quinn been delivered duds?

'No,' Miles said steadily. 'I would never do that.'

'You're a liar.'

'No.'

Quinn continued to glare at him through the fence. 'I got a call, Miles. From an associate of mine. A very important associate. A very fucking unhappy associate. You know why?'

'No.' But there was something in Miles's voice. A tiny tremor of uncertainty.

'His family is *dead*, Miles. I sent him a batch of plasma, like always. But what happens? Two weeks later they all get ill. Wife, son — both dead. Now, he can get a new missus, but he can't replace his son. I told him it was a one-off, maybe a bad batch. Then I get more calls. More people infected. So, I'm gonna ask you again — did you sell me shit?'

Carter saw the faint wobble of Miles's Adam's apple as he swallowed. 'I would never —'

Another burst of gunfire. Carter and Miles hit the ground. Sparks exploded as bullets hit the gate. When the noise stopped, they looked up. The security pad that controlled the entrance hung off it. The gate swung open.

Quinn stood just outside. 'That's how easy it is,' he said softly. 'For me to kill you all and take this place. But I don't. Because we had a deal. Now, tell me the truth before I turn your balls into mincemeat.'

Miles held his hands up and stumbled to his feet. 'Okay.' He nodded. 'I only found out recently —'

This was it, Carter thought. He was going to tell him that Jackson had been stealing plasma and leaving duds.

Miles took a deep breath. 'I noticed some issues with the plasma's efficiency.'

Carter gaped at him. '*What?*'

'It was minor,' Miles continued. 'A small lowering of antigens. Each extraction, it seemed to drop a little.'

'Meaning?' Quinn asked.

Miles sighed. '*Meaning* the extracted plasma is less effective at generating an antibody response. It may not work as well, particularly if presented with a different variant.'

Quinn continued to stare at them coldly. 'You messed up, Miles.'

Miles nodded. 'I know — and I've got a contingency plan.'

'And I've got fucking dead people. I let them down, Miles. You get that? Maybe they'll come for me, or my sons.'

'I know. And I'm sorry.'

'Your apology isn't worth shit. You tell me how you're gonna make this right.'

'We get fresh supplies. Untapped. We dispose of our current supplies and start again. I believe that will solve the problem.'

'Fresh supplies?' Quinn eyed him curiously. 'You

mean —' He glanced back down the slope towards the forest. 'Fresh Whistlers?'

'Yes.'

Quinn threw back his head and laughed. His sons chuckled a little awkwardly.

'You're a crazy fucker, you know that?' He shook his head. 'Okay. You've got one day. Twenty-four hours.'

'I need more than that,' Miles said. 'A day to get supplies. Then to process.'

'Okay, forty-eight hours. No more. I want fresh plasma. You don't deliver . . . you're dead. All of you.'

'I understand.'

'You fucking will.'

Quinn pulled his goggles down and climbed back on the snowmobile. Things 1 and 2 did likewise. In a rev of engines and a spray of snow, the three vehicles careered off back down the slope.

Carter and Miles watched them go.

'Well, that was . . . eventful,' Miles muttered.

Carter pushed himself to his feet. 'What the fuck, Miles? Why didn't you tell us?'

Miles spun around and pressed his gun between Carter's eyes. 'Don't question me, Carter. *Never* fucking question me. Without me you'd be dead already.'

Carter held up his hands and moved his head in a tiny nod. 'Okay, okay. I'm sorry.'

Miles lowered the gun, cleared his throat and took a deep breath. 'This is not an unexpected development.'

'So, what do we do?' Carter asked. 'It's going to take us a day to trek to the cable-car station and back.'

Miles didn't appear to have heard him. 'Nor is it a disaster,' he continued. 'We needed fresh supplies anyway. This has simply made that need more imminent.'

'But what about the power, the generator?'

'Change of plans. We get supplies first.'

Before Carter could argue or object, Miles turned and walked to the door. 'We need to inform the others.'

★ ★ ★

Caren insisted on coming with them.

'You need everyone you've got.'

Carter expected Miles to refuse. It would leave only Welland here, in charge of the Retreat. But Miles nodded.

'True. And again, I'm sorry, I should have informed you about my concerns with the plasma earlier.'

Caren's lips pursed. 'You should. But I understand why you didn't.' She regarded Miles intently. 'How protected are we, Miles? Quinn said people got infected and died. If we're going out there for supplies and we're exposed . . .' She let the sentence hover, not needing to finish. If they got exposed, would they get infected?

Miles took a while to reply. 'I honestly don't know. The doses we received previously should still offer some protection, and obviously we'll be wearing masks, goggles, but I can't give you any guarantees.'

What had already been dangerous was now virtually suicidal. But then, not giving Quinn fresh supplies was probably worse. They couldn't run because Quinn controlled the airport. They had no other viable transport and trying to get anywhere on foot was insanity.

Their existence here had always been a fragile balance. And now the pendulum had swung, the scales had tipped, and the house of cards had come tumbling down. Not to mention, metaphors had been well and truly murdered.

Getting fresh supplies was a suicide mission.

Not getting them was a death warrant.

Welland shook his head, sweaty curls flying. '*Man*, I can't believe this. You expect me to handle Whistlers without protection?'

Miles spoke calmly. 'The bodies must be incinerated, Welland. That is a greater priority than ever.'

'But what if —'

'Use all the relevant precautions you would normally take, and you'll be fine.'

Carter was sure he would. Some people, no matter how dislikeable, cowardly and selfish, always seemed to make it. While others, like his sister . . . he cut off the thought before it could grow and choke him.

Miles continued briskly. 'Right. We know the plan. We go in, seek out a group. They tend to rest more in the day, but don't assume that to be the case. I will tranquillize two, fast. Caren and Carter, you do what is necessary to scare the rest away. Then we load the supplies —'

'Could you stop calling them that?' Carter couldn't stop himself.

Caren gave him an odd look.

'Carter,' Miles said in a low, warning tone.

'All I mean is, Whistlers are still people, right?' Carter continued, trying to keep his voice steady. 'At least, they were.'

'We can't think of them like that,' Miles said. 'Not if we want to survive.'

'Miles is right,' Caren said. 'The way I see it, whatever they are, it's us or them, and I know which I choose.'

Of course. Perky, practical, perfect Caren with a C.

Carter sighed. 'Fine.'

Miles raised his eyebrows. 'So, if I may continue?'

Carter nodded, even though it wasn't really a question. With Miles it never was.

'Very well. We load the *bodies* on to the sleigh and bring them back here to the chambers, where we will start extraction.' Miles looked at Carter more intently. 'The Whistlers will be fed here, cared for. It's probably a better existence than the one they have out there, living like animals.'

But however harsh the existence, any creature would always choose the wild over containment, Carter thought.

Miles turned to Welland. 'You're in charge here in the meantime, Welland. Get the bodies into the incinerator and sit tight, wait for us to return.'

'What if you don't?' Welland whined. 'What if the power goes again? What if Quinn comes back up here?'

Miles handed Welland his gun. 'Then use this.'

Welland looked down at the weapon. 'But . . . I don't know how to shoot. I'll never hold Quinn and his sons off with this.'

Miles smiled. 'It's not for them.'

Hannah

She stared at the knife.

'Daniel. I can't. I —'

'Not Peggy. The baby.'

He held the knife out to her. 'I need you to save the baby.'

The implication sunk in. Hannah looked back at Peggy. Her swollen stomach. *No. Oh God. No.*

'I . . . I can't.'

'You're a medical student.'

'Yes, but not a doctor or a midwife. I've never done this.'

He thrust the knife towards her. 'You're the only one.' His eyes pleaded with her. 'Please. I can't lose them both.'

Hannah looked back at the girl. She would be dead within minutes anyway. Once that happened and oxygen was cut to the foetus, there would only be a tiny window to deliver the baby unharmed, alive, without brain damage. She had to act now.

But even if you manage it, how will the baby survive? No milk. The cold. And it will be an additional burden. Be rational, Hannah. Let them both go. It's for the best.

She looked back at Daniel. Saw the desperation in his face.

'The baby might die anyway.'

'I know. But *please*, just try. Doesn't it deserve a chance?'

Hannah. This is crazy.

Fuck off, Father, she thought. You're trying to kill

229

us all. So just fuck off.

Hannah took the knife and pressed it to the girl's distended belly. Christ. Her hand shook. She was sweating. Shit. She took a breath, tried not to cough. Okay. She could do this. Think what you know about anatomy, Hannah. Concentrate on the task at hand.

Of course, the task at hand meant slicing into the belly of a dying pregnant girl, without pain relief, undoubtedly killing her in the process. But Peggy was dying anyway, and the choice was to save a life. The life that had the best chance long term.

She pressed harder; blood welled beneath the knife. Peggy moaned, but it was weak. A last gasp. Hannah pushed the knife into her stomach and drew it hard across the belly, just below her naval. A gush of bright red blood spilled out from the wound.

'Daniel,' she said tensely. 'I need you to go to the bodies and remove their underwear for me to use as cloths. Get Cassie to help you.'

'Okay. What about Lucas?'

She hesitated. 'Don't tell him unless necessary.'

Daniel made his way up the coach. Hannah looked back at the incision. She wiped some of the blood with her hand, but it was still coming. It also struck her that she had just been scrabbling on the floor of a toilet. This was in no way a sterile environment to bring a baby into. But what choice did they have?

She needed to concentrate. Okay. Incise the skin and subcutaneous tissues. The next layer was the fascia overlying the rectus abdominis muscles. Hannah dug in with the knife. It was sharp but not scalpel sharp, and the muscles were tough. She felt heat course through her body again, sweat trickle from her brow. But she couldn't stop. She had to do this fast.

230

'I got you the underwear.'

She glanced around. Daniel had returned, with Cassie. To be fair, Hannah probably didn't really need the cloths. But she thought it was a good idea to keep Daniel occupied.

'Thanks,' she said. 'Drop them down.'

'Jesus,' Cassie muttered. 'Didn't have this on my Trapped in Coach bingo.'

'Yeah, me neither,' Hannah said. She used her fingers to separate the rectus muscles. Now she could enter the abdominal cavity through the parietal peritoneum . . . and yes. There it was — the uterus. Here, she might normally worry about how to separate the bladder, but in this situation the mother's survival or mutilation was not an issue. However, damaging the foetus was.

'Almost there,' Hannah said, fighting back another wave of dizziness and nausea. She pressed the knife into the uterus. Three layers. Outer layer (perimetrium), muscle layer (myometrium), and inside mucosal layer (endometrium). Again, she didn't need to worry about damaging blood vessels. She just needed to get in there and get the foetus out. Hannah sliced. Blood spurted out in a fountain, splashing hotly in her face.

'Fuck!' She stuck her hand out. 'Cloth.'

Daniel handed her a pair of thermal boxers. Hannah used them to wipe at her eyes and mouth but could still taste the metallic tang. She looked down.

'Is that —' Daniel asked.

It was. Hannah could see the deflated amniotic sac and the unmistakeable shape of the tightly curled foetus. She put the knife down and reached in with her hands, tugging the torn sac aside.

'Oh God,' Daniel murmured.

Hannah wrapped her hands around the foetus, barely daring to breathe. This was the hardest part. Before, she could just concentrate on the surgery. But now she was handling life. A tiny, delicate life. As gently as she could, she pulled the baby from the abdomen and lifted it out. She glanced at Daniel.

'It's a girl.'

She placed the newborn in Daniel's hands. He held the baby as if she was made of glass.

'I just need to cut the placenta,' Hannah said.

She picked up the knife and sliced through the tough tissue.

'Isn't the baby supposed to cry or something?' Cassie said.

She was right. Hannah glanced at the baby. Was she breathing?

'Here.' Hannah grabbed a cleaner pair of boxers and used them to wipe mucus from the baby's tiny nose and mouth. Then she gently but firmly rubbed her abdomen and chest. Hannah felt a small hitch and the tiny baby opened her mouth and let out a healthy wail.

'Oh, good,' Cassie deadpanned. 'That's better.'

'A baby,' Daniel whispered. 'Peggy, it's your baby.'

But his sister didn't reply. Hannah realized that she could no longer hear the girl's raspy breathing. Peggy's skin felt cold and her eyes were glazed. She was gone.

Daniel crouched down and held the baby to his sister's chest. 'Peggy.' He took one cool hand and placed it on the baby's body. 'She's beautiful, Peggy. Really beautiful. I'm going to call her Eva. Like you always wanted. Sean for a boy. Eva for a girl. And she should have your name too, right? Eva Margaret.'

The baby wailed again.

'She's probably cold. You should wrap her up,' Hannah said.

Daniel grabbed a thermal vest and carefully wrapped it around the baby. Hannah looked back at Peggy. Suddenly, it seemed obscene to leave her so exposed, stomach gaping open, like she was a used wrapper, a vessel of no further importance.

Sentimental nonsense, Hannah. She's dead.

Maybe so. But she was still a young girl who deserved some dignity. Hannah picked up the only spare coat she could see and draped it over Peggy's lower body.

Eva screamed harder. Yearning, high-pitched cries.

'D'you think she's hungry?' Daniel asked.

Possibly. But they didn't have any milk. Hannah tried to think, although exhaustion was making her head thick and mushy — what could you feed babies if you didn't have breast milk or formula? Cow's milk at a push, but they didn't have any of that either. Something stirred distantly. One of those random bits of information your brain picks up like fluff on a jumper.

'Pedialyte,' she said.

Cassie looked at her. 'Isn't that for kids that have the shits?'

'It's for rehydration,' Hannah answered. 'It contains minerals and salts.'

'Have you got any?' Daniel asked.

'No, but Ben did,' she said. 'Remember, he said he had Pedialyte in his bag.'

'Which is in the luggage hold,' Cassie added.

'I know,' Hannah said more impatiently. 'But we might have found a way out. Lucas accessed the space beneath the toilet. There's a hatch —' She paused.

233

Lucas. Where *was* Lucas?

Cassie had obviously been wondering the same thing. 'Where is our lord and master, by the way?' she asked.

Hannah turned and looked up the coach. Lucas must have heard the commotion down here, and he certainly must have heard the baby's cries.

'I don't know,' she mumbled.

They looked at each other. Hannah wiped the blood from her hands, stood and clambered up the coach. Cassie followed.

'Lucas?' Hannah reached the toilet and peered inside. Empty.

She squinted into the hole. The hatch at the side of the coach hung open. A beautiful blast of icy air blew in.

She looked back at Cassie. 'He's gone.'

And there was something else.

'Do you hear that?' Cassie asked.

Hannah did.

The same whirring drone as before.

The helicopter was back.

And closer.

Much closer.

The pair of them scrambled along the aisle to the front of the coach and peered up through the windscreen.

The chopper's dark shape loomed on the horizon, growing steadily bigger. The sound of its blades rose from a drone to a deafening roar.

'They know we're here,' Hannah said, raising her voice.

'No shit, Sherlock!'

Hannah peered upwards. The chopper was almost

right overhead now. Close enough for her to make out a pilot and one other figure inside.

'They can't land,' she said. 'The forest is too dense and the road is too narrow.'

'So why are they hovering?' Cassie asked.

Good question. Why not find somewhere else to land, come back on foot? As far as the men in the helicopter knew, no one in the coach was going anywhere.

Unless . . .

Something unfurled from the chopper.

'Shit,' Hannah murmured.

A ladder.

'They're not landing,' she said. 'They're sending someone down.'

Cassie stared at her, wide-eyed. 'What do we do?'

A figure in a green Department-issue snowsuit climbed out of the chopper and on to the ladder. A gun was slung casually over his back.

'Move!' Hannah cried.

They scuttled back down the coach.

'Daniel?' Hannah yelled, fighting down a cough. 'We need to get out of here.'

'But the baby?'

'NOW!'

Hannah turned and shoved Cassie into the toilet. 'You need to crawl out.'

Cassie didn't need to be told twice. She immediately crouched down and wriggled herself through the rectangular gap, squeezing past the holding tank and climbing through the hatch with relative ease. But she was small and slight. Daniel stumbled down the coach, clutching the newborn.

'You're next,' Hannah told him.

'What about Eva?'

'Pass her through to Cassie.'

'No.' He shook his head. 'You go next. I'll pass Eva through to you.'

'Daniel —'

'You'll be faster than me. If anyone gets left behind . . . it shouldn't be you.'

They stared at each other. Hannah glanced back down the coach. The windscreen exploded in a burst of gunfire. Heavy black boots swung through the jagged hole.

'Shit.'

Hannah dropped down and shuffled through the gap. It was tight around the tank, but she sucked in her stomach and managed to squeeze past. She wriggled out of the hatch and crouched on the upturned side of the coach. Cassie stood just below her, thigh deep in the thick drift.

The ice-cold air felt fresh and delicious. But Hannah didn't have time to savour it. She stuck her head back through the hatch and held her arms out. Daniel passed the tiny baby through. Hannah grasped the newborn and manoeuvred her gently outside. The baby stirred in her arms then settled again.

'Come on,' she hissed at Daniel.

She saw him squeeze through the gap in the flooring and attempt to push past the holding tank. But he was much bigger than her and Cassie, or even Lucas (wherever the hell *he* was, the deserting, cowardly bastard).

'I'm stuck,' Daniel groaned.

'Push,' Hannah urged. 'You need to push.'

He pushed. The holding tank creaked. Hurry, Hannah thought. *Hurry*. The gunman was inside.

It wouldn't be long before he realized what was happening.

'Come on,' she urged.

Daniel wriggled and squirmed.

'Here,' Hannah said to Cassie, holding Eva out.

'I can't —'

'Just do it.' She thrust the baby into her arms. Cassie clutched her like she was a bomb.

Hannah grabbed Daniel's wrists and pulled. There was a creak. Hannah pulled again, as hard as she could. Something gave. The holding tank burst free of its screws and both Daniel and the tank crashed out of the hatch in a stream of water, disinfectant and effluence. Hannah fell backwards on to the soft snow.

'Shit.'

Quite literally. But Daniel was out. Unfortunately, it was hardly a stealthy exit.

'*SCHEISSE!*', the gunman cursed.

German, Hannah thought, something flitting across her mind. Although that shouldn't be surprising. The Department was a global operation. And now wasn't the time to worry about the nationality of their would-be executioner.

She scrambled to her feet. The gunman's face peered angrily through the hatch. He cursed again and then disappeared. He wasn't going to risk getting stuck. He was heading back up the coach, Hannah thought. To climb out of the windscreen.

They didn't have much time. Hannah glanced towards the woods. It was several metres, and they would be exposed, both to the gunman and the still-hovering helicopter, but it was their only chance.

'We need to run for the woods,' she said.

Daniel sat up, gasping. 'It's too far.'

Cassie stared at her. 'He's right. We won't make it.'

'*HALT!*'

Hannah turned. The gunman jumped from the front of the coach, and advanced towards them.

Shit. Already too late. What to do? They had no weapons. Nowhere to hide. Hannah felt the frustration rise over the fear. They had got this far. They had escaped. *This wasn't fucking fair.*

And then she heard another voice: '*VERZEI-HUNG!*'

A figure suddenly appeared from the woods, stepping out from the shadow of the trees where he must have been hiding.

Lucas.

He stood in clear view of the gunman and the helicopter, the churned-up air snatching at his clothes and whipping his fair hair around his face.

As the gunman turned to him, Lucas held his arms up in a gesture of surrender.

'*Warte ab! Hören. Mein Name ist Lucas Myers. Ich arbeite für die Department.*'

'*Was tun Sie hier?*'

'*Ich bin hier um sicherzustellen dass die Operation rei-bungslos abläuft.*' He tapped at his wrist. '*Du hast den Bus wegen mir gefunden.*'

The gunman seemed to hesitate.

'What's he saying?' Cassie whispered, over the baby's head.

'I'm not sure,' Hannah said. She knew a little German, but from this distance, with the helicopter blades whirring overhead, she might be mistaken. 'I think he's trying to convince them he's on their side.'

'He's going to get himself killed,' Daniel said.

'Better him than us,' Cassie muttered, adjusting

238

Eva awkwardly in her arms. 'Could you take this back?'

Daniel reached out and stroked Eva's head. 'Just look after her a little longer.'

'*No*. Jesus. Why?'

'Because if Lucas dies, we're all dead.' Daniel lumbered to his feet.

'What are you doing?' Hannah hissed.

He offered her a small smile. 'I'll let you know when I work it out.'

Then he hauled himself up on to the half-buried coach and began to crawl along the side, now facing upwards. The gunman's attention was still focussed on Lucas, and even if the helicopter pilot could see Daniel, he was too far away to communicate with his colleague.

'*Warum sollte ich dir glauben?*' the gunman asked Lucas.

Hannah translated in her head: Why should I believe you?

'*Erkundigen Sie sich beim Professor.*'

The gunman stared at Lucas. Daniel inched along the coach's long metal body, snow shifting in his wake and revealing the Academy logo. He was almost parallel with the gunman, looking down on him.

'*Mein Befehl lautet*' — the gunman raised his weapon — '*Sie alle zu töten. Keine Ausnahmen. Keine Überlebenden.*'

No survivors.

'*Nein!*' Lucas cried.

Daniel threw himself from the coach, landing on the gunman's back and sending him sprawling to the ground, the gun flying from his hands.

'Fuck.' Cassie gasped. 'That's gotta hurt.'

239

The pair wrestled back and forth in the snow, fists flailing. But Daniel had the weight advantage. He rolled on top of the gunman, pinning his arms with his knees. Then he punched him in the face and head, again and again, blood spurting from beneath his fists until, finally, the gunman's body went limp.

Daniel grabbed the weapon and staggered to his feet. The helicopter still hovered overhead. Daniel turned and fired up at it. Hannah heard the ping of bullets bouncing off metal. The pilot decided to cut his losses. The helicopter rose into the sky, whirled around and disappeared into the distant clouds, sunlight glinting off its blades.

Daniel turned back to the unconscious figure on the ground.

No, Hannah thought. He's not a threat any more. You don't have to shoot him.

Daniel pulled the trigger. Again and again. The gunman's body jittered with bullets, spraying the snow red. Hannah winced. Daniel lowered the gun.

Lucas crunched over the bloody snow towards him. 'You saved my life. Thank you, my friend.' He held out his hand.

Daniel stared at the proffered appendage, turned and walked away. He sat down hard in the snow, staring at his boots. He looked like he might throw up again. Lucas shrugged and strolled over to the dead gunman's body.

'Wait here,' Hannah said to Cassie.

Cassie glared at her. 'What? You are literally leaving me holding the fucking baby?'

Hannah strode across the snow to Lucas. He was crouched down, rifling through the gunman's pockets. He looked up as Hannah approached and held up a small grey object, wires sticking out of the end.

'Explosive device,' he said. 'You were right. The intention was to kill us and destroy the evidence.'

'Shouldn't you be careful with that?'

'It is not armed. See.' Lucas pointed to a small button. 'I expect this will set a timer. If I press it —' His finger hovered.

'Put it down,' Hannah snapped.

Lucas smiled and slipped the device nonchalantly into his own pocket.

Hannah glared at him. 'You ran out on us.'

Lucas frowned. 'No. I exited the coach to look around and investigate the luggage hold. When I heard the helicopter, I hid in the woods.'

'How did you know the gunman was German?' she asked.

'I heard him speak.'

All the way from the woods?

'What did you say to him?'

'I barely remember. I was just trying to stall him. Why?'

Hannah regarded him coolly. 'My German isn't very good,' she said, '*aber für mich hörte es sich so an als hättest du ihnen erzählt dass du für die Abteilung arbeitest. Für meinen Vater?*'

Lucas stared at her.

'You said you work for the Department, for my father,' Hannah repeated. 'Is that true?'

'You are wrong,' he said.

'Really?'

'Yes.' Lucas rose and smiled briskly. 'Your German is excellent.'

'Hey!!' Cassie walked across the snow, still holding Eva. 'Will someone *please* take this thing off me?'

Lucas turned and blinked. 'Is that . . . a baby?'

Cassie rolled her eyes. 'Well, it's not Kermit the Frog — and it's not mine, before you ask.'

'Daniel's sister was pregnant,' Hannah said. 'While you were out here, I performed an emergency Caesarean.'

Lucas stared at her, letting this register. But nothing fazed him for long. 'A baby is an unnecessary complication.'

'Her name is Eva.' Daniel stood up. 'And she is not a complication. She's my niece.' He raised the gun.

Lucas eyed him carefully. 'Very well. In that case, time is even more of the essence. I have already been through the luggage, taking out what is useful. We should head into the woods, putting as much distance between us and the coach as possible. The Department knows we are alive now. That is not in our favour. This' — he gestured at the baby — 'will slow us down further.'

He turned and walked back towards the luggage hold.

Daniel slung the gun over his shoulder and held out his arms for Eva. Cassie handed the baby over. Daniel rocked her gently. 'We really do not like that fucker, do we, Eva?'

'Sweet,' Cassie said. She turned to Hannah. 'What did you say to Lucas?'

'Nothing much.' Hannah stared after him, frowning. 'I was just making sure we understood each other.'

Meg

We're all hiding something.

It jolted her from her doze. Like a sharp jab in the side. A sharp jab in the mind.

The cop.

Sean had called Paul/Mark 'the cop'. Before, he had always called him 'the security guy'. But during their argument, he had said: '*Maybe I killed the cop*'. Perhaps it was just a slip of the tongue. They had talked about the possibility of Paul/Mark being an ex-cop. But only she had known for sure. And Sean had said it with certainty. Had Sean known Paul? Had he been lying?

There was something else playing on her mind. The black tape beneath the bench. It bothered her. In the way that things used to when *she* was a cop. Things that were out of place. That was what you were taught to look for at a crime scene. Things that were wrong, that didn't fit the narrative. The black tape struck her as wrong. Why had that scrap been stuck under the bench? Had it been used to stick something there? Something someone wanted hidden, until they needed it.

Like a knife.

That would explain how it had got on board.

They had all been stripped. Searched. A knife wouldn't have been missed.

But if someone had inside knowledge, perhaps even an inside man — a disgruntled Department worker — who could sneak the knife on to the cable car before boarding, then that made more sense.

It also meant that the crime was premeditated. It had been planned. Thought out. Maybe even orchestrated with someone else. The killer had known Paul would be on board. Had needed to stop him getting to the Retreat. They had all been locked in their rooms upon arrival at the holding facility. No way to get to him beforehand. But if the killer had known what was going to happen to them, he could have faked being drugged and, while everyone else was knocked out, stabbed Paul.

But what about the gun? It didn't fit. It had to be connected, but she couldn't quite work out how. Or who? Karl hadn't struck her as the kind of criminal to mastermind a murder like this. Unless she had underestimated him. Or perhaps he was innocent, and the killer was still on board.

Meg sat up and slowly extricated herself from the group on the floor. Immediately, her body registered the lack of shared warmth. Sarah lay, curled into a ball. Sean lay behind her, body pressed close. Almost intimate.

You wouldn't think it was possible to nap at all in this cold, but lack of food and water was exhausting them. Making them sluggish. Their bodies were shutting down, trying to conserve energy for the most basic functions, as if for hibernation. Probably why her thought processes felt so much more laboured than usual.

She swung her arms to and fro as she walked across the cabin. Her fingers tingled. She couldn't feel her feet even in the thick socks and snow boots. The cable car creaked, but it wasn't rocking as much as before. The storm had abated, although the temperature wasn't rising. Her breath drifted out in ghostly plumes. Proof of life, Meg thought grimly. Even though, after Lily, she had felt more dead than alive. One foot in this world. One foot already in the other.

She walked over to the glass, staring out at the early-evening sky. Faintly, she could see the pinpricks of tiny stars. Planets in their final throes. Literally, a dying light. Was that what their world would look like when it finally gasped its last? Once, Meg had thought she would be happy to see the world end. Why should people continue to live their lives when Lily no longer had that privilege? Why should things just carry on as before? But now, she just felt sad at how easily the human race had succumbed.

Ten years. That was all it had taken for society to crumble. For the virus to ravage the globe. For the riots, the wars, the hatred. For the infected to become pariahs. For the Farms to become accepted, part of life. In a fight against a constantly mutating enemy, needs must. There had to be sacrifices. And some of them had to be human. Or almost human.

They're not like us. The infected. Whistlers. The dehumanizing had been gradual but deliberate. Fear was all part of the plan. It made it easier to forget that the Whistlers were once like us. Unlucky enough to be infected. Even unluckier to have survived. We're always closer than we think to the edge, Meg thought. Every day we're teetering on the precipice. We just never dare look down.

She felt tears well in her eyes. Why was she still here? Why prolong this? If her mission was to die, why not do it right now? Open the hatch, climb out and let herself fall. A breathless plummet to the icy snow beneath. It would be so easy. Almost too easy.

245

She heard movement behind her and turned. Sarah was sitting up. Max and Sean remained curled tightly in their suits.

'Hi,' Meg said neutrally.

Sarah stood and walked over. She rubbed at her arms, stretched out her limbs. Her face looked drawn, lips cracked, dark circles beneath her eyes. Hell, Meg thought, she was probably no oil painting herself right now.

'So, another evening drawing in,' Sarah said.

'Yeah.'

'Are you still planning to do what you said tomorrow?'

Meg looked back through the glass. 'I don't know.'

'You don't have to. I mean, it's probably pointless anyway.'

The woman's voice was dull. Meg recognized that tone. Defeated. It was how she had felt after Lily. Hope had drained away. You clung to it for a while. But hope was like sand. The tighter you held on, the more it trickled through your fingers.

Meg understood how people could die from grief or a broken heart, or how the elderly could just waste away. We don't realize, any of us, how much our existence depends upon hope and purpose, the promise of a new day. Take that away and we're just automatons, going through the motions until we wind down and die.

But she didn't say that. Because, as much as she disliked Sarah, she didn't have it in her to be cruel right now.

'The storm's cleared,' she said. 'There's still a possibility that the authorities have just been waiting for better weather to —'

246

'Don't,' Sarah said. 'You don't have to patronize me.'

'Okay.'

'I know you don't like me.'

Meg didn't reply.

'You think I'm a flake. A liability. A stupid, hysterical idiot.'

'I think you're scared,' Meg said. 'We all are.'

'There you go again.'

'Fine.' Meg sighed. 'No. I don't like you. Better?'

'Yes.'

Silence. They both stared out of the window. Sarah sniffed.

'I killed a man.'

Meg turned to look at her. Sarah's eyes were fixed in the distance, her face desolate.

'Yes,' Meg said. 'You did.'

'I didn't mean to.'

'If you say so.'

'I . . . I don't know what I meant to do. I thought I was trying to save him but . . . I don't know. Maybe I did want to push him.'

Confession. Right now, Meg didn't have the energy for it. She wasn't a priest. But guilt is an ugly boil. You have to lance it sometimes, let the poison flow out.

'Sometimes,' she said, 'we do things out of anger or fear. As a police officer, I saw a lot of that. Most people who kill aren't killers. They're just frightened, angry. Almost all of them regret it.'

Sarah nodded slowly, fingering that damn cross. 'You don't believe in God, do you?'

'Not so much.'

'I used to be like you.'

Somehow Meg doubted it, but she let the woman continue.

247

'In my twenties, I drank, took drugs, slept around. My mum had me young and she didn't make the best choices in life, or with men. I was fourteen the first time I ran away from home, after her latest boyfriend tried to feel me up one night. Don't get me wrong, she kicked him out as soon as I told her. But there was always another boyfriend, someone to give her money . . . it wasn't the most stable upbringing.'

Meg nodded. Her mum had been a single parent, but she had been strong, resilient, hard-working. She had died when Meg was just seventeen. Hit and run. The driver served just twelve months in jail. He was white, middle class, came from a 'good family'. A young man with 'his whole life ahead of him', the judge had the audacity to say. As if her mum hadn't. As if this killer, who had left the most wonderful woman she had ever known lying crumpled at the kerb like rubbish, had more value because of the colour of his skin.

Sarah was still talking. 'So, I got into a lot of trouble and then, one day, I overdosed. I should have died. I know it sounds corny, but I saw this light. And then I heard a voice telling me to go back.'

Meg tried not to snort. Stopped herself from saying that medical experts believed the light the dying saw was simply their brains shutting down.

Sarah continued. 'The next day I got myself into AA, accepted God and began my recovery.'

'Good for you,' Meg said, because it was. Addiction was a disease and not everyone managed to shake that devil off their back.

'I trained as a teacher. My mum was so proud of me. We even bought a place together.'

Meg looked at her curiously. 'So, if you got your

happy ending, why are you here?'

Sarah's face clouded. 'Mum got ill. Not the virus, cancer. But you know what it's like trying to get treatment. Hospitals bursting. Everything falling apart.'

Yeah, Meg thought. She knew.

'Except if you have money, if you can pay, then you're okay. So, when the men from the Department came around asking for volunteers for the trials, well, you know they offer a payment if you're voluntary?'

Meg did. It was a healthy amount. It meant little to her, but for many people it was an incentive.

'And I'd heard that they treated you well while you're there,' Sarah said. 'Nice room. Food. Facilities — gym, pool, a spa. I reasoned if I'm going to die for science, why not do it in style?'

'Even God wouldn't deny a girl a spa day.' A small, bitter smile. 'True. And if I don't make it, the money will go to my mum, to take care of her.'

Meg swallowed. She had taken against Sarah, still couldn't say she liked her. But everyone had their reasons for being here.

'That's good,' she said.

'Is it? If we die *here*, she won't get any of that. It will all be for nothing.'

'We're not going to die here,' Meg said firmly. 'We're going to get out of this.'

She sensed movement behind her and turned. Sean was awake, rubbing at his eyes. His hood had fallen back. In just two days his hair had grown, and his beard was thicker.

'Nice pep talk,' he said.

'I mean it.'

'Yeah.' His blue eyes found hers. 'I know you do.'

He stood and stretched. It dissolved into a shudder.

'Christ it's cold. Must be minus five.'

'Probably.'

'What time d'you think it is?' Sarah asked.

Meg glanced at the sky. Fading to grey, strung with ragged strips of cloud that masked a pale sliver of moon.

'Five, six o'clock maybe?'

It was hard to tell without their usual markers. Watches and phones.

'I need to piss,' Sean muttered. ''Scuse me, ladies.'

He walked over to the hatch, bent and yanked it open. Meg and Sarah looked away. But not before Meg had seen him unzip his snowsuit, revealing the tattoo on his chest again. The pretty girl with long dark hair. Meg frowned. Why did she look so familiar? Who was she — a lover, sister, daughter? Then, as Sean reached down, she averted her eyes.

The sound of urine also reminded Meg that she needed to go. Great. Urine-soaked snow boots or urine-soaked floor. Sean zipped himself back up and swung the hatch closed.

A freezing gust of air whisked into the car. Meg shivered. All three of them stamped their feet and blew out frosty breath. Max still lay, curled up on the floor. Meg looked at him. He hadn't moved. And now she noticed something else.

'Sean,' she said.

'What?'

'Max.'

He followed her gaze and frowned. Then she saw it register.

No plume of frosty breath.

'Shit.' Sean crouched down beside Max and gently shook his shoulder.

'What is it?' Sarah asked. 'Is he okay?'

Sean lifted Max's good wrist and checked for a pulse. Then he pulled back his hood.

Sarah stifled a gasp. Meg felt her heart buckle. Max's eyes were half open and already cloudy, his skin was bone white and his lips were blue.

Sean turned back to them, face grave. He didn't need to say the words, but he did.

'He's dead.'

Carter

He stared at her face. Her lovely, perfect face. Nothing like his, even before the accident.

She had got more than her fair share of the good genes. But he had never minded. He had loved her fiercely. Protectively. He would have died for her. Except here he was. Still alive. While she . . .

'Carter?'

Caren stood in the doorway. Carter scrambled quickly to put away the photograph he usually kept well hidden. But he was clumsy, and it fluttered to the floor, landing near Caren's feet.

She bent down and picked it up, glancing at the picture.

'Pretty. Girlfriend?'

'No. Sister.' He held out his hand, fighting the urge to snatch it from her perfectly manicured fingers.

She passed the photograph over, a slight frown on her features. 'I thought you didn't have any family?'

'I don't. She's . . . dead.'

'Oh. I'm sorry.'

'Why? You didn't kill her.' He slipped the photo in his pocket, meaning to put it back in its hidey-hole later.

'True. But I'm still sorry she's dead. What happened?'

It was on the tip of his tongue to tell her to mind her own business. Caren had never expressed any interest in Carter's life before and they had managed to make it through three years here without sharing

252

any confidences, so why start now?

But of course, he knew. They were probably all going to die today. That can weigh on your mind. Closeness to death is a great tongue loosener, among other things.

He swallowed. 'We were in an accident . . . we were supposed to be escaping, going somewhere safe.' He paused, and suddenly he could see it all again. The blood, the knife. He pulled himself back. 'It didn't work out. She didn't make it.'

'That's tough.'

He nodded. 'It was a long time ago. You?'

'Me what?'

'Family?'

'I had . . . *have* . . . a dad, brother and niece. They were supposed to be heading north, to a place Dad bought a while back. A safe place.' She shrugged. 'I don't know if they got there.'

'Why didn't you go with them?'

'And miss all this?'

He held up his hands. 'You're right. None of my business.'

She sighed. 'Fine. I have Huntington's Disease. I probably only have another five to ten good years. I thought if I volunteered for a trial . . . at least I'd have some control over how I died.'

'That sucks.'

'Yup.'

Carter opened his mouth to say something else, then realized he was all out of platitudes.

'So,' he said. 'Did you want me for something?'

She raised an eyebrow. 'A shag before we both die?'

He stared at her. She smiled. 'Joking.'

'Of course.'

Her face dropped. 'I didn't mean because of . . .' She made a vague motion towards her face. 'I meant, just that we're not exactly shag buddies, or friends, or —'

'I know. I get it. It's fine.'

Carter had thought he was past embarrassment or bitterness about his face but no, it could still hurt, even if Caren hadn't meant it to.

She glanced behind her and then stepped into his room, pushing the door to.

'Okay.' She looked at him steadily. 'Here's the thing — I don't trust you, Carter.'

A good start. He really hoped this conversation wouldn't end in him having to kill her.

'I hope there's a 'but' coming,' he said.

'*But*,' she continued, 'I trust Miles and Welland even less.'

'Well, we have something in common.'

A brittle smile. 'You didn't have much to do with Jackson.'

'I thought it was more that Jackson didn't have much to do with anyone else.'

'I used to talk to him sometimes.'

'Okay.'

'Jackson was an anti-vaxxer.'

'*What?* So what the fuck was he doing here?'

'Like a lot of us, I guess he had no choice —' She regarded Carter intently because they both knew that his presence here was under different circumstances to the rest of them.

'Right.'

'Anyway, he told me he wasn't taking his doses.'

Once they were all semi-proficient with a needle, Miles had let everyone dose themselves with the plasma. He had no reason to suspect they wouldn't comply.

'Fuck,' Carter said. 'You knew this all along?'

'No. This was just before he disappeared.'

'And did you know he was going to run?'

'No. But I got the sense he wanted out. Why else would he confide in me when I might have gone straight to Miles?'

'Why didn't you?'

'I didn't want to hand Jackson a death sentence.' She hesitated, then said, 'Like Anya.'

Carter stared at her. 'You know about Anya?'

'I don't know exactly what happened. Do you?'

Anya. Blonde, beautiful, angry Anya. Just twenty-six years old. She had been one of the original group, but she had been unhappy about keeping the infected staff for supplies. She had argued constantly with Miles about it. Told him it was unethical, that they were no better than the Professor. One night she had tried to release the Whistlers from the chambers. She hadn't succeeded but she had got herself infected. Then, she had tried to run.

Anya was dead now. Probably.

Carter still remembered her blood spreading out on the pristine white snow, gleaming in the light of the pale moon. The weight of the gun in his hand. Miles clapping him on the shoulder: '*Well done. It was necessary. Now, take her to the incinerator.*'

Carter had done what he was told. What was necessary. Just like he had done what he was told when Miles instructed him to kill Anya. That had been the price of being saved by Miles. But when Carter had returned to move Anya's body, in protective clothing and with the sled, she had gone. A trail of blood led into the woods and disappeared. Miles had been angry but deemed it more dangerous to find her. Now, no one spoke about Anya.

Carter shook his head. 'No,' he said. 'I've no idea.'

Caren nodded. 'I guess Jackson is dead anyway, so it doesn't matter. But the point is that he had absolutely no reason to steal plasma. He was against plasma extraction. The Farms. All of it.'

Carter swallowed. 'Sometimes people do things for other reasons. Perhaps he was sending them to someone else?'

'Perhaps . . . but it just doesn't add up. Also, someone aside from me and Miles had access to the basement.'

He tensed. 'Who?'

'Welland.'

'*Welland?* You're sure?'

She nodded. 'I saw him.'

'When?'

She looked a little sheepish. 'When I was down there.'

Christ. Carter had thought the basement was a stronghold, one only he had breached. Turns out it was busier than old Piccadilly Circus.

'What were you doing down there?' he asked.

'Just checking.'

'On what?'

'That Miles is being honest with us.'

Good luck with that, Carter thought.

'Anyway,' Caren continued, 'I was down there, in the office, and I heard the lift. I thought it was Miles and I knew he'd kill me if he found me.'

'Not even metaphorically.'

'So I panicked and hid under the desk. I heard

256

footsteps and someone came in, but it wasn't Miles. It was Welland.'

'What was he doing?'

'I don't know. I could only see his bottom half. He wandered around, then wandered out again. I crept out from under the desk and peered around the door. I saw him enter the isolation chambers.'

'*What?* But only Miles has the code for the isolation chambers.'

'That's what I thought. But Welland definitely went inside.'

'Could he have been doing a favour for Miles?'

A small shrug. 'I don't know. I didn't hang around. I ran for the elevator and got out of there.'

Carter frowned. Could Miles have entrusted Welland with his code and sent him to run some secret errand? It didn't seem likely. Personally, he wouldn't trust Welland to run a fucking bath.

'Should we tell Miles?' Caren asked.

He debated. If Miles didn't know, then Welland was in big trouble. A state Carter was perfectly comfortable with. On the other hand, if Miles didn't want *them* to know, then *they* were in big trouble. Less comfy.

'Let's keep a lid on it for now,' he said. 'If . . . *when* we get back, we can confront Welland then.'

She nodded. 'Agreed.'

They looked at each other and both managed a stiff smile. It felt weird.

'Right,' Caren said. 'I'll see you downstairs.'

'Yeah.'

She turned. He found himself saying: 'Caren?'

'What?'

He swallowed. 'I hope your family are safe.'

'Thanks.'

She opened the door and disappeared down the corridor.

Carter waited a moment. Then he got up and shut the door again.

What the fuck was going on? Jackson being an anti-vaxxer *did* tie up with the messages on his phone. But Welland having access to the chambers? No. That stank. Carter wasn't so naïve as to believe that he and Miles were friends. But he knew that if Miles needed something doing, secretly, then Carter would be the first one he'd approach. Welland was just the lackey who cleared up the mess.

So, what was Welland up to? How did he get the basement pass and the code to the chambers? And what else was the little shit hiding? Obviously, every-one here was hiding *something*. The only difference was the size of the secret and the depth of the lie. But Carter was starting to suspect that there was a lie here that went really deep. Right to the heart of their exist-ence at the Retreat.

The question was — what did that mean for him?

Carter had waited a long time to get here, been patient. And now, he sensed, he was reaching the end-game.

He pulled out the photo again. Scribbled on the back in faded biro, barely legible, were two names. *Daniel and Peggy. Invicta Academy.* He didn't need it, Carter reminded himself. He carried her face next to his heart. And if something happened to him, he couldn't leave this here to be found. Not by Miles. Not by Quinn. Not by anyone. Because if they did, it might lead them to *her.* The person he sent the par-cels to. The only remaining link with his sister.

Her daughter. His niece.

Carter took out his lighter, touched it to the corner of the photograph and watched the flames eat up the soft, crumpled paper.

The beautiful, brown-haired girl with the blazing smile curled up and died again.

Carter let the tears fall, extinguishing the flames.

Hannah

They traipsed through the dark forest, their strange little group.

Lucas led, Hannah followed, then Cassie with Daniel at the rear, tenderly cradling the baby. He had fashioned a sling from a jumper taken from the hold and tucked the newborn inside, pressed to his chest. He put his jacket over the top for added warmth. The baby dozed, lulled by the motion.

Lucas had been methodical in searching through the rucksacks in the hold, all eleven of them. He had separated out food, water and some milk (which also might do for the baby, at a push). He had also found three torches, two lighters and numerous phones. All dead, of course. No one had thought to turn their phones off when they handed them in, presuming they would have them back in a few hours. It was something none of the survivors had considered. Even if they could get a signal, without power to charge the phones, they were useless.

There were more clothes, of course. Again, Lucas had separated out essentials and spread them equally between four of the larger rucksacks. Hannah located the Pedialyte. Six sachets. It would be enough for the baby for now. There were also some cards and cash in the belongings. If they ever made it to a town, they could buy supplies. That's if they didn't freeze to death before then, or get eaten by wild animals, or killed by the Department. Or kill each other.

The forest was dark and dense. The thick canopy

of green shut out what little daylight was left. Their torches didn't seem to penetrate more than a few feet ahead so they walked carefully, conscious of needing to put distance between themselves and the coach but also wary of tripping or twisting an ankle, which would slow them down far more. There was no path, not even a rough one, so they meandered around the massive tree trunks, pushed their way through snagging bushes and climbed over the fallen skeletons of ancient pines.

It was hard to gauge if they were heading in the right direction, or any direction. For all they knew, they could be walking around in one giant circle. Lucas seemed to be checking his watch quite often. Perhaps he was trying to use it as a compass, or maybe he was just checking how long they had been walking.

It felt like days but had probably only been an hour. They were exhausted from trauma and lack of food. Hannah's chest felt tight and her breath short. Beneath her layers and despite the freezing cold she felt sweat soak her body. Her head felt heavy and clogged.

It occurred to her that she wouldn't make it. And the realization didn't feel as frightening as she had always imagined. Instead, it came with resignation and a vague relief. She wouldn't have to do this for much longer. Sometime soon, she could rest.

'Do you think we should stop?' Cassie asked. 'Try and make a shelter or something?'

'Not yet,' Lucas replied. 'We should keep going while we have the energy.'

'Yeah, well, hate to break it to you, but my energy is running low.'

Lucas glanced back. 'This is not a suitable area

to make camp. There is no space. We need to find a clearing. We keep moving.'

'Fine,' Cassie grumbled.

They stumbled on in near-silence, the only sounds their laboured breathing and the awakening murmurs of night. A distant owl hooted. The undergrowth rustled with things stirring into nocturnal life. Hannah shivered but concentrated on putting one foot in front of the other.

She wasn't sure how much time had passed when she noticed that the trees were starting to thin. More twilight filtered through their branches. Ahead of them, the forest opened out into a tiny clearing. But not just a clearing. Tucked into the trees, overgrown with moss and fungi, was the distinct shape of an old hunter's shack.

'Is that . . . a house?' Daniel asked.

'More like a witch's cottage,' Cassie said.

She wasn't wrong. The crooked shack did look like something out of a Grimm fairy-tale. Hannah knew there were abandoned shacks dotted around the forests here. Some had been built by hunters, some by survivalists back in the days of the first viral apocalypse.

This place must have been abandoned for some years. The windows were all gone. The wood was rotted, bits of tree poked through the roof and out of the lopsided chimney and it was creeping with so much greenery it looked like the forest had started to reclaim it.

'What's that kid's rhyme?' Daniel said. 'In a dark, dark wood —'

'— there was a dark, dark house,' Hannah continued.

But at least the shack still had a roof and walls and a chimney. Shelter.

They looked at each other. Lucas smiled.

'Shall we?'

★ ★ ★

The bad feeling struck Hannah as they climbed the rickety steps to the front porch.

It wasn't just the innate creepiness of the shack and the associations with fairy-tales and horror films. Hannah had never been someone given to flights of fancy or the heebie-jeebies. The dark didn't scare her. And gut feelings were usually down to indigestion rather than premonition.

But something was wrong here.

Lucas reached the door, rotten and half hanging off its hinges. He pushed it open and they followed him inside, torches held out in front of them. The shack was small and dark. Hannah could make out a sagging sofa and a rickety-looking chair, a couple of tables with half-burnt-down candles in bottles standing on them. No electricity, she guessed. To their left, a stone fireplace and . . . Cassie shrieked.

A pair of amber eyes gleamed back at them.

'Fuck!'

Hannah raised her torch. A stag's head was mounted on the wall above the fireplace. She swivelled her torch around the room. More glass eyes peered down from the walls. Animal heads. Deer, badgers, coyote. Her stomach rolled.

'Nice to have company,' Lucas said.

'At least they're not human,' Daniel offered.

Cassie scowled. 'Comforting.'

263

They moved through the living room/abattoir into the tiny kitchen. 'Basic' was one word for it. No cooker, or even a fridge. Just a rusted stainless-steel sink and an old camping stove. Hannah flicked the switch on the stove. Out of gas. Lucas opened a few cupboards. Some tins of beans, soup and canned meat. Probably out of date, but they might still be edible, if they were desperate, which they were.

They checked out the bedroom and shower room. The bedroom contained a stained mattress with a few dirty blankets flung on top and an empty chest of drawers. The shower room was just that. A faucet over a drain, with a filthy toilet and sink. Hannah turned the tap. It squeaked and a trickle of brown, foul-smelling water petered out. She wrinkled her nose. There was probably a water tank behind the shack, but if it hadn't been used in some time the standing water would have turned stagnant. No washing for them tonight.

They moved back into the living room.

'Well,' Lucas said, 'it is basic but more than we could have hoped for.'

'It's still fucking freezing,' Cassie said, rubbing at her arms. 'And what's that smell?'

Right on cue, the baby began to cry. Daniel shifted uncomfortably. 'I think it's Eva.'

Cassie rolled her eyes. 'Oh, great.'

Hannah cast her torch around again. The roof was intact in here and although the floor was hard and dirty — except for a cleaner square, perhaps where a rug used to be — it was still preferable to the stained mattress in the bedroom.

'Okay,' she said. 'Our first priority is light. There are candles in here, and we have lighters. Let's get the candles lit so Daniel can deal with the baby.'

'On it,' Cassie said, taking out a lighter. She moved around the room, lighting the half-burnt-down candles. The walls flickered with dancing shadows.

'Next — heat.' Hannah knelt and poked her torch up the chimney. It didn't appear to be blocked. There was ash and bits of burnt log in the grate.

'It's usable . . . but we need firewood —'

She jumped at a sudden loud *crrrrack* from behind her. She turned. Lucas had picked up the rickety chair and smashed it on to the floor.

He stamped down on it with his false leg. 'Now we have kindling.'

Hannah smiled thinly. 'Good. Cassie and I will search for more wood outside.'

'We will?' Cassie said.

'Yes. Lucas can get the fire going while Daniel changes the baby.'

Cassie sighed. 'Just like being back at Grandpa Joe's.'

Hannah stood. Dizziness swamped her. She leaned on the fireplace. She was breathing more shallowly, to avoid the hacking coughs. That and the pain in her chest.

'You ready?' Cassie asked.

'Yeah,' she said after a moment. 'Let's go.'

They traipsed out of the shack into the clearing. The sky had darkened in the time they had been inside. Twilight hovered. Insubstantial and transient. Soon it would melt away into night. Again, Hannah felt that shiver of unease. What was it about this place? Or was it her? Was the virus affecting her mind? She didn't think so. Her thoughts felt sluggish, but not fevered or corrupted. *Something wrong. Something*

265

forgotten. She just couldn't put her finger on what.

'Let's skirt around the edge of the clearing,' she said. 'We should be able to find some dryish bits of wood there.'

'Yeah, I know,' Cassie said. 'I used to do this shit when I was a kid. My grandpa had a shack just like this.'

'Oh, right.' They crossed the clearing to the woods and began to pick up bits of branch.

'You were close to your grandfather?' Hannah asked.

'Nope. Hated the crazy old coot. But he was my only living grandparent, so I was forced to visit every week. Dad had done well for himself but thought it would do me good to 'see where he'd come from'.'

'Oh.'

They moved slowly, scanning the ground with their torches.

'Yeah. By the time I was ten I knew how to shoot a shotgun, skin a deer and gut a rabbit. I could break a chicken's neck or slice a goat's throat so it would bleed out fast.'

'Sounds like quite an education.'

'Oh yeah. He was a real Mary Poppins.'

They started to work their way back round to the shack. Hannah's arms were full of musty-smelling wood. Dry enough to burn for a few hours at least. She stared around at the forest. It seemed still for now. Too still? Or was she just being paranoid? She glanced back at the shack. From a distance it looked almost homely. Orange candle flames flickering through the windows, the glow of the fire, smoke drifting from the chimney.

Wrong. What was it?

''Course, he was an old-school survivalist,' Cassie said, standing next to her. 'Basement full of guns and tinned goods. His 'apocalypse bunker', he called it.'

Hannah stared at her. 'What did you say?'

'Apocalypse bunker?'

The realization struck her like a sucker punch.

The candles burnt halfway down. The chimney that should have been blocked by birds' nests. The lighter square on the floor. Not a square. A *trapdoor*.

'It isn't deserted,' she muttered.

'What?'

'A basement,' Hannah said. 'We never checked for a basement.'

She dropped the logs and sprinted for the door, shoving it open. Daniel was nowhere to be seen, but Lucas stood in the middle of the room, near the fireplace.

'Lucas!'

He turned.

'What is it?'

The floor erupted beneath his feet.

Lucas was thrown backwards. He toppled and crashed into the lit fire. A filthy figure in animal skins with a mane of matted hair burst through the trapdoor. He screamed — a terrible, high-pitched whistle — pulled a gun from his belt and unleashed a hail of bullets around the room. Hannah ducked. Lucas rolled out of the fire, putting out the flames, but as he tried to crawl away, hair and clothes still smouldering, the figure let loose another round of bullets. Hannah saw Lucas's body jerk as they hit him.

She had to do something. And then she remembered — she still had the knife. Before the figure could turn Hannah pulled it from her pocket and launched herself at him, throwing herself on to his back and wrapping her legs around his waist. The basement dweller's stench was foul, almost unbearable, but Hannah clung on, raised the knife and drove it into his neck.

Blood spurted. He howled. Hannah yanked the knife out and stabbed him again, and again. He bucked and twisted. Hannah's grip slipped and he managed to throw her off. She landed hard on her back, sending bolts of pain shooting up her spine.

The figure whirled around. His face was bone white, teeth all but gone, eyes red and wild. Whatever he had been — hunter, survivalist — now he was pure Whistler. Blood poured from the wounds in his neck. He barely seemed to notice. He could well have been insane before the Choler corrupted what was left of his brain, but it was hard to tell.

He raised the gun and took a step towards her. Hannah scrabbled backwards on the floor. But there was nowhere to go. No help coming. Lucas was injured, Daniel and Cassie were both hiding, trying to save their own skins. Hannah braced herself for death. She heard the *crrrack* of a gunshot . . .

A red crater opened in the Whistler's forehead.

With a look of surprise, he fell to his knees. The gun slipped from his hands. Another shot. Blood exploded from his chest. The Whistler squinted at her, face puzzled, mouth working pitifully to find long-forgotten words. But all that bubbled out was more blood. Hannah stared at him, feeling a moment of pity. Then he collapsed forward onto the floor, twitching. Finally, with a soft, keening moan, he lay still.

Hannah looked up. Daniel stood in the bedroom

doorway, clutching the weapon he had taken from the gunman.

'Okay?' he asked.

No, Hannah thought. Far from it. But she was alive. For now. She nodded. 'Thank you.'

The front door creaked open, and Cassie peered in. 'You killed it.'

'*Him*,' Hannah said. 'And thanks for your help.'

To her right, Lucas moaned. Hannah crawled over to him. His shoulder was bleeding badly and his hair and face were burned and blackened. He was dying. There was no doubt about it. The bullet wounds were bad, but the burns would soon send his body into shock.

His eyes found hers.

'*Es tut mir lei*d.'

'What are you sorry for?'

Lucas's voice was a raspy wheeze. 'You understood. I work for the Department. My instruction . . . accompany the coach. Told . . . you were being driven to another location. Not the Retreat. Just . . . make sure it all went smoothly.'

'You lied to us?'

'I didn't know . . . about the crash. Nor . . . did the driver. Same instructions. I think he was *made* to crash.'

Hannah stared at him. But if the driver hadn't been part of it, then he would have had no need to escape or sabotage the door.

'You're sure?' she asked.

Lucas nodded faintly then coughed. Blood trickled from his lips. She was losing him.

His eyes widened. '*Die Zeit*.'

'Yes,' Hannah nodded. It was time.

Lucas strained towards her, lifted his wrist and wrenched off the watch. He pressed it into her fingers. '*Die Zeit.*' Then his hand dropped. Hannah felt the breath leave him. His head fell back and his eyes glazed. Death. *You came quickly*, Hannah thought. *While I take the long road.* She sat back on the rough floor, clutching the watch, trying to process Lucas's words.

The driver hadn't been complicit. Which meant he hadn't been the one to sabotage the emergency exit. That must have been done before they left. And now, something else leapt from her subconscious to the front of her mind.

Twelve students on the coach. But there were only eleven rucksacks in the hold.

The driver hadn't escaped. He had been with them all along. *An interloper.* Cassie had been right.

She turned slowly. Cassie was peering down into the basement. Daniel still stood in the bedroom doorway, holding the gun.

Hannah stared at him. 'When were you going to tell us, Daniel?'

He met her gaze, and she knew he understood.

'I'm sorry,' he said.

Cassie glanced between them. 'Tell us what?'

Daniel sighed. 'That I was driving the coach.'

270

Meg

Sarah insisted on saying a prayer. Meg wished she wouldn't, but then, this wasn't about her. Maybe Max would have wanted the accoutrements. Of course, what Max would have really wanted was to still be alive. Prayers couldn't fix that. Prayers couldn't fix a fucking thing, in Meg's experience.

Death was a horror, and everything we did — the ceremonies, eulogies, flowers — were just a way to try to convince ourselves otherwise. There was no such thing as a peaceful death. Those about to die regularly wet or voided themselves. There was fear in those final moments, as breath struggled to come and swallowing failed.

No one went into death willingly. That was a lie. Meg had lied to her little girl. *Just rest and Mummy will be there. Mummy will always be there.* But Mummy was not there. Mummy was still here. A betrayal that needed to be rectified.

As Sarah continued her holy mumblings, Meg and Sean moved Max over to the open hatch. Sean touched his lips then placed his fingers on Max's forehead, a gesture of affection and farewell. Meg wondered what she should do. She didn't believe in a god, had nothing to fall back on.

'I'm sorry,' she whispered to Max, leaning over to repeat Sean's gesture.

She paused. Their presumption was that hypothermia and infection had been too much for Max's body to cope with. But now Meg was up close she could see petechiae around Max's eyes. And something dried at the corner of his mouth. Vomit?

'Amen,' Sarah finished and crossed herself.

Burst blood vessels around the eyes. Vomit. Those were signs of suffocation.

'Ready?' Sean asked.

Meg glanced at him. He was watching her intently.

Had Max's death been more unnatural than they presumed? Had someone hastened his departure? Perhaps an act of mercy, or perhaps because they saw him as a burden.

'Meg?' Sean frowned. 'Are you okay?'

Good question. Not really. None of this was okay. And even if someone *had* killed Max, what difference did it make? He probably wouldn't have survived anyway. Chances were, none of them would. They were all just delaying the inevitable while Death kept their seats warm.

Meg turned away. 'Yeah. Let's do this.'

They grasped Max's body and tipped him out of the open hatch. He plummeted through the grey clouds, shrinking to a small dot and then disappearing into the darkness. Three down, three to go, Meg couldn't help thinking.

'May God look after his soul,' Sarah murmured.

'And may the devil never catch you leaving,' Meg finished.

Sarah glanced at her. Meg shrugged. 'Something my mum used to say. Just remembered it.'

And now Meg remembered something else her mum used to say: *'Be careful who you trust. The devil was an angel once.'*

'We should shut the hatch,' Sean said. 'Before the rest of us join him.'

They hauled the hatch back over and looked at each other. *All that remains*, Meg thought. Their numbers halved in less than forty-eight hours. Who would be next if they stayed here any longer? And what would get them first: cold, starvation, another 'mercy' killing?

'We're not going to make it another twenty-four hours,' Meg said bluntly. 'Tomorrow morning, I'm going to attempt to get to the station and raise help. Agreed?'

Sarah nodded. 'I don't see we have any other choice.'

Sean sighed. 'Fine. If that's what you want.'

'It is,' Meg said.

He turned and walked to the other end of the cable car. He cupped his hands around his face and peered out of the glass. The snow was melting, sliding down the panes, offering a blurry view of the station in the distance. A grey and glass semicircle sticking out from the mountainside. Like someone had crashed a spacecraft into the rock, Meg thought.

Sean craned his head to look at the supporting cable above them. Then he turned back.

'Almost two hundred and fifty yards . . . not much of an incline at this point, which is one thing. The wind might have dropped, but out there, it's still going to feel like it's trying to tear you off that cable.' He held his gloved hands up. 'These gloves have grip, but not much sensation. You could easily lose purchase without realizing. Plus, if you're holding tightly on to the cable, then it will slow your circulation and lower the warmth in your hands. So you need to keep moving as fast as you can.'

'Okay.' Meg stared steadily at him. 'You've given this some thought.'

'Yeah.' He looked her up and down. 'Your arms

273

are going to turn to jelly before you're even halfway. Physically and mentally, it's going to be torture.'

'Wow. Thanks for the pep talk.'

'I'm just preparing you. You need to understand how tough it will be. You need to know you might not make it.'

'Fine. Got it.'

He continued to stare at her, as if he wanted to say something else. Then he shook his head. 'You're stubborn as hell.'

'And that's one of my positive traits.'

He managed a small smile. 'Are you really sure about this?'

'I'm not scared of dying.'

His blue eyes found hers. 'That's what I'm afraid of.'

* * *

They slept again. A small death. A good description. Blissful oblivion. No thought. No feeling. No pain. Everything was nothing. There was comfort in nothing.

But it couldn't last. Faces floated in and out of Meg's vision. Lily, her mum, Paul. And a girl. A girl with long, wavy, dark hair. The girl in Sean's tattoo. Who was she? And how did Meg know her? The girl was drifting away. Meg tried to hold on. She was important. Meg had seen her somewhere else. Where?

And then it came to her.

The photograph.

The one Meg had found in Paul's pocket.

Daniel and Peggy. Invicta Academy.

It was the same girl.

And if it was the same girl . . .

Meg's eyes sprung open. 'He lied.'

She sat up. Silvery light filled the car. Early morning. Sarah lay beside her. Meg looked around. The realization unfurled slowly in her stomach, like poisonous tentacles.

No. *No, no, no.*

She pushed herself to her feet. Her breath puffed out like smoke. She walked over to the window and peered out. Mist caressed the glass. The grey shell of the station was barely visible through the drifting swathes.

You'd be insane to attempt to try and climb across the cable in this weather.

The fucker. The crazy, motherfucking fucker.

'Meg?'

Sarah was sitting up. She yawned, stretched and looked around.

'Where's Sean?' she asked.

Meg stared at her grimly.

'He's gone.'

Carter

They had been fucked almost as soon as they entered the forest.

They skied down to the point where the trees thickened, wind lashing at their faces, while more fast-descending flurries of snow obscured their goggles. Miles had managed to ski with an old sled tied to his back. At the edge of the treeline, where the snow petered out to a bed of mulchy pine needles, they stopped, and he dropped it to the ground. Carter pushed up his goggles. It was more sheltered here. But the darkness and suffocating smell of pine already felt claustrophobic.

In a dark, dark wood, there was a dark, dark house . . . and why the hell was he thinking of that old kid's rhyme right now?

Miles pulled a sharp knife out of his belt.

'What's that for?' Caren immediately asked.

'Breadcrumbs.'

'Sorry?'

'Have you never read *Hansel and Gretel*?'

'I gave up on fairy-tales a while back.'

Miles turned and carved an X into the tree trunk nearest to them. 'So we can find our way back.'

'Right,' Carter said, thinking it was optimistic to imagine that any of them would be making their way back, but hey, look on the bright side.

'So, ready?' Miles asked, taking out the tranquillizer gun.

'Ready,' Caren said.

Carter just nodded. He wasn't ready, but he was all out of options.

They trudged into the forest, every step increasing Carter's sense of foreboding. The trunks of the old trees were the width of two men, and the insulating blanket of pine needles overhead cut out light and deadened sound. Only a few flakes of snow penetrated through. The pine was making his eyes and nose itch. Their breath sounded like bellows.

Every few steps, Miles stopped and marked another tree. Carter looked back. He could see one rough cross behind them. Beyond that, just darkness, like the trees were softly moving, closing ranks in their wake. This was never going to work, he thought. They had no idea where they were heading, or how far they might have to go, or even . . .

Miles suddenly stopped and raised a hand. Carter almost walked into him, and Caren bumped against Carter's back.

'What?' she started to say.

'Shhh,' Miles hissed. He dropped to a crouch. Carter and Caren looked at each other and then followed suit. Carter squinted over Miles's shoulder. He couldn't see anything but more trees. And then he spotted it. Movement. What he had mistaken for another tree trunk was a figure, clothed in brown animal skins, dark green snowsuit bottoms and some kind of bizarre woollen knitted hat. And now he could hear it — a muffled whistling.

The Whistler paused for a moment, head raised to the air like an animal catching a scent. Carter could just see a white flash of skin beneath the hat. Then quickly, the Whistler turned and disappeared into the trees. Miles motioned for them to follow. They crept

277

forward, brushing past more thick trunks. Carter had lost sight of the Whistler. But he could see that the trees were thinning out. Patches of sky, flakes of snow. Not much. It was still twilight in the forest but ahead was a small clearing. And in the small clearing . . . a settlement.

Normally, the Whistlers lived a nomadic existence. Shunned by society for fear of infection. Hiding from those who would put them in the Farms. Many were infected with the Choler variant, which made them violent, unpredictable and dangerous. They usually lived alone or in small rag-tag groups. But there were rumours that some had formed more traditional societal structures, in remote places. Where they could live, undisturbed.

These dwellings looked sophisticated. Tents, obviously looted, a couple of rudimentary huts made from logs, a large fire pit in the middle of the settlement and another structure that seemed to have been constructed from scrap metal. Carter stared at it.

Lettering ran along one side: *INVICTA*.

The realization hit him like a punch in the gut. No.

He took a step forward. Distantly, he heard Miles hiss, '*Carter. Look out.*'

His foot caught on something. Glass and metal clanged and clunked loudly above him, shattering the still of the forest.

'*Shit!*'

Carter glanced up. Old bottles, tins and other bits of junk had been strung in the tree branches. He looked down. A thin piece of twine stretched between two trunks. *An alarm.* He had walked right into a trap.

Hooded figures emerged from the dwellings. Something came flying past. A rock. Then another. Out of the corner of his eye, Carter spotted someone raising a crossbow.

'Move out!!' Miles instructed, backing into the forest.

Carter didn't need to be told twice. He turned to follow Miles. Something struck his head above the ear, hard, and he staggered, falling to his knees. He clutched at his head. Wet with blood and it stung like a bitch. His vision momentarily blurred.

A hand grabbed his arm. 'Get up.'

Caren hauled him to his feet. He swayed, then steadied.

'I'm okay.'

She nodded. They started after Miles, who was already way ahead. First rule of survival. Know when to run and never look back. Also, don't be last. A rule Carter was royally screwing up. Caren was faster and fitter. He was going to get left behind. Left behind with the . . .

Something crashed down from the trees and landed on Caren's back, knocking her to the ground. A Whistler. She screamed in shock and pain. The pair rolled and wrestled on the forest floor. A mass of flailing arms and legs. In the twilight, Carter could barely make out who was who. A flash of blonde hair. A glimpse of white skin. Caren smashed her fist into the Whistler's face. The Whistler howled, a horrible, high-pitched sound.

'Shoot!' Caren screamed.

Carter pulled out his gun. But he couldn't. He couldn't get in a good shot. Not without risking shooting Caren. The Whistler grabbed Caren's hair and clawed viciously at her face. Carter pointed the gun. The Whistler turned. Female. White skin stretched

279

like gossamer over her skull. *Could it be?* He hesitated. The Whistler stretched its mouth wide, revealing sharp yellow teeth. *Smiling.* Then it ducked its head and tore a chunk out of Caren's neck.

'Nooo!'

Something whooshed through the air. The Whistler jerked upright. Another '*whoosh*'. The Whistler swayed and then crumpled on top of Caren. Carter looked up. Miles stood a few feet away, the tranquiliser gun in his hand. He *had* come back.

'Next time,' he said to Carter. 'Don't hesitate.'

He strode forward and pushed the prone Whistler off Caren with his foot. 'Although at least now we have something to show for —'

The Whistler reared up, teeth bared and lunged for Miles, grabbing his leg.

Carter raised his gun and shot it twice in the head. The Whistler collapsed to the ground and lay still.

Miles pulled his leg free. He glanced at Carter and nodded. 'Better.' Then he bent and slung Caren up over his shoulder with surprising ease. 'Let's go.'

They half stumbled, half ran back through the forest, Miles following the marked trees, Carter constantly checking behind them, even though he was pretty sure no more Whistlers were following. Caren was barely conscious on Miles's shoulder. Blood from her neck darkened the back of his blue snowsuit.

Finally, they emerged back out on to the mountainside. Carter bent over, panting. Miles laid Caren down on the ground. More red immediately stained the snow underneath her. Miles grabbed the sled and slid Caren on to it, securing her body with bindings.

'Miles,' Carter gasped. 'She was bitten. Didn't you see?'

'Yes,' Miles nodded, tugging a knot tight. 'I saw. We need to get her back before she loses any more blood.'

'She's *infected*.'

He looked up. 'So, you'd rather I leave her for *them*?'

'No. I —'

'We take her back,' Miles said firmly. His gaze was glacial. 'She's all we have.'

★　★　★

Carter and Miles dragged the sled uphill. With a body tied to it, this was laborious work. How had they ever thought they could manage two?

Their feet slipped and slid out from under them. The wind tried its best to huff and puff them back down the slope. Caren moaned and whimpered. She was fading, Carter thought. They all were. Maybe this was it, he thought. They would die here on this god-forsaken fucking mountainside. After everything he had done to get here, to make it, to survive, he would be lost to the snow and the stomachs of wild animals.

And then, just over the crest of a large snowdrift, Carter saw it. The dark silhouette of the Retreat. *Not today*, he thought. *Not this fucking day*. He dug in with his poles. Beside him, he sensed Miles upping his pace. They reached the electric fence and shoved the broken gate open, dragging Caren over to the door. Miles tapped in the code and the door opened. They stumbled gratefully into the hallway, just as the lift pinged and Welland stepped out.

He stared at them in horror. 'Shit, man. What the hell happened?'

'A trap,' Miles said. 'We were ambushed.'

281

'Fuck.' Welland looked at Caren. 'Is she dead? 'Cos I only just finished loading the incinerator, and it can't take another one today.'

'Wow. Your empathy knows no beginning,' Carter said.

'She's lost a lot of blood,' Miles said. 'But she should survive. We need to dress the wound, get some antibiotics into her to prevent the bite turning bad —'

'Wait!' Welland's eyes widened. 'She was bitten? By a Whistler? She's infected.' He backed away. 'No. No way. You can't bring her in here.'

'We need to get her to an isolation chamber.' Miles took a step forward.

Welland pulled out Miles's gun. He pointed it at them with trembling hands. 'You put her outside.'

'Seriously?' Carter exclaimed.

'Welland,' Miles said in an eerily calm tone, 'the only reason you're alive is to keep the power on. Right now, I have no good reason not to kill you.'

'Yeah. Well, I'm the one pointing the gun.'

'You've still got the safety on,' Carter said.

Welland looked down. Carter leapt forward and punched him in the face. Welland staggered backwards. Carter kneed him in the crotch. Welland *ooomphed* and buckled, the gun slipping from his hand. Carter snatched it up and pressed it to Welland's head. He clicked the safety off.

'I don't need an excuse, but it's nice to have one.'

'Leave him.' Miles said, carrying Caren past. 'We don't have time. And he's still useful — for now.'

The urge to pull the trigger was like an itch.

'You heard what he said,' Welland whimpered.

'Yeah.' Carter clicked the safety back on and stood. 'He said — *for now*.'

They put Caren in Isolation Chamber 4. Her neck had been bandaged. She was hooked up to intravenous antibiotics and sedated. She had lost blood, but not enough to kill her. With the right care, she would probably survive. Of course, she'd probably be better off dead.

Carter leaned against the glass. Her temperature was already rising. Direct infection was fast. Occasionally, even in her sedated state, Caren's body hitched as she coughed. Over the next twenty-four hours the coughing and breathing would worsen. Then would come redeye, fever, delirium, and if she survived . . .

He heard a noise behind him. Miles entered the isolation chambers, carrying more dressings.

'How is she?' he asked Carter.

'How do you think?'

'I think she's alive . . . and we were lucky. What happened out there?'

Carter shifted uncomfortably. 'I couldn't get a shot off without hitting Caren.'

'I don't mean that. I mean strolling into camp, triggering the alarm?'

In his mind's eye, Carter saw it again. That sheet of metal. The faded writing: *INVICTA*.

'I don't know,' he said quietly. 'I just got distracted.'

Miles sucked in his impatience through his teeth. 'And this is the result.'

Carter felt guilt drag his heart down to his toes. 'I know. I fucked up.'

A long pause. 'Not entirely,' Miles said.

'How d'you figure that?'

'Our task was to bring back fresh supplies —' Miles

turned back to the isolation chamber. 'As long as Caren survives, we have what we need.'

Carter stared at him 'Was that the plan all along? Get one of us infected. Bring us back?'

'No.' Miles smiled coolly. 'That was Plan B.'

'You really are a son of a bitch.'

'Do you have a better suggestion?'

Carter looked back at Caren. *With a C.* He clenched his fists. Then, slowly, he shook his head.

Miles nodded. 'Then, to quote Oppenheimer, now we are all sons of bitches.' He turned. 'I'll check on her antibodies later. With any luck, I should be able to begin extraction within forty-eight hours, as agreed.'

Hannah

'Put the gun down, Daniel.'

He glanced at the weapon as if he had forgotten he still held it. Then he looked up. 'You think I'm going to shoot you?'

'I don't know,' Hannah said. 'I don't know anything about you. Is Daniel even your real name?'

He sighed and then laid the gun carefully on the sofa. 'Happy?'

'Not really.' Hannah eyed him coldly. 'Why did you take the coach? What happened to the real driver? What the hell were you thinking?'

He glared at her. 'I was thinking that I didn't want my sister and me to be left to die because we didn't have a rich, powerful daddy to whisk us out of the Academy.'

'That's not fair.'

'Isn't it?' He smiled thinly. 'You can moan about your cold, unfeeling father all you like, but you still had money, privilege, the best education. And you' — he turned to Cassie — 'you can play the school misfit, but you don't know what it's like to be a real outcast because you're poor, you wear second-hand clothes and get free meals.'

'Yeah, well, if that's the case, Oliver Twist,' Cassie bit back, 'how did you end up at the Academy?'

'Because Peggy had brains, not rich parents,' Daniel said, his voice hard. 'She got a scholarship. She was clever as well as beautiful. It was her ticket to a better life.'

285

'And what about you?' Hannah asked.

'No brains. Certainly no beauty. I applied for a job — working in the kitchens and being a general dogsbody. Places like the Academy always need staff. Probably because the pay is shit and they treat people like dirt. They took me on, and it meant I could look out for Peggy, like I always had.'

'Guess you didn't look out enough to stop her getting knocked up,' Cassie said.

Hannah saw Daniel tense, his fists clench. If Cassie had been a man, she had no doubt he would have knocked her out. And girls like Cassie played on that.

'Why don't you just shut up and let him talk?' she said to Cassie.

Cassie held her hands up. 'Fine. I mean, this confession stuff is all very wholesome, but who really gives a shit? The only important thing is trying to stay alive.' She started down the steps into the basement. 'I'm going to check out crazy cabin guy's bunker.'

Hannah turned back to Daniel. 'When did you find out Peggy was pregnant?'

'When the outbreak in the Academy started. She was worried about the baby. She hadn't told me before because I'd have tried to persuade her to get rid of it. Then, it was too late. She was already eight months. She'd hid it well.'

'And the father?'

'She wouldn't tell me . . . because she knew I'd kill him. Predictably, he didn't want to be involved.' He shook his head. 'Peggy had her whole life ahead of her, could have done anything she wanted. But . . . what she really wanted was to be a mother.' His voice caught. 'So I promised I would make sure she and the baby got out safely.'

286

'You weren't on the evacuation list?'

'No. Staff were expected to stay. Only so many could be put on the list, even with a negative test. It was random, we were told. But we all noticed that those making the list were the fee-paying students, those with the most influential parents. Scholarship students and those with less money were being made to isolate on site.'

'Like Peggy.'

He nodded. 'So I had to find another way. The virus was spreading fast. Some students were falling ill after being allocated a place, but I'd heard that their names weren't being taken off the list. I got on a cleaning rota in the infirmary. A couple of days before the final coaches arrived, they brought in a girl who had been due to evacuate but had fallen ill. It was my chance. I stole her ID. Gave it to Peggy. Figured they wouldn't check the photo that closely. I was right. The morning of the evacuation, I watched Peggy climb on board the coach. I'd got her out.'

Hannah frowned. 'So how did you end up driving it?'

'The coaches were about to leave when I saw this guy go into the toilets — the coach driver.' A pause. 'I figured I had nothing to lose. I followed him in, smashed his head against a sink and knocked him out. Then I dragged him into a cubicle and locked the door. I took his cap, jacket and keys and climbed out. Tucked my hair up in the hat and kept my head down. The jacket was too small, so I just carried it. No one questioned me. No one took any notice of me. Hey presto, new driver.'

All her father's best-laid plans, Hannah thought. Spoilt by a coach driver with a weak bladder.

'And what was your plan once you got to the Retreat?' she asked. 'What would have happened when people realized Peggy shouldn't be there?'

'It would be too late by then. And I could look after myself.'

'But instead, you crashed the coach.'

He shook his head. 'It wasn't my fault. The route was dicey, yes. The storm was bad. But I was taking it steady. I wouldn't risk anyone on board. Then I came to a bend and suddenly there were headlights coming the other way, right at me. I hit the horn —'

Vaguely, Hannah remembered hearing the horn.

'— next thing, I'm trying to swerve and the coach is rolling. I'm thrown out of the cab, and I think I must have passed out for a bit. When I came to, my first thought was Peggy. I searched the coach and found her at the back. Straight away, I saw it was bad. That's when I called for help . . . and you came over.' He looked at Hannah. 'You just presumed I was a student. And I realized it would be easier if everyone thought that.'

Hannah continued to stare at him. He seemed to be telling the truth. But she couldn't be sure. And maybe Cassie was right. Did it even matter any more?

'And that's all there is?' she asked.

'Yes.'

But it wasn't. There was something else, something . . .

Cassie's head poked back out of the open trapdoor. 'Guys, you *really* gotta take a look down here.'

Meg

'*Gone?*' Sarah stared at her. 'I don't understand.'

Meg paced the car. 'He lied. The son of a bitch lied and went ahead of me.'

Sarah blinked. 'But isn't that brave of him? Now you don't have to risk your life.'

No, Meg thought. Sarah didn't understand. Because of the girl. The girl with the dark hair. She stopped and fumbled in her pocket. She pulled out the crinkled photograph. The one she had found on Paul.

Daniel and Peggy. Invicta Academy.

Meg squinted harder at the picture. This time focussing on the young man. She tried to add years, lose the weight, the long hair. *The eyes*, she thought. The startling blue eyes.

It was him. *Sean.* Sean was Daniel. Daniel was Sean.

Paul had his photo. So, he must have known who Sean really was. Or at least known he would be on this cable car. He was looking for him. But why? Sean had said he wanted revenge for the death of someone he loved. A girl. Was this her? Was that why he was here? Was the person he believed responsible at the Retreat?

'*When I find them, I'm going to make them pay.*'

If Sean had realized that Paul was looking for him, that was a good motive for murder. Kill Paul and let Karl take the blame. And what about Max? Had Max spotted something, or had he just been a liability — dead weight?

Sean hadn't taken her place because he cared about

289

her risking her life.

He had done it because he was on a mission. Revenge.

And a man who could murder, lie and deceive in order to achieve his goal . . . was that the sort of man who would send rescue?

Sarah was still staring at her. 'What is it? What's wrong?'

'I have to stop him,' Meg said.

'What are you talking about? If Sean has made it across, we just have to wait for him to send help. It will all be okay.'

Meg shook her head. 'You don't get it.'

She could see the hope in Sarah's eyes. Hope and desperation. She was clinging to that fragile thread and Meg was about to snatch it away.

'I don't think Sean is going to send help.'

'What? Why?'

'He killed Paul.'

'*Paul.* Who's Paul?'

'The security guard. Paul was his real name, and he was a cop.'

'How . . . how do you know that?'

'I knew him. I recognized him.'

'And you didn't say?'

'I wasn't sure it was relevant.'

Sarah regarded her suspiciously. 'And you thought we might suspect you?'

Meg sighed. '*Listen.* I think Paul was here because of Sean. I found this picture in his pocket.'

She held out the photograph. Sarah hesitated, then took it. She frowned. 'Who are these people?'

Meg pointed to the girl. 'Did you see the tattoo on Sean's chest?'

'Sort of.'

'It's this girl.'

'You can't be sure.'

'Look at the young man in the picture, Sarah. Really look. Doesn't he seem familiar to you?'

Sarah stared at the picture. Then she shook her head and handed the photograph back. 'It could be anyone.'

'It's *him*,' Meg said. 'You know it is.'

'No.'

Meg resisted the urge to shake the other woman's shoulders. 'Sarah, Sean is a killer. He is not sending help back for us. Why would he?'

'He can't just leave us here. I mean, someone would find out.'

But would they? Meg stared back out of the glass. What was the benefit to Sean of sending help, of increasing the chance of being discovered? Why not just make his escape? Save his own skin?

Meg felt the frustration build. She wanted to hit or kick something. But she probably couldn't afford to waste the energy right now.

And then she realized something else. She patted her pockets. Empty.

Sean had taken the gun.

She came to a decision.

'I'm going after him.'

Carter

Miles made dinner. Carter didn't feel like eating. Welland mumbled something about 'allergies'. But Miles insisted. And right now, Carter didn't think it was a good idea to say no to Miles, about anything.

Miles moved around the kitchen, putting pasta into water and stirring tinned tomatoes into a sauce. Fortunately, the hob ran on gas. The power wasn't back on in the living area, so it was lit by candles. Carter sat opposite Welland at the kitchen island. They stared at each other across the expanse of polished granite. Like the world's worst fucking dinner date.

'I hope you all like spaghetti Bolognese?' Miles said. 'I only have soya mince, I'm afraid.'

'Great,' Carter said.

'Soya gives me gas,' Welland mumbled, and reached for his Coke. He hadn't showered since his day's 'exertions' and Carter noticed dirt beneath his fingernails. He fought back a shudder of revulsion and threw back some beer.

'You get everything sorted today?' Miles asked Welland conversationally, like he was asking about a spot of light decorating rather than incinerating their friends' bodies. And also, as if they hadn't had guns pointed at each other's heads less than two hours ago.

'Yeah,' Welland muttered. 'They're all done. But that heavy load is gonna take its toll on the incinerator.'

'I'm aware of that,' Miles replied, spooning steaming piles of pasta into bowls. 'Which is why it's even

292

more vital that we retrieve the generator from the cable-car station tomorrow.'

'Tomorrow?' Carter queried.

'We can't delay.'

'But what about —' He faltered at her name. 'What about Caren?'

Miles brought the bowls over and set them down. The smell was rich. Carter's stomach rolled.

'Parmesan?' Miles held up a packet.

'No, thanks,' Carter said, swilling more beer.

Welland raised a steaming forkful of food and mashed it into his mouth without waiting for anyone else.

Miles brought his own food over, sat down and raised his glass of wine. 'To the survivors.'

Carter hesitated then raised his beer. Welland swallowed noisily and half-heartedly raised his can of Coke.

Miles looked around at them intently. In the flickering candlelight, it made Carter think of Hannibal Lecter. He could very easily imagine Miles casually strolling around the island, lifting off the top of their heads and scooping out their brains. *To eat with a nice Chianti.*

And then that made him think of Nate. Carter had barely given him any thought since he had died. Some friend. But then, survival meant you couldn't afford grief. Life hadn't become cheap. But it was certainly more of a bargain than it used to be.

Miles set down his glass. 'So, logistics. Our task to retrieve fresh supplies did not go exactly to plan. However, we do at least have a Plan B.'

'Could we at least call her by her name?' Carter said, stabbing a piece of pasta with his fork. 'Caren.'

'Of course. If Caren recovers —'

'No one recovers, man,' Welland said. 'You're either dead or a Whistler.'

'Or supplies,' Carter couldn't stop himself saying bitterly.

Miles dropped his fork with a clunk. 'And do either of you have a problem with that?'

Yes, Carter thought, but what choice did they have? 'Does it make any difference?'

Welland shook his head. 'Better her than us, man.'

'Exactly,' Miles said. 'And if we don't have enough regular supplies for Quinn, we're all dead.'

Something occurred to Carter. 'Do you really think you'll have viable plasma within forty-eight hours? Normally that takes three or four days.'

'I'm aware of that. If so, I can stall Quinn. But again, that's why it's important that our power is fully on and our security systems are working efficiently.'

Carter looked at him. 'So, we're still hiking to the cable-car station?'

'Not we.'

Carter's stomach dived. He shook his head. 'No.'

'I need to stay here to monitor Caren,' Miles said steadily. 'Welland needs to monitor the power.'

'And there's my asthma —' Welland started to say.

'Fuck your asthma,' Carter snapped.

Welland looked hurt. 'Hey. I have a condition.'

'You don't have asthma. I know those fucking cartridges you occasionally bother to carry around are full of nothing but air.'

Welland glared at him. 'Yeah, well, how about you? You're not even supposed to be here. I mean, Miles just finds you on the mountain, half frozen, your face falling off. Where the hell did you come from? You claim you can't remember, but I bet Carter isn't even your real fucking name.'

'Enough!' Miles slammed his hand down on the table. The cutlery jumped. So did Carter and Welland.

'We can't keep fighting among ourselves like this.' Miles eyed them coolly. 'If we want to live, we need to work together. Understood?'

They both mumbled affirmatives like chastised children.

'Carter,' Miles continued, 'I am counting on you. You are the only one who can retrieve that generator. I wouldn't ask you to do it otherwise.'

Bullshit, Carter thought. Miles would ask them to do whatever was necessary. And usually, he wouldn't even ask. However, Miles was also the only one who understood why Carter would rather scoop out his own eyeballs with a spoon than ever go back to the cable-car station.

He sighed. 'Yeah, I know.'

Welland shovelled a final forkful of food into his mouth and shoved his chair back. 'I'm beat, man. I'm gonna get some sleep. Big day tomorrow.'

Yeah, for sitting around doing nothing, Carter thought, but managed to stop himself from saying. He looked down at his own food, barely touched. He had even less of an appetite now. Welland lumbered to his feet, and Dexter, who had been curled on his 'dog chair', leapt up, tail wagging.

'I should let him out,' Carter said, glad of the distraction.

'As you wish,' Miles said, calmly sipping his wine.

Carter picked Dexter up and walked downstairs. He winced. 'Man, you really do stink, Dex. You need a bath.' Dexter panted happily in his face. Carter gagged and held him at arm's length, dropping him as soon as they reached the hall. 'Have you been eating wolf shit again?'

Dexter barked happily and ran to the door. Carter grabbed a thick coat and boots and shoved them on. He would often take Dexter for a last walk around the Retreat in the evening. They didn't go too far. Carter was aware that Dexter could be *part* of some wolf's next big shit if he wasn't careful. But their evening stroll gave him a strange sense of normality.

When he and his sister were kids, his grandparents had had a dog. A mongrel, or 'Heinz 57', as his grandad used to say. His name was Bruno. He was old, a little deaf and prone to the most excruciating farts. But Carter had loved that stupid mutt. Loved his unquestioning devotion, optimism and loyalty. Carter had been an awkward, overweight kid. Not so far removed from Welland — which, if Carter was ever being brutally honest, might be why he detested him so much. Bruno didn't judge, didn't care. Not about Carter's acne, huge belly or frizzy hair. It was the same sense of acceptance he got from Dexter. Dexter would never recoil in horror from Carter's ruined face or see the darkness in his ruined heart. Nothing in life was as simple or pure as a dog's love. Carter guessed that was why we put up with the crotch sniffing and bad breath.

He pushed open the door and Dexter bounded out into the trampled snow. The flakes floating down from the sky had slowed and the wind had lost some of its fierce insistence. By tomorrow, the storm should have abated. Carter took his torch out of his pocket and trudged after Dexter.

Since Quinn had blown the fence circuit, the security lighting was off and the grounds were in darkness.

They covered a fairly large area. Around an acre. In summer, when the sun rose high in the sky and the snow had all but melted away, the seven of them used to hang out here sometimes. Miles would set up the barbecue and pour Pimm's while Caren sunbathed, Julia and Nate chucked a Frisbee around and Welland bitched about the heat. Oh, and Jackson, well, he was usually around *somewhere*.

It couldn't last. Obviously. Nothing good ever did. But it had felt pretty okay to pretend that things were normal, just for a few hours.

Carter followed Dexter around the back of the Retreat. Just beyond the fence, he could see the woods. Somewhere within, the incinerator lurked. A second gate led out to it from the back. Carter didn't know why the incinerator hadn't been built within the grounds. Perhaps because it was a later addition to the Retreat. Perhaps because it offended people's sensibilities to smell the bodies being burned so close by. Humans didn't like being reminded of death, even when we brushed cheeks with it every day of our lives.

Cremation was essential. *Six degrees of infection.* Bury the bodies of the infected and you ran the risk of the corpses being dug up by predators, like wolves or coyotes, or even bears. Some natives in the remoter villages still hunted and ate the meat of those animals. Although infection through ingestion was rarer, it happened. The virus was clever. Blood, fluids, air. It constantly found new ways to travel. The Elon fucking Musk of infection.

Somewhere ahead, Carter could hear Dexter rustling and snuffling. Probably digging for something unsavoury. Carter stamped his feet and waved the torch around. He couldn't see the little dog. His grubby white-and-brown fur tended to blend in with the snow.

The torchlight illuminated the fence and the trees beyond. Just visible, the roof of the incinerator. Anya, Nate, Julia, he thought. All burned up in there. Flesh, skin, bone and whatever else we're made up of. All gone. All dust now.

And here he was, stuck with Welland and Miles. A sad fuck and a sociopath. Carter wondered again if one of them had stabbed Julia. Miles was cold enough, but Miles didn't do anything without a reason. And Carter couldn't think of a good reason for him to kill Julia. Plus, if Miles was to be believed, he had been locked in an isolation chamber when Julia was being stabbed. Which left Welland. Or Caren, Carter supposed. Caren was in no position to confess. And Welland? He was sure Welland would kill if it meant saving his own skin, just as long as it didn't require much effort or interfere with mealtimes.

But that still brought Carter back to the question of why. Why would someone want to kill Julia? And why was it worrying at him so much? He was no stranger to murder. He'd taken lives himself. For good reasons and bad. But there was always a reason. Senseless murder — that bothered him.

It wasn't the only thing. Even with Caren, their plasma source had dwindled. From three to two, and Supply 03 wouldn't last much longer. There would only just be enough for the three of them and Quinn. Any plasma going missing would be obvious. Miles would be on the lookout. Which meant that Carter would no longer be able to get away with sending his parcels. Of course, he didn't even know if the packages he sent were being received. Or used. But it was all he could do.

A sudden eruption of barking made him jump, and almost drop the torch. Dexter appeared out of nowhere, dirt and pine needles stuck in his fur, and pelted past Carter back around the corner of the Retreat. What the hell?

Carter sighed and jogged after him, chest feeling tight with the exertion, feet slipping on the flattened snow. He trained his torch in the direction of the crazed barking. Dexter ran up and down the boundary fence, hackles raised, small, sharp teeth bared.

Beyond the fence, a few feet away, stood Whistlers. Shit.

There were maybe a dozen. Clad in an assortment of looted clothes and animal skins. Hoods covered their heads. Only the white blur of their faces was visible. They held sharpened staffs and crossbows. They didn't move, but Carter could hear the sound of their breathing as they stood, staring at the Retreat. Like a distant wind whistling around the eaves.

Carter felt his own hackles rise. What the fuck were they doing here? Whistlers had never come this close to the Retreat before. And never so many. At the start, the odd loner had occasionally approached, maybe searching for food or shelter. The electric fence had soon taught them to keep well away.

Now the fence wasn't working and the gate hung open. However, the group maintained their distance. Perhaps they knew that their very presence here was a threat. Perhaps this was payback for invading their territory today. A warning.

That was a worry on two fronts. One — it meant the Whistlers were more organized and intelligent than Carter and the others had given them credit for. Two — it meant they were pissed off.

A figure stepped forward. Taller than some of the others. A straggly beard poked out from the tattered hood. Carter instinctively reached for his gun. In unison, three Whistlers behind the taller figure raised crossbows. Point made. Carter lifted his hand away from the weapon. The Whistlers kept the crossbows pointed.

The first figure held something up in his hand. Dexter whimpered and retreated behind Carter's legs. The figure took another step towards the gate. *Shit.* A few more steps, he could just walk in. Carter had a gun, but the Whistlers had numbers and ferocity.

The figure stopped. Inches from the gate. Carter held his breath. He could feel the Whistler's eyes on him. Then the Whistler dropped whatever he was holding in the snow and backed away. The armed Whistlers lowered their crossbows and, as one, they turned and drifted back down the snowy mountainside.

Carter let out a heavy sigh. Once he was sure the Whistlers weren't coming back, he walked up to the open gate, reached through and snatched up whatever their leader had left.

He frowned. A bundle of plastic lanyards. They were dirty and cracked but they had obviously once belonged to staff at the Retreat. *Former* staff. Nurses, cleaners, doctors. All dead now. *Ash and dust.*

But why did the Whistlers have them? The lanyards should have been incinerated with the bodies of the infected. And why had the Whistlers brought them here? Carter flicked through, staring at faces and names that weren't familiar to him. And then he paused . . .

A face he did know. All too well. But an unfamiliar name.

Carter stared at the lanyard for a moment, a coldness settling in his bones, and then he stuffed it into his pocket.

Things were starting to make sense.

He had known one of them was lying.

Now, he knew why.

Hannah

She followed Cassie down the creaky steps, Daniel bringing up the rear.

The basement was long and narrow. At the far end Hannah could see a sleeping bag, a camping light and assorted rubbish. Either side, makeshift shelves held stacks of tinned food, bottled water, candles and medicine. A small arsenal of weapons jostled for space on the walls.

To their right hung a row of lethal-looking hunting knives and two crossbows. To their left, a gun rack held three long shotguns, a semiautomatic and a pistol. Boxes of ammunition were piled underneath.

'See what I mean?' Cassie grinned. 'Grandpa Joe would have been in his element down here.'

'Who's Grandpa Joe?' Daniel asked.

'You don't want to know,' Hannah said.

She looked around. On the plus side, they could stock up on food and water. On the minus side, there was still something agitating her about Daniel's confession. He had admitted to smuggling his sister on board and impersonating the driver. *Is that all there is?* No, she thought. There was something else.

'Well, nice as this is,' Daniel said sarcastically, 'I should go back and check on Eva.'

He lumbered back up the steps, which groaned beneath his weight.

'I was thinking we could hide out here,' Cassie said. 'We'd have food, weapons. No one would find us.'

Hannah shook her head. 'If we found this bunker,

my father will. We should take what we need and move on as soon as it's light.'

Cassie's jaw set. 'I think you're wrong.'

'I'm not.'

Cassie looked like she was about to argue, but then she nodded and turned back to the guns. 'Fine. If you say so.' She took down a shotgun and studied it.

'You should be careful with that,' Hannah said.

'Oh, Grandpa Joe taught me all about guns as well as knives.'

Knives, Hannah thought. *That was it.*

The wound on Ben's neck. It couldn't have been inflicted with a piece of glass. It must have been made with a thin blade. A knife.

Like the knife that was still embedded in the Whistler's neck.

The flick knife that *Daniel* had given her.

'I'll be back in a minute,' she said to Cassie, and walked up the stairs.

Daniel knelt by the fire. He had made a makeshift crib out of one of the chest drawers and settled Eva in it. He cooed to the baby as he gently rearranged her coverings.

Hannah watched him, and then said flatly: 'Why did you kill Ben?'

'What?' Daniel swivelled on his heels, staring up at her. 'Ben killed himself.'

'No.' Hannah shook her head. 'The wound on his neck couldn't have been made by the piece of glass. And you're the only one who had a knife.'

She saw his face fall. 'The knife isn't mine,' he said.

'Then where did it come from?'

'I found it. When I opened the toilet door and saw Ben, the knife was on the floor. I picked it up, wiped it and took it. I don't know why. I guess I thought I might need it.'

Hannah studied him, searching for the lie. 'Why should I believe you? You've already lied about who you are and what you were doing on the coach.'

Daniel sighed. 'I did that for Peggy.'

'You worked in the kitchens — you handled knives.'

'No. I washed pots, mostly. I couldn't butcher a slab of meat. I certainly couldn't slit another person's throat.'

But there was someone here who could, Hannah thought.

'I could break a chicken's neck or slice a goat's throat so it would bleed out fast.'

'Cassie,' she murmured.

'You called?'

Hannah turned. Cassie stood at the top of the basement steps, the semiautomatic in her hands.

Hannah tried to keep her voice light: 'I see you settled on a different gun?'

'Yeah. I thought this one would be more useful.'

Hannah nodded. 'We might need to defend ourselves.'

'Nice try.' Cassie smiled. 'I heard you talking.'

'I was just —'

'— about to accuse me of killing Ben?'

'No.'

'Go ahead. Ask me.'

Hannah swallowed. 'I don't think —'

'*Ask me.*'

Their eyes met. 'Did you kill Ben?' Hannah asked.

'Man, you got me.'

'Why?'

The smile faded. 'Because he was a fucking liability

and he was going to die anyway. I just helped him along.'

'Really?'

Cassie sighed. 'Look, I got up to use the bathroom. Ben was already passed out inside. He'd tried to cut his wrists with some broken glass, made a fucking mess of it. So I just finished the job.'

'With a knife you smuggled on board?'

'Birthday present from Grandpa Joe . . . I was pretty pissed when I realised I'd lost it.'

'And what now?' Hannah asked. 'Are you planning to 'help us along' too?'

'You don't need to,' Daniel said quickly. 'I get it. I understand why you helped Ben to die. It was probably the right thing to do. We don't need to fall out over this, right?'

Cassie shook her head. 'Sorry, man. Wrong. See, here's what I'm thinking. The Department are searching for *four* survivors, right? And with crazy cabin guy here, there are four of you. So, if they find you all, dead, in a burnt-out shack, job done. While I get away without anyone looking for me.' She shrugged. 'I kind of *have* to kill you. It's just survival.'

'Cassie,' Hannah said softly. 'Please don't do this. You're not that person.'

Cassie's eyes narrowed. 'You have no idea who the fuck I am. Here's the other thing my grandpa taught me. You're either a good guy or a survivor. And the earth is full of dead good guys.'

She pointed the gun at Hannah. The baby wailed. For a split second, Cassie's eyes flicked in that direction. Hannah took her chance. She sprinted for the kitchen, throwing herself through the door and landing hard on her hands and knees. The floorboards

305

behind her splintered with gunfire. She heard Cassie curse. 'Fuck!'

'*Stop*, Cassie. Please!'

Daniel's voice. Hannah glanced back. He had stood up, holding the makeshift crib in front of him. Cassie swivelled with the gun.

'Wait,' Daniel said, sounding desperate and scared. 'Kill me if you want. Kill Hannah. I don't care. But spare the baby. Please. Take her with you.'

Cassie shook her head. 'Sorry — but that thing is just dead weight.'

'In that case —' Daniel threw the drawer at her. 'Catch!'

Cassie fired. Wood exploded in the air. Hannah screamed before realizing that the drawer was empty. While Cassie was talking, Daniel must have carefully taken Eva out and laid her behind the sofa.

Now, he darted forward and grabbed the gun he had left on the cushions. Cassie re-aimed, but Daniel fired first. The bullets struck Cassie in the stomach. She bucked and staggered backwards. Daniel fired again. Cassie stumbled against the wall of the shack and gradually slid down it to the floor, the gun slipping from her hand, her eyes wide and surprised.

Hannah pushed herself to her feet and walked out of the kitchen. Her legs felt shaky. Daniel stood over Cassie's body. Hannah could see that the girl was leaking blood but still breathing, just. Daniel stared down at her.

'My grandad taught me to shoot too. You know what else he taught me? If the earth is full of dead good guys . . . hell is full of fucking bitches like you.'

And then he raised his gun and shot Cassie in the face.

Meg

Meg watched the emotions cross Sarah's face. Fear, desperation, denial.

'Come with me,' Meg said. 'We can both do this.'

Sarah shook her head. 'No. I can't. I won't make it. I'll fall before I get halfway.'

'It's not that far.'

Sarah shook her head harder. 'I could never even do the monkey bars as a kid.' She blinked back tears, voice catching. 'I'll fall and I will die.'

'If you stay *here*, you'll die, Sarah. Rescue isn't coming.'

Sarah clutched the cross. 'Well, that's God's will.'

'*No.*' Meg stared at her angrily. 'It's yours.'

'I can't do it,' Sarah repeated. 'Please. Respect my choice.' She glanced out of the glass. 'You go. If you make it, try and get help.'

'I can't just leave you here.'

'Yes, you can.'

They stared at each other.

'I have to do this,' Meg said.

Sarah nodded. 'I know.'

'I can't just wait here to die.'

'And I can't kill myself out there.'

Shit. Meg sucked in her breath. And then, awkwardly, she leaned forward and hugged the other woman.

After a moment, Sarah hugged her back. 'I'm sorry.'

'I'm sorry too.'

They released each other and Meg looked up at the

307

hatch. 'Okay.'

She stepped up on to the bench. This was crazy, she thought. She was suffering from food deprivation and dehydration and here she was, about to try and climb a quarter of a mile along a steel cable a thousand feet in the air in sub-zero temperatures. Totally crazy. And a small part of her responded: *Hell yeah.*

She reached up towards the hatch and pushed at it with her fingertips. Now it wasn't weighted down with snow, it flipped back easily. Immediately, Meg felt an icy blast of air, and a few light snowflakes drifted in. She shivered. Her legs felt weak. But she had to do this. She couldn't trust Sean. He was a murderer, twice over probably. He had let another man die. How could a man like that be counted on to save them? As ever in this life, if you wanted to be saved, you had to do it yourself.

'Sarah,' she said, glancing back. 'I'm going to need a bit of a boost to get out of the hatch.'

'Okay.'

Sarah grasped her buttocks and shoved. Meg scrabbled for purchase on the roof but slid back.

'I'm going to have to get on your shoulders,' she said.

'Fine.'

Sarah crouched. Meg climbed up. Sarah attempted to straighten and wobbled. She was right, Meg thought. She wasn't strong. She was thin and frail, and hunger was only making that worse. But then she heard a grunt. With an obvious force of effort, Sarah gripped a pole and pushed up enough so that Meg could lever her top half out on to the roof. Meg wriggled on the slippery metal like a landed seal and managed to drag her legs out after her.

She lay there, on the top of the car, spreadeagled, breathing heavily. The worst of the storm may have passed, but up here the wind still whipped and tore furiously around her, trying to wrench her from her perch. If Meg moved at all, it felt like a sudden gust might peel her from the roof and toss her idly to her death. And if she wanted to get to the support cable, she would have to stand. To climb up the metal arm that attached the car to the cable, then swing out.

Sean had been right. Lunacy. A suicide mission.

Had he made it? Or was he lying dead and frozen in the snow below them?

Meg had to believe he had done it.

Because if that bastard could do it, so could she.

'Are you okay?' Sarah's voice drifted up through the open hatch.

No. *I'm scared,* Meg thought. And she hadn't expected that. She had thought she would welcome death. But this wasn't just about her now. Someone else's survival depended on her. Someone she didn't even like but who was still a person, with a life, who wanted to live it for a little longer. *Damn.*

'Fine. I'm going to close the hatch.'

'You sure?'

'Yeah.'

Meg shuffled back a little. Her feet were near to the edge of the roof. She reached over with one arm and grasped the hatch door.

'Good luck,' Sarah called up. 'Godspeed.'

Meg swung the hatch closed with a solid *clung.* The cable car swayed. Meg pressed herself to the roof, stomach rolling and head spinning. Vertigo. She needed to get a grip, both literally and metaphorically. Deep breaths. Calm. Focus. One step at a time.

309

She raised her head, squinting against the wind. Okay. The car was attached to the cable above by a thick metal arm, taller than she was. A ladder ran up along the side, presumably for technicians and rescue teams (hah!). Meg would need to crawl over to it. Then, pull herself up on to the ladder and climb to the top to reach the cable. From there, she would need to swing her legs up and monkey-traverse the cable all the way to the station. The ascent was shallow at this stage. Further down the line it would have been far too steep.

She could do it, Meg told herself. She *had* to do it.

She started to wriggle on her belly across the cable-car roof. She reached the metal arm and grabbed the first rung of the ladder. She pulled herself up on to her knees. Dizziness threatened again and she closed her eyes and counted to five. Then she stood shakily and placed her foot on the bottom rung. The wind buffeted her. She clung on tighter. *Don't look down. Pretend that this is a training exercise. Police boot camp. The obstacle course. Horizontal rope climb. You beat the guys at this. You can do it. You've done it before.*

Meg climbed to the second rung. The third. Her breath was coming fast, heart hammering. She felt weakness in her legs. Part lack of sustenance. Part fear. She remembered running a marathon. The same sensation. It wasn't physical. It was mental. She gritted her teeth and climbed the final three rungs. She was at the top of the ladder now, the cable-car roof below her, the thick steel cable to her right.

The wind buffeted her again and the cable-car groaned. Meg knew the feeling. The cold was already getting into her limbs. She couldn't stay here. She needed to move and keep moving. She looked down.

And felt herself sway. White below her and, just visible, the tips of pine trees. It seemed impossibly high. *Top of the world, Ma.*

Meg reached for the cable. It was thick. Her hands, in the cumbersome gloves, would only just wrap around it. That would make holding on even more perilous. But without the gloves her hands would be numb with cold within seconds. She needed to get a firm grip and manoeuvre her legs up.

But she couldn't do it. Her body was frozen. She had hit the wall. And every second she stood there the less likely it was she would be able to do this. The cold was eating into her bones. Time was eating into her resolve.

Move, damn you. Move.

But her feet remained firmly planted on the ladder rung.

The cable car swayed again. Meg could feel her fingers numbing. She had to move before she was too cold to hold on.

Think. Think about something to break the paralysis.

'*You can do it, Mummy.*'

She glanced down. *Lily*. Her daughter stood at the bottom of the ladder, looking up. Snowflakes had settled on her curly hair. She wore her pretty, yellow sundress. Of course. Like the line from that old Disney film. *The cold didn't bother her.* Why would it? She was dead.

'Lily?'

'*You can do it, Mummy. It's just like the monkey bars.*'

Her little girl smiled at her. A ghost. A spectre. A symptom of her deteriorating mind. Lack of food. Hypothermia, maybe. Meg sniffed back tears.

'I'm scared.'

'*I know, Mummy. But it's okay.*'

'I never thought I'd be scared of dying.'

'*You're not — you're scared of failing.*'

Because how dare Meg be scared of death when her little girl had accepted it so bravely?

'I want to be with you, sweetheart.'

'*I know, Mummy. But not yet.*'

'Lily?'

But she had gone. A ghost of wind and snow. Meg sniffed again. She stared ahead at the cable-car station.

You can do it.

She gritted her teeth, grasped the cable and tried to swing her leg over it. Her foot slipped. Shit. Meg scrabbled and managed to get it back on the ladder. Fuck. She needed to get more momentum. She inched her hands further along the cable, wedged her feet against the solid mechanical arm and this time managed to hook one boot over the cable. Then the other. She was up. Clinging on for dear life. Although not necessarily her own.

Now, the trickier bit. She needed to move. Meg slid her hands along the cable, wishing she had more feeling through the gloves, hoping they didn't start to slip. She shuffled her feet along behind her. The wind rocked her like it wanted to shake her off. The tendons in her arms ached already. She needed to move faster. The momentum would help her resist the wind. Once she got going, she could keep shimmying along. Shimmy, Meg thought a little hysterically. *Shimmy, bitch, shimmy.*

She moved her hands again, inching her legs along behind. Then, again. A little faster. The cable car wasn't beneath her any more. Below, nothing but air and snow, snow that might seem like a soft, fluffy blanket but would be as hard as concrete if you hit it from this height. A stone-cold landing.

Don't think about it, Meg told herself. Just concentrate on the task at hand. Get a rhythm. Once you've got a rhythm, it gets easier. What was that old tune they told you to sing when giving mouth to mouth? 'Staying Alive'. Yeah. *Oh, oh, oh, oh*. Move on the beat.

Meg inched along. *Oh, oh, oh, oh*. Her arms burned, but she couldn't think about that either. *Sing to me, Barry. Sing, baby.*

She must be halfway. She craned her neck. But as she did, one foot slipped. Meg's heart jumped. Adrenalin spiked. Her other foot followed. A scream rose and died in her throat. Pain shot up her shoulder blades. She held on. Just. But now she was hanging, swaying, the wind rocking her. She needed to get her feet back up. But her arms hurt so much. She wasn't sure she had the core strength to do it.

You can do it, Mummy. Just like the monkey bars.

She swung. Not far enough. *Fuck*. The wind buffeted her. But it was coming from behind. She could use it. And she only had one more shot at this before her arms gave out. Meg swung harder, kicking up her legs. *Yes*. She hooked one heel. Then the other. *She was back.*

But her energy reserves were less than zero. She needed to move. Keep going. *Stay alive*. Keep going. *Stay alive*. Meg's arm muscles screamed in agony. She wanted to cry but she didn't have the energy. How much easier it would be to just let go now. To fall. To join Lily.

No. She wouldn't give in. She was not a quitter. And then there was Sean. She was damned if he was going to get away.

Keep going. The wind seemed to be lessening. White clouds above her replaced by the shadow of grey. Struts. A grey metal roof. The station. Meg was under the cover of the platform roof. She was going to do it. *She was going to make it.*

She craned her neck around. Now she could see another problem. Ahead was the mechanism that attached to the cable car and hauled it into the station for disembarkation. Meg couldn't climb past this, so she would need to let go and drop just before she reached it. But that put her right at the edge of the platform. If she missed, she would fall on to the snowy mountainside below. A big drop. She might not die but she would probably break a limb or two, which would leave her useless to anyone, for anything.

Her head touched metal. A large wheel the cable wound around. Okay. She needed to let her feet drop, then manoeuvre herself so she faced *towards* the station then swing herself out to try and land on the platform.

Meg gripped the cable tightly — one, two, three — and released her ankles. She grunted. Pain shot up her shoulder blades. Her arms were now taking all her weight again. Meg's muscles raged in protest. She just needed to hang on a little longer. She managed to rearrange her grip so she could see the platform edge. At present she was hanging a few inches shy of it. If she simply dropped, she would miss.

She needed to gain some momentum. Then jump. Fuck. Meg clenched her stomach muscles and started to swing her legs. Back and forth, back and forth. *Staying-a-fucking-live.* Back and forth. Just one more and she should have enough propulsion to let go and

314

jump. *Now or never, Barry.*

With all her effort Meg flung herself forward, throwing her feet out and — *yess* — hitting the platform, right at the edge. She skidded, her left ankle twisted awkwardly and she fell, landing face first on the concrete. But she was down. She had made it. Terra firma.

For a moment she just lay there, breathing heavily, wondering if she should kiss the fucking ground. Instead, she rolled over, staring up at the ceiling. *A ceiling.* Not the sky. Meg's whole body started to shake. And then she began to laugh, shivers of cold and exhaustion becoming shivers of delirium. She lay, shaking and laughing, until both started to fade. Crazy. Impossible. A fucking suicide mission. But she had done it.

And now what?

Meg sat up and looked around.

The station terminal was a large, semicircular area. Overhead was the giant wheeled mechanism that hauled the cable car into the terminal. Meg could already see that the haulage cable had snapped, thick steel threads exposed and frayed. The huge motors that powered the system were located at the ground station. Meg supposed that if the haulage mechanism was jammed or stopped somehow at the top, the resulting tension from the motors at the bottom could have caused the cable to break. But had it been an accident, or sabotage?

Meg couldn't see a control room up here, but it might be behind the passenger disembarkation area. She couldn't hear anything either, she realized. No noise of machinery running. No voices. And the station felt dark, despite the daylight streaming in. No lights.

Meg hadn't expected a welcome committee. But it was more than that. The emptiness felt ominous. Unnatural. She pushed herself to her feet. Her legs felt as insubstantial as jelly. She stood for a moment, letting the dizziness fade. Her ankle felt sore too. She had obviously twisted it when she landed. On the plus side, the pain meant she was alive. For now.

She walked forward slowly, careful not to put too much weight on the sore ankle. The rubber soles of her boots squeaked on the concrete floor. Ahead of her a sign read *Café and Viewing Deck* with an arrow pointing left. Beneath this, another sign read *Toilets*, with an arrow to the right.

Ridiculously, at the same time, Meg's belly rumbled and her bladder clenched. The idea of relieving herself in an actual toilet instead of a ski boot was suddenly enormously fucking appealing. And what if the café had food in it? Of course, that wasn't why she was here. She was here to see if she could summon help. But could it hurt just to use a washroom and then see if there was any food or water? Food and hydration were essential, after all. So was toilet paper.

Meg walked across the terminal and turned towards the *Toilets* sign. The corridor was dark. The sound of her boots seemed louder; the sensation of emptiness even stronger. She reached the toilets. The signs were worn but she could just make out F for Female. She shoved the door open and walked inside. Sinks lined one side of the room. Three cubicles on the other. Never enough women's toilets, she thought. The sinks were stained and cracked. The taps looked rusty. She turned to the cubicles. All the doors were closed.

Meg raised a boot and kicked the first one open. It gave with a creaking groan, revealing a dirty toilet

316

stuffed with dried-up loo roll. She walked to the second and pushed at it with her boot. Another stained toilet bowl. Obviously, cleanliness had not been top priority here. Just the third door left to try. Like the Goldilocks of public toilets, Meg thought.

She raised her boot and shoved. The door stuck on something inside. She shoved again. The door gave, slamming open . . . and a body spilled out.

'Fuck!' Meg leapt back.

The body was female, dressed in a green Department-issue snowsuit. Blonde hair, matted with dried blood. The woman had been shot in the head. Close range. There was a large red crater in her forehead and not much left of the back of her skull. Just a mess of gristle, splintered bone and blood.

Christ. Meg turned to the sink and heaved. She had seen worse. But that didn't make it any better. Her stomach convulsed, even though there was nothing in it but bile. It stung her throat and nose. She waited, taking deep breaths through her mouth, and then spat several times, before turning on the rusty tap. A thin dribble of water trickled out. Meg splashed some into her mouth. It tasted stale but okay.

She turned back and knelt down next to the body. Just one bullet to the head. *Executed*. Meg could see it in her mind's eye. Recreating the scene. The woman running from the gunman (or woman) and shutting herself inside the cubicle, cowering, hoping she wouldn't be found. Then the door opens . . . *bang*.

Could Sean have done this? Meg examined the woman more closely. Her limbs were stiff but not immovable. Rigor mortis was wearing off. Plus, her hands and the back of her neck were mottled purplish-red where she had been slumped against the toilet. Livor mortis. The woman had been dead for around forty-eight hours. Of course, the cold temperatures would slow decomposition, so it could be longer, but not less. That ruled Sean out, and put the time of death close to when the cable car had stopped. Unease gripped Meg. Something was wrong. Very wrong.

She exited the toilets and hobbled back along the corridor towards the café. And then she stopped. To Meg's right was another, shorter corridor. She must have hurried straight past it before. She could see two more doors. A sign on the first read *Staff Only, Restricted*. The control room. It had to be. Meg debated with herself then walked towards it. As she drew closer, she saw that the lock had been shot out. She pushed at the door and it swung open.

Two bodies still sat in their seats at the control desk. Not that there was much to control, from the looks of it. The small area had been trashed. Cables ripped out, wires hanging loose. Computer monitors smashed. And the operators killed with a swift bullet to their backs as the killer burst in. Like the body in the toilets, these guys had been dead for a couple of days.

Meg frowned, trying to piece together the timeline. The crew at the station must have been alive to authorize the cable car's ascent. But at some point, after the car left the base station, something had happened up here. The operators had been attacked and the cable car sabotaged, its occupants left to die. But the stoppage had only been temporary. Perhaps one of the operators had survived for long enough to try and get the car moving again, to save them. Unfortunately, that was when the haulage cable had snapped.

A piece of luck for the saboteur.

But why stop the cable car?

The obvious answer was to prevent those inside from getting to the Retreat. But maybe it was more than that. If the car was sabotaged en route, there was no other viable way up to the mountains, not any more. Perhaps the intention had been to stop *anyone* getting to the Retreat.

And whoever was responsible for the sabotage here, if the Department suspected that something had happened at the Retreat — an outbreak or an attack — they would shut it down. Cut the place off. No one in or out. The group in the stranded cable car were expendable. Which is why they were chosen. Who would risk lives and resources to rescue a group of guinea pigs?

It made sense. But it still left unanswered questions. What exactly had happened? Why kill all the people in here? But perhaps it wasn't the time for hypothesizing. One thing was for certain. Whoever had done this was dangerous and armed. On top of that, Sean could still be here. Also dangerous, also armed.

Meg turned her attention from the bodies to the desk they were sitting at. There were drawers underneath. She pulled open the first one. Inside, pens, Post-its, paperclips and a Tupperware box that contained a half-eaten sandwich. Her stomach growled. She opened the lid and took a couple of bites. The cheese was dry, the bread like cardboard but, right now, it tasted delicious. Meg rammed the remainder into her mouth, swallowed it down and tried the second drawer. Locked. She frowned. In her experience, locked drawers usually contained one of four things — porn, private papers, cash . . . or weapons.

She bent down beside one of the bodies and patted his clothing. She felt something in a side pocket. Her glove was bulky, so she tugged it off and gingerly slipped her hand inside. The body felt unnaturally cold and stiff, even through the thick material. Then Meg's fingers closed around something bulky and metallic. A keyring.

She took it out. There were five keys of varying sizes on the metal ring. Four were labelled: *Generator, Control, Maintenance, Snow 1*. The final key was unlabelled and much smaller. It looked about the right size for a drawer. Meg slipped it into the lock. Her luck was in. The key turned smoothly and the drawer slid open. She had been right. A small handgun lay inside. Meg took it out and checked the chamber. Fully loaded. Maybe the operators here hadn't just been employed to keep the cable car running.

She stuck the gun in the pocket of her snowsuit. Then she exited the room and walked back along the corridor. Ahead of her, Meg could see double doors. *Café and Viewing Deck*. Not used by the general public for a long time. Tourists hadn't journeyed up here to enjoy the luxury chalets and crisp white slopes for over a decade. Places like these had been the first to fall. And then they had been repurposed by the Department.

But the Department's needs were utilitarian. Paint peeled from the walls, the concrete floor was pitted, a stale smell hung in the air. This place was a shell. But was it a completely empty shell?

Despite the freezing temperatures, Meg was sweating in her snowsuit. She pulled out her gun and tried to peer through the glass at the top of the double doors, but it was too dirty. She could just make out a few haphazardly stacked tables and chairs.

Gun still poised, she pushed one of the doors open and stepped inside.

A floor-to-ceiling window took up the opposite wall of the semicircular room. Jutting out over the mountainside, it was probably meant to feel like you were floating in the clouds, the world spread out before you. A heavenly vista. Except the world had gone to hell. And the last thing Meg needed to see was more fucking sky.

The view wasn't what had caught her attention though.

A solitary figure sat on a chair facing the window, feet up on a table, sipping a beer.

Meg limped slowly over. As she drew near, he raised the beer bottle in greeting. 'Nice of you to join me.'

'Wouldn't miss it for the world.'

Sean turned. 'I mean it. I'm glad you're not dead.'

'Wish I could say the same.'

'Harsh.'

'Yeah, well, I tend to be harsh to liars and killers.'

Meg reached into her pocket and flipped the crumpled photograph on to the table.

'I know who you are, *Daniel*.'

He picked up the photograph and stared at it for a moment.

'Who is she?' Meg asked. 'Your girlfriend?'

Sean shook his head. 'My sister. Her name was Peggy.' He laid the photograph down. 'I took this when we first arrived at the Academy. Ten years ago. Our whole lives ahead of us.' A bitter chuckle. 'Guess that didn't work out so well.'

'Why did you kill the cop?'

'You want the whole confession?'

'I want a good reason not to blow you through that window.'

Sean tipped up the beer and took a long sip. 'I told you. I made a promise. To find the man who caused Peggy's death and kill him —' He broke off, looked at the beer and grimaced. 'Man, the end of the world is nigh and all they stock is warm Estrella.' He turned. 'Want one?'

Before Meg could react, he spun and hurled the bottle at her.

She ducked as it whizzed over her shoulder. Glass exploded on the floor. Meg straightened, fumbling to re-aim her weapon, but she was too slow. Sean's gun was already in his hand.

He clicked off the safety. 'And I'm really sorry, Meg . . . but I can't let you stop me.'

Carter

He was ready early. Snowsuit and boots, mask, goggles, compass, a rucksack full of tools and a sled which he would have to drag up to the cable-car station in order to drag the generator back down. Oh, and a fully loaded gun. Just in case.

'You know what you have to do?' Miles asked.

Carter nodded. They had been over it several times. 'Disconnect the generator. Don't damage anything. Make sure I check for gas canisters. Also, there should be another battery back-up. If it looks usable, take that too.'

'Right.' Miles glanced at Welland. 'Right?'

Welland grunted and nodded. 'Sounds about right.'

Carter eyed him coolly. 'Wow. Could you run that tech advice by me again? It was a little too detailed the first time. After all, you are the expert.'

'Hey, I wasn't in charge of the cable-car station.' Welland glared back at him. 'S'all pretty straightforward.' He rubbed his belly. 'I gotta go. I really need a shit.'

He turned and wandered off. Carter let out a long sigh. 'One day, I'll have a good enough reason to kill him.'

'But not today,' Miles said briskly. 'We still need him.'

'Do we? Really?'

Miles eyed him curiously. 'Is everything okay?'

Carter looked at him. No. But it could wait, he thought.

'Fine. Dandy.'

'Carter, I know you don't want to do this. And I know why —'

'I said, it's *fine*. It's probably time anyway, isn't it? Confront those demons. Lay ghosts to rest. All that shit.'

'Yes.' Miles nodded. 'That really is a pile of shit.' He fixed Carter with a steely gaze. 'Just remember — if you let me down, demons will be the least of your concerns.'

Hannah

They crouched by the glowing fire. They had taken what they needed from the bunker and then shoved the dead bodies down the steps and shut the trap-door. Out of sight, out of mind. Nearby, Eva dozed, wrapped in dead people's clothes. This is who we are now, Hannah thought.

'Do you think we'll make it?' Daniel asked.

She coughed and covered her mouth. 'You might. Not me.'

'You're infected?'

'Yes.'

'So I probably am too.'

'Maybe not. You've come this far without any signs of infection. Some people are less susceptible, depending on the virus strain.' She glanced at Eva. 'And infants are far less likely to catch the disease.'

'I don't care about me,' Daniel said. 'I just want to get Eva to safety. I couldn't save Peggy. I have to save Eva.'

He shifted and reached into his pocket. He pulled out a piece of paper — a photograph. Hannah glanced at it: a picture of Daniel and his sister, when she was alive and beautiful, not carved up like a slab of meat. Hannah swallowed.

'I took it when we first arrived at the Academy,' Daniel said. 'It seemed like a fresh start. Our whole lives ahead of us. Now Eva is all I have left. I have to make that mean something.'

He stared at the photograph. The firelight lit half

of his face in orange. Shadows carved black hollows from the other side.

Hannah came to a decision. 'Once it's light you should go on without me.'

He half turned. 'Are you going to say you'll only slow me down?'

She managed a faint smile. 'Something like that.'

'Are you sure?'

No, she thought. She wanted to live. But there were no miracle cures for this virus. They might be able to prolong her life. But what sort of life would that be? She didn't want to become one of *them*. A Whistler.

She nodded. 'Yeah. I'm sure.'

The fire crackled.

'Aren't you angry at him?' Daniel asked.

'Who?'

'Your father. If he loved you, he could have saved you.'

'Science saves people. Not love. That's what he always used to say.'

'That's not an answer.'

'I know,' she said. 'I suppose it's only what I expect of him. I used to be angry at him, but then I realized it was a waste of energy. It didn't affect him. Emotions bounce off my father like Teflon. You can't hate someone who doesn't care.'

'He sounds like a piece of work.'

'He is. He's also brilliant at what he does and, if anyone will beat this virus, it will be him.'

'At what cost?'

Hannah smiled grimly. 'Whatever it takes.'

'And the little people don't matter.'

'Not to him.'

He stared at her. 'No offence, Hannah, but if I ever

326

meet your father, I'm going to kill him.'

'No offence taken.'

They both turned to the fire. The flames were ebbing now. Neither of them had the energy to restart it.

'How much time till morning?' Daniel asked.

'I don't know.' Hannah glanced towards the windows. It was still dark, but she could just make out the outline of trees now. Dawn was gradually seeping in. Hannah realized she still had Lucas's watch on her. She fished it out of her pocket.

The hands read three minutes past eight. That couldn't be right. It must have stopped. And yet Hannah had seen Lucas looking at it in the forest. She frowned.

Die Zeit. The time.

Had Lucas been trying to tell her something? She had thought he just meant that it was time for him to die, but what if there was another reason he had wanted Hannah to have the watch? She examined it. The face was thick. Too thick? She ran her fingers around the edge and found a catch at the side. She pressed it. The face sprung open, revealing a small compartment. Inside, a smaller black device, pulsing red.

'What's that?' Daniel asked.

Hannah's heart plummeted. Shit.

'I think it's a tracker,' she said dully.

That was how the Department had found them. Lucas — all along. Perhaps, while the storm was bad, they couldn't fix on the transmission, but when it cleared they didn't even need to search. Just followed the signal.

'Lucas was working for *them*?' Daniel asked.

'Yes. He told the gunman the truth.'

'So that means the Department know where we are.'

And if they could track the signal, Hannah thought, they didn't need to wait until it was light to search for the survivors. In fact, wouldn't it be better to ambush them in the dead of night or the early hours of the morning?

She stood and crossed briskly to the window, eyes scanning the semi-darkness outside. It looked still and quiet out there, but were those darker silhouettes moving within the trees? Hannah squinted, leaning against the rotten window frame . . .

A burst of bright white light blinded her and sent her staggering backwards. The hum of electrical equipment powering up vibrated through the shack. One by one floodlights cranked on around the edge of the clearing, bathing them in light, turning night into day. Between the dazzling beams, Hannah could just make out men in hazmat suits, holding guns.

The baby started to wail. Hannah turned. Daniel stared at her with wide eyes. 'They've found us.'

'HANNAH!'

The voice echoed over a loudhailer.

Hannah turned back to the window. A figure walked out of the daze of lights and into the centre of the clearing. Dressed in a Department-issue green snow-suit and face visor. But still instantly recognizable.

Professor Grant. Her father. He raised the loud-hailer to his mouth:

'Hannah. I know you're in there. I believe there are at least four of you, and one or more of you may be infected. It's vitally important that you let us help you.'

Daniel walked over to her, holding the gun.

'What do we do?'

'We can't fight,' Hannah said, mind struggling to work through the fug of the virus. 'There are more of them. A shoot-out will only put Eva in danger.'

'So we just give up?'

'No.'

Something came to her. 'The explosive device Lucas found on the gunman. I need you to get it. It's still in his pocket.'

Daniel nodded. 'O–kay.' He walked over to the trapdoor, flipped it open and creaked down the stairs.

Hannah looked back out of the window. There were at least half a dozen Department agents out there. They must have driven as far as they could then trekked through the forest.

'Father?' she called out.

'Yes?'

'Tell your friends to lower their guns.'

'Hannah. One of *your* friends killed a Department agent. Right now, you are complicit in murder.'

'And what about your plan to crash the coach and kill us all? Did the Department sanction that? Does the Academy know?'

'Hannah, you're confused. Our only aim is to get you all to safety.'

Daniel emerged through the trapdoor, carefully holding the small grey device.

'What now?' he asked.

Hannah took the device. 'I'm going outside to talk to him.'

Daniel's face fell. 'Are you *nuts*? He'll kill you.'

She nodded. 'Maybe. But he'll let me talk first.'

'Why?'

'One thing I know about my father — he believes

that he is an honourable man.'

Daniel snorted.

Hannah's eyes found his. 'I can't promise that I can save you — but I *will* save Eva. He won't kill a baby.'

'Are you sure?'

Not a hundred per cent, she thought. But it was all she had.

'As sure as I can be.'

Daniel looked back at Eva, who was still crying. He walked over and crouched down, trying to soothe her. After a moment he said, 'I guess that will have to do.'

Hannah shouted back out of the window. 'I'm coming outside. I will be holding an explosive device — the one your agent tried to blow the coach up with. If you shoot, I will trigger it. I believe it will probably take out everyone in the vicinity.'

She saw her father's face falter.

'Hannah, that is not necessary.'

'Yes. It is.'

She pushed open the door, blinking against the light, shivering in the cold. It made her head swim. Despite the freezing temperatures she could feel her hand growing clammy around the device.

Slowly, she walked down the steps, clutching the rickety banister with her free hand. Just a little bit more, she told herself. Just a little longer. She walked towards her father, holding the device aloft. As she drew closer, she coughed.

Her father placed the loudhailer on the ground and watched her, hands in his pockets. 'You are not well,' he observed.

'No. I'm infected.'

He nodded. 'Put the explosive down, Hannah. Let me help you. I can take you and your friends to a treatment centre. We've many new experimental drugs.'

'So we can be your lab rats?' she said. 'I don't think so.'

'Hannah, you know the alternative.'

She glared at him. 'Listen to me, Father. For once, just listen. There is only me and one other person left . . . and a baby.'

Her father's eyebrows shot up. 'A baby?'

'One of the students on board was pregnant. She gave birth on the coach before she died. The man in the shack is her brother. Promise me one thing — save the baby.'

He sighed. 'Very well —'

'*Promise me.*'

He looked at her with his cool grey eyes. A trait they shared. 'The baby will not be harmed. You have my word.'

Hannah nodded. It was the best she could do. There was no point asking her father to save Daniel — he was expendable, like her. She bent forward and laid the explosive device carefully down in the snow. Her father picked it up and slipped it into his pocket.

Hannah coughed again, her vision wavering.

Her father gazed at her sadly. Then he held out an arm.

'Come to me, Hannah. You are still my daughter.'

Hannah hesitated and then realized, for the first time, she wanted to be held, just once. She walked forward and leaned against her father. He wrapped his arms around her.

'I'm dying,' she whispered.

'I know.'

Tears squeezed from her eyes. 'I don't want to die.'

'I know.'

She felt something pressing into her back. She looked up. 'Fath —'

A muffled bang. A feeling of intense heat in her side. Hannah's legs gave. She couldn't feel them any more. She slid out of her father's embrace, falling backwards into the snow.

He looked down at her, still holding the small pistol. 'But we all have to die sometime, Hannah.'

She tried to reply, but blood was clogging her throat. All she could do was lie there, her side throbbing, breath coming wheezily. Around her, boots crunched in the snow.

'What shall we do with her?' someone asked.

Her father's voice: 'Burn everything. Leave nothing but bones.'

'What about the others?'

'Take them.'

'Alive?'

'Yes. I promised my daughter . . . and they could both be useful to us.'

Distantly, more commotion. Shots. Hannah was aware of cries and shouts. Once, she thought she heard Daniel's voice: 'Okay — I'll come. Just don't hurt the baby.'

A figure crunched up to her. Something wet and caustic splashed over her face and body. Accelerant. Gradually, the voices and noise faded. Hannah was alone. Unable to move, she stared up at the small circle of sky, watching it lighten. The beginning of a new day. Her last.

She didn't feel cold any more. She was aware of the smell of burning and the crackle of flames around her. But she didn't feel the heat either.

Comfortably numb.

Except . . . there was something.

Hannah could sense a presence.

Death, perhaps, lingering close by.

You can come now, she thought. *I'm ready.*

Soft steps in the snow.

A shadow fell over her.

And then . . . whistling.

Meg

Meg stared at the gun. 'I'm not here to stop you. I just want to get help, for Sarah.'

'I'm not sure our needs are mutually compatible.'

'But they could be. We could work together.'

Slowly, Meg turned her gun round so she was holding it by the barrel. Never taking her eyes off Sean, she stretched out her arm, placed the gun on the table and stepped back.

She waited, heart thumping. Sean nodded at the handgun. 'Where did you get that?'

'Dead guy in the control room.'

'Resourceful.'

Sean considered her for what felt like an eternity, then clicked the safety on and laid his gun beside hers. He stood. 'I need another beer.'

He walked over to the counter. Meg glanced at the handguns on the table and wondered if this was a test. Could she grab one in time? Did Sean have another gun on him? Did she actually want to kill him?

Sean opened the fridge and glanced back. 'Want one?'

'To drink?'

He grinned, took out two bottles, popped the lids off on the countertop and walked back over. He held out a bottle to Meg.

She accepted it and took a swig. Warm, stale, and Estrella. But still fucking delicious right now.

'So should I call you Sean or Daniel?' she asked.

His face clouded. 'Daniel was another life. A lot of

blood under the bridge since then.'

Meg regarded him with more sympathy. 'What happened to your sister?'

Sean sat back down. 'You ever hear of Invicta Academy?'

Meg frowned. Again, that distant bell ringing.

'Exclusive school in the mountains,' he continued. 'Ten years ago, a coach carrying students from the Academy crashed in a snowstorm. They were all killed, including the daughter of Professor Grant, the famous virus guy, head of the Department.'

Meg nodded. '*Yes*. I remember now. It was on the news. Only the driver survived. He went to jail.'

Sean threw back his beer. '*I* was the driver.'

Meg stared at him. 'You?'

'I wasn't meant to be. I had to knock the real driver out and lock him in a toilet.'

'Why?'

'Long story. The short version — to get myself and my sister to safety. Otherwise, we would have been left behind to die with the rest of the infected.'

She stared at him, confused. 'I don't understand.'

'There was an outbreak at the school. But it was kept quiet. The fee-paying students who tested negative were evacuated. I was working in the kitchens. My sister was there on a scholarship. Our names weren't on the list.'

'Jesus. And your sister died in the crash?'

He shook his head. 'About half a dozen of us survived the crash, including my sister, Peggy. But she was badly hurt. And then we found out that some of the students on board were infected.'

'How? You said only those with negative tests were evacuated?'

He gave her a grim smile. 'Money can buy you a lot of things, including a ticket out of lockdown. The rich parents bought their infected kids out of there. Or at least, they thought they had.'

'How do you mean?

'The Department pretended to be evacuating the kids — keep those rich, powerful parents happy — but they never intended them to reach the Retreat. They engineered the crash.'

'But Grant's daughter was on board. He was going to let his own daughter die?'

Sean nodded. 'Everyone is expendable to him. But Hannah, his daughter, worked it out. She tried —' he broke off. 'She tried to save us. To save Peggy.'

'But she couldn't?'

He shook his head and then said softly. 'But she saved Peggy's baby.'

Meg stared at him. 'Peggy was pregnant?'

He nodded. 'A little girl.'

'What happened to her?'

'We almost made it. Me, Hannah, the baby. We escaped the coach; we were trying to make our way to safety. But then they found us.' Meg saw his face close down. 'Grant and the Department. He shot Hannah and took the baby.'

'Why did they let you live?'

'I was the scapegoat. The evil imposter who killed the students the Department was trying to rescue.'

'They could have killed you and still spun the story,' Meg said.

'But far better to be able to parade a sacrificial lamb in front of the press. To put a face to the evil. To hear him say, 'Guilty'.'

Meg stared at Sean. That was *why*, she thought.

Why that picture had stuck in her mind. Why the overweight young man and the beautiful girl had seemed so familiar. Meg must have seen them in newspapers, on television screens. Ten years ago, but the brain is a hoarder.

'Why didn't you tell people the truth?' she asked.

Sean sighed. 'Because I *was* guilty. And they had Eva. They promised me she would be looked after. They would even give me updates, a chance to see her grown up . . . if I played along like a good boy. They kept their side of the bargain' — he swigged more beer — 'and I bided my time.'

'For what?'

'Revenge.'

He said it as if it was the most obvious thing in the world.

'How did you plan on getting revenge from prison?' Meg asked.

A thin smile. 'People think you're cut off from everything inside. In fact, you have access to a lot of stuff others don't. Inmates aren't there because they're innocent bystanders. They know things. A lot were Rems. I picked up plenty of useful information from them over the years. I found out how to get inside the Retreat.' A pause. 'And I found out where Eva was.'

'How?'

'There's always a man. Wherever you are: he might be a white man, a black man; might even be a woman. The principle is the same. There's always *someone* who runs things. Someone who has the power. You just need to know the man.'

'And what did you have to do for 'the man' to get this information?'

His face darkened. 'You don't want to know.'

'Maybe I do.'

'Really? You want to hear how I sucked, fucked and stabbed my way into his favour?'

Meg swallowed drily. 'I'm sorry.'

Sean threw back the beer. 'Don't be. I did what was necessary — I got what I needed. And then I got myself a get-out-of-jail-free card by being picked for a trial. And not just any trial. It had to be this one. The Retreat. Because that's where he is. Grant. The Professor.'

'And when you've killed him, what then?'

'Then I go and find Eva. She's ten now. She should know about her mum. Know her family.'

Meg sipped her beer. She wasn't so sure about that. But now was not the time. She had other questions: 'What about Paul?' she asked. 'Why did you kill him?'

'Paul?'

'The cop on the cable car. That was his real name.'

'How do you know?'

'I used to be in a relationship with him.'

Sean stared at her — and then he burst into laughter. 'Man. Guess we all have our secrets.' He tipped his beer at her. 'I'm sorry for your loss.'

'No, you're not, and it wasn't a loss. I hadn't seen him in five years. But he didn't deserve to die.'

'It was him or me.'

'And what about Karl?'

'I didn't want that to happen.'

'But you were happy to frame him.'

'I didn't —' Sean shook his head. 'It wasn't how it was meant to go.'

'And how *was* it meant to go?'

Sean sighed. 'I got a tip-off that there was going to be a cop on board, looking for me. Somehow, word

338

got out I was going after the Professor.'

'How?'

A shrug. 'No honour among thieves, like they say. While the man was feeding me information, he was feeding someone else information about me. I half expected it.'

Meg stared at him. 'So you smuggled a knife on board to kill Paul?'

'No. I'd already arranged for the knife to be on board. I knew that we'd be drugged before being put on the car. Stripped, possessions taken. I didn't know if I'd be able to get hold of a weapon once we got to the Retreat. So I arranged to have a 'friendly' Department worker hide the knife in exchange for some drugs I'd scored. I poured the food and drink I was given down the toilet and faked being out of it when they came for me. When we got into the cable car, I checked you all out. I knew right away who the cop was. The gun was kind of a giveaway.'

'Paul was carrying the gun?'

'Yeah.'

'He was drugged?'

A slight hesitation. 'Yeah. I guess he wanted to play along, or he didn't get the memo.'

Meg's throat tightened. 'So you stabbed him while he was knocked out?'

Sean shot her a black look. 'He'd have killed me if he got the chance.'

'But he didn't, did he?' Meg felt her voice catch and gathered herself. 'And then you hid the gun and planted the knife?'

'I had to think quickly. I had a bloody knife to dispose of, and a gun to hide. My only option was to dump them both out of the cable car. But then it

339

occurred to me that the gun could be useful, so I had an idea. I took the tape that had been used to stick the knife beneath the seat, opened the roof hatch and stuck the gun to the roof, figuring I might be able to get it later.

'I was about to ditch the knife when the power cut and the car stopped. I got thrown back into the car, and the hatch slammed shut. That's when you started to wake up. I had to make a quick decision, so I shoved the knife in the pocket of the person nearest me, curled up on the bench and pretended to be out of it.'

Meg let this sink in. It all made sense now, in the way that a crazy man's plans made sense. Or maybe not crazy. Just grief-stricken and obsessed.

'You had the key to the hatch all along. You pretended it was locked.'

'Yeah.'

'And Karl was just collateral damage.' She eyed him more sharply. 'And what about Max?'

He looked down. 'He was a dead man walking, Meg.'

'So you helped him on his way.'

'He was a liability.'

Meg shook her head, a nasty bitter taste in her mouth. 'All of this, just to kill one man.'

Sean stared at her. 'I thought you might understand.'

'Me?'

'You lost your daughter. If you knew *one* person was responsible for her death and you had the chance to kill them, wouldn't you?'

Meg opened her mouth to reply and realized she couldn't, not honestly. After Lily's death she had seen one of the doctors who had failed her daughter. Getting into her car in a supermarket car park. It was late, the car park was deserted. Meg had started to approach, fists clenched. In that moment, she had wanted to see terror in the bitch's eyes. To say, *This is for Lily*, and smash her fucking brains out.

But then someone had called her name. An officer Meg knew, crossing the car park with his shopping. The moment was broken. Sanity restored. Meg had walked away and got in her car, commending herself on her restraint. Except it wasn't her conscience that had stopped her, but a witness.

'I understand the need for revenge,' she said to Sean. 'But it wouldn't have taken away my grief. Lily would still be dead.'

'It's not about grief,' he said. 'It's about justice. For Peggy — for all of those Grant has killed.'

'At any price?'

'There's always a price. Just like there's always a man. You just have to decide if you're willing to pay.'

'Were you ever going to send help for us?'

Sean rolled his eyes. 'What help? From where? Look around you, Meg. This place has been completely trashed. You saw the bodies.'

She nodded. 'I thought you'd shot them at first. But they've been dead for far longer than that.'

'I guess whoever stopped the cable car must have killed them.'

'Do you think that person is still here?'

Sean shook his head. 'I've had a look around. This place is empty.' He gave her a sharper look. 'No one is coming to help us, Meg. Face it, someone wanted to stop us getting here. Permanently.'

Meg stared back out of the huge window. The cable

341

car hung, toy size, in the distance. 'Sarah is still stuck out there.'

'Her choice,' Sean said.

'I can't abandon her,' Meg said, more desperately. 'If I could get hold of some climbing equipment, I might be able to get back across the cable and lower her down out of the hatch.'

'Seems like a lot of effort to save a woman you don't even like.'

'I'd do it for you.' Meg leaned towards him. 'Sean, please. Just help me. You can kill whoever the hell you want afterwards. I'll even lend a hand. Just let me try and make this right.'

Sean swigged his beer. 'You're a better person than I am.'

'Am I?'

She saw the conflict in his face.

'Fuck!' This time he threw the empty beer bottle at the picture window. It bounced harmlessly off the reinforced glass. He stared at it and sighed. 'Well, that was a wasted gesture.'

He looked back at Meg. 'There's a snowmobile around the back. I was going to use it to get to the Retreat . . . but we could probably both fit on it.'

Meg smiled. 'Thank you.'

Sean stood and then paused. 'Just ask yourself one thing, Meg — who exactly are you trying to save?'

She frowned. 'Sarah.'

His blue eyes bored into hers. 'Fine. Keep telling yourself that.'

Carter

It took three hours to trek up over the mountains to the cable-car station. It wasn't that far, but the terrain was steep and treacherous. Once, snowmobiles had provided quick and easy transport. But they had gone a long time ago.

Carter sweated and panted as he dragged the sled up the mountain slope behind him, occasionally stumbling, often swearing. The snow had all but stopped but a damp mist hung low, thickening into dense pockets in places, obscuring the way ahead.

Making the journey on foot was hard going. The endless white and identical mountain ridges made it easy to get lost. There were sudden gullies and at some points the mountainside dived away into sheer rockface.

Halfway, Carter paused to catch his breath and ease the ache in his weary legs. The air was thinner up here; he could feel his heart and lungs having to make more of an effort to get the oxygen into his limbs. His phantom nose and exposed mucous membranes stung with the cold. He buried his face further into his scarf and resumed the trek. Finally, he crested another small ridge, and saw it. The circular grey hub of the cable-car station.

Once upon a time, the cable car had brought tourists from the hotels and train stations in the main town to the more exclusive ski resorts higher up the mountains.

Those resorts had been closed for over a decade.

343

The town below had fallen to crime and dereliction. Most of the buildings were ruined and uninhabitable. But the cable car had found a new purpose: it had been the only secure way to bring recruits up to the Retreat.

Built into the mountainside, the huge, curved wall of glass offered views over the forest and valleys beyond. The main level contained a viewing deck, café and dock. Below this, a small engine room housed the generator. Carter was pretty sure it was where he would find gas canisters, and a spare battery too.

He pushed on, staggering and stumbling down the rocky slope to the entrance at the side of the station. Around the back, he could see a ramshackle maintenance shed and the burnt-out skeleton of an old snowmobile. Carter swallowed. He was sweating inside his snowsuit. He didn't want to do this. But he *needed* to. And not just because Miles would kill him if he failed.

The automatic doors to the entrance foyer were jammed half open. Carter propped the sled against the wall and peered inside. It was dark. Snow had drifted in, piling in the corners and coating the floor in slippery flakes. Carter could just make out a small, unused ticket desk, a row of fixed plastic seating and, ahead of him, a corridor that led further into the station. A dank smell drifted out, like bad drains.

Face those demons. All that shit.

Yeah, it really was shit.

Forcing down his trepidation, Carter stepped inside.

Meg

Sean walked ahead. Meg followed. She had let him take his gun back. She kept hers in her hand. They didn't know for sure that there wasn't a killer hiding out here. And they still didn't fully trust each other. *Who are you trying to save?* But he was all she had.

Sean pushed open an emergency exit door and they emerged back out into the freezing cold. It hadn't felt exactly toasty inside, but Meg had forgotten just how bitter that wind was up here on the mountainside. It grappled with them, snatching breath, clawing and tugging at their snowsuit-clad bodies as if trying to fling them from the mountain's rocky face.

Meg found herself wishing for diver's boots, weighted with concrete, to keep her planted firmly on the ground. She bowed her head, keeping close behind Sean, using him as a human shield as they rounded the corner.

Here, the wind abated, its fury muted by the grey hulk of the station building. Meg raised her head and saw that Sean had been telling the truth about one thing. A dirty red-and-blue snowmobile, a number '1' stencilled on the engine, squatted outside a small building with a sign that read *Maintenance*. They walked towards it.

'It's got petrol in it,' Sean said.

'How d'you know?'

'I checked.'

'So why are you still here?'

'Spot the problem.'

And Meg suddenly did. 'No ignition key.'

She glanced towards the maintenance shed. 'Have you searched inside?'

'No. I thought I'd go and have a beer and wait for a woman to come and suggest something obvious.'

'That's what men usually do.' Meg smiled sweetly at him. 'Couldn't hurt to look again though.'

She shoved the door open and stepped through.

The 'maintenance' shed was obviously a dumping ground for a lot of crap. Meg could see straight away what had become of snowmobiles 2 and 3. They had been stripped, various parts lying on a large worktable in the centre of the room, along with an assortment of tools. Either someone had been trying to repair them or to use the parts for something else.

Meg stared around. Maintenance uniforms and a couple of dirty ski jackets were hung on the walls, along with more tools. She patted down the pockets of the grubby clothing. Empty. To her right were two tall cupboards. Meg pulled the first open. Inside, two sets of skis and poles.

'Can you ski?' she asked Sean.

'Not well. You?'

'Pretty rubbish, but I might be able to make it a short distance without falling over.'

'As long as your destination is downhill.'

'Yeah. There is that.' She turned back to the cupboards. Sean propped himself on the other side of the worktable. 'You don't give up, do you?' he said.

'I thought I had. But I was wrong.'

She reached for the second cupboard and pulled the door open.

'Before you get your hopes up,' Sean said. 'It's not in there.'

Meg stared inside. Keys hung on labelled pegs: *Generator, Storage, Snow 2, Snow 3.* The final peg was empty: *Snow 1.*

Meg stared at it, something niggling in her mind. And then it came back to her. *Snow 1.* The keyring in her pocket. *Of course.*

'I've got it,' she said.

'What?'

She fumbled excitedly in her pocket. 'I took a keyring off the dead guy in the control room. I didn't realize what it was.'

'You've got the snowmobile key?'

'Yes!'

She turned. Her grin faded. Sean stood, his gun pointed at her chest.

'I knew you were worth waiting for.' He nodded at the gun in her hand. 'Put that down carefully on the worktable.'

Meg hesitated.

His face softened. 'Please.'

Reluctantly, she laid the gun on the table.

Sean held out his hand. 'Now give me the key.'

'You were never going to let me come with you, were you?' Meg said. 'It was just a ploy to get me off guard.'

'Pretty much.'

'And now you're going to kill me.'

'No. You give me the key. I'll tie you up in here so I can do what I need to. Then I'll come back.'

'If you don't get killed first.' Meg stared at him in despair. 'The Professor might already be dead, Sean. Have you thought of that? All of this could be for nothing.'

He nodded. 'True. But I made a promise to my

347

sister — and I have to keep it. Now give me the key.'

She tried again. 'Don't tie me up. I'll freeze in here. I can't come after you if you take the snowmobile. Please?'

Sean sighed. 'I'd like to agree, but you admitted it yourself — you don't give up. I think you'd still try to stop me.'

Meg stared at him, letting tears fill her eyes. 'Yeah.' Her shoulders slumped in defeat. '*Damn right.*'

She kicked out at the worktable. It tipped back, crashing into Sean, knocking him off balance. Her gun flew off the table and hit the floor. Meg grabbed it and bolted for the door, sprinting outside into the freezing air. She glanced to her right. The snowmobile. She ran towards it. A shot rang out behind her and something hit her in the shoulder, spinning her off balance. She fell to the ground, shoulder burning. *Shit.*

Sean emerged through the door. Ignoring the pain from her shoulder, Meg rolled and fired off a round. Wood splintered near his head.

'Fuck!' He ducked back inside.

Meg pushed herself to her feet and half ran, half staggered down the slope towards a thin copse of firs. She crouched behind one of the trees and peered around the trunk. She saw the shed door swing open, Sean using it as a shield.

'Meg!' he shouted. 'Don't be stupid. We shouldn't be fighting each other.'

'Okay!' she shouted back. 'Then let me take the snowmobile.'

'I've got a better idea. You let me take it and we might both get out of this alive.'

'No can do.'

'Why? You can't save Sarah, Meg. Even if you

could, your daughter is still dead.'

Anger rose in her throat. 'Fuck you. You think murdering another man will bring your sister back?'

'No, I think it will bring her justice. He deserves to pay.'

'And what if other people try to stop you? Are you going to kill them too? How many more have to die, so you can get justice?'

A long silence. Meg clutched her gun, fingers numb with cold. Her shoulder throbbed, blood seeping into her snowsuit. Too much blood. *Fuck*.

'Meg,' Sean said in a softer tone. 'If you try and make it to the snowmobile, you know I'll have to shoot you.'

'Ditto.'

She heard him laugh bitterly. 'So, this is stalemate.'

'Guess so.'

A long pause.

'What are we going to do about that?'

Meg stared at the maintenance shed, then back at the snowmobile.

Only one of them could make it. Or neither.

She made her decision. She stood, edged around the tree, aimed and fired. Twice.

The second bullet hit its target. The snowmobile's petrol tank exploded in an eardrum-rupturing burst of orange-and-blue flames. The force and heat, even at this distance, sent Meg staggering backwards, shielding her face. She felt her hair crisp. Shards of molten metal nicked her exposed skin. And then, a second eruption blew her off her feet completely.

Gravity snatched her, tipping her down the steep, snowy slope, rolling her faster and faster towards the edge of the mountain. Meg tried to turn and slow herself, digging in her heels, scrabbling for purchase in the snow. Her feet slid off the precipice just as her hands managed to grab at a small outcrop of rock.

Christ. She lay there for a moment, feet dangling in thin air. Then, cautiously, she clawed her way back from the edge. She glanced behind her. A sheer drop, and nothing but sky, the sun slowly sinking behind the mountains. It glinted off the roof of the stranded cable car in the distance. As Meg watched, she thought she saw a speck of darkness fall from the bottom. *Sarah?*

Meg felt something inside her ache and settle. She turned back. Her gun lay half buried in the snow. She picked it up and pushed herself to her feet. On shaky legs, she stood, braced against the wind, shoulder still throbbing, gun clutched in her hand. Ready.

Sean approached through the shimmering heat haze of the explosion. He looked different, face distorted by the haze, skin blackened by the smoke. He staggered down the slope and stopped a short distance away, panting, gun held loosely at his side.

He stared at her through red-rimmed eyes. 'Why? Why did you blow up our only chance of escape?'

'Someone had to stop you — from hurting anyone else.'

'Why the hell do you care?'

'Because . . .' Meg struggled to find the words, forcing them out against the wind and pain. 'Because caring is all we have left. If we stop caring — about life, about other people — who are we? What have we become?'

Sean shook his head. 'I always knew you were one of the good guys . . . I've got to tell you, it's a major pain in the ass.'

They looked at each other. One intent on death.

One on retribution. Perhaps it had always been going to end this way. In blood and bullets.

'You know you're going to bleed out if that shoulder doesn't get attention,' Sean said.

Meg nodded. 'And you're weak and exhausted. You're going to die of starvation and exposure on this mountainside before you get anywhere near the Retreat.'

'Guess we're both fucked then.'

'Guess so.'

His eyes found hers. 'I don't want to kill you, Meg.'

'I know.' She raised her gun. 'I wish I could say the same.'

Sean fired. Once, twice, three times. Meg felt the bullets pierce her body, little eruptions of fire. She smiled. Her feet lifted from the mountainside, and then she was falling. Falling and falling.

A hand caught hers.

She turned. Lily floated beside her. No longer in yellow but a shimmering dress of white snowflakes.

'It's okay, Mummy. I've got you.'

Meg squeezed her daughter's hand. 'I know, honey. And I won't ever let you go again.'

They pulled each other close. The sky rushed by. The world dissolved into white.

Meg buried her face in her daughter's soft curls.

'I'm sorry it took me so long,' she whispered. 'I just got a little stuck.'

Carter

He walked along the corridor, boots kicking up dust from the cracked and crumbling concrete floor. The waft of stale drains was coming from the toilets. He held his breath as he passed them.

Ahead of him, a faded and cracked sign on the wall read *Café and Viewing Deck*, with an arrow pointing straight on. A shorter corridor branched off to his right. He turned down it. Along this corridor there were two more doors. A sign on the first read *Staff Only, Restricted.*

Carter hesitated. The control room. He pushed the door open.

The small area had been trashed. Cables ripped out, wires hanging loose, computer monitors smashed. The bodies still sat in their seats at the control desk. Not that there was much left of them now. Empty eye sockets and lipless mouths gaped. Wisps of hair clung to yellowed skulls and skeletal fingers poked out of green jumpsuits. Ragged holes in the material bore testimony to how they had died, shot twice in the back.

Miles was a brutal and efficient executioner.

After the outbreak, he had trekked up to the station to prevent anyone else from reaching the Retreat. The crew were unaware of the situation. A storm had interrupted communications. Miles had ended them permanently. Then he had sabotaged the cable car that was already on its way, leaving everyone inside to die.

But he had come back a few days later . . . and

352

saved Carter's life.

Miles had found him, lying face down in the snow, collapsed from hypothermia and exhaustion, near to death. For some reason, Miles had dragged him back to the Retreat. Why? Carter would never really know. Miles only ever said: 'You looked like a survivor. Survivors are useful.'

Carter had spent those weeks recovering from frostbite and hypothermia in one of the isolation chambers at the Retreat. Miles had saved his life but, even with his medical knowledge, there was little he could do for Carter's face.

For a while Carter had worn a surgical mask to cover the worst of his mutilation. Gradually, he began to take it off more often. The others in the Retreat stopped recoiling at the sight of his face. And eventually, so did he.

Carter gave the long-dead crew a final glance then walked out into the corridor. He turned and followed the signs for the café and viewing deck. At the end of the corridor he pushed open the double doors.

The spectacular view was more muted these days, the wall of curved glass coated in layers of grime. Exploded bottles in the defunct fridge lent a ripe, wheaty smell to the air. Carter negotiated his way past the stacked tables and chairs, stepping over a broken beer bottle, and stood in front of the dirty window.

The cable car still hung there. Blood red against the whiteout of the sky. Rusted, battered by the storms . . . no more than a carcass. But clinging on. Like him. A survivor.

Behind him, a boot crunched on glass.

Slowly, he turned . . .

'Returning to the scene of the crime, Sean?'

Carter

She looked just like he remembered her: dark hair tangled, face bloodied but determined. More blood stained her blue snowsuit. In several places there were ragged holes where his bullets had penetrated the fabric.

'I really didn't want to kill you.'

Meg shrugged. *'If it's any consolation, it was you or me.'*

'Yeah.'

'And it should have been me, obviously.'

'You were one of the good guys.'

'But not a survivor.'

'You wanted to stop me. I had to find him.'

'And you have, so what now?'

'I'm going to kill him.'

'And then? Where does it end?'

'When he's dead.'

She smiled sadly. *'You keep telling yourself that, Sean.'*

And then she was gone, dissolving into dust that drifted down to the floor. Nothing left of her now, except in his mind, where she lived with the others: Peggy, Hannah, Lucas, Anya — and more. There were always more. A lot of blood under the bridge.

After Meg had died, he had considered, for the briefest moment, following her over the precipice. But the survival instinct was too strong, the need to finish what he had started too great. He had come this far. If the road to hell is paved with good intentions, it's also a one-way street. No going back.

354

He had staggered back up the mountainside and into the maintenance shed. The cold was already biting through his snowsuit. He knew he would need extra layers if he was to stand a chance of making it. He had grabbed one of one of the grubby ski jackets off the hook and shrugged it on. A name had been sewn into the lapel.

P. Carter.

At some point, after his rescue, Miles had asked what the 'P' stood for.

He had smiled. 'Doesn't matter. Most people just call me Carter.'

A new name, another new life. But one thing didn't change. His desire for revenge.

Carter had been patient. Prison had taught him that. He had bided his time, recuperating, regaining his strength, learning to live with what remained of his face. He had found out all he could about the Retreat, tried to make himself useful, to earn Miles's trust.

And it had worked.

Eventually, Miles had told him the truth about Isolation Chamber 13.

Unlucky for some. But for Carter it held a certain serendipity.

Because Carter had waited thirteen years to kill the man held inside.

And now, it was almost time.

The Devil Was an Angel Once

1

The light was failing by the time Carter reached the Retreat compound, dragging the generator, battery and two gas canisters on the sled behind him.

He was sweating inside his snowsuit and his chest felt tight, probably from the exertion and altitude. He was struggling to catch his breath. His legs trembled as he staggered the last half mile. It didn't help that the wind was getting up once again, snowflakes swirling around his face. A fresh storm was coming.

As Carter reached the gate, something cracked under his foot. He looked down. The old sign. It had come off its hook and lay half submerged in the snow. Carter crouched down and picked it up:

THE RETREAT
Property of D.R.I.F.T
(Department of Research into Infection and Future
Transmission)

Carter stared at the battered sign. Then he drew back his arm and threw it as far away as he could. Man, he hated fucking acronyms.

He trudged up to the door and tapped in the code. It didn't open. He tried again. The door still wouldn't budge. He yanked off his gloves with his teeth and tapped the pad once more, in case he had somehow got it wrong. The door remained locked. *What the fuck?* Carter glared at the pad, like it was deliberately screwing with him. A power problem again? But that usually *released* the locks. Unless Welland had messed something up, which was a high possibility. In irritation, Carter hammered at the door with his fists.

'Hey! Welland! Miles! The pad's bust. Can you let me in?'

He waited. Nothing. The door was thick. Maybe they were both in the basement or in another part of the Retreat. Carter cursed and kicked at the door. Fuck. He stepped back and looked around. He was tired and hungry. He needed to get inside. But the Retreat was secure. No way to break in, or out.

Carter stomped around to the front. He could see the shimmering blue of the swimming pool through the plate-glass window. Above it, the decking area and huge curved glass window of the living area. He took several steps back and craned his neck up. He couldn't really see inside the living area but . . . he frowned. *Were there lights on in there?* Yes. Definitely. Which must mean that the power was back or Welland had fixed the generator. Either way, if the power was on, why wasn't the front door opening?

Carter walked back around and stared at the door. Really, there was only one other explanation. Someone had changed the code. He hammered at the door again, for several seconds, yelling and kicking at it, loud enough to 'wake the dead', as his grandad used to say. Still no response from within.

'Fuck this.'

He stood back, pulled out his gun and fired into the security pad. The plastic jumped off; the electric wires sparked. Carter shoved at the door. This time it opened. Carter entered the hallway, gun still drawn. Empty. Silent. He pushed the door shut with his foot.

If he had made a mistake, there would be hell to pay from Miles for fucking up the front door, but Carter didn't think he had. Something here was wrong. Carter could almost taste the wrongness in the air.

He yanked off his goggles and mask, kicked off his boots and quietly unzipped his suit, shedding it on the floor, all the time keeping his gun steady in one hand. He padded across to the stairs and up the spiral staircase, trying not to breathe too hard. At the top he looked around, gun held out in front of him. Carter's heart leapfrogged into his mouth. *Fuck.*

A body lay, face down, in the middle of the living area. Bulky, dressed in a heavily blood-stained T-shirt and baggy jeans, a cloud of frizzy hair sticking up, more blood pooling underneath him.

Welland.

It looked like he had been shot multiple times. Carter had often wished for this moment, but now, staring at Welland's body, he didn't feel any satisfaction. Just pity. And puzzlement. Only one person could be responsible. But why?

Had Miles discovered that Welland had been down in the chambers? Killing him for that seemed extreme, even for Miles. Perhaps Welland had attacked Miles and he'd been forced to shoot him in self-defence. But then, you don't usually shoot someone in the back if it's self-defence. And if Miles *had* killed Welland, why just leave him lying up here? Miles hated a mess.

Carter frowned. This wasn't right. And there was another thing he was missing. Dexter. Where was the little dog? Carter had a very, *very* bad feeling about this.

He turned and padded back down the stairs. He considered checking the pool area, but in his gut he knew where he would find Miles. Down in the basement.

Carter walked over to the elevator. But he didn't press the button right away. Doubt remained. Did he really want to do this? Maybe he should just get the hell out of this place, while he still could. But where would be go? Quinn was hardly going to help him get away and Carter didn't want to take his chances out there with the Whistlers and whatever else roamed in the wilds.

There was only one way.

And it sure as hell wasn't up.

Carter called the elevator. The doors opened right away. He stepped inside and took out his own pass from the hidden pocket in his jeans. He pressed it against the panel. The elevator slid smoothly down. His heart pounded. The doors opened.

Gun drawn, Carter stepped into the familiar chill of the corridor. The lighting was back on. Bright, white, sterile. It made him feel exposed. He walked cautiously forward, poking his head into the rooms as he passed. Empty, empty, empty. As he neared the end of the corridor, he realized he could hear a noise. An odd, grunting sound. Even from a distance it made his stomach churn. Carter rounded the corner and stopped. The door to the isolation chambers was still open. The noise was coming from within there.

Carter tightened his grip on the gun, advancing slowly, heart hammering. He reached the entrance. From here, he could see that the doors to all the chambers were open again. *Fuck*. What the hell was going on with the system controls? Was *that* why Miles had killed Welland? To override them?

He stepped inside. The guttural sound was louder.

And familiar. Carter could see that Chamber 3 was empty. He approached Chamber 4 with a sick feeling and stared inside.

Caren lay on the bed, sedated, barely conscious. Her jumpsuit had been yanked down to her knees and Supply 03 lay on top of her, his own baggy blue jumpsuit around his ankles, snow-white buttocks pumping up and down energetically.

Carter didn't wait, didn't think. He strode over, grabbed 03 by his greasy hair and dragged him off, throwing him to the floor. 03 screamed in impotent rage. Carter raised his gun and shot him in the crotch. 03 howled and writhed, clutching at the bloody mess between his legs.

'Yeah? How d'you like that for kicks, you sick bastard!!' Carter fired again and took out 03's left kneecap, then his right.

Supply 03 wailed and screamed. Blood spurted from his pulverized knees, pooling on the floor. He would bleed out in agony. With any luck.

Carter walked over to Caren. He grabbed a blanket from the end of the bed and covered her body. Her eyes flickered. Her breathing was ragged. Her skin already looked pale.

Carter stroked her hair. 'It's going to be okay. I'm going to take care of this.'

But if he did, it really was over. No more supplies. For them. Or Quinn.

Fuck it.

Carter placed the muzzle of the gun gently against Caren's head and pulled the trigger.

Then, he turned, kicked 03 in the crotch and walked back out into the corridor.

Only one chamber left.

363

Carter had never seen inside Isolation Chamber 13 before. The door was the only one not made of glass. Instead, it was smooth and white, set seamlessly into the wall. If you didn't know it was there, you would never find it. An entrance keypad was similarly well hidden. Like the other chambers, only Miles had the code, and he changed it regularly.

The inhabitant of Chamber 13 wasn't infected or dangerous. But he was valuable. A brilliant, ruthless genius. A man who believed he could save the world, and that those who got in his way were collateral damage. Like his own daughter. And Carter's sister. A man who was as despised as he was revered.

Professor Stephen Grant.

The world believed he was dead.

But Carter knew differently.

The door to Chamber 13 was open. Carter stepped inside. A large double bed faced him. To his right was a small, separate bathroom. To his left, a large book-case and a small desk, lit by a single lamp. A figure sat at the desk. Carter could make out only a silhouette and a bald head, gleaming in the light.

He raised his gun, taking aim with both hands.

'Turn the fuck around, Grant. I want you to see the person who is going to kill you.'

Slowly, the chair swivelled around.

Carter stared at the man sitting in it. Shaven-headed, dressed in a clean blue jumpsuit, pointing a gun right back at Carter.

'Hey, man.' Welland grinned. 'Snap.'

2

Carter gaped. 'You're not dead.'

'Man, you are observant.'

'But . . .' *The body. The clothes . . .* 'The hair.'

Welland ran a hand over his freshly shaved dome. 'Yeah. Fooled ya, right?' He giggled. 'Man, I wish I could have seen your face when you found Miles.'

'That was . . . *Miles*?'

'Yup. Dumped my hair on his head. Padded him out with cushions and dressed him in my old clothes.'

'Why the fuck would you do that?'

A shrug. 'I thought it would be funny . . . kind of a welcome-home present.'

'But . . . you changed the lock code to keep me out.'

'Yeah, but I figured you'd still get in somehow. You're fucking persistent like that.' Welland grinned. 'And I like that about you, man. I really do. You don't give up. Even with that abomination of a face, you're still here, like a fourth-rate Freddy Krueger.'

Carter continued to gape, mind struggling to get with the programme. 'I don't understand. Why did you kill Miles?'

'Why not? I'd waited long enough.'

'What for?'

Welland shook his head. 'You really don't get it?'

Carter needed to make up some ground here. 'I get that you're a liar,' he said. 'You told everyone you worked here in maintenance. But you were just a cleaner.'

The grin faltered. 'How did you know that?'

'I found your lanyard, with your old name — Barry Coombes. I guess you must have tried to dispose of it at some point.'

Welland nodded slowly. Then his grin widened again. 'Yeah. Funny story, man. I got the job here just before the outbreak. When I arrived, the cleaners' overalls they'd got me didn't fit, so I borrowed a pair from a guy in maintenance: Welland. Nice guy — a Whistler ripped out his throat. Anyway, they liked to colour-code us here. Guinea pigs in blue, nurses in light green, doctors in white, cleaners in grey and maintenance in dark green. When the shit hit the fan, I hid out in the utility room. Miles found me there, put a gun to my head and asked if I could keep this place running. What was I gonna say? I said yes — and learned fucking fast.'

'And the name change?'

A shrug. 'I always fucking hated Barry.'

Carter stared at Welland. Simple as that. Just the wrong overalls. But then, as he knew himself, most best laid plans were usually just dumb fucking luck. 'That's why you couldn't fix the power when it started to fail,' he said. 'You didn't know enough about the systems.' 'I knew some stuff. I mean, I fooled you suckers for long enough.'

And now, something else started to make sense. Julia.

'Is that why you killed Julia? Did she come down here when the power failed? Did she find you out?' 'Yeah,' Welland nodded. 'That was a shame. I liked Julia. Nice tits.'

Carter frowned. 'But there was no blood?'

'Overalls, man. I always kept a set in the utility. I

366

put them on, dumped Julia in the pool, mopped up and changed. Stuffed the dirty overalls behind some shit in the utility till I could dump them. I thought I'd have to try and pin her death on one of you, but then all hell broke loose.'

'And the knife?'

'Miles wouldn't let me have a gun. Thought I was too pathetic to handle one. So, I kept a knife.' He looked at Carter slyly. 'Man, I cannot tell you how often I considered stabbing you all in your sleep . . . but Miles is a pretty light sleeper. I wasn't sure I'd finish the job without getting shot.'

'And we all lock our doors.'

'Sweet how you thought that kept you safe.'

'What d'you mean?'

'I may only have been a cleaner, but I watched, and I learned. Dreyfuss, the head maintenance guy, kept a book with all the default system codes in. He wasn't supposed to, but he liked a drink and had a shit memory. After he died, I stole it. I could walk into your rooms any time I wanted.' Welland winked. 'And believe me, I did.'

Carter swallowed. 'And that's how you got into the isolation chambers too.'

A flicker of surprise. 'You knew that?'

'Caren saw you.'

'Ah, sneaky little Caren with a C. Not so high and mighty now.'

'She's dead.'

'Damn. She had a great ass.'

Carter felt his revulsion rise. 'Your empathy is commendable.'

Welland's face darkened. 'Hey, don't play the good guy with me. I know about you, Carter. I know about all of you. Man, you're so fucking dumb. Saving your personal stuff in your 'secret hideaways'. Even Miles. Did you know Miles killed over twenty patients when he was a doctor? Kept his own press stories. Oh, and your good pal, Nate — he liked 'em young. Real young. Found the pictures. Julia cut herself. Caren took laxatives. And I know that Jackson was arranging for his Rem friends to come up here and take the Professor . . .' Welland nodded at Carter's shocked gaze. 'Yeah, I know all about the Professor. The great genius who just disappeared, presumed dead. But *we* know where he ended up, right?'

He held his arms out wide. Carter just stared at him.

'Hey, don't be coy, man,' Welland said. 'You wanted to get inside 13 as much as me. And your reasons are far more noble, man. The whole avenging your sister's death stuff —'

'You know about Peggy?'

'I told you. I watched and listened. I found your photo, saw your tattoo. Plus' — Welland lowered his voice to a whisper — 'you talk in your sleep.' He chuckled. 'And believe me, that motive has some heart. I mean, sounds like you killed some folk along the way, but you did it out of love. If this was a movie, people would forgive you. Everyone loves an anti-hero, although it usually helps if they look like Brad Pitt and not some fucked-face freak like you.'

Another wild giggle. Carter realized he had got Welland wrong. He had always thought he was a selfish, good-for-nothing sack of shit. Now he was pretty sure Welland was totally fucking insane.

'So we're both here for the Professor,' he said.

'Like I told you — snap.'

'So, where is he?'

'Playing Hide and Seek.'

'Seriously,' Carter said. 'What did you do with him?'

'Nothing. That's the joke. And it's on us.'

Carter tried to batten down his anger. He needed to keep calm. 'What the hell are you talking about?'

Welland sighed. 'He isn't here. No one has ever been in here. Look.' He picked up a notebook from the desk and blew off dust. 'This place has been empty for fucking years.'

Carter walked forward and brushed a hand over the bed cover. Not a crease. And coated in more fine dust. A hollow opened up in his stomach.

'Empty. All this time?'

'Yeah. Miles lied. How 'bout that?'

Carter let this sink in. 'Miles used to come down here, bring food and water.'

'Guess he washed it all down the toilet.'

Carter's legs felt weak. 'Grant was *here*. At the Retreat. Before the outbreak. I know it.'

Welland shrugged. 'Maybe he was. I never saw him. Guess he's dead now.'

'So why did Miles keep up the pretence? Why tell us he was keeping him a prisoner here?'

'Because it suited him,' Welland said, as if it was obvious. 'He knew the Prof was the ultimate bargaining chip. Lots of people want to get their hands on him, for a lot of different reasons. He didn't want any of us ruining his fall-back plan.'

It made sense. Knowing Miles.

'And what did you want with the Professor?' Carter asked Welland.

'He was my ticket out of here, man. Once I found Jackson's phone and knew what he and his Rem friends were up to, I went to talk to him. Caught him coming back from an early-morning run. I told Jackson I knew what was going on. I reckoned we could make a deal, help each other out.'

'But Jackson wasn't buying it?'

'No.' Welland looked affronted. 'He attacked me. I mean, I had to defend myself. It was self-defence.'

Something began to register. 'You killed Jackson,' Carter said.

'It was him or me, man.'

'Yeah. That sounds familiar.'

'I dragged his body down to the woods,' Welland continued. 'I figured the animals would soon get him, or the Whistlers.'

'He wasn't dead.'

'He's alive?'

'Not any more. I shot him.'

Welland chuckled. 'See, you and me, we're a lot alike.'

'We're nothing alike,' Carter said, feeling the lie catch at the back of his throat.

And there was something else, niggling at the back of his mind, but he couldn't think what.

'So, with Jackson out of the way, you decided to deal with the Rems yourself?'

'Yeah.' Welland nodded. 'I deliver the Professor in return for a safe passage out of here, and a nice wad of cash.'

So the final the call on Jackson's phone had been made by Welland, after Jackson was dead.

'Why leave the phone hidden in the shower pipe?' Carter asked.

'Safest place. Only I knew it was there . . . and if anyone else did find it, Jackson would get the blame.'

Little fucker thought of everything.

'And how did you plan to get to the Professor?' Carter asked.

Welland leaned slightly forward. 'You all thought I was so stupid not fixing the lags . . . but I didn't *want* to fix them. I figured if the lags got worse, the automatic locks would release, and I could get inside 13. You see, 13 was the only chamber that I didn't have an override code for.'

Carter thought about this. 'But it didn't work out like that. Because 13 is also the only chamber that doesn't open if the power cuts. It has a back-up battery. Miles checked it every day.'

Welland shook his bald head. 'I gotta tell you that was a bummer. Fortunately, the shit that went down from the supplies getting loose took care of a lot of my problems. Caren getting herself infected was the icing on the cake. I *knew*, when you left for the cable-car station, it was a perfect opportunity.'

'Make Miles give you the codes, kill him and get inside 13.'

'Bam! Cool, huh?'

'Except, you don't have your prize.' Carter smiled. 'And when the Rems get here you won't have anything to give them, which, I'm guessing, they're not going to be happy bunnies about.'

Welland's face crumpled like a petulant toddler's. 'Fuck Miles. I should have known he'd given up the code too easily. If I hadn't already killed the fucker, I'd go and kill him again . . . and do it slowly this time.'

Carter's mind was ticking over. He detested Welland. He was a psychopathic fucker. But right now, it looked like they had other problems.

'When are the Rems getting here, Welland?'

'Well . . . the storm probably slowed them up a bit —'

'*Welland?*'

'Any time now.'

'*Shit.* We need to get out of here.'

Welland's eyebrows raised. 'We?'

'I suggest,' Carter said steadily, 'that for the moment we put our homicidal feelings for each other on the back-burner and concentrate on getting out of this alive.'

Welland considered. 'Yeah — you might be right.'

They looked at each other and both lowered their guns.

'Okay,' Carter said. 'The electric fence is bust.'

'But the building is secure.'

'Not really. I shot the lock out of the front door.'

'Fuck, man! So, the Rems can just walk in?'

'Unless we stop them.'

'We could just stay down here,' Welland suggested. 'We're safe here.'

'For how long? How long before they override the elevator controls?'

Welland shrugged. 'I don't know. I was just a cleaner.'

Carter took a deep breath. 'Let's go.'

Welland still looked doubtful. 'I'm not sure.'

'Fine. While you sit down here and jerk off, I'm going to try and save my ass.'

He headed for the door.

'Wait!'

He turned. Welland looked down at his gun. Then he stuffed it into the back pocket of his jumpsuit. 'I can't believe I killed everyone but you.'

3

They hurried down the corridor, past the isolation chambers, the labs and offices and into the elevator. Carter hit the 'up' button. When the doors opened at the top, they both drew their guns. And now Carter could hear something. Distant, but growing closer. They locked eyes. A helicopter.

'Guess they're right on time,' Welland said.

'Shit.' Carter ran up the stairs to the living area, Welland puffing behind him. The huge picture window revealed nothing but flat grey sky and snowy mountains. But the whirring was louder now. Really loud. Almost right overhead. Carter stepped closer to the window, staring out. He raised his eyes.

The grey bulk of the helicopter swooped down in front of the glass.

For a fraction of a second it hung there, like a giant grey bird. The pilot lifted his hand.

'Hey,' Welland said. 'He's waving. Maybe —'

'Hit the ground!' Carter yelled.

They threw themselves to the floor as gunfire exploded from the chopper and the picture window shattered inwards, raining a tsunami of glass down on them.

'Christ!' Carter threw his hands over his head but still felt the sting of the razor-sharp slivers.

'Fuck, fuck, fuck,' Welland wailed.

'Run. Now!' Carter told him.

Without waiting to see if Welland had heard,

Carter scrambled to his feet and ran for the stairs. More gunfire roared. He smelt the burn of cordite, winced as broken glass crunched under his feet and sliced through his socks. As he charged down the staircase, he almost slipped on his own blood.

Welland half ran, half fell down the stairs behind him. 'What the hell do we do?' he whined as they reached the hall.

Carter turned. Welland's bald head was speckled with shards of glass. Like a cut-rate Hellraiser.

'We get the fuck out of here,' Carter said.

'But we won't survive out there.'

'And we'll die in here.'

Carter grabbed his boots, tugging them on and wincing in pain from his lacerated feet. He thought about the chopper. The pilot dressed in green combats. The guns. He swallowed, a brutal realization fighting its way to the surface.

'They're not Rems, Welland.' He grabbed his padded coat. No time to clamber into his snowsuit.

'What?' Welland looked confused and panicked.

'Jackson wasn't a Rem,' Carter said. 'Or if he was, he was double-crossed. Those fuckers are Department.'

'DRIFT?'

'Got it in one.'

Which meant they weren't here to negotiate, or to bargain. They were here to get the Professor and kill everyone else. Carter grabbed a jacket off the rack and threw it at Welland.

'Stay close to the building. We'll head around the back. Hide out in the woods. Pray they don't find us.'

Carter yanked the door open. Too late. The helicopter had settled on a flat area just outside the

374

electric fence. The whirring blades died with a low whine. Three guys in combats were already out of the chopper and running towards them. They all held machine guns. Shit.

Carter looked at his handgun. It might as well have been a water pistol. They'd never make it around the back of the building without getting cut down.

'We're fucking dead,' Welland muttered.

For once, Carter didn't disagree.

He started to raise his hands. And then he heard something else. The high-pitched whine of engines. He turned. Three snowmobiles sped up the mountainside. Jimmy Quinn and his sons. They must have seen the helicopter fly in and realized they were about to lose their golden goose.

The snowmobiles skidded up to the chopper, spitting out snow and machine gun fire. Two of the Department guys staggered, chests blooming red, and crumpled to the snow. The third fired back, hitting one of Quinn's sons, who toppled from the snowmobile. It spun around in circles, riderless, knocking him down as he tried to get up. Another burst of gunfire kept him down for good, soaking the snow crimson.

Carter and Welland crouched beside the door, not daring to move as bullets sprayed the air. More armed men jumped from the chopper. Quinn howled and bombarded them with gunfire, hitting one in the back. Son number 2 jumped from his snowmobile and blew the head off a second, whooping in triumph. His victory was short-lived. A burst of heavy ammo from the helicopter guns lifted him up, legs jittering, and opened up his torso like a piñata. His guts spilt out in a steaming lump and he fell to the ground.

After this, the pilot had obviously had enough. The

blades whirred. The chopper started to rise. Quinn ran after it, still firing manically, his gun spitting out bullets. They sparked off the blades. The whirring slowed. The chopper tilted in the air, rising and dipping as the pilot desperately tried to maintain control. Then, with an ear-shredding mechanical squeal, the blades stuttered and stilled. The chopper started to spiral, faster and faster, before crashing back into the mountainside and bursting into flames.

Carter ducked his head and threw up an arm to shield his face from the heat of the blast, still hot enough to make his hair crisp from several metres away. After a few seconds, when he didn't think his eyeballs might melt, he lowered his arm and looked up.

Just one man was still standing. White snowsuit flecked with red spots. Fur hood pulled up over his head. Orange snow goggles like giant insect eyes. Jimmy Quinn.

He strode through the carnage, stepping over bodies, machine gun held aloft. Flames and smoke rose into the air around him.

'Shit,' Carter muttered, wondering why the hell they hadn't run when they had the chance.

Quinn stepped through the gate and pulled back his hood. 'Lose the guns, lads.'

Dutifully, because they didn't have much choice, Carter and Welland chucked their weapons into the snow.

Quinn nodded. 'Where's Miles?'

'He's dead,' Welland whimpered.

'Good. Saves me the fucking trouble of killing him.'

'Mr Quinn —' Carter started to say.

'*Shut the fuck up!*'

Carter shut his jaw with a snap.

Quinn regarded them grimly. 'We had a deal. You give me the plasma. I let you live here quietly. In peace.'

'I know —'

'Does this look fucking *peaceful* to you, Carter?'

Carter shook his head. 'No —'

'You brought the Department *here*. To *my* fucking door. And now my sons are dead.'

'I'm sorry,' Carter cried desperately. 'If you just give us another chance —'

'You want another chance' — Quinn raised his gun — 'pray for reincarnation.'

The sound of a shot echoed in the air. Blood and brain matter exploded from the centre of Quinn's forehead. His eyes widened in surprise, then he dropped to his knees and toppled forward, falling face first into the snow.

A blackened and burnt figure stood behind Quinn's fallen body. The helicopter pilot. Or what remained of him. Smoke rose from his crisped and charred skin. Even from this distance, Carter could smell the sickly-sweet aroma of cooked flesh.

'Jesus,' Welland moaned. 'He looks like a fucking hog roast.'

As they watched, the pilot raised his gun and aimed it at his own head. He pulled the trigger. A dry click. He tried again. His eyes found Carter's. They stared out desperately from his melted, featureless face.

'Shoot him,' Carter said to Welland.

'What?'

'Do something good for once in your life. Shoot him.'

Welland reached forward and picked up his gun.

He aimed and fired once. It hit the pilot in the chest. He staggered but didn't fall.

'Again.'

The second shot took the pilot down. He twitched and then lay still.

Welland sniffed. 'That was brutal.'

'Yeah,' Carter nodded. 'One word for it.'

He picked up his own gun and tucked it into his belt. They stared around. A dozen bodies lay scattered in the snow, staining it crimson. The smell of blood, gunpowder and hot metal clogged Carter's nostrils. A thick plume of black rose from the stricken chopper and the burning engine oil had melted half of the mountainside back to green. The air shimmered with heat. After the drone of helicopter blades and the roar of gunfire, the silence was deafening.

'What do we do now, man?' Welland asked.

'Okay.' Carter took several deep breaths, trying to think. 'First — we need to get rid of these bodies. They'll attract predators. The incinerator is going to be working overtime.'

'Yeah.' Welland scratched awkwardly at his head. 'About that.'

'About what?' Carter snapped.

'The incinerator isn't working.'

'It *what* now?'

'It's a heap of junk. Dreyfuss always said so.'

Carter tried to keep his voice steady. 'And when did it *stop* working?'

Welland looked thoughtful. 'Well, it's more like it never really *started* working — not properly. I mean, it chucked out a bit of smoke but burning bodies, nah.'

'*What?*' The anger caught in Carter's throat. 'So what the hell did you do with the bodies?'

'Just dumped them. Out in the woods, around the back of the incinerator. None of you guys ever went out there, not even Miles. He didn't like to get his hands dirty. I figured animals would eat them or they'd rot eventually, right?'

For a moment, Carter wondered if he had misheard. 'You've been dumping *infected* bodies out in the woods ever since the takeover?'

'Yeah. Pretty much.'

And that explained the lanyards. The Whistlers must have found them. Was that what they'd been trying to tell him? That the bodies were out there. A risk to all of them. Had they been trying . . . to help them?

'What about the six degrees of infection?' he asked Welland.

Welland rolled his eyes. 'What's the worst that could happen? Some wolf or bear eats the bodies and then some hunter kills them and eats the meat. They die. Big deal.'

'*Or* they sell it to Quinn,' Carter said. 'We bought meat from Quinn, Welland.'

He shrugged. 'I know. That's why I'm vegetarian, man.' He pulled a face. 'Although soya *does* really give me gas.'

Carter stared at him. He could feel the fury boiling inside.

'What?' Welland asked.

Carter shook his head. 'I guess it's only just sinking in that it's just the two of us now. Stuck here. Together. For however long.'

'Yeah.'

A pause. They looked at each other and both reached for their guns at the same time.

Welland got there first. He pointed the barrel in

379

Carter's face. 'Guess this place isn't big enough for the both of us.'

'Guess not.'

'I just want you to know, before I kill you — you're *fucking* ugly, man.'

'Thanks.'

Welland pulled the trigger. Carter closed his eyes.

Nothing happened. He opened them again.

Welland yanked on the trigger again and again. Nothing but empty clicks.

'What the —'

Carter smiled. 'I guessed that you put at least four shots in Miles's back. You just wasted your final two on the burnt guy.'

Welland's lip wobbled, realization sinking in. 'No. Please. Don't kill me, man. We can work together. I can be useful.'

Carter considered. 'I suppose you could be. But here's the thing' — he pointed his gun at Welland — 'I really fucking hate your guts, *man*.'

He shot him in the face. Welland's brains exited messily out of the back of his skull. He landed with a heavy thud on the ground.

Carter let out a long breath. He'd wanted to do that for three years. Now, after all that had happened, surrounded by all this death and destruction . . . it still felt pretty damn good.

He looked back at the carnage. What a fucking mess. Without the incinerator, he couldn't get rid of all these bodies. And leaving corpses lying around was just inviting trouble. Wolves, bears, Whistlers. Carter could probably set up the generator himself, get the power back, maybe even get the electric fence up and running. But with the window blown out, the Retreat was still vulnerable. How long before more Department choppers came, or more of Quinn's cronies?

No. He couldn't stay here. But where could he go?

And then it came to him. The cable-car station.

It had shelter, facilities. If he took the generator and the battery back with him, it had power. Carter could certainly camp out there for a while. Something else occurred to him. The Quinns' snowmobiles. He had transport. That would make getting there a hell of a lot easier. Maybe he could make it even further. Carter had heard rumours that there were some remote settlements that had stayed infection-free. It was a possibility. There were always possibilities. You just had to look for them. Luck and ruthlessness had got him this far. Maybe it could take him further. Maybe even back to Eva.

'I guess we had a good run, right?' Carter looked down at Welland. 'But new beginnings and all that. Just me, myself and I again.'

He chuckled. And then he heard a noise. A bark. Carter turned just as a brown-and-white bundle of fur came careering out of the Retreat.

'Dexter!' Carter grinned. 'I thought you'd run away. You've been hiding inside? I don't blame you. Come here.'

The little dog leapt up into his arms, slathering his face with wet, smelly licks. Carter laughed and grimaced at the same time. 'Man, your breath isn't getting any better, but right now, you're the best god-damn thing I ever smelt.'

Dexter wagged his tail furiously, body wriggling wildly from side to side. 'Okay, okay. Calm it down, buddy.' Carter dropped him to the ground. 'C'mon. Let's go get our stuff.'

Dexter whined and trotted a short distance away, looking at Carter expectantly. Carter raised his eyebrows. '*Really?* You need to go for a walk right now?'

Dexter ran towards the fence and back again. Another whine.

Carter shook his head. 'Okay, fine. Let's take a stroll.'

Dexter barked and ran off around the side of the Retreat. Carter crunched wearily through the snow after him. The air was still ripe with the smell of ammunition, heat and death. And yet, overhead, he could see patches of blue between the clouds. The air felt a little warmer. It even seemed like the snow might be softening beneath his boots. *After the storm, the thaw*, he thought.

He rounded the corner of the building and looked for Dexter. He realized he couldn't see him.

He called out: 'Dexter?'

Nothing. He looked down. Dexter's paw prints tracked to the boundary fence, where they suddenly stopped. Weird. Carter crouched down. Closer now, he saw it. There was a hole in the fence. Small, but big enough for Dexter to wiggle through. *Damn.* Dexter had been sneaking out.

'Dexter?' Carter called again, and heard a distant bark from the direction of the trees. He rolled his eyes. 'Yeah, I'll just come to you, right?'

He got up, let himself out of the back gate and traipsed into the woods. It felt darker within their pungent folds. He picked his way along the rough path, breathing heavily. As the trunks of the pines thinned into a clearing, Carter could see the ominous grey oblong of the incinerator directly ahead of him.

This was the closest he had ever been to it. Welland was right. None of them ever came out here.

Why would they? There was plenty of space within the Retreat. Who the hell wanted to stroll around the place where they burnt the bodies?

Except Welland *hadn't* burnt the bodies.

Carter stopped. He had a bad feeling. Or maybe that was just because he could *smell* something bad. Sweet and slightly rancid. Rotting flesh. He heard rustling and jumped. A flash of white and Dexter bounded out of the undergrowth.

Carter let out a shaky laugh which turned into a cough. Probably the fucking pine. Getting in his throat. 'Way to go, Dexter,' he croaked. 'Give me a fucking heart attack.'

Dexter barked and dropped something on the ground.

'What you got there, boy?'

Carter stepped forward. Dexter immediately snatched his exciting discovery — probably a shitty stick or a dead animal — back up.

Carter frowned. 'No, man. I'm not chasing you for it. Drop.'

Dexter bared his teeth.

'Hey,' Carter instructed more firmly. 'Drop it. Now.'

Dexter eyed him sulkily and then, with a snort, dropped his prize. Carter bent down . . . and immediately recoiled. '*Jeesus!*'

A human hand. Mostly skeletal, with a few stringy bits of flesh and muscle attached.

Before Carter could pick it up Dexter grabbed the hand and scampered off, back through the undergrowth. *Dammit.* Carter followed, dodging trees, pushing through brambles and sharp, spiky bushes. He was sweating inside the thick coat and struggling to catch his breath. Maybe he should have hit the gym more, like Caren with a C. Should have done a lot of things. *Shoulda, coulda. Don't mean shit. Didn't anyone tell you, Carter? The devil was an angel once.*

He burst through a thick clump of undergrowth. The incinerator loomed in front of him. A large grey metal box, tall chimney pipe sticking out of the top. Dexter darted down the side and disappeared around the back. Carter paused, then traipsed, reluctantly, after him.

Behind the incinerator, the ground dipped away into a natural hollow. The rancid smell was worse back here. Much, much worse. Dexter looked back at Carter, panting happily, and then scrambled down into the dip.

Carter pulled his jacket up over his nose and mouth, guts churning. On heavy legs, he walked to the edge of the hollow. He peered down.

Branches had been dragged over the shallow grave to try and disguise it. But Carter could still make out the jumble of rotting corpses. Some, like Nate and Julia, were just about recognizable. Others were barely more than skeletons, yellowed bones and leering skulls, wrapped up in tattered rags.

This was where Welland had dumped them.

'*Out in the woods, round the back of the incinerator.*'

What the hell had he been thinking? *Six fucking degrees*. Christ, even Carter knew the risks infected bodies posed, and Welland must have dumped, what? A dozen or more out here. How long did they remain infectious? How long could the virus live on in a plague pit like this?

As Carter stared at the bodies, Julia's arm twitched. Carter leapt backwards, swallowing a scream. Dexter emerged from under her armpit, dragging a foot.

Then he lay down and started gnawing happily on the rotting toes.

Carter's stomach lurched. '*Christ*, Dexter. No wonder your breath stinks —' He broke off.

It struck him, like a hammer blow.

He raised a hand to his face. He thought about all the times Dexter's rough, smelly tongue had licked it all over, slathering him with saliva.

He looked back at the pit of bodies. *Infected* bodies.

He thought about his cough, the breathlessness, the sweating.

'*Fuck.*'

Carter's legs gave way and he sat down abruptly on the cold ground.

After a moment, he began to laugh. He laughed until his stomach hurt and he could barely breathe. He wiped at his sweaty forehead. Man, he was hot. *Hah.* Of course he was. What would come next — delirium or redeye?

He stared over at Dexter, who was chowing down on the stinking little piggies.

'I gotta tell you, buddy — licked to death by a mongrel with a foot fetish was not what I had in mind for my epitaph.'

Dexter looked up, pink tongue lolling, and wagged his tail.

'You're right,' Carter agreed. 'Could be a lot worse.'

He pushed himself to his feet.

'C'mon, bud. Let's go home.'

Four Days Later

Carter stood at the edge of the precipice.

The wind whipped around the mountaintop. Sweat coated his body. The cough was worse, a hacking, insistent thing that tore at the delicate membranes of his throat. His thoughts were feverish, like his body. Occasionally, he felt himself consumed with rage.

This morning he had shot Dexter. He couldn't leave him alone.

It was time.

Carter had considered other ways, but it had seemed fitting that he should come back here. For the final time. To join the others.

He stared across at the cable car's rusted shell. He thought about the crashed coach. The people who had struggled to survive within. All gone now.

Had it been worth it?

Maybe. Maybe not. You could ask that of anyone's life. What did I achieve? What did I make of this tiny space carved out in time? Did I leave a permanent mark, good or bad? Or did I simply leave a footprint in the snow, all too soon obliterated by the next fresh fall?

Ultimately, there is only one day after another. Some good, some bad. There are moments of unexpected pleasure and times of unbearable grief. For every action there is an opposite. For every piece of good fortune, a random bit of shitty luck. Every silver lining has a cloud. The devil was an angel once.

Carter turned so that his back was to the drop. A

group of figures stood a short distance away. Ghosts? Whistlers? Carter couldn't be sure any more. The past and present seemed to be merging. The living and the dead becoming one. Peggy was there, and others he recognized. Meg, Hannah, Lucas, Miles.

A tall figure in a hooded cloak of animal skins stepped forward. The same figure who had dropped the lanyards outside the Retreat's fence. He pulled back his hood. Eyes blood red, face thin and white as a skull. But Carter still recognized him.

Grant. He held out a skeletal claw. Beckoning like Death. *Come with us.*

Carter smiled. Then he lifted his hand, raised his middle finger . . . and stepped back.

A moment before he fell, he realized that the mountainside was empty.

The cold air rushed past him. Memories, faces, past lives. It seemed to last an eternity and a millisecond. Time had become irrelevant. Gravity had become irrelevant.

When Carter finally hit the ground, he didn't feel his bones shatter or his organs pulverize. His brain was already shutting down, turning out the lights.

Carter has left the living. Thank you, and goodbye.

He lay in the crisp white drift, legs and arms splayed, a perfect snow angel. His failing retinas stared up at the bright blue sky. The storm had passed.

When the first crow landed and poked its beak into his eye, he didn't blink.

Later that night, bigger predators would come. By morning, there would be nothing left but a ragged carcass.

A week later, a hunter would shoot a wolf. A sickly-looking thing, but wolf meat was as good as any to feed his family.

Soon afterwards, the hunter would fall ill and die. Then his family. Then his family's friends.

And the crows would fall from the sky.

3,500 Miles Away

'So, you understand why you're here?'

She nodded. 'This is where you keep the kids whose parents are dead or have been sent to the Farms.'

'We don't like to call them that.'

She shrugged, fingering the chunky silver locket around her neck. 'Suit yourself.'

The man stared at her, not kindly. 'More specifically, do you understand why you are here, talking to me?'

'I guess something was up with my tests?'

'Indeed.' He glanced down at a small tablet on his desk. 'Tell me again, how long did you nurse your parents once they were infected?'

'A week or so.'

'You are unvaccinated?'

Her face tensed. 'You've got my details. You know my parents were anti-vax.'

He swiped down on his screen. 'Your immune response is remarkable.' He looked up at her. 'We would like to keep you here to run some further tests.'

'You want me to be a lab rat?'

'You would have your own room, entertainment, a choice of food. Privileges not extended to other young people here.'

'I don't think so.'

A small smile. 'You seem to think you have a choice.'

'I do.'

'Really?'

She held up the locket. The kids here had been

389

allowed to bring one item of their own into the home. 'This was my mom's. Well, she was my adoptive mom. It's all I have left of her.'

'It's nice you keep a picture —'

'It's not a picture.' She clicked the locket open and slipped out a small vial of red liquid. 'It's her blood.' The man's face fell. 'Her *infected* blood.'

She gestured as if to throw it at him.

He shrank back in his seat.

She chuckled. 'Worried your precious vaccine might not protect you?'

His Adam's apple bobbed. 'Put that down.'

'No. First, you take off your clothes and lay them carefully on the table.'

She waved the vial at him again. He started to undo his shirt.

'What do you intend to do?' he asked.

'Tie you up with your belt, put on those lovely green fatigues, take your car keys and security pass and drive out of here.'

A sneer. 'Good luck with that.'

'Gee, thanks. Now strip.'

★ ★ ★

The security guard barely glanced at the car as she drove through the gates. Lucky that her dad had taught her to drive in his old pick-up. But her luck was unlikely to last. Luck never did. Soon alarms would sound. People from the Department would be looking for her.

She put her foot down. There wouldn't be much time. She needed to head back to her old home first. The plasma and medicines were still hidden there.

Her mom had never explained who sent the packages, or why she saved them, but she was grateful. They would be useful currency.

The plan was to ditch the car and take her dad's old trail bike. That way she could travel off road. She wasn't sure exactly where she was heading yet. Maybe she would camp in the woods, or find an abandoned property to sleep in. She'd get by. She always had.

Her parents hadn't always been kind, but they had taught her to be tough.

Or maybe she got that from her real mom.

Eva smiled, blue eyes gleaming. She was a survivor.

Acknowledgements

I had the idea for *The Drift* back in Autumn 2019. I pitched it to my agent as 'a triple-locked-room mystery/post-apocalyptic horror thriller'. Back then, no one had heard of Covid, and the idea of a global pandemic was still very much in the realms of fantasy.

Fast forward to Spring 2021, when I actually sat down to write *The Drift*, and the world had changed. Many aspects of my idea had become a terrifying reality, and I wondered if anyone would want to read a book with a virus theme, however fictional and far removed.

I wouldn't have blamed my publishers for thinking the same.

That's why I would like to thank Penguin Michael Joseph, Ballantine, my wonderful agent, Maddy, and my ace editors, Max and Anne, for their unwavering support of *The Drift*. They could have tried to get me to change tack or hold back but they didn't, for which I am eternally grateful. Kudos to Anne, whose initial reaction upon reading the first draft was, 'Wow. Holy f**k!'

That was when I knew it was all good.

Ultimately, I found that I really *needed* to write this story. It gave me a chance to let loose creatively in a way I hadn't before, as well as unload some pent-up stuff. There's a lot going on in the book, but at its heart it's about loss and how we hold on to hope and humanity in the face of terrible events.

(Okay, that's the serious stuff done).

Thanks go as always to my ever-supportive husband, tech support and first reader, Neil. Also, to my amazing daughter, Betty, for being fierce, funny and most of all, kind. There are no two people I would rather be stuck in a cable car with.

Practically, I would like to thank Claire Hall of JG Coaches in Heathfield for arranging for me to come and poke around their vehicles. Special thanks to Nathan Petty who showed me around the coaches and talked to me in detail about the feasibility of aspects of my plot. Some authors visit exotic locations for research. I visit coach toilets.

Also, many thanks to my proofreaders and copy-editor who had the unenviable task of ploughing through this book picking out typos and continuity errors. Plus, marketing, design and all the folks who basically make me look good!

Everyone at the Madeline Milburn Agency — you are brilliant. Thank you, Liane and Valentina, for negotiating all the foreign rights and arranging trips with my publishers abroad. Thank you also, Hannah, for your amazing work on the TV stuff.

Thank you to my author friends for the laughter and listening to me sound off. Everyone needs a safe place where they can spout crap.

Huge thanks, once again, to you, lovely readers, and I'm sorry there has been such a long wait between novels. I hope it was worth it.

I've never been someone who likes to keep doing the same thing again and again. Hence, why I've had so many jobs in my life. It's the same with writing. This book is a departure from previous novels and the next one will also be completely different. Because that's the joy of writing. It can take you anywhere. Past, present, future. You can create whole worlds in your mind and play with them. It's a bit like being a god except with less smiting and more tea and biscuits.

On which note, I'm off for a cuppa.

It's been a blast. See you in 2024.

I'm thinking Alaska . . .